754

OCCUPATIONAL HAZARD

By the same Author

Three For the Road
Eager Beaver
To The Manner Born
Bottom Line
To Europe with Love

Occupational Hazard

John Chaloner

This first world edition published in Great Britain 1991 by
SEVERN HOUSE PUBLISHERS LTD of
35 Manor Road, Wallington, Surrey SM6 0BW.
First published in the U.S.A. 1991 by
SEVERN HOUSE PUBLISHERS INC of
271 Madison Avenue, New York, NY 10016

Copyright © 1991 by John Chaloner

British Library Cataloguing in Publication Data
Chaloner, John *1924-*
    Occupational hazard
    I. Title
    823.914 [F]

    ISBN 0-7278-4227-7

Printed and bound in Great Britain by
Billing and Sons Ltd, Worcester

CHAPTER ONE

If working in television you actually appear on the box, for example over thirty years, you are known by far too many people. Which is not to say you are famous. Or even infamous.

"And never, at least in this house, will you be a Television Personality!" said Chloe.

TVP became a password between us. Chloe, my second wife, mother of our two daughters, Chloe overweight and over-fifty, who still smokes cigarettes because she says they are the only thing that stop her smashing the TV set.

When the telephone in the kitchen rang I was half-way across the hall and stopped, because I knew she had hooked the receiver off the wall. "Thanks I'll tell him!" she hung-up as I appeared, "TVP! They are sending a taxi for you!" Chloe said.

I was genuinely surprised, "I know they want me badly or I wouldn't be back on the job. But not this early! Was that Owen? You were a bit short with him."

"His secretary. The driver's on his way now." The Beeb never had cars even for TVP's. They had taxis on contract so you could wait awhile.

"Did they really not say anything?" I was fretting now.

"Nobody sends a taxi for prison-visitor, housewife-mums! There you are Mr. Tolly!" Chloe crossed the kitchen, having brought in our tray lunch from the terrace, and put it by the sink. "I'm off!" I got the Chloe kiss on her way out – Irish, with Spanish Armada ancestry, and a whiff of Georgia. "Get me some cigarettes love, on your way!"

Which was why I told the mini-cab driver to drop me off at the newsagent-tobacconist not far from Lime Grove studios.

They would all be shut at the hour I normally finished on the Newswatch programme.

Somehow I disliked even purchasing the things. Even for my wife. I was aiding and abetting seriously damaging her health. As the Surgeon General wrote on every packet. Wrong, I thought as I entered the shop. That was the United States. Here it was the whole Government that was agin her.

A woman coming out of the shop looked at me, blocking the way. Middle-aged and with a tight blonde perm, she smiled. What followed was routine.

"I know we know each other!" She opened her eyes wide and spread out one hand that bore several rings, across an overlarge bosom. "Really I'm getting terrible! I just can't remember names. Is it Oxfam?"

"No," I said. "Felix Tolly. Tonight on Newswatch. Don't miss it!" And I slid past her into the shop.

Bright, authoritative, kindly. This was TVP manner. It had taken years to acquire. Back in the sixties, they had said right away that I was a natural. "When you do a newscast, you still look as though you were conducting an orchestra." the Beeb Controller at the time had put it. "As though you now arranged the world! The sensitive pixie face, the big, schoolmaster glasses, the soothing, authoritative voice! In fact the world is your oyster Tolly and you're giving it to them!" Everyone seemed to prefer Tolly to Felix, but what the hell? One of a small handful, in those early days, who brought that big world into the drawing room, or the bedsit, to be seen and believed. Black and white then of course. Perhaps more graphic or gripping because of it, and on the way up I started newscasting, then special correspondent, then the big interviews, the politicians, the Royals, the scoops.

Now, I pressed in fast to the counter, where the man who ran the shop whom I knew, put the two packs of cigarettes into my hand and changed the note I gave him.

"OK Mr. Tolly?" The shop was empty and he had heard the doorway encounter. "You must wish you could put on a mask sometimes! – Like they do at these fancy balls! Come to think of it, I've got a few funny masks left over from Bonfire Night! Scare your fan club off they would!"

2

I thanked him, just naturally soothing and authoritative, and walked on round the corner into Lime Grove, the inconspicuous street with its nose-to-tail lines of parked cars, famous itself only for the built-out entrance to the TV studios.

The fan club would never be scared off. All of three girls of an age that should have been at school, if my own two daughters were anything to go by. But with a second marriage you get confused about the young, and these three wore make-up, and one had red-hair and another white bobby socks and high heels. They weren't my fans, they were Lime Grove Groovies, ready with their autograph books for anybody.

"It's Felix Tolly!" Bobby socks had got it right, and when they do, I can tell anybody who wants to know, that it is still, and always will be, a great feeling.

"You don't want an old has-been like me!" I said, but I was scribbling away on the pink and pale-green pages that were held up to me, as were the bright soft faces, innocent and happy.

Then I remembered a piece in one of Hemingway's books, that it was not the policemen looking younger, but the girls, that remind a man of his age. I have forgotten which Hemingway character felt that this was so significant, or what happened as a result, but these three so obviously believing that anyone and anything connected with the television world was truly special and different made me wish that I believed it too, and was their age again. Instead of the synthetic clone I had almost certainly become.

Inside, the two reception porters looked up as I passed by, on my way to the old fire-escape ascent to the studios.

"Evening, Mr. Tolly sir!"

This caused interest among the few people sitting around in reception, which was encouraging again, so that when I reached the fire-escape stairs I took the first steps two at a time. One of the things about being an old hand was that you wouldn't want the fire-escape changed, and you knew why a part of Lime Grove was called the Polish Corridor because originally the studios belonged to the Ostrer brothers of dear old Gainsborough Films.

3

I reached the floor on which Nightwatch ran production. This was the programme for which I was standing in for Lawrence Brill, the normal number one presenter or Anchorman as this role is called. Jane Milward, secretary to Owen Owen the editor of Nightwatch, was at her desk.

"Why the fast-forward treatment Jane?" I asked.

"The Editor wants you on stand-by! There may be an early splash."

Jane called Owen Owen the Editor, just as she called the Director the same way, and the Producer and the Controller. She also did "pro-speak" about Camera and Lighting and Research. Who were all people. Because that was Jane, bright-blue eyes that matched a denim jacket, who had been with the Beeb all of three years. But she was looking at me over the top of a word processor on her desk, not a typewriter, so things were moving on.

"Where is Owen?" I said.

"He's in Studio A Mr. Tolly. And if you'd like coffee I'll get it sent up. I think you'll be interviewing in Studio A, if you don't mind."

Jane Milward knew that I would know this meant that I would be interviewing live. So something must be on the running order already, and I could have told her that it made no difference where I interviewed. I had done it, as the car-window stickers nowadays say, in a cellar, under the House of Commons, up a palm tree at the Shangri-La, or from the broadcasting box in Westminster Abbey. Wherever the magic camera of TV functioned, I functioned too. The success of any programme is always people, and in my particular case my face and voice, that pixie face, that warm voice persuaded people to reveal, to give of themselves, for those unseen millions who made up the ratings. Long ago, on what people are now pleased to call steam radio, I had first learned. From Ed Murrow for one. There were probably not more than a handful of us then, who could do it as it should be done. Dimblebys, Ludovic Kennedy, Robin Day. There were good new younger ones coming along too. Again, I remembered the beginning days. One big timer, an American, had been kind, and again you don't forget. "You have it all going for you Tolly!" he said. "With those big goggles of yours, and is it

4

the kissable mouth? The girls love it, because you've got a jaw line too, that says no nonsense babe! And the big intelligent forehead bit, so that altogether nobody quite knows how old you are or whether you're an egg-head or not. Just don't wave your hands around like a bloody Continental, that's all!" he had added. "And if you must wear a bow tie, get somebody to fix it properly for you!"

I went to find Owen Owen, whose Welsh parents must have anticipated the one-name society. Currently he was producing the end of the day news round-up called Nightwatch. He too was a different generation. Cambridge, Fleet Street, Radio Wales, New York then back again. And all of thirty. Tall, sallow, stylish, grey crumpled suit, the quick, easy smile. He leaned against the long work table at which a half dozen of the editorial crew sat, most of them busy and wearing earphones.

"Jane sent the taxi for you?"

"She did." I waited. You wait for producers if you are old school.

"It's the assassination story! We should have plenty by the time it's all come in! I'd be glad if you'd help me sort out how we run it."

"What? Who?" I said, now I had it. "Who's been assassinated?"

"Nobody! But it was a damn close run thing! Might have touched off another war if you think it through!" Owen handed me a fax sheet with the large easy-to-read script lines.

"Immediate, 1300 hrs London." I read aloud, like it was a rehearsal. "Attempt on United States Ambassador by unknown terrorist gunmen thwarted by swift action of – oh no!" I looked up at Owen without any sort of acting. "Not Max Beaumont! Not the major making his own headlines again!"

"You know him, don't you?" Owen spoke quickly, with only the faintest Welsh music.

"Yes," I said shortly. "I know him! He was in Germany with me. After World War II."

"Maybe we can fit that in. Let's go to your office." Little personal links like that, carefully worked into the script, the ratings people had discovered, made for audience participation. Their phrase.

5

The Anchorman's office was a small glassed-in partition in a corner of the main news room.

"Don't you ever listen to the radio?" Owen grunted as he switched on a standard tape recorder, and as Jane Milward brought in coffee. The spools started turning.

"For once Chloe didn't have it on at lunch," I said. "We had quite a bit to talk about. The driver didn't have the radio on in the car for once either!"

"This is all we've got at the moment," Owen said tersely. "It's a flash from World at One. The lads in the recording car come on later. Listen!" The spools turned slowly, then the rounded voice of the radio reporter filled the small glass-panelled room where the three of us stood, because there was only one chair.

"This is Radio Four! We interrupt our programme to bring you a news flash. Reports are coming in of an assassination attempt on the life of the United States ambassador in London. It was foiled by the swift and dramatic action of a passing motorist, who succeeded in knocking down the motorcycle gunmen making the attack. This is all we have at the moment, but for listeners who stay tuned, we will pass on any further details as they reach us!"

"Dear Robin!" said Jane Milward, and I noticed it was not Mr. Day. "He would make doomsday sound as though he had it all under control!"

Owen, who had pressed the cut button, moved other controls on the tape machine. "The next bit is from the news at two o'clock." He grinned. "They had the radio car outside the House of Commons – turfed out some MP who was about to do his piece, he wasn't pleased – and they were up there in Belgrave Square in minutes!"

"Is that where it happened?" I asked shortly.

"Outside the German embassy," said Owen. "This piece is radio car to off-the-air control at Four, then the news at two, then some more. Listen!" Owen's finger stabbed again, and the spools rolled.

The radio car reporter was plainly tense, but keeping his professional cool. I knew how he was feeling. Belgrave Square for him was no different from Lebanon, Hanoi,

Suez, Cuba. For the press boys it was easier, they could write it up afterwards. On the air you were there.

"Hullo Newscom? This is three-four Tony. Bill's trying to get more on this thing, he's out there now. But he's briefed me so far."

"Three four, position!"

"Sorry, OK! We've been shifted by the fuzz twice already. West side Belgrave Square. They've taped off the action and all traffic is being diverted, but I can see quite well from here." The reporter was shouting now.

"Is there danger of any more shooting or big bangs?" Control was laconic, but I recognised the form, which was the usual war or peace, when the other end doesn't want transmission going off the air in a gurgle of blood and bullets. Listeners don't like that, and it can't be used.

"No, I'd say it's clear. D'you want what I've got? It's the basic. About three minutes!"

"Have one to get it straight, then read! Unless Bill comes back with more. But we'd like it for two-o'clock which is only ten now." The spools hissed, then jabbered its gibberish on fast wind.

"Now!" said Owen quietly, as the reporter's voice resumed.

"This is Tony Jackson reporting from the BBC radio car here in Belgrave Square in the centre of London. An attempt to assassinate the ambassador of the United States as he visited the German embassy was foiled by the cool nerves and swift action of a passing motorist. It is now known that the driver of the car is the well-known Fleet Street and international publishing personality, Max Beaumont. In actual fact whether he *was* driving the car himself, or someone else, is not clear, but we know that he was in the car. The car, a big dark-green Bentley Mulsanne Turbo, its front now mangled, is up against the railings of a house about four along from the porticoed front entrance of the German embassy. There is a big police presence in the square now, you can probably hear sirens, and the whole of that side of the square is cordoned off. From where I am I can see an ambulance, and a big sheet has been draped over the front end of the car. According to my colleague Bill McKewan, who was earlier able to inspect the scene, and talk with

7

police, a motor-cycle was invo.ved, and is under the front end of the car, under that sheet. We understand that two people were killed or wounded. But whether one or more were bystanders is not clear. At this point the police are not yet issuing a statement."

The reporter was now delivering with the quick, neutral voice of the professional newsreader, keeping an eye on the sweep-hand clock in the car. So much easier than when facial expression as well as voice has to come across to viewers I knew, from my own conveying of death and disaster, good news and bad. But now the studio newscaster was on the air. Guiding, questioning.

"Has there been any shooting Tony?"

"Not as far as we know. People who happened to be in the square say it all happened very quickly – otherwise there might have been. But plainly this was a major attempt to assassinate the United States ambassador!"

"Do we know what he was doing in Belgrave Square?"

"It seems the ambassador was making an unofficial call on his counterpart for Germany, and using the old front door on the corner of Belgrave Square. As is prudently necessary these days, the appointed representative of the United States was travelling incognito to visit a key European ally, doubtless to discuss all the current topics of concern."

Incognito I knew, means no Cadillac with stars and stripes flying up front. Plain black Ford with another close behind as bodyguard buggy, other guards in the front car, two British police outriders, one in front, one behind, possibly armed, but always difficult to get that bit denied or verified.

Now the reporter in Belgrave Square was speeding up, and his voice rose.

"The action came as another motorbike shot into the square. Probably looking like any one of the growing army of bike messengers that harass the nerves of London road users. The only difference was that this one had a second rider, on the pillion seat. As the ambassador stopped in front of the embassy entrance, and the bodyguards sprung out, and the police escort stopped in mid-road, this other bike slewed to the kerb, the pillion passenger seen whipping a machine pistol out of the despatch box, the first figure

8

already swinging his weapon out of the front of his black leather jacket.

According to eyewitnesses, this was the moment when Mr. Beaumont's Bentley motoring round the square rocked into full lock, seeming for a moment that it might roll over. It lifted the bike and the riders across the pavement, and smashed against the railings of the Country Landowners Association, just four doors up from the embassy! The noise, according to those who were nearby, was like a bomb going off! Clouds of steam from the car's shattered radiator immediately enveloped the scene. Out of it staggered two men who were seized by some of the police bodyguards. The ambassador's men with drawn sidearms had instantly hustled him into safety, and that, at the moment, is all we have got, here in Belgrave Square in London!"

I looked at my watch. It was twenty past three. Owen pressed buttons on the recorder and the spools whirled and whispered on rewind.

"There must be more since then?" I said.

Jane Milward got up from the stack chair on which she had sat listening to the tape, silent, her expression carefully composed throughout.

"I'll be back at the desk," she said collecting cups. "Unless anybody wants more coffee?"

"Thanks," I said.

"Jane, me too please –" said Owen. "Tell the desk to go on keeping tight tabs on that driver. He's our ace for to-night," Owen said to me as Jane left.

"You mean Max? You've got Max for Nightwatch?" I swivelled round in the one decent chair the undersized office offered. "Do we know it was Max Beaumont who was driving the car anyway? And what was that bit about World War Three I heard?"

"Well, like I said. Think it through!" Sometimes Owen Owen was like his Oxbridge dons.

"I've thought it through," I said evenly. "All by myself! But it depends where those two murderous bastards on the bike came from – or who was paying them! Has any outfit claimed they were responsible yet?"

"No, because it was a failure! But with our usual taps into

9

the anti-terrorist squad – who are being unusually tight about this one – it's pretty certain they were Arabs."

"They like London squares for murder scenarios!" I said, remembering Gaddafi's effort. "That was WPC Yvonne Fletcher they killed!"

"The one on the back of the bike was a girl!" Owen said shortly. "That's unofficial at the minute. By the time you're handling this it will be confirmed I'd guess. Of course, we'll be following the earlier news and the evening papers. But perhaps with your personal link with Max, we could fill it out quite a lot. If he's allowed to talk."

It occurred to me to remember that Owen was managing me. He was Producer. It was his programme, and it was nice that he had agreed to the suggestion that I should come back as stand-in anchorman. It had to be a suggestion, although I had been the TVP, regularly pictured in the *Radio Times*, in black and white, if you can remember what that looked like, while Owen Owen was but still in his crib.

"So you *have* got Max?" I asked. "In studio? Or is it Fleet Street? Or that little pad with the polo ponies at Richmond?"

"We haven't got him." Owen was drumming his fingers on the table, and the other hand ran through his thick black hair as he watched the staff of Nightwatch through the glass panels. Because the office was effectively soundproof, they moved about, like in a dream sequence.

"We were onto that right away, although obviously Max will give an exclusive to his own people to-morrow! And you can't blame him. Alternatively he might not. And it will be a straight piece. He's not like some of these other Press Barons running himself as news. You've known him," Owen repeated, almost angrily. "Have you kept it up? I mean this story has actually gone to the sixth floor at Wood Lane I was told earlier, because if he is going to appear, it's a question of bidding against ITV. That could mean big money or several other kinds of power talk!"

"You mean someone might buy Max a new Bentley?" I said.

"I don't think Max likes ITV," Owen said slowly. "They take his advertising from the papers, and he doesn't own any TV in this country, only abroad." He got up to open the door as Jane Milward approached with renewed coffee mugs on a tin tray. As she put them down on the desk the telephone rang. It was one of the new ones that make a noise like a curlew.

"Mr. Tolly's office!" Jane said. But it was for Owen, and she gave him the receiver. For a while he listened, occasionally still ruffling his long hair. Owen was jumpy which was unusual for him. Then he said: "OK! Great. Thanks!" I noticed too that he gave the receiver to Jean to put down for him.

"Interesting! Felix you'll like this! Look, let's go round to my office! Jane you come too – because we'll need a bit more space. Get Geoff! And get Cindy, and whoever's running Cameras in Studio One!" I got up out of the only chair, which I had considered was mine to occupy and we moved into the main Newswatch office with Owen still talking. "And Jane! Fix it so that the Running Order titles has Menu One timed for ten minutes, not five. That's yours Felix!"

I liked to hear Owen being good at his job. When we reached his office I realised I didn't actually know very much about the rest of his life and style. The poor Beeb needed good people, but the money – in what the House of Commons call Another Place – and in TV that is several other places – is usually a lot more. And a lot of people have left for it. And what I realised too, is that I needed people like Owen Owen to keep me going, because it is one thing to have been Prime Time, as America first called it, and another to keep the rating, the personal standing, when for even a short time, you have not been on the box every week.

"It's nice to be in on a big one again!" I said to Owen. "And I'm doubly glad that you're handling it." You have to go carefully with a new generation.

"I feel about the same way." Owen Owen gave me a lop-sided grin. "You've got the name to make anything big, Felix! When the others come we'll get down to it."

"I suppose that was TV Centre on the phone?"

"Right! Controller's right arm. It's interesting. Here you are!" Owen was pushing out the chairs with a foot under the table.

I knew the other three – one man and two young women – by sight from earlier Newswatch programme work, and we nodded at each other, while Owen looked at his clipboard.

11

"We've got quite a bit of outside camera now. Some of it will be on news at six. We don't know what ITV and Four have got, but the general idea is not a lot, because the foreigners have been begging and buying from us, which is always a good indication. It seems we managed to get camera up into a front-facing window of the *Director* magazine on Belgrave Square as, having no other publishing connections, they gave us a freebee seat in the stalls. It seems Max Beaumont *was* driving the car himself, and there's a tele-lens shot of him getting away from the scene, apparently insisting on being allowed to keep his lunch date round the corner, although accompanied by some plain clothes. After all he had in fact just killed a couple of people."

"Do you know that? For definite?" It was the research girl. "I remember some scenarios when they like to keep them guessing whether some wounded are around because they talk!"

"Gruesome, but true" said Owen. "Everyone seems to know both the man and the girl were killed. Bill McKewan – he was senior on the radio car you remember, Felix – got it from more than one fuzz on the job, before they clamped down. Reuters, and who else, have put out the official police statement which *is* ambiguous – maybe for the purpose somebody just said. Anyway here's the point. The first effort to get Major Max to appear for us this evening has failed. The only comfort is, we're assured by his own PR people that he isn't going to ITV. It could be that he's on some technical charge, or it's all sub-judice until a coroner has had his say."

"Owen, what about this might-have-been-the start of the next world war bit I heard you say?" I insisted. I wanted plenty of time for thinking at that level. "Do you want me to take that line? Is Jane scripting me for this evening? I haven't seen any film yet, remember!"

"Put it this way." Owen was himself weighing up what I was asking. The responsibility was his and the Beeb's, if it was wrong. "If they were Libyans, and they had got the ambassador, that previous knuckle-rapping air raid by the Yanks would have been kids play. They'd lift Libya off the map. If a couple of our cops had been mown down – and I

12

suppose there were a few hand grenades to discourage pursuit for a bit, could we refuse air-base usage? And if he was visiting the German's Embassy could they refuse planes based there? And if there was a whiff of Syrian backing and they caught any backlash, and the Soviets didn't like that, or the Shi'ites are involved and they and their Iranian pals pull in some more hostages – go on! You're the international guru Felix!"

I shook my head. The story – the whole incident, stark, scary, messy – had it really happened? Sometimes TV seems like that, even on the inside. From the time I had heard the taxi was on its way for me, and walking through the old Polish corridor, getting ready to be TVP, I knew something big must be around. Why else would they want me early, and with a touch of the old star-billing treatment? But not a guru – they could foretell the future as well as the past.

All I could do was measure up to my own reputation for handling the big stories, because this was, after all, only my third night on a brief return to Newswatch, which hadn't even existed as an in-depth reportage programme in the days when I ran the big weekly probe feature in black and white. Now the young generation were looking at me, and I had to say something that was pro. The awful word that is short for professional and not just profile.

"I don't think we can really play that one," I said, slowly. "God knows, the world probably will all go up one day, on another Archduke assassination! I'll get together with Jane for scripting what ever might be used as evidence against the idea!" I looked at Owen. "But don't ask me to get through the Beaumont barrier on the grounds of old times!" I was trying to puzzle out a feeling that Owen was holding out on something. That phone call, taken in my glass bowl cubby-hole, the one from TV Centre.

"Does the name Bob Dasher mean anything to you?" Owen asked. If it did, it was too far away for quick recall. The young man beside me, the one who was a reporter rather than a researcher, had the answer. He too had his clipboard, and was looking down at his pencilled scribbling.

"He's Max Beaumont's driver! The other man in the Bentley. I got that from the radio car. It seems definite he was not driving, at the time I mean, but he has been Major

13

Max's driver, minder, nursemaid and tail-gunner for a long time. They're about the same age."

Which of course was all I needed. Memory, names, faces and places make a photofit session look child's play in my job. Sergeant Bob Dasher was opening the door of Major Beaumont's staff car for him back in Hamburg in 1946.

"Sergeant Bob Dasher!" I said.

"You'll be meeting him again!" said Owen. "Because we have got him for you! And he'll be delivered here by Beaumont's people about ten minutes before we run, and after that they take him away again. That's the deal with the police and Beaumont's PR. It's up to you what you get Felix!"

The taxi and driver who took me back from Lime Grove after Nightwatch were both different. The man was called Bert, opening the door as soon as he saw me. I had known Herbert, not as long as Sergeant Dasher had performed the same function for Major Beaumont, but as a regular with the taxi outfit.

"Still living in the same place, Mr. Tolly?" he asked as we moved off.

"Same old Barnes," I agreed. "Still on the night shift then?"

"Quite a story you had on to-night – couldn't help seeing that while I was waiting, sir! Glad it wasn't me driving with Mad Max! Although that chap you were talking with, the one that was his driver – he said they were alright with the safety belts! Rather him than me! One way to write off a Bentley I suppose. But a couple of seconds later, those bastards would have been shooting!"

We slowed for traffic joining at Shepherds Bush, and crossed over into Hammersmith. I was sitting in the back, and Bert was looking in the rear mirror, to see if he could continue.

I leaned back in the seat and closed my eyes. Knowing Bert was an advantage, because he knew what it meant. I was tired. In many ways the sight of Dasher and the time with him in the cocoon of bright studio lights were still inside my head, telescoping decades rather than years, and bringing Max Beaumont back from the past, from a time when during the occupation of Germany after World War II, everything seemed violent, the unexpected and the perverse a natural backcloth.

Why he kept the title Major, after all these years God knows. Perhaps it was the alliteration that pleased him. Or the media. Certainly the Mad Major and the unpredictability it implied always amused him. I think, precisely because his real character was exactly the reverse. In those days when we first met I had worn the uniform of the Fleet Air Arm, and in the situation in Belgrave Square, I rather fear I would have followed my own training for observation, and pulled up just to see what was happening, whereupon perhaps I, and others, would have been shot or blasted with hand grenades. Max Beaumont was always different. Basically I hold the view that the world has had a few nasty jolts all through mankind's history, but it is also on the whole, a good place. But then my parents weren't killed in particularly unpleasant ways by the Nazis.

Eyes closed in the back of that taxi I was remembering when my own Mother died, fading and wasting away, with the gramophone beside her bed, still playing the recitals and concertos she had lived by and loved. It was only a little more than a decade before the arrival of the penicillin that might have cured her. I only knew a move to Putney, where Father's mother had a large, damp house near the towpath, and enough servants to exclude some quality that I have always associated with home.

In spite of Father's thought that I might follow the musical inheritance, it was the Royal Aeronautical College, then in Sydney Street, Chelsea, that I persuaded him held my real future. I wanted to learn to make something more substantial than balsa wood and tissue paper creations and fly a larger machine than my beloved Frog model aeroplane. Eventually, in the war years, with the Fleet Air Arm it was as a radio op., when all the subterfuge in the world couldn't get me past the eyesight test for pilots.

A stick of German bombs meant for Lotts Road power station wiped out the Putney house and those in it, and nostalgia turned to a kind of cold, lost feeling. I wondered, if at all, it was the way Max Beaumont had felt.

15

It was when I came to London to work in the BBC that I met my first wife who was an assistant editor on the news side, while I had returned to music through an old friend of Mother's. We had three rooms in Earls Court, handily placed for the tube station, and in those days it was called the Polish Corridor, for different reasons than the one in Lime Grove studios, but because most of General Anders' Polish army survivors had come to settle there, before they moved on.

First wife's idea of home was that it served as a useful base for eating out, and there was not much point in making a bed if you were going to sleep in it the next night. This was before the age of the duvet. The launderette and the cinema were also planets, in the orbit of those three rooms in Earls Court, and I seemed to spend nearly as much time in both as I spent working to join the radio orchestra. On our break-up, it was my wife who kicked the radio set across the room, having thrown it onto the floor for the purpose.

It was dear, fat, cigarette-smoking Chloe who taught me once more what real home was all about, some years and several false starts later. I moved into her inherited small house at Barnes. Chloe who cooked like a professional, and tried unsuccessfully to slim, and worked on the BBC World Service when I decided to quit music for her side of things. But with the big difference that it was the new world of TV. Also Chloe wanted children, without which she said, nowhere was home. "Not a proper home," she had said firmly.

When I began to make the serious money, Chloe had found our present house. It was one of the larger early Victorian residences in Barnes, white-painted, with an ancient mulberry tree and a library and fine curved staircase with polished rails. It had an outside verandah that ran the length of the downstairs.

"This is how we lived in India when I was a kid," Chloe said. "Relaxed, spacious, half out of doors!" She looked down the long garden. "We could have a pond, and there would be a heron!"

"No punka-wallah?" I said. "No peacocks?"

"Now that I'm pregnant there will be room for an au pair at least." Chloe never rose to taunting. "Felix darling, that you

16

can afford! Perhaps we could get a house couple! He could do the garden and look after your clothes."

We did in fact do all those things. The two girls had been born in the first two years. Jennifer that summer when I was held up by fog, flying back from New York, and Angela who was very nearly presented to me on the verandah, if it hadn't been for some fast work by Hammersmith hospital. After that they said Chloe would have to stop. On account of her weight they said. On account of my great age she told everyone.

I grew to like the big rambly house, and especially the verandah which, never mind the Indian hill country, reminded me of a big country barn. It had the same smell of old, dry wood, compounded of dust and sealed in by sunshine and creosote.

Chloe had found some rattan furniture, a rocker and a long table and some ordinary chairs with basketwork backs. She added ferns in brass pots and the sort of dracina and yuccas that will grow outdoors in England, given a bit of warmth and shelter. We used to sit there and drink Pimms and Singapore Slings, and when the Filipino couple actually were on the scene to start with, my dear wife persuaded the little man to wear an alpaca jacket, and appeared herself in the multi-coloured Memsahib's dresses that she loved.

Maybe it was drifting and remembering some of this that had me sufficiently far away not to realise that the car had stopped, and Bert was opening the door for me, and even offering a hand, to help me out. It was, of course, near midnight. Newswatch was a late show, and there had been a longer than usual post-mortem. I thought of the Filipinos now long ago, who, whatever the hour, would have come down the steps from the front door, smiling and ready to carry the kind of gear and papers I often had in those days.

Now Chloe opened the door and stood waiting in the shaft of light from the hall behind her. The resident au pairs – two for safety, Chloe said – would have gone to bed long ago. Maybe they had stayed up to watch me. "Staff stay up, if you're on the box," Chloe had revealed.

"Do I see you to-morrow Mr. Tolly?" Bert was moving round to his driving seat again. "I'm on the late shift all this week."

"Then you probably will. Thanks! I'm glad not to drive myself after those shows." I didn't add that I always reckoned I'd earned myself a studio drink or two before leaving.

"I saw it," Chloe said. "You were good darling! Lost none of the old charisma!" Dressed in a large Kimono-type dressing gown, she moved round the big room that we called the library, which was the room where I worked, turning out wall lights and putting on others, my desk and the side table. It was the changing shadows this caused, and the voluminous gown that gave her a swaying effect.

"You're swaying!" I said. I sat down in the high-backed leather chair at the desk and looked across to where she was moving towards the corner cupboard. She looked round and said: "Scotch? Soda? Then bed. You look more tired than usual Felix."

"A glass of scotch, a dressing gown and thou, and that were paradise enow! And to hell with the book of verse," I told her. "If you come near enough to give me the glass I might get under that dressing gown and surprise you with how tired I wasn't!" I got the glass at arm's length, then Chloe settled in a nearby armchair. She had made this room for me too, a proper study, a room, if not with a view, enough space for books, from floor to ceiling, and corners for papers and magazines and the battery of videos, recorders and two TVs, one portable, one rented property.

"Quite a story you got yourself! For your third run of Newswatch I mean!" Chloe sipped a cup of tea that must have gone cold. "You know Max Beaumont don't you? You mentioned that. The chap you interviewed this evening – the grey-haired tough-looking type. Dashpot, or whatever his name was? He seemed to know you? Why wasn't Max Beaumont there? I've got it all videoed by the way. I know you have the studio recording but I thought you'd like this one." Chloe paused, looking at me over the rim of her raised tea cup. "It's sort of different you being on again! Like the early days!"

"It's the same." I agreed, and sucked down a quantity of scotch and soda. "Remember when we sat around like this when I first started *Periscope*? And then *Roundup*?"

18

Chloe smiled, and she hunched her shoulders. There was still a little fire left in the grate, and she stared at it, seeing her own memories. "You were away so often then, and I couldn't come. I hated it!" But she changed the mood quickly. "You must have learned a good bit more this evening – more than actually came over I mean – I thought the Dashpot was being careful. You could have grilled him a lot more than you did!"

"Dasher – Sergeant Bob Dasher – used to be Max Beaumont's sergeant," I said. "When he was starting the newspapers in Germany, and I was doing the same thing with radio, and there were other people resurrecting cinema, theatre – all those sort of things. In the British Occupation Zone."

"Why was Beaumont driving and not his man then?"

"I only had him on camera for five minutes," I said wearily. "You know how it goes. It was a special deal that got him our way. I hear that ITV got the head of the anti-terrorist squad, and he didn't do them half as well. Max Beaumont himself isn't allowed to make any statements at the moment, and I doubt if there'll even be much from him direct in his own papers to-morrow. Correction, to-day," I said, looking at the clock on the desk. "The question darling!" Chloe said.

"Well, they were going in the car to a business lunch at the Carlton Tower. You know the place, just round the corner from Belgrave Square. One of the Major's favorite watering holes, the Chelsea Room, it seems he often goes there for small private dos when he doesn't want to use the office set-up. Doesn't like the fashionable French *boîtes*, no privacy, and thinks the Connaught and Claridges are for Americans. The Major drives the lovely turbo Bentley *to* lunch, and Dasher drives him back. Like you and me."

"Except that on the way to lunch he crushed those two and their motorbike against the railings of that house like a mincing machine. In one second flat! Do you think that left him with an appetite?" Chloe's eyes had what I called her fakir look. Like when she told me one of her prisoners had hung himself at Wandsworth, an hour before she visited.

"The car looked a write-off. I saw the clips on the programme' " she said. "Did the two of them just get out unscathed?"

19

"I think Dasher admitted he was what he called stunned for a few moments. Hanging in his safety belt he said. Then he saw the Major, as he still calls him, taking a casual look round the front end of the impact. In a Mephistophelean cloud of steam. That's my bit not his. Just as police and all sorts of American and German minders and shoot-from-the-hip types came yomping in. The Major had picked up one of the weapons which had been thrown clear, and all Dasher could tell me was that he was looking at the bloody thing, in what Dasher called a bitter sort of way, and shaking his head. He was saying it was an Uzi."

"What's that?" Chloe asked.

"Israeli sub-machine gun. Nine millimetre. Dasher again. But old Max chucked it down pretty fast and put his hands up when the heavy mob started pointing their metal at him. Sort of occasion when they shoot first and find out who did what afterwards. After that, as you heard on the programme, there was quite a session, and Max insisted on walking round the corner to his lunch date and nobody seemed to have the rule book to stop him." I looked down into my glass and swirled the bubbles. "I got the impression that Mr. Dasher had instructions to put his boss across in a good light, whatever else. What you'd expect."

I could see and feel now that both of us were getting tired enough to be near ready for bed.

"You saw the programme," I said wearily. "It's all hedged around with legal caution at the moment. But off camera, the way the Dasher told me, they were tooling into Belgrave Square where the German embassy is on that corner, and saw this BMW bike begin to pull to the kerb, and the little convoy with the police bikes stopping, and first bodyguard types jumping out, the way they do. Max was always a motorcycle buff his man said, and this machine, the BMW, came across his car like a rocket, braking hard. What made him notice was that for a messenger service it was odd that there were two riders. As they stopped, the back one had a weapon out of the box, and the one in front had the same, coming up to his shoulder."

Bob Dasher said the car had turned and picked up that pair, Uzis, BMW and all, and crashed into the railings before he could think. There were a few hand grenades rolling around too, which had come out of the messenger box so the bodyguards were lucky, because they were meant for them, and the police bikes and any other pursuers. After that, crunch, wow, zap! As Mr. Warhol would have said." I finished my drink and got up, and in the silence that followed, the ash in the fireplace slipped, and made a tiny imitation of the sounds I had just evoked. We both looked automatically to see that no sparks had hit the rug.

"There were two phone calls," Chloe said after a silence. "I didn't mention them because it's too late to call back anyway."

"My contract doesn't say twenty-four hour availability," I agreed. "Not any longer."

"One was on the ex-directory number, but no name. Sounded like a Beeb governor, but that's just the well-tuned ear. The other was a ladybird." This was Chloe's language for a female not on her wavelength. "She said they'll call to-morrow."

"You mean a Royal We will call to-morrow?"

"I don't think it was Buck House."

"Pity. My K is really overdue. It's time TV scooped another!"

"I don't think I would want to be Lady Tolly. I couldn't honestly go on prison visiting, as Lady something." She pulled her dressing gown tighter round her shoulders and sat hunched for a moment. "What d'you think Max Beaumont will get? The Purple Heart or the Iron Cross?"

"Probably both," I said. "Or," I paused for a moment, but Chloe knew today's world.

"He'll move to the top of the hit list with the other side," she said. Now she stood up, and moved to turn off lights. "Jennifer got best bonus in the office to-day."

"That's great." I said, "Me, no K, no prizes, no bonus. But wait a minute! In the kindergarten where I never got top marks in anything, I once I got a prize for embroidery!"

Perhaps embroidering things was what life in the great media game was all about I reflected, as we went upstairs.

21

CHAPTER TWO

Breakfast had been laid on the verandah table. Chloe did this whenever the weather in Barnes was even half warm. The breakfast Durbar involved some elaborate sepia-coloured table-cloths and place mats, added to by an earthenware teapot, and a brass container for a vibrant palm or fern, I never knew which. Some of its larger relations were permanently stationed in suitably larger urns round the verandah rails.

All three of my women had left for various destinations, but that I was not entirely alone was signalled by the noise of a vacuum cleaner upstairs where Mrs. Braxton was already at work.

I began my own, by leafing through the stack of daily papers. That they front-paged the Max Beaumont story was inevitable. More surprising was the generosity with which his publishing competitors gave tribute, albeit in the inevitable breathless-deathless prose, to his part in the incident, while his own majestic rag carried no "Exclusive to *The World* by its Owner scoop". True, Max Beaumont's style had never been that way – an example that more than one of his tycoon chums might have emulated to the advantage of their public image. But, all the stories were embroidered. There were brief fillers on the Mad Major's well-known rise to fame, or notoriety (depending perhaps on whether the reporter or editor has ever worked for Max), then there were dark suggestions about the meeting of the two ambassadors, and leaked information, hinting at the assassins', origins.

So far no-one had claimed them. As Owen Owen had surmised, only success was worth claiming. Also the only pictures that were any good had come from TV clips, because by the time the ordinary camera boys had got to the scene the police had put up their barriers and plastic screens, and what went on behind them as the terrorist corpses and the Bentley were scraped apart was, as one thwarted editorial pen put it, "unlikely to be released for public consumption."

I made coffee for myself in the kitchen, and brought it out, and the aroma mingled with the verandah's faint scent of dust and hot wood that seemed to epitomise Chloe's private passage to India. At that moment the telephone rang, and I reached for the radiophone extension that was an automatic part of the breakfast table equipage.

"Felix Tolly?" The voice was male, solemn and to be fanciful I could almost smell expensive aftershave. I hesitated. Some instinct in these matters told me that I was in this morning. And that it was not a day to be my butler in answer to phone calls.

"Himself," I said, and sipped hot coffee and waited.

"Mr. Tolly this is Al Chemmy! I could spell that for you if you like. We have met, although I daresay you might not recall that. On the House of Commons terrace, and a *Life* magazine thing, for one of their films, in which you were participating in New York for instance."

"Mr. Chemmy," I said. At that moment I had hardly a hazy recollection of both those occasions. The name had a familiar ring about it, something that might be public relations, or near to Madison Avenue. I was guessing, without much difficulty. Even over the breakfast table I could image Al Chemmy, and I knew instinctively that he was not yet in his office either. I knew with certainty though, that he was not in his dressing gown as I was, but had poured himself into the ink-blue mohair suit, fixed the full head of natural hair, possibly grey, and was even now, pushing a manicured finger to the bridge of his overlarge spectacles. As I was doing, in reflex at the thought.

"So good you remember, Mr. Tolly, and I am sorry to trouble you this early! I am senior executive of the PR division of World Media." It seemed to me, listening so far, that this was a worried voice. From the sort of person who was normally used to calling the tune, but who on this occasion was playing grandmother's footsteps.

23

"That," I said, "is of course, one of Max Beaumont's holdings! Could that be why you are calling me Mr. Chemmy?"

"I think Max would have called you himself." Al Chemmy was saying quickly. "He spoke of knowing you as a friend of many years, but after that amazing business yesterday, well, he is now under pressure. Well I guess he always is. But he did want me to send you his very best regards. I may say he does speak of you with real affection Mr. Tolly! Which he says goes right back through – was it in the army?"

"After the war," I said, "In Germany. And may I say, if you are seeing him, please say I think of him too, which is not difficult, when his exploits and acquisitions in publishing, television and radio worldwide have been so well publicised over all the intervening years. You do a good job Mr. Chemmy!" I said.

"Well now, that's kind of you Mr. Tolly!" This conversation was beginning to purr. "We were in conference most of last night, because of the attention being focussed on Mr. Beaumont after his exploits yesterday. There's the other media, some of them competitors. Then there are aspects that might be political. Or sub-judice or anything that is no good to us."

"Max does like the right kind of publicity," I said baldly.

"You've hit the nail right on the head! As a matter of fact, your name came up directly at the conference, and Max said you were about the only person who would be able to handle this thing the right way."

"What thing would that be?" I had been waiting for it. It was bound to come up. TV would want do something big on Max Beaumont. Commercial and the Beeb. Whichever could get there first.

"A full profile treatment. I can imagine this will not surprise you Mr. Tolly?" The heavy stalking was going on. "You are the only person he could possibly work with on such a project, MB said. And I'd like you to know that he considered there was a hell of a lot more status in being programmed on BBC than on any commercial! How do you like that?"

"I'm sure TV Centre would like that a lot," I said politely.

24

"We don't want to pull too many strings. Handle it all informally Max said. Because right now – and this is important Mr. Tolly at this present time – it is vital that he does get the right kind of programme. MB and World Media are going to need all the right kind of thinking – by the public – about him I mean – over the next few months. I wish I could talk to you about this personally, and not just on the phone." This Al Chemmy was fretting suddenly. "I could meet you anywhere for that purpose!"

"Max Beaumont is moving onto something big?" I guessed.

"Well, that's a fair guess, I'd say! But maybe you and I should get together, like I said."

I could tell that Max Beaumont's top PRO was experiencing a certain amount of angst. It was beginning to come across in such a way that I knew there was almost certainly trouble for Al Chemmy if he did not get what he wanted. I also got the impression his dentures could be loose. It was the anxious hissing of breath.

"I tell you what," I said. "I have quite clear memories about Max Beaumont, but I have not seen anything of him recently except to exchange a few words on public occasions over the years. Just what exactly is it Max wants?"

"This incident of yesterday," Chemmy began to sound brisk. "The way the whole thing and the man himself is portrayed to the public. We don't want Max to say the wrong thing. We know how you handle people on TV. But Christ you're the top! Max knows you and trusts you! You could draw him out the right way. Pull out what has made him the achiever, the extraordinary man that he is! Unravel his life, show a big audience his past, his motivation, Mr. Tolly! Can I say this. MB is not just one of your tough small-minded tycoons. He is unique!"

"Chemmy," I said. "You have done your job with me. But you may have to talk with the TV Centre!"

There was a sad silence at the other end of the phone.

"Then you'll think it over? I could say it had your support?"

"Yes," I said. "You could say that."

When the phone rang again I was still on the verandah, still thinking and remembering.

25

The girl's voice was authoritative. "Mr. Tolly? I have Mr. Girsten for you!" The phone played with its own static for a moment while I waited. Graham Girsten. Network Controller. Which meant he could keep me waiting.

"Felix! It's far too long – when was the last time?"

"Brussels," I said, because I had had time to be thinking about that too. "EEC wavelength conference for you. Interviewing Euro MPs for me."

"Felix, that memory of yours! That marvellous total recall system. I wish I had it!"

"Where you are now, Graham, you have to keep your brain clear for big innovative thinking!"

"I know! And your wife was with you!" Like the chat with Chemmy I wished Girsten would get on with it.

"That's Chloe," I reminded him. "Used to be with World Service."

"Dear Chloe," Graham put his best into it. "And the kids OK? You really will have to come over to our place, that's all of you, because we have the pool now and it would be great if you could make it, and meet my wife Jilly again. Jilly often mentions Chloe, and says we haven't seen you for too long." I knew too, that it was Jilly's family money that had paid for any swimming pools.

"You were running Radio then Graham," I said kindly. "Top admin is busier I would guess. They're not kids anymore by the way! All busy working, like me, doing anchorman on Newswatch, for a bit."

"It's funny you should mention that, Felix! I should say of course, from my end, that I know – well I have to know – just about everything of importance in programme changes and the leading personnel. Well, you're more than that. After all there's only one Felix Tolly."

"Go on Graham, I like it," I said. I looked across the table where Chloe had silently crept in, sat down and lit a cigarette. Her errands over, she listened and her expression became increasingly suspicious. Unseen by Graham Girsten I waved to her across the table. I knew Graham on the telephone. It always gave him a special sort of pleasure to talk into instruments, and decades ago we had been radio reporters together. Even then he took a long time to come round to a

26

point, only sometimes holding listeners on the way. He had moved almost naturally to Administration.

"I liked your piece last night. The big one. Major Beaumont wages war again. It's things like that you do so well, Felix! I envy you. Being just staff these days."

"But at the top Graham!"

"Have you heard from Max Beaumont, Felix?" So, like Al Chemmy we were getting to it now. I had known Graham's mind for longer, and how he could go on like this, but seeing Chloe's face, decided the time had come to stop rolling the dice.

"I have had a public relations figure on the phone here this morning, a certain Al Chemmy. I thought it was rather a good name – if you think of PR as I do, as a sort of alchemy."

"You didn't tell him that clever thought, Felix?"

"No Graham I did not. Knowing how much the Beeb needs all sorts of PR help, especially these days. And knowing he was making suggestions on behalf of Max Beaumont. And that he would speak to you." That, I thought was quite good.

"As a matter of fact, I realised we should be getting onto Beaumont after I saw you handle the story last night. And learned then that you know him, or rather you used to know him pretty well, isn't that right?"

"It's being talked about," I said brightly.

"What I hadn't realised was that Beaumont was so keen to get onto the air with us, and not the other side. And a lot of that seemed to be the notion that his friendship with you, personally, counted so much. Frankly, Felix, his PR guy didn't mince words about that."

"Let us not either," I said. "What have you got in mind?"

"Felix, you could handle him in a big one, like your old *People in the News*. Remember? I've had a word and everybody agrees it's important. How about it?"

"If Major Max will give it the time. It wants scripting really."

"That could be the snag," Graham said. "If it goes on in two and a half weeks, that will just get it in to the *Radio Times* for proper presentation. Even so it'll push something else out."

27

"So that's about two weeks for me – assuming I come off Nightwatch. That's a short tightrope, Graham."

"Owen Owen is keen. I can release him as Producer."

"Does Owen want me?" I was genuinely surprised.

"Yes. He suggested Joe Bailey script. Right?"

"Listen," I said. "Why don't you get to work on those details?"

"The real point is that Beaumont wants only you!"

"Thank you, Graham." I said politely. Chloe looked at me and I turned off the walkie-talkie phone. My wife has long, dark, thick hair which really does frame her strong, bright face, like mahogany. She tossed it about habitually and did so now.

"I do like it when you are nice to people I can tell you don't like!" She put a dimpled hand across the verandah table to cover mine. "You gave in!" Chloe said. "Whatever it was – less time here that means I know!" She looked at me sadly. "But darling! I've been meaning to say this for some time, but I think you ought to find another tie, still a bow one I mean, but not spotted, like the one you had on last night. I meant to mention it earlier. Sometimes, when you get a bit excited, like when you wave your hands, the light catches the spots on that tie and they seem to jump all over your face!"

"Perhaps I could go on in my dressing gown, like this?" I said. "Informality is everything these days. Old Tolly's Teatime Talkabouts!"

"I like it," said my wife. "Then they'd know it was really time to pension you off!"

Mrs. Braxton appeared in the wide doorway onto the verandah, carrying a tray. She wore a white overall, which I always thought suggested a mental home, as I had told Chloe, when she had bought them for Mrs. B and the au-pairs, again as part of the Plain Tales From The Hills scenario.

"Can I clear away now?" Mrs. B always croaked, which she said was from her childhood in damp housing. "Or will Mr. Tolly be wanting more coffee?"

"It is still hot in the pot," I said. "So you can leave just my cup and those sugar pills. Although they don't seem to do a damn thing for my weight."

28

The table was cleared, and Chloe and I sat on. Breakfast and thereafter, had been for so long the only time we had together, which is the usual fate of television and newspaper workers who have no evening time. Chloe's prison visiting hours were in the afternoon as a rule, and if we were lucky we both saw something of the two girls, rather briefly, after their work. Neither seemed in a hurry to marry. Home was comfortable, and cheap.

"You learn a lot, in prison, I mean," said my wife. "Those people were just persuading you about Max Beaumont, Tolly Wolly!" Chloe only used that when she was about to be deadly serious. "Don't get too close to that man, however well you know him! Not in the near future I mean."

"Do you pick up things in Her Majesty's gaols that I ought to know about him?"

"He's killed two of them." Chloe's mouth was pressed into a thin line. Her hair tossed again. "They'll try to get him! Their pals will I mean. And you might be in the way."

"I'll look under the bed every night," I said. "And so that way will take care of you as well. As for Max, well I have a feeling he would know how to take care of that sort of possibility better than most."

"How did you come to know him? I heard you once talk about Germany and after the war." Chloe pulled herself up from the table, and went and sat on a big tapestry-covered settee further along the verandah. There was an inlaid ebony table in front of it, and she had picked up the coffee pot and carried it over, so that I was more or less obliged to follow.

"Put the inside phone onto the tape and come over here where it's comfortable and tell me, darling!"

I did as she said, and when I came back onto the verandah, I sat beside her on the big broad settee.

"I remember the first time I saw him," I said. And then stopped. Perhaps it was just as well that even without Chloe's prompting, I should do some serious recollecting – about Max Beaumont.

In July 1945 I was in Hamburg, a city that had been nine-tenths destroyed. It looked, when I first saw it, more like ten-tenths. I had been seconded, while still in the uniform

29

and with the rank of Flight Lieutenant, Fleet Air Arm, to an ill-assorted group of technicians and German speakers charged with the task of resurrecting steam radio in the British Zone of Occupation. Nobody called it steam radio then, in that virtually pre-TV age. The Germans surviving in the ruins on less than a thousand calories a day, were keen to hear what was going on in the world they had so nearly devastated. They were beginning, in a dazed way, to realise that Reich Propaganda Minister, Dr Goebbels, had not been telling them the truth.

In Hamburg, Hanover and Dusseldorf, various other teams in Allied uniform were working on press, theatre and cinema. We all had the problem of finding taint-free Germans, those who had not been members of the Nazi party or affiliated organisations, who might become the new editors, broadcasters, film-makers. At the time there was a general no-fraternisation order in all the zones of occupation. The military police picked up sad or alcoholic soldiers who forgot that the pale, hungry and therefore willing *frauleins* – and *fraus* for that matter – had until so very recently, been their enemies.

The Information Control Units were on a different footing, we were seconded from navy, air force or military units, to what was called Military Government. After all you can't control demolition squads, hospitals, schools, food supplies, local government and the hundred or so other aspects of a shattered, broken, defeated country without talking to at least some of the inhabitants. Non-fraternisation did not last for long. Our command level was one below the German Desk at the Foreign Office in London.

"You'll have to go on to Berlin," my immediate boss said soon after I started. "Short of flying, the road route is the autobahn through Helmstead. Which is under Hanover ICU. We've found a useful chap in Berlin, non-Nazi, religious programme producer – that's why he's *partei-frei* as they say." A major in Army Intelligence sat with him, looking at me.

"Who do I meet in Hanover?" I asked.

"There are two chaps in Berlin who are wanted," said the I. Corps Major looking down at the desk. "The other is lined

30

up for press work. You and the Hanover Press Chief will go together. He'll have his C.O.s staff car and driver. A tank type called Major Max Beaumont. He knows Berlin. He used to live there."

I drove south to Hanover in a unit Jeep, with a transport-section lance corporal. We shared the driving. The American Jeeps were fun still. But the road was not. Pot-holes, bailey bridges, military police checks, dust, diversions. What now takes about three hours, took over seven.

In Hanover I found the 30 ICU easily enough. The mess and living quarters for officers and other ranks were in an undestroyed street called Stingerstrasse on the northern side of the city, a virtually untouched outskirt of the ruins. Because Hanover had been hit by American flying-fortresses like Hamburg, it had been virtually wiped out.

I was shown a bedroom in one of the two-storey houses along the street, that belonged to a Scottish officer working on book publishing. He in turn was travelling elsewhere. His spare kilts and a pair of trews hung in the plywood wardrobe. There were no curtains in the windows, but by now it was late and dark outside and tired from Jeeping, I fell into the Scotsman's bed and, with the taken for granted camaraderie of those times, a slug direct from his bedside bottle of whisky.

Because there were no curtains, the sunlight was early, filling the little first-floor bedroom with bright light, spilling round the whitewashed walls. I kicked aside the bedclothes, and moved across to the metal framed windows and pushed them open. Outside I saw Stingerstrasse in the clear morning air as I had not really taken it in the night before, and it was suburbia as though there had been no war. Below, there was a small front garden to the house, with a path to a quiet, tidy street. A low rise block of flats opposite, still with window panes and curtains in place. The only thing that was different, as the early sun cast horizontal light over this peaceful scene, was the nearby existence of a cornfield. As in other countries at war, every available piece of German land had been utilised for food production. A winding path ran through the middle of the crop. At that time of year ripening barley, faintly gold in colour, and moving in the morning air.

31

A lone figure was striding through the corn and a ray of sunlight seemed to pick it out like a figure of fortune. Major Max Beaumont was coming back from his early morning ride, maintaining, as the cavalry did, the fiction that they had not really fought the war with petrol or diesel. I looked. It was the jaunty set of the peaked cavalry cap, the flared riding breeches of that time, the polished brown riding boots. The wearer strode easily along a path in the golden sea of corn, slapping the boots with the end of a riding crop as he went, and made me curiously envious.

We had breakfast together that morning in Stingerstrasse, the golden youth and I. A middle-aged foreign mess waiter with a pale face, red hair and dressed in a jacket and trousers made of grey army-issue blanket, served us coffee and the standard eggs and bacon.

"He's Hungarian," Max said. And I noticed his own very faint trace of accent in those days. "Used to be a Count, so he says."

That is all that I can recall of the conversation at that breakfast. As he was senior in rank and in age by perhaps a year, it was customary to defer not only to that, but as in all services messes, talking and breakfast did not go together.

His service dress uniform, in which he obviously proposed to travel to Berlin with me that day, was of olive green. It was well pressed, although its elbows and ribbons looked well worn. One was the MC. His rich, black hair and the pale, bright blue eyes were the unusual feature of a lightly tanned face, somehow already made older by lines around those eyes and above the high, taut cheekbones. Others had formed around his mouth, which was curiously sensual, with lips which twisted sardonically when he smiled. His teeth were made more white by an unshaven chin at that hour, with its centre cleft like a knife cut. His own acknowledgement of this was to say that we would leave when he had shaved. I can remember too, when we got up to depart, and the Hungarian Count, if he was one, asked if we were travelling far. "Just a little way along the road of life!" Max Beaumont had said, lightly. And afterwards, "Don't trust any of them, at any time!"

32

There was no dividing glass partition in the Humber staff cars, at least only if you were a Major General, Max explained, as he introduced me to the sergeant who was to drive us.

"This is Sgt Bob Dasher!" he said. "Lieutenant Tolly speaks some German, but if the Russkis try it on, none of us do, OK?"

"That's easy for me, Sir!" The sergeant, square-shouldered and square-jawed, drove out of Stingerstrasse at a steady speed.

The row of semi-detached houses on our right hand were not all requisitioned for military occupation, after about half-way along the street, and as we both sat side by side in the back, I noticed Max had wound down the car window on his side. He looked, and he waved. The cavalry cap had been taken off, and was resting on his knees. I looked too.

From one of the little houses, still occupied by civilians, a young woman waved from an open ground-floor window on the right-hand side, so that she seemed quite near. Even seen quickly, and at that distance, she was also without any doubt beautiful, with auburn hair that tumbled to her shoulders, which were bare, and because she still had on what plainly was a white nightdress, there was even more on display as she leaned on her elbows at the window sill. She did not wave. But as an *auf Wiedersehen* pose it was dramatically unspoken. Max wound up the window.

Crossing the zonal-border in those early months after the war was not the tedious and sometimes formidable business it soon became. It was a matter of known fact that the Germans from the Russian side were slipping through the *grünnergrenze* – the wooded area to the south of the Hertz mountains – at the risk of being shot if they were seen or caught, but there was no Berlin wall and Churchill had not yet identified the Iron Curtain, and the Russians were supposedly still our allies.

That bright, early autumn day we had bumped along the length of battered autobahn, eaten some packed food and drunk some beer. I found the courage to ask if Max had found anything of Berlin that he remembered. I knew so

33

little of such things, I enquired if either of his parents were alive. Then wished I had not.

"They were killed," he said, almost lightly. "Not by us – by the Nazis." I asked no more.

There was a second check of our identity cards and vehicle papers before entering the British sector of Berlin.

The only papers Max had shown me authorised our purpose by a standard order, signed by the General who was head of the Information Control services, to transport two named individuals, who were qualified for radio and press purposes, from any other of the allied sectors of Berlin.

There were few military vehicles of the British, American and French to be seen as we moved into the ruined and rubble banked streets of the Russian sector. Occasionally a heavy red-starred truck lumbered past. I had only been to Berlin once, and then by air, but Max said he had been several times. He seemed subdued and I took it that he was preoccupied with route finding, as it was nearing dusk. It was also now beginning to rain in a dispiriting way.

The staff car turned a corner, and Max spoke quickly. We pulled up in a street where a few dark houses clustered together, some more damaged than others, and none with light in the windows.

It was a street and a scene that has since become familiar to every le Carré and Deighton fan as Smileys have smiled, and spies have come out of the cold. It was Berlin 1945, and I was there, with Max Beaumont and his driver, Bob Dasher. Both, if I was not mistaken, suddenly tense, watchful, totally quiet, as the engine was switched off and the lights dowsed, as we said in the Navy.

Two men, the ones we were to collect, were suddenly and equally silently there, as only a dim memory now, but they seemed to come from different doorways in that dark, stage-set street. One minute they were at the windows of the car, the next they were sitting on the back seat beside me and we were moving off, with Max in front now, giving brief instructions. Not the way we had come, a different way, turning and then quickly turning again. Stopping and reversing, for the route was blocked with rubble, and then jerking forward again with only sidelights on, giving scarcely any vision through the windscreen. I thought it was the rough passage of our vehicle that had brought our two passengers into a crouching position, practically kneeling on the floor below window level. Then I realised they were staying that way, and it was only when we were in the British sector, which I could not have known we had reached, that Max turned in his front seat and shook hands in the unfailing German manner and told them, in German, that they could sit up, and that they were safe.

When, that morning on the verandah at Barnes, Chloe said that she couldn't really understand what this bit about Max Beaumont really meant, I stood up, and moved round a bit. I put a hand on Chloe's shoulder. Plump, round and comforting, I could feel the bra strap.

"Not a happy place then, Berlin," I told her. But my memory was again of Max there, at that time, in Berlin with its ruins and sights and smells and the quality of war and the defeated Germans, to which he seemed peculiarly to belong. All so different now."

"What about your radio man?" Chloe asked. "Was he any good?"

"Except that he was not a radio man. Nor was the other one for press work. Max had known all along I think, because he produced all their papers for them when we picked them up. Perhaps it was better that I didn't know."

"What were they? Spies?"

"German rocket scientists, Von Braun's kind. They were beautiful and different and very truly sought after then."

"A Just So story!" Chloe observed.

CHAPTER THREE

Chloe always said the answer machine was an invention of the devil, and I told her she could do better than make cliché comments against the onward march of civilisation.

"Quite truthfully," – it was Chloe's most used emphatic – "I'm spooked by that machine! Because there's something deceitful about it! You can be there, and pretend not to be. And the other way round! So time and tide *and* telephones wait for no man! Who knows it isn't someone dying? Or one of the children? Or the Prime Minister wants you, and ten minutes later is too late! It's like that thing you've got in the studio, for when they can't remember the lines, and the poor public can't tell!"

I pushed the tab, and the tape spun and stopped. Then started talking. There was Jane Milward for Owen Owen, who would like me to telephone – she would never say call – Mr. Owen as soon as I could. There was another message, a seductive voice of the kind that costs more money than the Beeb pays, doing the same job for Mr. Chemmy. Also the control-tower female who got telephones connected for Graham Girsten.

"Nobody dead," I told Chloe. "Nobody has passed Go, and nobody has collected two hundred."

"I'm going!" She stood in the doorway to the hall, wearing a bright-red mac, looking at the watch on her wrist. "Darling, just you remember that bit I said about the bow tie!" When she had gone, I pushed more buttons, on the phone I called Girsten first.

I was put through to him without delay and there were none of last night's pleasantries.

"Felix! You're OK? I wanted you earlier. This Beaumont thing has moved fast. I'd no idea how the man worked and

36

who he knows. I suppose I might have asked you. People have called, like a couple of the governors for instance. You know the form here at the Centre, especially since all the shake up with the new boss! And the Deputy DG's seemed to have got into the act. It's a funny thing, and I don't know whether I ought to mention it, Felix, but something was said that kind of implied that Downing Street was not disinterested in whether the BBC was going to publicise Max Beaumont as a great and good cause?"

"Not even a slight rise of my well-known eyebrows at this end," I told him.

"Here's what you're going to like, Felix! I got hold of Max Beaumont himself, OK? And personally this time, he made the point that he wanted you to do the programme. He said he didn't want to appear difficult, but he brought up your name immediately. He said because of your former connection you could conduct him through this thing."

"That was the way he put it?" I said. "Max Beaumont doesn't need conducting!"

"Perhaps he was thinking of your musical past, Felix. Well, you have Max Beaumont for the top slot on One, Thursday in two-and-a-half weeks' time. That gets it into the RT, which I always say is a must."

"Usual finance for a special?" I said.

"No problem," Graham agreed, "unless the producer has extravaganza in mind."

"Owen Owen coming off Newswatch, for a bit of economy, and he has a useful girl with him," I said. "I want a scriptwriter for a one-off on Max Beaumont. I'm not going to do this unscripted, and frankly Graham, I think he'll want it pretty tight in advance too!"

"I'm glad you suggested that, because we had the feeling here it would be good not to get any misunderstandings. You suggested Joe Bailey." I realised Graham Girsten had made notes after our first talk. "And, Felix, listen." There was a pause, and it sounded like Graham had put his hand over the receiver at his end. He was back on quickly. "Yes right! Well, just hold yourself ready on this, but I think it is most likely that you will be asked to get into action this evening, because Beaumont will be inviting you and any of the crew you want. I get that from his PR people but I suppose they may contact you direct. Anyway, just play it along – God knows you've done enough of this sort of thing before!"

"Yes, Graham, thank you, I have." I rang off.

I certainly had done enough. Over the years, one way and another. But somehow, that morning, it struck me as odd that I had never thought I would have to prepare a major project on Max Beaumont. For some reason that was part of his character, Max had always kept away from this sort of thing, from the limelight, from the big Sunday paper features.

He was different from the other media tycoons in a lot of other ways, although I might be guessing. As anyone could, I had kept up with his success since our time in Germany. He seemed to have had an almost ordained, relentless march forward. From Fleet Street to international publishing, radio, TV, plus the extensions into paper, print, property. As we seemed to be moving towards a reunion, he was more a Medici, I fancied, than a Caesar, although there was an Anthony about him in those early years, and I certainly knew one Cleopatra in his past. But people said that his dealings had a code of behaviour that was almost like the British army's King's Regulations.

I called Al Chemmy next, to get a dose of reality.

"Felix, that's good of you to call!" The voice of public relations this morning seemed solemn, weighed with responsibility, but not excluding destiny and great events. If Chemmy was chameleon rather than alchemy in the matter of voice, he was unperipatetic on subject. "Max Beaumont – you've heard?"

"Go right on!" I said.

"MB is pleased – although I think he put it some better way– that you are going to run this programme, that is! That last bit, which he did say, but you and I know the fact is, Felix, if you know him – he will run it! Now Felix the way we have to work this – and your Controller, is it? said you were going to have a producer, name of Owen. Did I get that there were two Owens?"

"Two Owens, one person," I said. "Told to be the Producer".

38

"Are you there?" Al was fretting again. "Well, Max seemed to think we could get things sorted out if we all met at his place for dinner, and that would be to-night! Now don't tell me you can't make it at short notice! And he did ask especially if Mrs. Tolly would come with you. Because his wife will be hosting, and she has asked especially that one or two ladies be there. She and Max are both looking forward to meeting you and Mrs. Tolly."

"Is this a work session by chance?" I asked coldly. "Because for all I know right now, and I'm probably the last to be told, I am still on Newswatch this evening!"

This time the pause had a tactful hesitation, even a fraction of something that amounted to caution. You can measure pauses if you specialise in it, and you do in radio and TV.

"We had understood that you were being dropped out of Newswatch to take this assignment, Felix! That is, if I understood Shepherds Bush, that is TV Centre. The decision was taken there, and I guessed you were cognizant of that."

Somehow, in spite of myself, I found I was grudgingly accepting Al Chemmy and his style. I recognised a professional doing his job.

"Besides which," Chemmy continued on the brave, new realism line, "there's Max Beaumont, and at least you should know him if you were in uniform together! Like this effort that's just got him into your hands, Felix. Wham bam! He wants action fast!"

I thought I would not like to do Al Chemmy's job.

"Is this dinner proposed, a working occasion?" I persisted. "Who else will be there? I take it you will be? And was it mutual friends from TV Centre? Or will they be toasted as absent friends? And by the way, where is the Beaumont residence? And if we are not getting a RSVP card, what sort of time? And," I said, thinking of Chloe, "what sort of tie?"

The fact is, that after years of talking, probing and fact-seeking for interviews on radio and TV, you guard against semi-social dates, I like to get the balance straight from the start.

Chloe, surprisingly to me, was graciously pleased to be invited. By early evening she was floating round the big living room in one of the Memsahib balloony evening dresses that suited her and gave a sort of ethereal style to her movement.

"So you will be with me for the evening instead of Newswatch? Well I call that super! And not far to go?" Richmond I told her. In fact Richmond Park. I had written down the address, and even a telephone number that Al Chemmy gave me.

"A car is being sent," I said. "A Beaumont car. Why are people always sending cars? Probably because they think I cannot afford a car, or cars?"

"Or that you will almost certainly be intoxicated," said Chloe. "Anyway a change from Beeb mini-cabs."

"Whose side are you on?" I wanted to know.

"Well never mind drink! What do you think we shall be eating? Clam-chowder? Finger bowls? Brown hash?" Chloe said. "Will the car be a Rolls or a Cadillac?"

"Mrs. Beaumont – and I am pretty sure they have been married for thirty years, because she brought some inherited publishing holdings with her – is American," I agreed. "But my guess is a Mercedes. The Bentley will be off the road after all."

It was. Chloe and I were driven silently away, sitting behind a driver in uniform dark blue that matched the car. It was not the gallant Bob Dasher whom I had met for the brief Newswatch interview, so I presumed it was not a Max Beaumont substitute for the Bentley.

"This is one of Mr. Chemmy's cars, sir!" Professional drivers communicate subliminally. "Mr. Chemmy is coming himself in one of the other cars, sir, and he said to expect a call while on the way, sir."

But it was not until we had nearly reached Richmond Park that the car phone squeaked and winked its little red light, the chauffeur listened, and then passed it back to me over his shoulder.

"Glad you're on your way, Felix!" the voice of Al Chemmy was loud and cheerful. "Now I hope you and Mrs. Tolly are enjoying the ride, and I am just now coming near to the Roehampton Gate. The house backs onto the park, or rather the grounds do, so they do not unlock the gates for us. It will not be a big party, Felix, and I shall not have Mrs. Chemmy with me to-night. But you will find Max Beaumont and Mrs. Beaumont. Now is it Mr. Owen Owen?"

"We've gone through that, Al," I said wearily. "You're right, he doesn't stammer! It must have been his parents. They have managed to get someone to hold his Newswatch spot, I suppose TV Centre did that."

"Well, that's thanks to you Felix, and he knows now, it will all be handled the right way." Chemmy was using my first name now. "There's some research girl. A Miss Milward, is that right? And a writer, like a Mr. Daley?"

"Joe Bailey! He's scripting. You've got the best," I told him.

The chauffeur took the talk box from me and replaced it in its special nesting place.

"Dear," said Chloe "Look out of the window now! Isn't it wonderful? And so near London. You could be in the Highlands!"

The driver, again without turning, spoke into his rear view mirror. "From the house, madam, you can see the park and the trees and often the deer from the terrace of Mr. Beaumont's place. I think it was a bit of the park once. There's a few of those big places along there that were."

"I wonder if Mr. Beaumont rides a horse out of his place?" I said, thinking back.

"I know he gave orders to feed the deer, sort of to keep them near, because the secretary told me," said the chauffeur. "We're nearly there now, sir!"

The car was slowing to a crawl as we approached a tall entrance of buff-coloured, square-shaped pillars, and as we passed between them there was plenty of time to read the black, painted letters on the front of one, Poincienna Lodge. The Poinciennas, three of them, reared up above the drive from their twelve-foot thick trunks, the genuine redwoods of the Pacific coast.

"Not planted by Mrs. Beaumont," said Chloe, knowledgeably, "not unless she is a hundred and eighty or thereabouts."

And then I was noticing the drive, which was not the scrunching gravel, but the kind of flat cobble stones, a blue-grey colour, the sort you find in front of small Scandinavian castles. Or Charlotenburg in Berlin.

41

"If that's the lodge, where's the house?" Chloe, in the same mood, was showing mild social apprehension.

"That is the house, madam," the chauffeur said. We were now behind two equally slow moving cars, a flight of three, circling to a control-tower landing.

"There's Owen in front, and I would guess that's Mr. Al Chemmy in the one ahead," I said.

We stopped and while the driver hurried to open the door on Chloe's side, I looked up at a front with palladian columns and a roof over an equally wide flight of steps that led to a terrace and the main doors. The columns were obviously an addition to the basically Georgian architecture, that meets with world-wide approval, a combination of elegance without ostentation, even with the bigger residences like this one. Having seen in the course of three decades of working round the globe, everything from maharaja's palaces to adobe huts, I reckoned Max Beaumont and his American wife must have combined taste and finance on this one.

"Just a little home from home," I said to Chloe quietly as we got out of the car. Owen Owen and Al Chemmy came forward. I introduced them to Chloe, and all four of us mounted the steps together.

I could see Max just inside the doors. He was speaking with a man in a cream-coloured jacket, who was also, I was glad to notice, holding a tray with filled glasses. But it was Mrs. Beaumont who suddenly appeared, and did the greeting at the top of the steps without waiting inside. It was in line with the best American hostess tradition. I had seen pictures of her, the ageless, firm, bright and well-travelled power, that stays behind the throne, but has the assurance from combining the two sorts of money that Americans understand, old and new. Her jewellery and clothes were also old and new. A soft grey silk dress, with a high collar, held up by a choker necklace of gold links and blue stones.

As I introduced Chloe, I could see Max Beaumont was now busy with the other two men.

"Max has told me about you!" said Mrs. Beaumont. It was the classic line. "As if most of us didn't have you in the living room most nights! Now do I call you Felix or

Tolly? Because Max seems to use them as though they were both first names?"

"Most of my friends from the old days do," I said, but she had already turned to Chloe, "My, now isn't that a sweet dress!" And although Chloe was not unfamiliar with the wonderfully morale boosting line of Americana, she knew better than to return the compliment, and said instead:

"It was really kind of you to ask me to come too!"

"Well my dear, I really didn't know who was coming, but I did say to Max that I would not like to be the only woman!" It was years of putting people at ease, and she did it well.

We moved into a big circular hall with an overhanging chandelier, and a sort of entourage gathered beneath it, including Owen Owen and Jane Milward and the plump, solemn Al Chemmy. And then Max was with us, and he did not shake hands, but stood and smiled at the group of us, and looked at me and then at Chloe. The years had dealt with him too, but his face, it struck me right away, was still hard and handsome. There was the same devastating combination of dark thick hair and clear blue eyes. The hair of course, a little grey here and there. Nor was the face the acquired distinguished elder statesman. I might have known he would never look like that. The small, fine nose, the strong cleft in the dark chin, the odd swing to the straight shoulders were still there.

The two dogs, wolfhounds, not much more than a year old, moved round the group of us with rapid film motion gait, back and forth.

"What are those dogs doing?" So easily he held the stage. "Beating around here! Now Debby it was you who asked me to keep them out of the way, and I told Rinski! Where is that man?"

"You must excuse him going on about the dogs!" Mrs. Beaumont said. "Max forgets everything and everybody when it comes to dogs and horses! Now does everyone have a drink? Here's Boris with the tray. Al, you can lead the way, as you know where everything is."

"I'm going to have a talk out here for a moment with Tolly. We've a lot to catch up with!" Max said. Together we moved to one side, and he put a hand on my shoulder.

43

"I don't need to look at you – we see that face often enough! Quite a time, Tolly! Since Berlin and Hanover I mean!" His head turned with the old, quick abruptness, but the chin line tautened. He was seeing the others were being taken care of as they moved away. "You've been about the world, as well as sitting in front of those cameras. Has it done you any good?"

"I haven't got a pad like this," I nodded up at the chandelier. "And you still ride horses?"

"At the back, straight into the park! Past the polo and stuff now though!" He smiled the old, quick charmer's smile. He must have had a fuller, bigger day than I, but he didn't show it. He guessed what I was thinking.

"Well, how do I look, Tolly? Damn it! I've got to appear on the box with you! Tell me!"

"You've been through a bit, the last day or two," I said carefully.

"Kindly put. Make it a decade or three! I really don't know what the world is all about. Nobody took much notice when I pushed those damned flail tanks up the beach in Normandy, and just because I was going round Belgrave Square on the way to lunch and they can't give me a bit of ribbon for that, they turn me over to you!"

"I thought you volunteered, Max?" I said quietly. "You didn't have to do it!"

"Done it all my life!" He was moving us both after the others now, but he gave me the cool, slightly chilling look that had always lurked in those blue eyes.

In the drawing room he took a heavy cut-glass tumbler of whiskey, gave it to me, and took one for himself. The man called Boris poured Malvern water from a bottle for us both.

"There's one more to come," Al Chemmy said. He looked at a small piece of paper in his hand. "Joe Bailey. Is that right?"

"He's script-writing," I explained to Al and to Max Beaumont, that for a one and a half hours, peak-viewing time, big profile, we had a script writer, although to the viewers the questions and probing would appear spontaneous. It all had to be gone over first. "Joe will do a lot of what is really rehearsal work and get it onto paper. Then the producer and I can cut it and move it around and improve it. Most people are going to be careful what they say on a this-is-my life kind of thing. If they want time to remember, or are too cautious, it goes flat. Also I want to look at the sequences and dig a bit deeper here and there, and I can do that too. But the Producer is in charge of the whole thing."

"Mr. Beaumont has been on the box, here and abroad," Al Chemmy said dutifully. But Max was looking at me, again quizzically, intently.

"Not like this. Only quick bits. When I bought *The World*, when I backed the British Olympic riding team, or was buying into American TV and chunks of Hollywood. The Kruschev interview, union hassles, that Onassis scandal."

"I remember them all," I said truthfully. "But I think you'll find Joe is good. We both need the whole team," I told him.

Max Beaumont looked at his watch. Almost automatically, Al Chemmy and I did the same.

"Nineteen thirty-eight," said Max. "This Bailey had better get here soon! "He picked himself up quickly, and patted my shoulder. "Sorry, Tolly! I'm trying to take over again! This is your show, so next time just put me down will you? I'll join the rest, till we go in for dinner."

"If Mr. Tolly and I could just have a few minutes now – just to run over the programme," Al Chemmy said. "Could we use the library?"

"You know where it is." As Max Beaumont, shoulders square, turned away, once again I thought he really did not look his age. Life is unfair in these things. He was wearing a lighter coloured version of that drab olive army battle-dress that perhaps helped to sustain the younger image, still in my recollection. But now there was a cream silk shirt, with cuffs showing thin gold links, his beautifully polished brown shoes had metal tips, and they clicked on the flagged hall between the carpets as he moved away. You looked for these details in my world.

"Let's go!" said Al Chemmy. "We've got about quarter of an hour."

When he and I were alone in the library, I looked round curiously. The windows were the only side not book lined. We were like secret agents, fresh from the man we had been following.

45

"If I can kick off." Al Chemmy was not bothering about sitting down. "My idea of presenting him is this – and I hope you'll agree with me! Max Beaumont adopted this country – fought for it, and worked for it. He may be half-Jewish and half-German but he's a straight, clean, hundred per cent good guy!" Al Chemmy, looking at me, was appealing.

"OK Al," I said tactfully. "But that background alone means a lot of digging. I want to know about that name for instance. And early days, and to find out what makes Max Beaumont tick. My interview programmes are warts and all. What made his whole approach to action, judgement, risk taking? A lot of people have said he never got over his time in the army and the war, and has gone on like that ever since. Is that so?"

Al Chemmy became plainly unhappy, "You knew him quite a bit in those early days!" He looked round. With his short, thick neck this was difficult. He took off his spectacles and polished them briefly, with the handkerchief from his top pocket, and when he put them on, his large, beak nose was close to me, the secret agent again, keeping his voice down.

"The thing is, you can't portray people like Max in ordinary terms! You've met Mrs. Beaumont?"

"For the first time this evening."

"There have been a lot of other ladies in Max's life." His voice was even lower.

"There were one or two in Germany I remember. But hasn't he been married for thirty years to this one?"

"Sure, sure! It's just to get a bit nearer to what I want to say. I will tell you, but total confidence of course, Felix, that Max Beaumont is right at the point of doing something sensational in the way of newspaper publishing. Maybe you didn't know that, Felix? Something that will make history! It could also make him a hell of a lot of enemies. He needs all the public approval and support and understanding he can get. Like this programme of yours. That's what I mean!"

"I can't make anyone what they aren't. How many people know about this big deal, or whatever it is?"

"It's more than just a deal. Listen, Max himself would be quite upset if he knew I'd even talked about it. There's only a few, maybe less than half a dozen, very close to him at the

46

top, who have the whole scenario, the whole jigsaw. It's like cell work."

"Aren't you getting a bit dramatic, Al?" I said. "This isn't Dallas. It's real life."

"Maybe! But I'm just saying, don't push Max about his private life. Because it might screw up the whole thing. He needs the right kind of publicity, but if he was pushed on some areas he could refuse to go at all!"

"What are you worried about?" I asked. Chemmy rocked on his heels, and swirled the drink in his glass. "Things you might uncover. That this Joe Bailey might. The probing game."

"Joe Bailey is a pretty serious sort of worker. We all are still at the Beeb. Not even mildly like one of Max's own tabloids, say *Flash*, or some of his local rags in Australia and the States!"

"I know, and you're perfectly right. Do just forgive my putting it to you straight, Felix! Just any bit of dirt could stick to someone with a life like Max Beaumont. Especially if you moved the goal posts on the actual night."

"I don't like that, Al!" I said. "And I don't really deserve it. I'll brief Joe Bailey and I have a big say with the Producer on the question and answer script." We were both silent for a moment.

"Well, I guess that's it then, Felix. And thanks! That's a weight off my mind."

I decided, while we were clearing the air, to change the wavelength.

"While we're on the job together, Al," I said, "and I think you're planning to stay close all along, I'm not too sure I like this 'Al' bit. Is it Alan? Or Alfred?"

For a moment the round composed face of public relations went sad, then smiled, and he placed a hand on the side of my arm. "Neither. It's Albert! I can't be Bert. Or even Bertie. Not here, nor in the States – well you know! So it's always been Al."

That evening had other unexpected qualities and as a basic, I felt sure that others beside myself could not feel really at home in the surroundings, because a lot of Max Beaumont was as carefully put together as his beautifully cut clothes and his wife's ability to put everyone at ease. None of us had lived in this sort of setting. Chloe knew about silver, and candlesticks, linen and glass, even Indian servants. But we could not entertain that way, even in the big house in Barnes. Food wise it was different. These days everyone eats everything everywhere. It was Beluga caviar on the smoked salmon I noticed. Also, that Joe Bailey, now having arrived, was already talking to Max Beaumont, looking at him over his heavy rimmed glasses like a doctor studying a patient on whom he was shortly to operate.

I had been seated on Mrs. Beaumont's right hand as she took one end of the table, and I can still remember, almost as though Jane Milward was already taking notes for me, exactly what she said. The man Boris, with the help of two girls, moved round, wine was being poured and when all the rest were talking she spoke as though we were alone.

"I owe it to you that Max is at home for dinner you know!"

"I think my wife would like that," I said.

"This dining room is really a repeat of one we both liked in upper New York state, when we rented there one season," she went on. "It was the time Max had those TV deals, and we were spending time on that side of the Atlantic." Mrs. Beaumont I saw was drinking mineral water, while the rest of us were now on champagne. "Your wife looks really happy and at home here, Felix! I just hope, if you are going to spend more time on this assignment here, and I understand from Al that is the idea, then I shall see more of you both! You know, we've always moved around a good deal, Max's work was always international. But I don't think even in this home he feels settled. I don't think he ever will, anywhere."

I nodded, storing the information. But it was when dinner was nearly over, and there was one of those sudden silences at the far end of the table, and I heard Al Chemmy speaking, that what he was saying made me uneasy.

"You've got to understand by that," the PRO was saying, "Mr. Beaumont doesn't mean he thinks war is a good thing! Or that peace is like war, and justifies a sort of ruthlessness."

Then I realised that Max Beaumont, owner of great newspapers and television and radio stations around the world, had been seated with other members of the media all by himself at the far end of the table. And I saw the anxious face of Al Chemmy, and Joe Bailey putting a finger to the bridge of his spectacles, and looking at Max in that expressionless way he had, while the others were staring, in either embarrassed or puzzled fashion. Only Max Beaumont's face was set in the smile of a Medici mask.

"I wasn't making a broad general statement," he said. "Bernard Shaw put it that the state of marriage only survived as an institution, because it combined the maximum of temptation with the maximum of opportunity, and it seems to me, that making big business work, and getting rich, could be that way too. Now old Clausewitz would understand me, and a bit nearer our own time, so would Moshe Dayan. And for that matter, Kipling. *If you can trust yourself when all men doubt you, yet make allowance for their doubting too.* Remember? Acquiring power, and aiming to reach what we used to call the high ground, is a professional thing. But people always doubt your purpose. World Media Plc, or Pty or Inc, or whatever it has to be called in different parts of the world, moving fast forward – well that's still like moving armour across country. Perhaps my only formal training. I never went to Harvard or the LSE you see. I think this old dog learned to jump through the right hoops, and some of them were on fire at the time."

Joe Bailey's glasses glittered in the candlelight, and I saw him nod meaningly at Miss Milward, who had her notebook on her knees out of sight, under the table.

"I do see very much what you mean," Joe Bailey was saying. "I never heard it put that particular way before."

"Well, it was sort of asked for," Max Beaumont replied.

I had an instinctive guess that it was Chloe who had started this off. She was staring at the man fascinated.

"The belief is you have to be not only ruthless but dishonest and downright inhuman to get where I have. I never saw leadership that way!"

Mrs. Beaumont had pushed back her chair quite quickly and stood up, and more slowly I did the same.

"After that very excellent dinner," I heard myself saying in the voice that had filled a million screens with warm integrity,

49

"I would like to say our thank you, and now we should get our working show on the road before breakfast."

I was glad that Max and Joe Bailey both laughed and as we all got up from the table I joined Owen Owen.

"Are we going to be long?" Max was asking him. "I had guessed you might want to make a start, so we have coffee and drinks in the library. I thought we might set up the schedules this evening and then fix more time around the next two or three days, which incidentally are looking tough for me."

Owen told Joe Bailey to take over, once we were in the library, and he did it very well. Owen asked Max to sit with me.

"I've only got one thing," Owen said. "We have a still cameraman waiting outside, and we need to get just the one picture of you with Felix, sitting together, and that's for the Radio Times and advance programme flashes. Can we get that over now?"

"Go right ahead," Max said as coffee was brought in. "I can't pretend I'm not used to it. But I never like it."

The cameraman came in, and was quickly organised by Owen Owen. I sat close up in a chair by Max, and after the flashes had produced the usual spots in front of our eyes it was over, and the man left in the charge of Boris.

"It probably may seem rather like being interrogated," Joe Bailey said. "This is just to explain how we get going. Next time we'll have a tape, although anything you don't like is off the record."

"Which isn't the way we always go about it," said Owen Owen, meaningfully.

"It doesn't really matter where we start, when we do," Joe Bailey said, and I saw he too was looking round the library. The books were genuine, by which I mean you could tell most of them had actually been read at some time. Some had bindings with fine tooled leather work. If Joe was looking carefully, he would know they were worth several times his annual pay. There was a mahogany book ladder, a world globe on an ancient mounting, a small oval table and some upright chairs beyond where we sat. A fine painting of Richmond Park with deer and horses, looking like

Stubbs, hung above the fireplace and a striped zebra rug was on the floor by the window.

"One of the things I like least about violence," Max was saying, "is that a lot of beautifully made and precious things often get damaged and wrecked. Like that Bentley for instance."

"Just one question then, on that to kick off." Joe Bailey's face was a total blank. "I want to know, what did you personally think, you yourself, at the actual moment when you saw that one of them was a girl? And that you had killed her?"

"What did I think?" Max Beaumont's voice was still as I remembered it, over the years. The light, even drawl that slowed, only fractionally, into the over-perfect articulation of an acquired language. "Well now, I can tell you what I thought, Mr. Bailey, because as a matter of fact it was a new experience. I had often wondered. Car safety belts, did they really work? Well they do!"

CHAPTER FOUR

It is strange how even a short interval of time changes the look and feeling of a room. The Richmond library the next morning, when Max Beaumont has agreed we should reassemble, was in daylight, and there was a different atmosphere, calmer, with the big windows bringing the view of the great park, which had been curtained off the previous evening, almost into the room.

The man Boris had shown me in, and a moment later Al Chemmy came through the door apologising. Owen and the two others had been there some time.

"M.B. will be around ten minutes," he said. "But you've got him then, through until noon. How is Mr Bailey this morning?"

I had to avoid a grin that might have hurt Al's feelings. I knew he had heard about Joe's questioning the previous evening, and Al was worried.

Joe was certainly special. I had known him on the job, on and off that is, for quite a while, in the seemingly close, but probably casual way you do in newspaper and TV work. I had first met him in Washington when he was working for Canadian Broadcasting, and then in Paris, when he was doing some work for *Time Life*. When that brought him to their Bond Street office, he sought me out for some help on a piece he was doing privately about the Royals for *The New Yorker*. Like others he had moved almost accidentally into the talent hungry maw of TV.

Joe was in his late forties, tall, sandy haired, and pale faced, wearing heavy dark-framed spectacles and looking more like an archetypal city editor. But Joe was worth all of his high salary. Independent television had tried to snaffle him more than once, but Joe stayed loyal. He had some

Scottish in him somewhere, and a terse, economical style, getting to the point without pushing, and from all I heard the news side liked him, as well as the features crowd.

Owen Owen took over as we sat down. He was certainly not going to allow Al Chemmy any leeway in production, but he was nice about it. "As we have time, and you're here for a while, Al, just before we start again how about basics?" He used his teeth to take the cover off his ball-point pen. "Reference, usual stuff, or have you got that, Felix? Do you work in what, and who, the man is, for those who ought to know?"

"Probably will," I said. "Shots of office, boardroom, presses, that kind of thing. Quick *mélange*. Will you work on that? Obviously Al will help."

"There is – and its rather interesting – much less on library and film tape about Max Beaumont than I thought," Owen said. "Plenty on the others, his competitors if you like to call them that. But he's kept very much out of the limelight. Now he's hit his own and every other headline as a result of the other day. Now a lot of people want to know about him. And I'll tell you what I think." Owen took up his clip pad and wrote something at the top of the paper. "In my experience, if you'll allow me – these sort of people, lots of power, lots of position, also have lots of past. Including things they don't care to have known about. What makes Mr Beaumont tick? What skeletons are there? Really, what motivates him? Do we go for those sort of answers, Felix?"

"Just run through the library facts we need to have first," I said for Al's sake. "And then make some copies for when we go on, and I need to check anything that may come up."

Owen flicked papers on his clip board. "Born in Berlin, 1924, mixed parentage, school over here. Now that's something you might think was unusual. Look, let's save time with the obvious biography stuff, and I'll read out the shape of the empire today. Here – that is in this country – he is controlling shareholder and chief executive of World Media, that is, chairman and managing director. WM publish the *Daily World* of course, and the *Sunday World* and their colour supplements, and in addition the other national daily *Business News*, and the tabloid *Flash*.

53

"In this country again. The locals he started, with the West London, North and South News, each separate but same management, and provincial weeklies in Yorkshire, Glasgow, two in Wales, two in the West Country. There's some other small stuff. A big trade magazine outfit, all separate companies, oil, computers, textiles, design. Jumps into the USA where some of them came from, and where he has bought similar publishing. Plus his big one, *Family*, and a lot of local radio and TV. One big daily in Boston and the lucrative ad. agencies that own subsidiaries in Europe with PR affiliates."

"Al, you have got to be good then!" I said helpfully. Although I think we already knew that. "Is that the lot?"

"Leaves only Europe," said Chemmy. "But you've got it basically."

I saw Owen Owen looking at me curiously. "Are we really going to get the story of the real man behind all that?"

I hesitated. "Whether he'll respond with everything significant, I can't say. What Joe doesn't ask, I'll take to the limit, but I don't want Max walking out on us! He has a kind of curious indifference, a sort of private side I think, that's more the word. He's at heart, after all, German. But half-Jewish. He's ruthless, but that's not quite the word either. He's still almost a serving officer – that's the feeling I get! It's all mixed together – technical skill, honour and a tireless drive. He doesn't suffer fools gladly, but then he is not cruel to them. He has hired and fired people all the time, but he's gentle with the failures and the wounded, and he pays the good ones the earth then drives them hard." I stopped and thought over what I had said. "I believe we'll have to see whether Max Beaumont is going to come out like that, or something different. But I think being Jewish and German, the war, and his Sandhurst upbringing, was the catalyst. He sort of belonged to both sides in that war, rather as though he was born from its experience and meaning."

"What meaning does war have?" It was of course Joe Bailey, laid back, provocative. It was the Vietnam bit again, from his generation.

"Life or Death," I said. "For people like Max."

"Is that the same as Success or Failure?"

54

Because Max Beaumont came in silently through the door then, he must have heard that last bit by Joe.

"You treat those two imposters both the same!" he said in the high clipped tones that were sometimes all rounded vowel sounds. Unsmilingly, he made for the big, tall backed ivory leather chair next to the fireplace, where logs already burned with established glow and low flame. He sat down and faced the others, sitting opposite on the settee. Off to one side in another chair I watched them all.

"Eleven thirteen!" said Max Beaumont. I had the feeling that he would have liked us to have got to our feet on his entry, but even Al Chemmy had stayed put. "Who's on parade today, Tolly?"

"Only the Floor Manager is away – he's fixing a few things – we shall have to have technicians in, maybe tomorrow or the next day. Then we'll have to decide all the time when we want to think of location shots for back up and change of rhythm. We can't just have two heads talking in the studio you understand?"

"When do we get started?" Max Beaumont asked.

"OK," Joe Bailey said helpfully. "It doesn't really matter when strictly. Why not start telling us where you were born, and about family? I mean tell us everything you can and want to as though you were thinking to yourself."

"I don't mind, as long as you'll stop me if I go off the kind of thing you want," said Max Beaumont. "Now, I notice you're using a portable tape there . . ."

"Not switched on," Joe said.

"And Miss Milward, isn't it? She has her notebook, so that's two to one. I have a tape slot recording in this armchair, so that's all fair! Looks like an ashtray in the arm. The reason for that, is a lot of people have said things in this room, and denied it later. Or tried to quote me for reasons I didn't like. So now that's settled I'll talk all you like. I was brought up in Berlin. Do any of you know Berlin? I suppose, Felix, you've been back there?"

"Quite a bit," I said.

"More west than east," said Joe. "I never really saw it in the immediate post-war days. As a ruined city I mean."

55

"I'm talking about Berlin pre the second world war," Max said drily. "A different city. Maybe a different world, back in those days of the early twenties, when I was born. The great war, the fourteen–eighteen one, had only been over for six years, if you can think of that. My father had been a regular army colonel in the great war to end all wars. He was Prussian. If you know what that means."

He waited, expectantly, but no one spoke. "It was the joining of Prussia with the Austro-Hungarians that made Berlin the natural capital. The Prussians were the backbone of the German military, even before Blücher's time, when he came to the rescue of the Iron Duke at Waterloo, although not all the history books write it that way. My father was awarded the Iron Cross in that first great war. Not with diamonds, but a good one all the same. Later, in the second war, they were dishing them out like – well, like Purple Hearts. He was a von Klieschen, the old man, and there have always been von Klieschens in Berlin as far as I know, although the main estates lay up in north-east Prussia. There were really big estates then, back in the previous century, the kind of thing we shall probably not see again, anywhere. I've never been back there, since I visited as a small child, and even then I can't recall much of it, except that there seemed to be a lot of cold stone passages in those big houses and beautiful colours in the trees when the first snow came in the autumn. And horses. Maybe hundreds of horses. It was a special kind of life, living in Prussia. But I was a city kid. And my mother was Jewish," Max paused. "How am I doing?"

I, in fact at that moment, was doing the usual TV interview watch, for expression, give-aways, eye movements and mouth. Full face, side face, head tilting, the real smile, the put-on one, the defensive surprise, the suppressed anger, fear, pain. They could all be caught or made to appear. I realised how many men I had known of Max Beaumont's age, and, to some extent his type, with qualities that could apply to Swiss, American, German of course, but especially the aquiline and very smooth Italians. They also dressed with careful, studied nonchalance, modelling their suits and shirts, cufflinks and hair styles on an international stereotype of the town and country Englishman. It took money and

56

fastidiousness, and for those over fifty, unlike Max Beaumont, most of them missed it, and had instead an indulgent, decadent look that went with a cunning eye and unsuitable perfumes. The kind that are always there, posturing in the expensive restaurants, on planes and in hotel foyers.

His parents' paths and mine might even have crossed, I thought. My mother played twice in an orchestra in Berlin, shortly after that first great war. And my father had spent time there in some deal that involved early electronic sound techniques being developed by Siemens. Which was why German was always taken as a serious language in the Tolly family.

"*Toll*," I remember my father saying to me, "is, after all, German for funny."

"You're doing all right, Max," I told him.

There were always von Klieschens in Berlin, Max Beaumont had said. They had been in banking and the Baltic timber trade, and somehow in silver, as well as the military and in the judiciary, and some of their tombstones were there, in what was left of a small cemetery he had looked for and found, in 1946. His grandfather on his mother's side had been a Schönberg, but he had been buried in Frankfurt. He didn't know too much more about that side of the family except that they were German Jewish and had always been in merchant banking for generations.

He had no brothers and sisters, although there were some family in Paris and Geneva, and connections in New York City, and it was, of course, through them that much later he had met Debby, his wife.

The house in which he had been brought up was pretty sizeable by any standards. For some reason that was not unusual in the Berlin of those days, it was painted pink, three-stories high, and stood on a corner site formed by Stulerstrasse and Klingelhofstrasse. Big windows of the early 1800s when the house was built, looked over the Tiergarten, so that with trees outside, and cobbles in front of the main entrance, the Prussian estate feeling was perpetuated. It had been the town house of a Prussian civil servant in

57

the 1870s. He had borrowed money from the Schönberg bank, and used the house as security. When Otto married Viola Rosa Schönberg, her father sold him the house, it was not given but the bargain price was dowry. They were married in 1922, and in 1924 Maximilian Daniel was born.

Of course, it was difficult with what happened afterwards to ever feel the same about Germany and a whole lot of other things. But it was a pleasant home, there on the Tiergarten side, for a start. But it was complicated to unravel feelings and memories when one of your parents was Jewish, and the other very much old school Prussian. A lot of people afterwards, couldn't believe that such a marriage was possible, but that was because they knew Germany only after Hitler came to power, and all they had heard about that time. Back in the very early twenties his parents' marriage had been regarded on both sides as a most suitable union between two dynasties. But it was also very soon to be that period of frantic inflation, with people carrying suitcases of banknotes to buy a loaf of bread. So that the von Klieschen background of landed wealth, and the Schönberg merchant trading and connections set such families apart. The big house by the Tiergarten was also partly in exchange for certain securities, in timber and land tenures, and an agreement that the Colonel, again in return, was to devote more of his time as a director of the bank, although still on the army reserve.

All this had to be explained, Max said, if the life of a small boy, and an only child, in the Berlin of those days was to be understood. Berlin was in many ways, for people in those circumstances, and as a place to live, one of the main cities of the civilised world. In the 1920s it was the most lively place in Germany. Still a young city that had developed too fast, everything concentrated in the capital. Politics, literature, the arts, press, theatre and cinema, and in the field of science too. Within a stone's throw of the von Klieschen house was the Kaiser Wilhelm Institute, which then had collected more Nobel Prizes than any other such place in the world. True it was the city of the Hohenzollerns, but it was also the capital of German working-class freedom, with not only the barricades of 1848, but the revolution that had ended the 1914–18 war, and the streets of workers'

58

bleak tenements that housed the communist masses, already involved in sporadic fighting with the unofficial armies of Hitler's illegal stormtroopers.

Max Beaumont was sheltered from all that sort of thing, at least to start with, living in the big house which was his world, but he would always remember the sounds and smells of that house. The city outside he saw only when he went with his parents to visit relations, or later was taken by Papa to ride a pony in the Grünewald under the tuition of plump, corsetted Frau Bloch, who wore a squat black top-hat and black satin jacket.

There were quite a lot of other figures who loomed large in his early memories of the von Klieschen world. A lot of his time was spent in the room that served as bedroom and playroom, ruled over by Maria, who as *Kindermädchen* had him as her special charge. There were other servants, plenty of them, in those days of post-first-war unemployment and depression, all like himself suffering from that overworked German word *Disziplin*. As an only child, the smallest person at the end of the line, and subject to correction by everyone it seemed, he could early tell the special authority of his parents.

"Maria," his mother said, "you need not take Maxi to bed yet! I would like him to be here with me for another ten minutes, he is helping me with my petit point!"

He loved his mother and the memory of her. She always seemed certain at first that everything would be all right if you spoke gently but firmly to people at all times. And that was true for a while, at least in the world of the big house. His mother was undoubtedly beautiful. She had given him the thick riot of black hair, that although it was worked round to the back of her head to look short, as was the 1920s fashion, could also be let down.

When she came to see him in his room, she would lean over his bed, with its short wooden sides, and her hair half hid those big, dark eyes. She had high cheekbones under the tawny colouring of her skin. The ends of her hair tickled his face, and the scent, that she wore at all times, filled the bedroom. It seemed also to pervade the small airy morning room where Max found the embroidery skeins she wanted,

59

or sat on her lap and was read to. Best of all he was allowed to play with Miska, the miniature Poodle. Then sometimes the noise and excitement would endanger the many small tables, set out with ornaments and objects, and again *Disiplin* would have to be asserted.

His father, on return from the bank, and having handed coat, hat and stick to old Herr Biene, his former army manservant, who waited in the hall, would enter this drawing room, sliding his feet across the carpet. He held out both hands to his mother, who would rise and tiptoe across to him so that they embraced in front of Max. Then, inexplicably Max would feel lonely.

He could remember the smell of the fire in that room, for there were usually more cold days in Berlin than warm ones. There was certainly no central heating in the large houses, only the big blue and white tiled country style *Ofens*, taller than himself, that stood in the corner of the big room and there were others in the hall, the main receiving room and the dining room with its high gallery.

"Now young man!" said his father, which was always understood to mean, "And what have you done today!"

"He has been helping me, Otto!" his mother would answer pacifically, because it seemed his father grew quickly impatient with Max's own accounts of his day.

"I had a walk in the park with Miska, Papa! Maria talked a long time with the other nannies in the Tierpark, and then I had lesson time with Miss Dorothy, and then I went with her to post Mama's letters in the yellow box in the wall at the corner of Klingelhofstrasse, and I am tall enough now to put the letters in the box without anyone to lift me!" He was out of breath at the end of the telling.

There will probably always be some particular scene when the curtain goes up on anyone's career, and probably any of those evenings when Papa returned home and stood in the big room would be about as good an introduction as any, to the life and times of Maximilian Daniel Schönberg von Klieschen.

To be tall would have seemed important, for his father, with his close shaven head which seemed oddly small in proportion to the rest of him, stood with a curiously upright stiffness that made him tuck in his chin to look down at his son. Max knew that Papa had been a colonel in the Kaiser's army. Sometimes he would still appear in the uniform of the Reichswehr for some reunion, and before Max was put to bed by Maria he would be allowed to admire the Iron Cross, the other orders, and buttons and *epaulettes*. On one side of Papa's face, the skin was taut over the cheek bones, and bright red, and on the other side where the skin was almost white, it was pitted with little blue marks.

Max had asked about the face colour and the marks, and was told: "Those are also war-decorations. A present from the Russians!" He pondered about this, but asked no more.

Once, while he was waiting in that same hall, with his mother and Maria, and old Biene, Max had circled round the big, dark, oriental carpet, imitating his father's walk, the stiff arm movements and the slight limp, with such accuracy as to cause dreadful consternation. Mama had taken him quite fiercely by his arm into her own downstairs room, but then she had relented and told him never to do that in front of the servants. Nor Papa himself. Because it would hurt his feelings. And Max was old enough to know how his own feelings could be hurt, if people made fun of him.

The best evenings were when Papa was pleased with what was reported to him of Max's day, especially progress with the work set by Miss Dorothy. She marked his two separate school books, and left them on a brass tray on one of the hall tables for *Der Freiherr* for it was she who told Max that Papa was a baron, as well as an honorary colonel.

"Sums!" said Papa, in his clipped, oddly high-pitched voice, picking up one of the books. "*Good* for sums I see! We shall need people who can add up, to deal with what is going on now! Ah! *Very good* for English, today I see! *Wie sagt man Zug auf Englisch?*"

"Train!" shouted Max excitedly, because this was known to be one of Papa's jokes, that had a special meaning. His father nodded, and smiled the thin-lipped, lopsided smile, as he took from a waistcoat pocket a long thin key.

"Only half an hour and not a minute more, Otto!" said Mama. "Then it is bed for Max! Uncle Paul and Tanja are coming to dinner, and we must change."

61

Father and son went through a doorway, down some stairs that turned into a lower floor. The long thin key unlocked a door, and the light switch was flicked on. There, stretching across the whole expanse of the cellar room was, to Max, the most special thing in his world, an unbelievable display, an Aladdin's cave. It was a *Märklin* train layout, with all the precise glory of the greatest of German model makers. The gleaming double tracks, the bends and straights, points and sidings, engine sheds and stations. There were long distance trains and goods engines, the tiny figures of railway staff and waiting passengers, tunnels with trees and hedges and even toy countryside, with farmhouses and animals. But, this was not Max's playroom. It was Papa's. It was Max's reward, when his daily report was good, or when Mama or Maria added their own commendation, that he was invited to share the fabulous train room that was the former Colonel and Freiherr's hobby, his way of unwinding after a day in the *Bankhaus*.

The Colonel moved the transformer switch that set everything going. Lights went on and a small goods train moved slowly forward.

"What is the English for *Frachtzug*?" It was not all playtime.

"Freighttrain!" said Max impatiently. It was more a catechism than a lesson. "Can I move the points Papa?"

"To the north track, when I say the word!" There was no left or right in the railway room, that could have led to accidents. "Do you know north?"

"Where you are standing, Papa!"

"So if I move to here, that is north?"

"No, north is where you were standing just then!"

"*Na, gut!* And what is the opposite?"

"South! And there is west and there is east!" The small boy knelt upright on the leather topped stool, proud, his outstretched arm pointing. Then his hand moved to the track switches. "Now?"

"Now!" said the Colonel. And both of them watched the little black freight engine, with its red wheels turning and silver couplings clinking. It moved onto its new line, towing the assorted goods wagons.

62

The big room had been designed for billiards, and the full-size table was still there, acting as foundation for the railway layout. The long electric lights hung overhead still, from brass chains secured to the high ceiling. The Colonel did not care for billiards, and the room had remained neglected and in dustsheets from when he and Rosa Schönberg had moved in at the time of their marriage in 1922. The Freiherr Colonel von Klieschen had bought, or transported, such additional items of furniture from his own family estates as were needed, to complete the marital home. When he looked back at the big square house on the corner site, as he left for the bank in the morning, the Colonel always felt a degree of satisfaction. In those days, so soon after the end of the Great War, a marriage of such shrewd significance as combined the Schönbergs' banking interests with the von Klieschen's Prussian family estates was regarded by many as a symbol of Berlin's traditional past and hope for the future. Rosa Schönberg's side of the family were, in any case, less secular than others, her father and his brothers were a small sect of Calvinist Jews. But cosmopolitan enough by banking prudence, to have family, and connections abroad.

All blessed the varying degrees of providence that had ordained a son. The first name of Maximilian had been the choice and decision of the Freiherr. It was after the famous soldier and first German Kaiser. The Daniel, after a grandfather Schönberg, was as his second name. The von Klieschens claimed long ago family ties with the famed Emperor, and this having been accepted, the boy was christened in a family chapel in one of the distant von Klieschen estates. Then again in Berlin in the synagogue on the corner of the Bismarkstrasse and the Hardenberg.

During the World War, as it was called by both sides, Otto von Klieschen had followed family tradition again into the cavalry, and command of a squadron of hussars on the Russian front. There were plenty of opportunities for shelling cavalry, and he had been an early casualty. This damaged the side of his face, and for a time embedded shrapnel in his spine. On recovery he was seconded to the transport staff, promoted to full colonel, and although trains were not horses, his tall, upright limping figure with the Iron

Cross and high-buttoned collar with its staff badges created an image of command efficiency on the railways.

When Schlummers great toyshop that had revived so quickly on the Leipzigerstrasse, showed the first *Märklin* electric railways, so greatly superior to any clockwork models, the Colonel had stood stiffly by the window, with a crowd composed as much of other adults as the horde of small boys. The former transport staff-officer watched with ice-blue eyes that lifted only at the corners, noting how everything was under remote control. The precision of the miniatures, perfect in their replica of the real thing, consoled the smouldering bitterness of defeat that was in every German officer's heart. Shortly afterwards the billiard room in the big house on Klingelhofstrasse was transformed.

Max as soon as he could walk, was allowed in there, not to touch but to observe. Later came participation, linked with instruction and practical tuition, as part of what Colonel von Klieschen saw as the right way to educate a son born of curious circumstances and far from the broad estates under the high, fresh skies of his own childhood.

When Papa lit a cigar, those evenings down in the railway room, Max knew where the matches were.

"Can I light it for you, Papa?"

"If you are careful yes, but not if you drop the match! Strike it that way – away from you! Ah!" The match was put into a big brass ash tray on a pedestal, that was partly formed from a shell case, which fact Max held in awe. The blue smoke from the cigar curled up round the long, green shaded lamps that had formerly overhung the billiard table, and the railway room always had a special smell, compounded of the cigar smoke, which was strong and not Havana, as he later knew, and an odd mixture of warm metal, oil and electricity that came from the network of trains and tracks and buildings. Papa had a special smell too, of the rough uniform coat that he put on in the railway room, the kind of coat that station men wore. There was also an extra smell of lavender, on the handkerchief he put in the top pocket where hung the whistle on a chain.

There was another delight, a gramophone, with its own turntable and a big crinkly horn, and this was used to play a special record of train noises, made by *Deutsche Grammophon*. Steam hissed, the cranks slowly rotated, the speeding rhythm of the wheels on the metal tracks, the Bahnhof loudspeakers that nobody could understand. And piercingly, in between, the train siren or the station master's whistle.

"Can I blow your whistle, Papa?"

Carefully it was pulled up on the chain, the Colonel pressed switches that set two engines in motion at different ends of the track, and Max, puffing out his cheeks, bit on the cold steel and blew. That was always a great moment. Even Papa looked pleased, and when this happened he patted Max's head, and smiled, his mouth a small tight V shape.

"*Na, Rosa!*" he said. Mother appeared round the door, with all the elaborate over-acting of a lady disturbing two gentlemen in a club room.

"Max is up too late! Maria is waiting, Otto!" she said reprovingly. "And now Uncle Paul is here with Tanja and they are saying Max should join us for dinner. Of course they have older children or they would understand better!"

Another figure, old Biene, appeared through the doorway. The Colonel had bought a Horsch *cabriolet* so that Herr Biene – who was always spoken of as *Die Biene*, the bee, had to drive sitting on a special cushion being so hunchbacked and short. With his pale face and rasping voice he sounded like a bee anyway. *Die Biene* had taken in more than a whiff of phosgene gas on the Russian front, Papa had explained, and this had not helped his lungs.

"The Freiherr has a bath waiting!" rasped Die Biene indignantly. He was allowed more liberties than any of the other servants.

"Maximilian can make his manners to his Uncle," declared Papa. "I shall take a quick bath and change. And you my dear, can be kind enough to see that Maria collects our *junger Mann* in ten minutes. Biene! See to the lights and things here!"

So commanding Papa! So firm, so kind, so splendid. And everyone moved swiftly to his bidding, so that Max went off happily with Mama, holding her hand, smelling her different, sharper perfume, jumping happily up the staircase that led to the big hall. Uncle Paul had promised

65

a bicycle for his next birthday, and that was only a week away now.

"Can I ask about the bicycle, Mama?"

"Paul has not forgotten, he mentioned it to me." His mother squeezed his hand. "It is going to be delivered, he said, so do not speak about it!"

Actually the birthday, apart from the bicycle, was not so happy. It was the day when Mama was suddenly taken unwell.

Uncle Paul had come with the bicycle, but now looking far from happy, with his dark black curly beard and tissue paper grey face he stood in front of the big, stone-flagged open fireplace. His wife, *Tante Tanja*, sat upright on the high backed settee, her gown, with its tiny buttoned front making a pattern at Max's eye level. She was Mama's younger sister, and Max made first a *diener* to her, with the quick down-bobbed head, not yet being old enough for *Küss die Hand*, and then again to his Uncle.

"Rosa has at the moment a slight indisposition," Papa had entered the room, accompanied by Maria, and Die Biene, who, wheezing desperately, hurried forward to place new logs on the big open fire. "The Herr Professor has gone, and she will be with us in a moment. Biene! You can tell Cook to hold dinner for quarter of an hour." The Colonel made all his pronouncements and orders in the same clipped, precise, unemotional tones. "She is all right, dear Rosa. I think perhaps the stairs in this place make her short of breath."

"*Zum Befehl, der Freiherr!*" The bent, scuttling figure of the Biene made for the big door, pulling its heavy curtain and rattling wooden rings behind him. Max could always hear the sound of those curtains on their heavy rails that covered the inside doors against drafts and noise. Maria remained behind, her hands clasped on her apron.

"Maximilian, he should come now!"

"Let him stay a little longer, dear Maria," Aunt Tanja spoke, again with the permitted manner with close servants that was the accepted tradition. Also, in the matter of children and nannies, his aunt could without question overrule Papa. "He will kiss good-night to his mother."

66

"Please to ring the bell!" said Maria, with only the slightest toss of her head, and she too left through the curtained door.

When Max's mother reappeared, she was holding the arm of her own companion and dressing maid, a tall, strong, flaxen-haired young woman with the same Grecian face that featured on a marble bust that stood at the foot of the big staircase in the hall. This was Max's private thought, but he had never asked whether Annamarie had modelled for the bust, or if, for some reason, it went the other way round.

"*Na*, Rosa!" Papa stood, holding out his own arm, stiffly, while the statue-faced Annamarie wheeled Max's mother round into the chair opposite Aunt Tanja.

That scene remained for Max like a tableau, with Mama, leaned back in the tall chair, her own, normally strong-featured, dark-hued face suddenly masked and pinched, pallid papier-mâché, the thick black ringlets of her hair twisting from under the two heavy combs as though in their own agony. Her eyes were closed. Her lips, thin and straight, opened briefly.

"It will pass. *Es geht schon!*"

Annamarie held her wrist hoping to take a pulse reading, and stared unseeingly. Papa stood in the centre of the floor, almost as though to attention. He looked down at his wife, the bright blue eyes like glass, his sharp nose lifted, like a small national eagle. Aunt Tanja waited, motionless, both hands with their many rings, holding the ends of the chair arms.

Uncle Paul was the first to speak. He folded his arms, and the artificial lights made his large face paler, and his eyes small and dark. It seemed that his tongue was used to push words from between his thick lips.

"At least it is not the lungs! That is right, Otto? That is what the Professor said?" Although his brother-in-law was the senior partner of the banking union the Freiherr found him irritating. He had stayed safely in Berlin during the war, advising the government. Doubtless effectively, but also probably dealing mainly with the obvious.

"It is circulation. The tablets are helping." With a sudden understanding he turned and put one of his large hands on the shoulder of Max who was standing still beside him.

67

"Mama will be all right! Won't she, Max? Take her hand! There! That will help her *Kreislauf*!" And Max remembered how that word was always there, over those following years, as his beautiful Mama recovered and declined, improved and faded.

Kreislauf. The circulation. That was the diagnosis of the solemn doctors and Professors. The heart, of course. And the blood pressure that had never been really right since Max was born. Although nobody said it in so many words when he was around. But health, or the lack of it, and a morbid obsession with illness and symptoms seemed an inseparable part of life in those times, so soon after the Great War. There were many cripples in the streets. People begged, children even, of his own age. Max passed them on his way to the Tierpark or when he took Miska for a walk with Maria. Children who had grey faces and dragged rickety legs along, or leaned against the railings of the big houses or sat on the kerbstones waiting, with buckets and little shovels, for the horse droppings.

Max was too young then to know anything of the other side of *Grosstadt Berlin*. That other side of neurotic, unstable, fashionable decadence that paraded sometimes openly, but mostly hidden, in the bars and cabarets, the famous *Adler* and other hotels, and the many private salons. That legacy of death, the unbelievable casualties and carnage of the war still stalked in Berlin. But it became real for him suddenly, the occasion starting as a promised treat.

"I shall take our *junger mann* down to Schlummers, and we shall buy some things for the railway!" Papa announced.

His mother was in her chair in the small morning room and she held out a hand to him. He went to her and stood close by the chair. He could smell the sweet mixture of scents that combined when she was close. The eau de cologne, the faint smell of her freshly ironed blouse, like warm, baked bread. The frilled, sleeve cuff tickled his forehead as he kissed her hand. When she kissed the top of his head in return, he could tell she had just taken her after-breakfast medicine.

"You must take care my men!" she said. "Maria says there is a lot of *Krach* in the side streets. There was fighting with the police in the night! I shall stay here with Miska to guard me until you come quickly back."

68

"We shall go in the Horch," Max's father said. "Die Biene will drive us there." This was an extra part of the treat because Father had only recently acquired the Horch, an 835 Cabriolet model.

"Uncle Paul does not approve of the Horch!" Father said, but did not explain. His father never minded about saying such things, and Max loved him for it. The idea that travelling in that wonderful car with the roof down, so that people stared as they passed, added to a feeling that it did not matter what Uncle Paul thought.

Die Biene dropped them off not far from Schlummers. He had to get petrol, and there were not so many petrol stations in those days. He would return for them again, outside the toyshop.

Max held his Father's hand as they waited on the brink of the Charlotenburger Chausee, the broad avenue which flowed dead-straight from West Berlin to the grey pillars of the Brandenburg Gate. The Kaiser had intended it as a victory avenue down which all conquering armies would march home in triumph. All Max could see now were streams of cars, trams, motorbuses and horse traffic that normally bore down this magnificent speed track.

Today it was oddly quieter, and there was no difficulty in getting quickly across. There was still quite a lot of horse transport in Berlin in 1931. You had to avoid treading on the little piles of steaming droppings or the spread flat kind. Max watched the small, dirty-faced boys, darting with bucket and scraper between the traffic to scoop up the dung. Maria had told him they sold it for two pfennigs. It was to help make flowers grow, she said, matter of factly, which made it seem better.

It was when Max and his Father were in Schlummers and had finished buying things that were to extend even further the glory of the toy railway, that the noise from outside reached them. There were few customers in the shop that day, and all of them on the ground floor moved quickly to the main doors.

A half dozen Weimar police in heavy coats and with the coal-scuttle *picklegruber* spiked helmets were spread out along the pavement. An uproar of noise, with hundreds of shouting voices and chanting was all Max could hear, unable to see anything, squeezed between his father and the other grown-ups. There were whistles blowing, a strange sound, wooden rattlers, not unlike machine-gun fire, and then a fearful sound of hundreds of feet running along the pavement and out on the street and there was screaming and shouting. Men as well as women were screaming. The policemen seemed to disappear in a melée of bodies, arms and legs, as the shop doors were quickly closed, with Max and his father and a press of other customers on the inside. There was a splintering crash as the shop windows were shattered, the glass collapsing like great sheets of ice. But the doors seemed to be of tougher stuff.

It was curious how at such moments things seemed to stand still. There was the ice-glass falling on the toys in the window, his father lifting him up, and with one hand holding Max's head down on his shoulder. He could smell the bay-rhum that Father used on his cropped grey hair, and did not feel afraid. Outside, the battle between the police and the mob raged down the Leipzigerstrasse. He might have thought of it in recollection as a nightmare, but it was always like that even afterwards, Max said. When it was real, he felt only a sort of cold detachment. It was waiting, or imagining, the unreal things that brought on the shakes as he called it.

They came this time, when he and Father were safely back in the big house, to which they had walked, after Father had spoken to a police inspector, some way apart from Max.

It was darker even than usual in the receiving room and there were candles lit. Apparently electricity had failed in parts of Berlin, and Mother was there with Maria and Annemarie, and her sister, and Tante Tanja. Two of the women were crying, and Max lay on the floor cuddling Miska the little dog, which seemed to be upset too. His Father spoke, and said only one thing.

"They killed Biene!"

Then Max cried, and sat on his Mother's lap, and she pressed his face in turn to hers and he could not tell whether the salt of her tears was what he tasted, or whether they were his own. It was really like a dream as his father had told it, something that was not true.

70

"On the Leipzigerstrasse. It was the communists of course! They came out of the back streets in hundreds, more like thousands! There have been five thousand camping in the Grünewald you know, Paul saw it the other day he said, living like the old-time armies, laying siege! In tents and tin-can shacks!" Father's voice shook slightly, as he sought to light a cigar. "Biene was sitting in the car outside, waiting for us. They were coming and he got out and tried to run, but they caught him, and killed him, kicking him on the ground and swarming over him! One of the police saw it. I saw some of them badly hurt too! Lying on the road. Madness! The car is finished of course, turned over and set on fire! *Verdamnt! Das neue Horch! Und der kleine!* With one lung gassed out, crippled already! He had seen real fighting! And the bastards had to get him because he was driving an expensive car! What in God's name is it all coming to?"

"Otto, Otto!" His mother cried, and he felt her stiffening and twisting under him. Max felt he had to stand up. On Mother's knees he was small and crouched and vulnerable, like Die Biene.

"Why did they kill Die Biene?" He remembered his voice high pitched as though it was someone else's in the big dim living room, with everything moving in the flame light of the candles.

"Because they are against the rich people!" said Mama. She sought to hold his hand again, but he twisted it behind his back.

"Are we rich? Was Die Biene rich?"

"He worked for us!" His father was not looking at anyone. He stood straight-backed and distant, staring at the far wall of the living room where the dark, heavy portraits of his own ancestors hung in gilt frames.

More times came later that year, when other things happened that Max did not understand then, but could remember. And not so much his own feelings, but a perception of the adults' feelings. He must have been seven, or would it be eight? About then, he was allowed to join the grown-ups when visitors came to the big Klieschen house, usually for dinner in the evening, or for midday on Sunday.

There were various customs and inhibitions that involved both these eating times, and days of the week, or months of the year. He heard some light-hearted exchanges between his parents. Either if her relations were dining, or some of the Prussian family, of which there seemed fewer. Papa made wry remarks, and Max remembered once that Mama had her lace handkerchief to her eyes over something that was said, and again Father had stared blankly out of the big windows which overlooked the entrance on the Klingerhofstrasse side waiting for guests to arrive.

It was about something called Kosher, which Max at first thought was like *Küss die Hand*, or making a *Diener* which was the little head-dropping bow he had to make to all grown-ups when he shook hands, whether they were family or not. But never to servants, some of whose hands he might shake and others not. Like Biene who had shaken his hand, and Maria, but not the cook or the man who came to do the gardening. Max found it all very complicated.

On these dining occasions some of his cousins were there, all like himself, dressed in best clothes, the girls in black or red velvet with lace collars and cuffs. The boys, who were Uncle Paul's sons, and one who was Uncle Herschel's, in tunic coats, and although their hair was the same strong black texture as his own they wore it long, like some of the portraits of the older ancestors that were in the dining room. At first he liked this new world of being grown up.

About that time he went to a fancy dress party that he had been invited to by the physician who attended Mother and who had a large family. They lived in a smaller house in a road nearby. Mother and Maria had made a costume for him, not unlike the ones that his cousins wore, all velvet and buttons, and a hat with a feather plume. He was given some sheet music to carry and told that he was *Der junge Beethoven*. This Max felt less happy about, especially when the grown-ups at the party had asked if he could play the music, and he had to admit that he could not. But there had been the marvellous discovery of ice cream, and one of the doctors' daughters agreed to exchange pink and white coloured, and they sat together. She had said: "Open your mouth," like Maria did. And it was a strange feeling when she put the ice cream on her spoon slowly between his open lips. Did it start so early and intensely for everyone? That cold spoon, turning slowly in his mouth, while the plump little girl looked at him steadily, with expressionless face.

The first time Mother had put him in the sailor suit for lunch was different. The cousins had put their tongues out quickly behind the grown-ups' backs. They were a little older than he, the Schönberg cousins, with their handsome sallow faces and dark bright eyes.

"Where is your ship, Admiral?" whispered the Herschel boy, and it was again like being Beethoven who could not play. At table the children were separated, sitting between the various adults to prevent what was called whispering and being rude. Manners were everything, and included keeping hands in sight on the edge of the table and never under it, when it was considered they might be up to all sorts of mischief. When Max had once asked Maria why, when he was alone, and what sort of mischief she had coloured up, and replied that he was never to mind, and to eat up his soup.

"You *drink* soup!" said Max, eyeing her over his spoon. He knew this because Mama had told him.

"It is eating!" said Maria. But he could tell she was unsure.

"Perhaps eating is not Kosher!" Max had said kindly, spooning away. And again Maria had looked uncomfortable.

At the family gatherings, the adults talked as though children were not present. This was not so much that the younger members were treated as inferior. They were old enough now to learn about more things than were taught in the nursery, and by listening, and not being allowed to talk among themselves, the children would become informed and *gut manieriert*. That was the idea. Sometimes the conversation moved in a way that led one or other of the adults, generally Uncle Paul, who was the Bank *Präsident*, to say something in a foreign language. It was not English that Max was already learning, it was in fact the universal *Pas avant les enfants*. One summer evening all caution was

73

abandoned, as even the servants hung anxiously round the long table, making excuses to linger and overhear anything they could glean.

Something had gone wrong with money. The children had to keep quiet anyway, and Max remembered pretty well everything about what went wrong with the Reichsmark, that July of 1931. The Saturday evening, that summer weekend, it seemed that most of the family were there, perhaps twenty adults plus the young, and there was no great interest in food or any of the usual topics. It was rare that bank business made conversation at the table, but that night it was nothing else.

It was interesting what Papa had to say. It seemed that much of the day he had spoken on the telephone. Because it was acknowledged that his English was the best of the members of the main board, he had been put into contact with those English and American banks with which the family had closest contact. It had not been easy, Father had reported. He looked round the table, keeping the monocle in his eye, his back straight as he talked. Such things Max remembered, because the other men, who seemed to wear unrelieved black with high white collars, as though it was an agreed uniform, crouched, or held themselves with their arms on the table. He noticed how Uncle Paul crumpled, and slowly broke up, his little roll or bread all the while that Father talked.

"They are difficult to reach. They are avoiding us! That much is quite clear. I was asking for information only, at first. We have worked together with some of these concerns for over a hundred years, that you know! A few of the top people are personal friends – Paul you, and you Jacob! You have spoken with some in New York. I spoke with Chicago and London. You took Paris. It is the same story. It has nothing to do with the war. That is over now. Not forgotten, but a long time over, and we are going down the drain! It is too big for them to help us!"

The two sons of Uncle Paul at the table that evening, had adult faces now, immobile, high cheekboned, silent. Their wrists rested correctly on the edge of the white tablecloth, while their eyes moved like small, dark marbles from one speaker to the other. Then Max saw Mother was crying, quietly, noiselessly into a small ball of handkerchief held in her hand.

"I have my money box!" Max cried, almost shaking with the braveness that he had pluck to speak up at all. "I know because I looked this morning. You can have my money box!"

It was the only time that strange evening that there was anything resembling laughter, and he could remember his Father looked at him for a moment, then thanked him, gravely, and he was the only one who was not smiling. His Mother next to him, took his hand, and then, with the two aunts and his girl cousins got up. Servants pulled the chairs, and he had to follow behind her long skirt, out through the big doors, although the men, and the two older boy cousins, stayed.

It was the following Monday that was really the start of everything else that followed. Black Monday it was called.

It was quite impossible for Max not to know what was going on. The telephone, still a relatively new device in even a wealthy household, hung from a box in the hall. When it rang, one or other of the servants answered with a stock phrase. "*Hier Residenz von Klieschen!*" If Mother was wanted, she would be called to the hall.

It was worrying for all the female relations whose husbands were in the same position, and most of them came to call and would drink small cups of coffee with Mother in her private salon. When his schoolroom work was finished, Max hung about with them.

"There are queues of depositors that run around the block!" Aunt Tanja was saying. "Paul says every bank has crashed!" She paused and looked at Max. Her voice became a whisper. "Have you heard?" She mentioned names, men whom she and Mother knew. "At least, he has not been heard of since yesterday! Von Schuter drowned, that is in the Grunewald, and poor Brugger cut his wrists in the bath they say!"

"Enough! Quite so!" Mother gave Max a push. "Maxi – go and find Maria and tell her you need to get some fresh air! A walk in the park will do you both good."

"They must take care!" Tante Tanja, put out by the interruption brought about to her stories, wagged a cautionary finger. She wore a considerable number of rings on both hands, and now she tossed her head, swinging the black natural ringlets that descended from under the small peacock-blue hat. "It is not safe in the streets, Rosa! Not anywhere! I came in the car, and made big Emanuel drive it. On the streets there are crowds, looking for trouble, I can tell you! There are thousands more, camping out in the Grünewald, they say, and your Tiergarten is a place where they are marching. Not the communists but these Stormtroopers! The ones in the black uniforms!"

"They are not supposed to wear uniforms!" Mother said. She looked very pale, and Max gave her a kiss and hug that made her cry out, so he had to kiss her again, and then a *Küss die Hand* for Aunt Tanja, and a *diener* before he left the room to go and find Maria.

Father seemed more prepared to talk with him in a new and different way, in the weeks that followed Black Monday. Max asked why Biene had been replaced by another man called Dieter.

"I must have a driver," Father explained. "It is as simple as that, Max! I am not a motor mechanic! Sometimes your mother needs driving out, visiting, or shopping, and the Dieter will drive her. Now that the Horch is gone and times are hard the Bank will not supply another, and we have to make do with a Mercedes."

"I like the Mercedes," Max had said. "I like the star in front! It is like we have on top of the Christmas tree!"

His Father had looked at him coldly, unamused. He seemed to carry himself even more stiffly these days. His pale face and his grey hair cropped short, made a striking contrast with the Schönberg uncles.

Mother was anxious for both of them. "These are not good times for any of us, Maxi!" she said. "Papa is very greatly worried and now he is sleeping badly, and dreaming of the war again. When he comes back this evening, if it is a reasonable time, you will ask him to play with the soldiers! Tell him you want to be like him! He would not admit it, but he likes that!" Already Max knew instinctively that his

76

parents bridged gaps of their unusual marriage, and what he meant to both of them.

Papa seemed pleased when he asked, and they went to the study, a special room that was also on the first floor, past the big salon. There was heavy brown furniture and a dark-blue carpet and matching velvet curtains. The single window looked out towards the Tiergarten, and there were books that went up in shelves to the ceiling. And there were the library steps, that Max used to climb up and come down again when he was allowed into the study, until his Father would say: "Come on, Max! Stop performing like a circus bear!"

Max used this as a lever to say: "If I stop, can we do the soldiers?" He had learned that play was not the word one used for soldiering.

The soldiers were made of lead, and beautifully modelled and painted, standing on other shelves in assembled rows, as separate regiments, even separate individuals. Especially the ones on horseback or the commanders. Some of these were under glass cases that were carefully lifted down by Father.

Papa knew everything about them all, and they were solemnly paraded on the big desk top, while Max sat in the high-backed armchair and watched.

"You will have to be a real Maximilian!" His Father said that evening. "It was I who gave you that name because the first Maximilian was the first Kaiser of The Holy Roman Empire! He was the last of the Great Knights, a Hapsburg of course, and his kingdom included Burgundy in France and Austria as well! Think of that little Max! Your Mother accepted the name, because he was also a friend of artists, including Dürer. Do you see Dürer's picture of the old knight on the wall there? Mama named you Daniel after her Grandpapa, and you have also your other family name of Schönberg because that is the name of the Bankhaus of which I am also a director." Father seemed to need to talk. He moved the soldiers and looked strained and tired.

"As Emperor, you may join the Archduke Chalers-Walgren who defeated Napoleon!" said his father stiffly as he put the little equestrian figure on the desk, and as though as an afterthought, straightened and clicked his heels. He turned back to the silent miniature ranks on the shelves,

77

handing down each little lead soldier with great care, and
Father's fingernails were always clean, cut blunt and square
ended.

"Here is the other Emperor! Franz Joseph! He was also
a Field Marshall of course." The second little mounted
figure wore a great hat with a big plume of green feathers.
"Now here come the troops!" First were the famous White
Guards, with the eagles on their helmets. "Here are the
Black Huzzars! *Die Totenkopf Huzzaren*, and some Uhlan
officers of the same period. 1900, although you know, Max,
they went into action at the start of 1914 looking like that!
Now these are much older."

The ranks of mounted and infantry regiments were beginning to cover the desk top. Outside the window in the
Tiergarten it was dark now, and a rain shower was beating
on the glass, but the blue velvet curtains were still undrawn.
It was a special moment of closeness with Father.

"These are Coldstream Guards – about 1712. And here is
the Artillery Corps! That was my outfit, after the Hussars
until I went onto the Staff. See that Fusilier! Pink facing to
grey uniform, cocked hats, knee boots!" There were more
and more in the collection.

"Here is the best piece!" Papa always said this when he put
down the much larger mounted figure. "That is an Uhlan of
the Napoleon time! Look at that plume on his helmet, and
you see he carries a flagged lance *and* a sabre. *Ja, dann war es
etwas*! That was the time to be a soldier! None of the shrapnel
and machine guns and gas."

Now he seemed to notice the window behind the desk for
the first time, and slowly drew the curtains. "The girls will
not do it when I am in here," he said. He mostly called the
female servants *Mädchen*.

"Tell me about the shrapnel, Papa." He knew now it had to
do with the little blue marks on the backs of those big hands
and the pale side of the face. And it was then for the first
time that he was allowed to take hold of one of the hands,
and study the little purple-blue flecks on the pale skin.

"Was that shrapnel, Papa?"

"Actually a mine. *Schrotten!*"

"Did it hurt?"

78

"Actually not that badly. I was lucky."

"I would like to be a soldier, Papa!"

There was another pause. His father was looking at him in a strange way, looking down at the crowded desk with its miniature lead army.

"That will not be so easy! Probably there will never be armies again." Max had cause to remember that, not once but many times.

"It would be better to be a banker, my boy! Look at the present time, a sort of war – a financial war! Because we are bankers we can still eat, and pay the servants, and a few more things. Ordinary money is worthless."

"What do we pay with, Papa!"

"Dollars. And gold. The bank has both."

"What are dollars?"

"American money."

"Do the Americans give us their money?"

"Certainly not! They have sold it to the bank."

There was a small knock at the door, and Father turned quickly, so that the light glinted on his monacle. "*Herein!*"

It was Maria, who stood quietly in the door, bobbing to the Colonel, who stood stiffly in front of the assembled army.

"If I go to bed, can I have my pocket money in dollars?" Max asked.

That winter Mother went into hospital. What exactly was the matter no-one seemed to know. She had been in the big bed in her room for over a week before moving into the *Klinic*, and when the time came she kissed Max, and said she would soon be back. Papa drove off in the black Mercedes driven by the new chauffeur Dieter, with the private ambulance following behind.

Max had tried not to cry when the ambulance had gone, and Maria took him on her lap, a thing she did seldom, and cradled his head on the dark-blue starch of her bosom. Max felt the underlying softness and the familiar special scent of Maria. Staff did not take baths so frequently, and Maria smelt faintly of perspiration and lavender. To Max it seemed that all the grown ups smelled of something identifying. His mother of cough sweets and eau de cologne, Father of

79

shaving soap, and his suits of wool and sometimes mothballs. Mother must have noticed it too, because she would say: "Otto, you must get Dieter to hang out your suits before you wear them! Biene would always have done so!" And this was understood to refer to the mothballs, which Father found in his jacket pocket and would give to Max. It was one of his early jokes.

"They are cannon balls to kill the moths!"

"It is something wrong with the Kreislauf." Maria soothed Max, "Herr Professor will put it right!" Max had started recently to wash all over with cold water. It was to improve his Kreislauf, he knew, because Father said it could affect every part of the body, and every organ.

Maria sought to cheer him up by reading to him from *Struwelpeter* with its lurid-coloured illustrations. It seemed to be a book that amused all grown ups, but Max found little that was amusing in the cautionary tales, and much that was frightening. When it came to Little Suckathumb and the cruel tailor whose scissors went snip-snip-a-snip, he slid off Maria's lap and ran down to the big hall behind the front door, to stare out of the window and wait for the return of his father.

Those weeks when his Mother was in the hospital, which he visited, sometimes with Papa and once or twice with Maria, meant inevitably that he was more often alone with the servants, in the big house. The new governess who had been brought in by Mama just before she went into hospital, became the person who figured largest. She was called Frau Lingwurst, a middle-aged thickset, widowed lady. There were a great number of widows like Frau Lingwurst in post-1918 time. She had been the wife of an officer, and had taken up private teaching. Thus, approved by both parents, she was not as well accepted by the servants, and even gentle Maria was spiteful. Behind her back they called her the *Wurst*, leaving out the first part of her name.

Wurst being the German for sausage, even Max thought this funny, and when she rebuked him on their first or second morning, in what was now called the school room, and had been one of the spare bedrooms, he told her she was a sausage, and he would eat her. He also threw his pencil at her, the books on the little desk he scuffed on the floor, and drummed his heels on the carpet. Frau Lingwurst, scarlet, slapped his face.

All this was reported to his Father. Max had been called to see him in the big drawing room, where both stood facing each other, and Max looked at his Father's toe caps. They were highly polished, under the pale chamois leather spats Father wore. It was winter, and the streets were wet and slushy for walking.

"I shall not tell Mama! It would make her very unhappy to hear how you have behaved! When she is so unwell that is a poor return to her and myself. Is it not? *Ja oder nein*?" His Father was shaking, as Max could see from his hands, as he started to look up. Father's face was pale, he never flushed, but his short cut grey hair seemed to bristle, his neck twisted and turned in the high stiff collar.

"You are a big boy now, and your lessons are important! Germany will need all the intelligent people it can get. Most were killed! Soon you will be a man and you will not be rude to women! Not to Frau Lingwurst! She is teaching somewhere else this afternoon, so tomorrow morning you will say you are sorry! I shall be here when she comes."

"Yes, Papa."

The Colonel pulled the old-fashioned bell rope by the fireplace, and in silence they waited. It was Maria who appeared, as though by arrangement.

"You will take the young man, and put him to bed. He will go to bed now!" Papa had turned away, not even wishing him goodnight.

Max wished Mama had not been in hospital. Small and lonely he got into bed between the cold sheets. Maria returned. She carried a bright-green apple.

"There! I suppose I shouldn't. Now eat that and go to sleep! Your Father is right to be angry, but of course it is because he is worried about your Mother, and we are all sick about the stupid money and the reds and blacks fighting."

"Tell me about the fighting, Maria?"

But Maria had retired, switching out the one light by the brass switch at the door, and leaving behind only the scent of starched uniform, mingled with perspiration. The apple tasted extra sweet in the dark.

When Mother came back from the Klinic, she still had to stay in bed, and Max came to see her in the morning, before his lessons, and then again at midday, when she had a small meal on a tray. In the evening when Papa came home, Mother kissed Max when it was time to leave her room. Max could smell that she was unwell, in spite of the lavender and eau de cologne.

"Will you get better soon, Mama? I have a new skipping rope! We skip in the Tiergarten by the skipping fountain. Maria knows the other ladies there and I can play with their children."

"Perhaps I can see you skipping soon, Maxi! The Herr Professor says I may get up for a little while next week. Now you must go to bed and leave Papa and I to talk."

The house became strangely full of furniture, and when Max asked Maria why, she shook her head. Mama explained, in a way he could understand, that the various pieces belonged to desperate friends and distant relations, who now had only such things to sell to anyone who could pay in money that would buy food and other necessaries. His Father had accepted a magnificent silver clock to go in his study.

"What do I need a clock for?" he said testily to Max, who was with him when the delivery had been completed, and the clock stood shining gently where a regiment of lead *Dragoner* had held the shelf space. "I have my pocket watch which is enough, and that confounded thing is going to ring the hours like the church in here!"

"It is to help people who are poor," Max told him firmly.

"You sound like a communist, young man!"

"What is a communist?"

His father paused, looking at the displaced *Dragoner* now forced to thicken the ranks on the other display shelves. "Biene was killed by them. Of course we must help the less fortunate. I have bought a quantity of wine for the cellar from the widow Leipuss. The poor man committed suicide – he killed himself," father explained.

Max wanted to ask more questions, but the look on his father's face was not encouraging.

Once again Mama was back in the Klinic. Now Father had the other men of the family, and male friends to dinner. At the table, when Max and the cousins were allowed for the meal itself, the talk was as usual intended to inform and develop their precocious intelligences but strictly on the "do not speak unless spoken to" principle.

"It is all very dangerous!" Uncle Paul's head with its carefully parted hair was bent over his soup spoon. "Can you explain, Otto, how that man Helldorf – supposedly an aristocrat as he is a Count, has become chief of the Stormtroopers? And released from the Criminal Court after a trial to prove that he led the smashing of Jewish shop windows? Eh?"

Max looked to his father, but saw his face had gone into the old, staring familiar mask.

"This Schickelgruber," said one of the other relations. "He is trying to persuade the Chancellor to give him power to put these communists down, but we must be careful! Paul is right! He says that Jewish business and Jewish banking is financing socialism! It suits them to say that of course."

The Colonel, at the head of his own table, sat stiffly, his fingers turning the stem of his glass, and he spoke shortly. "The man is hoping to win an election for his party on any basis that he can! He was a corporal! Do you think Hindenburg will trust a corporal?"

"That chief of his bodyguard, what's his name . . .?" One of the family friends emptied his wine glass, and Father signalled to the Dieter, who functioned as wine waiter, and refilled the glass with the spare hand latched behind his tail coat.

"*Sepp Dietrich!*" said Father grimly. "A sergeant of Bavarian cavalry, I found! Corporal Schickelgruber claims the Iron Cross!"

"We know about that!" A bald-headed man with a black patch over one eye and a scar, also a friend of his father, and whose villainous appearance fascinated the boys, spoke in his clipped Berlin-Prussian. "He is supposed to have taken fifteen Frenchmen prisoner, single-handed! Of course they were all shell-shocked and half-starved in the trenches."

Uncle Paul shook his head. "It is not as simple as all that. Part of this gang, or entourage, or whatever you wish to call it, is Prince August Wilhelm! Consider that! Yet they call

themselves National Socialists! One thing is for sure, dear
family and colleagues. None of them is on the side of a
Jewish bank. But we are Germans! Yes, Germans too! For
generations!" Uncle Paul passionately hit the table, making
the cutlery jump.

"Don't let it keep you awake, Paul." Father looked with
sympathy down the table to his older brother-in-law. "The
bank has a lot of the money abroad already!"

"They could hold us hostage, to get it back, if they get into
power," Uncle Paul said slowly. Max could see his small, sad
face with the black eyes, like currents in the sallow pudding
of his skin, dart momentarily to where his own sons were
sitting.

"Paul, come! There is Weismann," said Father. Do not
forget he is state secretary of the Prussian Ministry of the
Interior! I know confidentially that he plans to disarm these
stormtroopers of this Hitler, as he calls himself. Now that
is very confidential, and I should not have spoken about
it here. Corporals and sergeants! Bavarian and Austrian
rabble!" Father signalled for his own glass to be recharged.

Mother's health did not improve, and the family went away
to the coast that summer, to Heringsdorf on the Baltic where
Uncle Paul had a house that his side of the family had made
use of for two generations.

Heringsdorf was elegant and expensive, more like the
English resorts had been in Regency days. The little black,
red and gold flags of the Republic flew from walls of sand
which each family heaped up round their basketwork beach
shelters, the *Strandkörper*. The next resort along was Bansin,
where the flags were black, white and red or the maltese cross
and eagle of the old Imperial navy. Because now there was
no peace by the seaside either. At night, and sometimes
even in daylight, the young braves of Bansin stole out and
wrecked the sand castles of Heringsdorf. They tore down
the "jew banners" and wrote obscenities in the sand with
sticks.

On one daylight occasion, even Father appeared uneasy,
and stood up as the sound of gunfire, brief shots, sent women
to clutch children, lying on the sand, or scrambling back
towards the houses behind the beach.

84

"Lunatics! Where are the police? This is no place for shooting!"

"It is the *Deutsch National* rowdies from Bansin!" One of the Schönberg cousins, squatting on the sand beside Max tried to sound calm as he tossed two round stones in his hands, and looked up, squinting at Father in the sunlight.

"The police are on their side, Uncle! Everyone says so!"

Eventually an ambulance party came, and from where they now all stood could be seen a small group carrying a covered stretcher crossing the empty beach.

After that Mama's health seemed to decline rather than improve and they all returned to Berlin early, but whenever afterwards, many years later, Max heard the strolling lilt of "We do like to be beside the seaside" he saw the sunlight on the waves at Heringsdorf, and heard the cries of alarm of the families on the beach in 1932.

That autumn he was eight, and his father decreed that he should start school. There had been much discussion as to whether he should go to the *Gymnasium* or to a private school, where he might be expected to get more attention. Uncle Paul's two went to a private academy, but then they had been to a *Volkschule* from when they were five. Their school was too far for Max to travel each day.

"Full-time school will be a strain for Maxi," his Mother said. He sat on a small stool by her bed, while they debated almost as though he were not there. Frau Lingwurst had finished her task earlier in the summer, and had rewardingly declared that *der junge Mann* had surprisingly good English and even better maths "as becomes the son of such an eminent banking family". For this verdict, the servants said, the sausage had received a fine handshake in negotiable currency.

"He can walk to the *Vereinschule*," Papa declared. He stood in front of the bedroom fireplace in his usual way. "After he has been a few times with Maria or Dieter. There is no need for the car, but he needs to be sure of the way. I know Maria is your maid now dear," he said to Mama, "but she can be spared in the afternoon, and Dieter can do it in the morning. After that Max will probably find one or two others who come from this way. We shall see. He is a big boy now, and in any case he needs the exercise!" Papa coughed;

which was his usual signal that the discussion on the matter was over. But he went on to make a second decision. One for which Max had been grateful all his life.

"The school is not so good on games and sport. That I agree is one disadvantage compared with the *Volkschule*! But as you will have two afternoons off, or that finish early, I have arranged for you to start riding lessons with Ritmeister Mocher in the Grünewald! I know Mocher. He has the best establishment. You will also ride on Saturdays. That will prevent those shoulders from getting round – and teach you a lot of things you don't learn in a classroom. Na-ja!" This was another of Father's terminating noises.

"Otto!" Mother made a small wail. "You must go yourself and see that Max is able! He must not ride alone!"

"Of course he will not ride alone!" Father seemed almost to snarl. "I have done my cavalry school, it is not like that! There is no danger, just some good hard work and discipline – yes, and some sport too!" Max had already jumped up from the stool and impulsively flung himself round his Father's leg. Not unkindly he was detached.

"Tomorrow we will go to Leipzigerstrasse. To Wertheim's. Breeches, boots, hat! And school things, the boy will need . . ."

On that expedition they had indeed bought enough to warrant a shop assistant carrying bags to the waiting car outside. In those days he learned, there was no question of jodphur boots, it was knee boots and small flared-cut breeches, and a hard hat something like a postman wore.

Max set off for the first day of school with the correct satchel, an absurdly big affair with a furry flap, that sat with cross ties high up between his shoulders. Maria escorted him that first time, over the Ladwehrkanal by the Cornelius-brucke, and the name of the bridge was comforting, that first day, on the way to school. *Babar the Elephant* by Jean de Brunhof had just been translated into German, and Max was given the book by Aunt Tanja. He had come to love Cornelius, the oldest elephant.

"Will it be horrid at school, Maria?"

"Of course not! The Sausage said you were a clever boy!" She squeezed his hand when they separated at the cloakroom door. Shoes were changed, and special school overalls were put on.

After a week Max looked forward to it. There were less than a hundred pupils, some a year younger than he was, some of the girls going on to fourteen. The teachers were all women, except for two masters, both part-time, one taking music and the other dancing. Max was not to have either, at least not for the time being it was decided – the Colonel's decision again. Perhaps because of the lead soldiers, Max liked history especially as the teacher had identified his name in class with the first Kaiser of all Germany, which made him feel special. His English, thanks to the sausage, was by far the best in his class.

The riding lessons were a completely different world. Intense, demanding, absorbing, they involved total pain and pleasure in a way nothing else in his life up to that point had ever done.

The stables on the west side of the *Grünewald* were owned by Herr Mocher, the Ritmeister, who stabled about thirty horses, some at livery and some for tuition, and from where there was constant riding out in groups or alone. Some of the horses seemed very big, and dangerously ill-willed to Max, with their flaring nostrils and shoes striking the cobble stones of the yard like pistol shots, their riders like the mounted figures in the lead soldier collection. He could not know that a fair proportion of the private owners were ex-cavalry officers, who wished to make that impression.

But it was a magic world to which he would always return – the smells of the yard, the muck-heap steaming, the sweat of worked horses, the exciting scent of leather polish on the gleaming tack, rows of saddles, girths and bridles in the wonderfully ordered tack room of Ritmeister Mocher's.

His own instructor was Frau Gertrude Bloch, a strong, stout, well-corseted lady, dressed in black. She, too, was a widow like the Sausage. He knew that she was called Gertrude, because Ritmeister Mocher spoke to her that way, but of course Max called her Frau Bloch, and said *Sie*, and she used the diminutive to him. "*Du, kommaher!*" she cried with clipped authority, and there was lots of lipstick on her mouth which opened and shut like a wound in her face.

They rode out in the Grünewald. Frau Bloch lowered a black veil which was wound round her gleaming fat top-hat, and it flowed out behind. Frau Bloch also had a most handsome bosom, restrained by the tight shiny tunic top, which buttoned up to her neck. It was quite the most splendid bosom Max had ever seen. He was beginning to notice such things with strange feelings of interest, differences that took his attention between the girls at the school where several of the older ones plainly had something different about the shape of their blouses or overalls.

Sometimes, when they were going out in the forest, Frau Bloch would insert a small rosebud between the top buttons of the bulging tunic.

"Such a nice rose, Frau Bloch!" Max said, driven by what he hoped were good manners. For this he had received a tap on the seat of his rising breeches from her long, thin dressage whip, but she smiled with the red painted mouth.

Frau Bloch rode side-saddle, at all times, and as they walked and trotted along the woodland rides of the *Grünewald*, her legs and bootees were elegantly concealed on the near side under the voluminous side-saddle dress. She always rode an iron-grey mare that had a heavy, arched neck and distinct stride. Max trotted on her offside, on a small, slightly subdued pony, at first on a lead rein. After three weeks came the permitted day for him to ride out, reining his own mount. Not so scared, because he had overheard Frau Bloch telling the Ritmeister that "he had a natural seat". From then on, her control of pupil and pony seemed to be not only by a stream of instructions, but by use of the long thin whip now carried on the offside. This sometimes touched-up the pony, when Max's efforts seemed inadequate, but as often, seemed to touch up that natural seat itself, especially when Max moved into the rising trot. Whenever this was done and he looked around, Frau Bloch seemed to be smiling her most enigmatic smile. She knew everyone on the rides they took.

"*Guten Morgan, Herr von Reissel!*"

"*Morgan, Frau Bloch!*"

"Keep your contact!" This to Max. "Heels down! Don't lean forward!"

"*Tag Herr Doktor! Morgan der Herr General!* Keep your balance!"

"Please Frau Bloch!"

"What is it?"

"When do we gallop? I have seen two, smaller than me, galloping on the other side of the lake."

"You will when I say so!" It was at this moment that Max's grey pony stopped trotting. He tried to kick it on. His instructress had stopped too.

"Rise in your stirrups and whistle."

Such was equestrian obedience that Max did as he was told, the only whistle that came to his head being the one he used to call Miska the dog.

"Why do we do this, if you please?"

"Because your mare wants pee-pee!" Frau Bloch looked scornful. "Can you not hear? Now she has finished!" Before Max could resume his seat she had touched his stretched pants with the tip of her long stick. "Now! You show me how good you are! We make the first canter!" And away ahead went Frau Bloch, fixed firmly sideways in the saddle.

Max Beaumont said he enjoyed telling about how he first learned to ride, because it was a long time ago, but if anybody was interested, horses taught you a lot about people.

He didn't tell these stories often, but then that was what he was here for on this particular morning, wasn't it? And they were there to listen, and very good listeners they'd been. He turned to me.

"I expect you'll stop me, Tolly? If I get off the track, the way you want it?"

With the others I was silent. It was taking a while to come out of that long-ago Berlin. Max had been talking for over two hours, and all of us had made notes, but increasingly had just listened. Jane Milward was looking at him with a new, strange expression.

"It's fine, so far," I said encouragingly, and even this sounded faintly condescending. "The thing is we are going to

89

get the questions worked out that will pull in your responses. It's like cutting and editing."

"We're going to want locations," Owen said. "Shots or film, and quite quickly. I want to know if we can get background flash-backs. The house for instance?"

"*Kaput!*" Max Beaumont looked at him, his lips in a straight-lipped smile. "Bombed flat!"

"The school? That store – what was it?" Joe Bailey turned back his notes. "Wertheims?"

"There is another Wertheims in Berlin today, but nothing like the emporium that was in the Leipzigerstrasse."

Now that my ear was tuned in again to some German place names and phrases, I listened to Max Beaumont's too World-Service-sounding English. With the Beeb obsessed with regional accents, it sounded almost old-fashioned. Only a finely tuned professional ear could detect a certain over-perfection of the elocution moulding. Somehow surprisingly, in spite of all the subsequent achievements and influences in his climb upwards, he had not made the transfer to media-transatlantic. It was my turn to look at my watch, and he got up, not suddenly, as though called to order, but with an uncoiling grace that was almost feline. I found myself remembering it was the way he had always moved. Now it was also the movement of someone who was used to terminating meetings, and in that way we all got to our feet. Max must have pressed a bell – I could see one on the table by his chair. A tall, lithe-looking woman, with blonde, straight hair, came through the door, carrying a filled basket tray of papers.

"Liz Charlton, my PA!" Max said. "The one who makes me work. Is that all signing, Liz? I'll introduce you to BBC television in a minute . . ."

"We've spoken on the phone," Owen Owen said to her.

The tall blonde put down the basket and made two heavy gold bracelets jangle. She smiled at all of us.

"I remember! So nice to have your name doubled up! So that people can be chummy or distant all in one?"

"I'd like to check round the whole of Beaumont Holdings," Joe Bailey said suddenly. "I must get background, visuals, locations. For Owen, and you Felix! We ought to get film plus dialogue in a few places where the Beaumont powerhouse is functioning."

"Don't fail to get Mr. Beaumont riding out across Richmond Park on a misty morning!" Liz Charlton said lightly, while he sat, signing and initialling some of the papers, glancing at and dropping big sheets of computer stats onto the floor.

"He'd like that, you know!" Liz's voice was husky. She was one of those strong woman, who are also beautiful, but there was no footsy here, between her and the boss, I was sure of that, in an instinctive way.

"That's Al Chemmy," said Max, answering Joe Bailey, but without looking up. "The guided tour bit! Is he outside, Liz?"

"Together with Messrs. Cheswick and Mills. Top finance," she said to Joe. "And two German friends. You haven't reached their telex yet," she told Max, "but they have to be on the plane to New York by five. And at this point you need them, more than the other way round!"

"We're going," I said, before this all got too sycophantic. "Joe here can talk with Al outside, fix up what he wants. Tomorrow I'm off Nightwatch!"

"As a programme I'm not," Owen said. "But will be soon."

"How about here tomorrow then?" Max looked up. "I don't like business breakfasts, but coffee at ten?"

It was as though we were spirited away by Liz Charlton, with a twirl of her woollen skirt, and bangled wrist reaching for the door knob, she saw to it that we were.

Outside, it seemed several people were sitting on chairs in the large sized hall. Two chauffeurs with hats on their knees, other figures reading newspapers or talking.

"Thanks Liz. Can I call you?" It was Owen.

"Call me what?"

"Liz, dear!" Owen fell into the Welsh lilt he used when he had to move fast to keep up, which must have been rare.

"I follow him around!" she said. "And that's the real truth, so try Park Lane which is his top pad. Ask for me there, and they'll know where I am. Always!"

In the Beaumont car offered for our return to Lime Grove, I sat in front with the driver, and Owen and Jane Milward sat in the back.

"What's the number, Jane? Back where we've just been? I want to call Joe as soon as we get back."

There was a rustle of notebook behind me, and she gave the number slowly.

"OK, get that for me when we're in." Joe came to the phone almost at once when I called from Jane's desk.

"I'm glad you're hanging on a bit there," I told him. "And I'll be quick. I don't think you'll get much out of that perfect personal assistant, Joe, but Max Beaumont is up to something!"

The phone played with its own static for a few moments while Joe Bailey waited.

"We're not scrambled," he said at last.

"I know, so just listen! Two things – those Germans waiting for him. They're not publishing or banking, they're electronics, at board level, if you get me. Something they said – my German may be rusty, but it's still there, attached to a pair of big ears. Also the Liz said something to Max when she put down the work basket. She used a codeword if I'm not mistaken. Max and I did a job during the Occupation time together, and the operation codeword we had to use was the same. It's yiddish for Get Out, just one of those things that sticks in your mind. We can talk again, but you listen in there!"

"Nothing like life with the haunted aquarium!" Joe Bailey rang off.

CHAPTER FIVE

"How did it go yesterday?" Chloe asked. "Such a pity the weather's changed, we could have had breakfast on the verandah." She fretted on, and I saw she was smoking already. "I never know whether you like this morning room for breakfast? Those two girls are in the kitchen with the au pairs."

I gave a small piece of toast to the dog, and in exchange got back my napkin which had fallen to the floor.

"He's as straight-backed as ever," I said. "And looking ten years younger than I do. Which is unfair, when I think of the stress he's been under all the years."

"Didn't you say Max Beaumont rides each day and swims and stuff?" Chloe overweight and cheerful, puffed at her cigarette, and poured more coffee.

"It's a sort of inner resilience. Unusual. So far, we're still at school in Berlin. Maybe I shall learn more."

I decided to get to the Richmond estate earlier than the agreed time. I might trade on the earlier special relationship, be invited in, and could talk more confidentially. Even with Mrs. Beaumont if he was not available.

Chloe seemed inclined to hold me still. Perhaps I never did consider enough how the things I worked at for a living were likely to make a more interesting day than hers.

"Is he really a good guy? Or is he a baddy like most of them, with power and money?"

I sipped coffee and stared back at her, thinking.

"You're not really listening to me!" Chloe said. "You're composing while you're listening."

"You tell me," I countered. "You've met him! What does the womanly intuition say?"

"I think he's not even tough. In the orthodox sense! I think

93

he calculates, which is different, and he's cool – although he has a battened down temper which implies passion. So which is the Jewish side?"

"A sense of humour. Jewish humour is odd."

"I know what you mean. I was talking to Ruth MacLeath. We met in Barnes High Street. You know he works at Shepherds Bush, and has done for years?"

"He does personnel management, although he must be retiring soon I'd guess."

"He is Jewish," Chloe said. "Same thing, I mean German-Jewish. He got out just in time, as a Hitler refugee, and came over here, but when the war broke out, we arrested him! She seemed to want to tell me about it when I said you were on the Beaumont thing.

"It was when Hitler was going to invade," I told her. "Nobody knew who was real and who wasn't. They could all have been spies, traitors, fifth column."

"After that he was sent to Canada," my wife persisted. "Nobody seemed to care that he had Hitler as an enemy before anybody. He stayed there, chopping down trees and stuff until they brought him back here, later in the war, and he was allowed to join the army. The pioneer corps, Ruth said. It was full of famous musicians and judges and people like that. And he stayed a private all the time till the end, doing dirty jobs. And another thing – his name in German – he changed it to a Scottish sort of name, because if the Nazis had ever captured him in uniform, or any of the others, they would have shot them, or cut their balls off!"

"That's enough good after-breakfast talk!" I said. "I'm glad she explained it all. I shall have to try and fit that into the programme!"

"Stuffy and important as you are, I am ready to take you to Richmond!" Chloe got up.

"Listen!" I said. "I am glad to hear what you just told me. Nobody has ever got much on Beaumont, and he doesn't chase after personal publicity like the others. We shall have to pan a lot to get the gold. When he and I were together in the Occupation time, there were a lot of people doing strange jobs and it was a strange time. And a lot of them had strange pasts, and didn't particularly want to talk about them. I didn't want to tell people that I was born in Putney necessarily. And a lot of people didn't want to tell me they were born out of wedlock in Yugoslavia, or had been specially let out of jail because they were good at murdering. Surely as a prison visitor – "

Chloe kissed me quickly. Then she drove me to the Beaumont residence and dropped me off at the gates.

Another car, a Jaguar, pulled into the drive as I reached the steps, and Liz Charlton, wearing a dark-green Loden cloak and carrying possibly the same wire basket, came lightly down the broad front steps towards me. A uniformed driver got out of the Jaguar and opened one of the rear doors for her.

"Early birds get the worm, Mr. Tolly!" she said. "He's round at the stables. Just got back. You're not due for half an hour, and he was reckoning to do some work in between. But it's been a fine morning for a ride in the park." She smiled, a small tight smile. "After all, I must remember, you are working here!"

"What sort of worms are in that can?" I nodded at the contents of the wire basket.

"Yes I expect you'd like to know that!"

"Would it help my programme?"

"It might, or it might ruin it. I told your Mr. Bailey yesterday to watch his step. Max is funny about publicity. Personal publicity, I mean."

"What has made him change his mind now? The killing that happened the other day? Does he want the world to really know what sort of man he is? After that?"

Liz Charlton's shoulders under the Loden cape lifted, so that the turned-up collar covered the lower half of her face, and the cool grey eyes looked up at me over the edge.

"Clever Mr. Tolly!" She spoke indistinctly.

"Do you speak German?" I asked her.

"Yes, and French. Will you want something translating?" She was pushing down the collar now, turning and stooping to get into the car, while the po-faced driver held the door. "But that's Swiss finishing school you know! Like all nice girls! Don't look any more, Mr. Tolly. It's impossible to get into one of these bloody low cars without being indecent. I don't know why he can't buy a private taxi like Mr. Gulbenkian!"

But I looked, and the chauffeur looked, and then the car carried Liz away.

I walked round the side of the house, seeing nobody else and hoping I was heading in the right direction for the stables.

It is always worth identifying the moments when time telescopes, either backwards or forwards, because I came straight out through a door in a brick wall, into a cobbled stable yard. And there was Max Beaumont, whacking his boots with his riding crop, as he had done, through the corn, that long ago morning in Hanover. Could it even be that he remembered too? Because he grinned in an unusual way when he saw me. Max rarely laughed. When he did, it was oddly high-pitched, because you expected a deeper sound. But when he smiled, it was pure sex-appeal, and shone in those bright blue eyes.

"Tolly! I suppose you're looking forward to taking me apart again?"

A pretty stable girl was washing off the feet of a large chestnut mare, and Max Beaumont turned to her.

"Thanks, Mary! These TV tyrants aren't giving me much peace as you can see."

"Will you ride tomorrow, Mr. Beaumont?"

"If Tolly here will let me!"

Max turned, and put an actor's arm round my shoulder. Together we walked the back way round into the house.

"How many have you got? I asked him.

"Girls or horses?" He stopped walking, and his arm round my shoulder fell away. "I'll tell you how it is Tolly!" he said. "For years and years they've been trying to pin the women one on me, find out something, yell it in the headlines! Maybe I had a certain reputation earlier, I don't know. Even some of my own people, on my own papers! Maybe not to use, but to keep a job secure. In the States, in Germany, in France! And the competition as you can guess. Telescopic cameras, privacy invasion, the lot! Now you're prising me apart. Are you . . .?"

I faced him. "I want to know who you are Max! What you are, and what has got you to where you are! I shall ask questions, and before that I need to know what has happened

96

to you up to now. But you won't tell us everything! I know that already."

Max did not reply. He opened a large panelled door which led from the stable yard into a tiled hall. He hung his riding hat on a peg, pushed the stick among others in a stand, and spoke as though I had said nothing.

"There are six horses in the stables since you ask. And I remember you doing part of the Grand National commentary one year! I nearly phoned you afterwards. You could still come and work for me much better than hanging on at the Beeb!"

"Years too late!" I said.

"Go through that door, and they'll give you some coffee. I'm going to get a shower, and I'll be with you. There's a girl called Liz who is my PA, and a great girl she is too – she'll look after you."

"She's left already. I met her round the front. Said she'd had enough of you!"

"Go easy on me Felix Tolly!" Max was working off his riding boots. "I might not play!"

"You want this show," I said. "I don't know why, but you do!" I knew I was right. You get to discern those who want to appear on TV. Big money is not for BBC pundits and senior anchormen, but you are near to it a lot of the time, and I saw Max smile in a familiar way, a distinctly wry, mock humour twisting of his lips into quick wariness. Like when he had shown our papers to the Soviet officer as we crossed over in Berlin that time.

"I've never been in such a damn curious position before! Being invited to take an ego trip, go back to the beginnings, plaster myself all over millions of TV screens! That's risky!"

"You've always taken risks!" I said.

"I have succeeded in keeping hull down – but that's a tank expression. Nearly out of sight. Except for a relatively small number of my working associates, people I have needed. I can print millions of copies of newspapers, magazines, books – even run some overseas TV and radio too, but nobody knows me." He stood his boots up as Boris came through the inside door.

"There you are Boris! Not so bad today eh? Take them

97

away! Hey, Tolly!" Now he took my arm, all charm again, as Boris bore away the boots. "Let's go and see if half a bottle of champagne doesn't get us straightened out! I don't like coffee at this time of day. And Debby doesn't like me on the half bottle at breakfast!" He called after Boris in a clicking tongue that I thought was probably Polish. Except for the word Bollinger.

There was quite a team waiting in the library, but with the addition this time of a cameraman and lighting engineer, and another, all of whom I knew. They were introduced by Joe Bailey.

"Owen can't make it this morning! But he'd just like to get the room and the light and the subject sized up. For an out of studio clip. Jim here is floor manager."

"There'll be at least a couple of other locations. The bits in Germany Owen will take care of separately," said the man called Jim.

The lighting engineer walked to the big windows behind the chair where Max had previously been seated, pacing the distance, and on the way back looking at a meter in his hand.

"Would you use a film camera?" Max Beaumont asked.

"Could do. Sixteen mil. Arriflex probably."

"You used to be keen on camera." He was one of the older hands so I risked it. You go carefully with crew.

"Might do a video – a Sony Ikegami. How are you Jim? Done?"

"Four red-heads, one blonde." This was lighting talk, but of course Max had to rise to it.

"That sounds like one each then? And one of us spare for Miss Milward?" There were polite smiles.

"Do we check the other locations with you, Mr. Tolly? Or Owen?"

"Probably only one other in Mr. Beaumont's boardroom," I said. "Or maybe Fleet Street. Owen says we'll have a first running order by the seventeenth, and we're likely to use your takes on advance publicity flashes."

When the men left, and Max Beaumont was standing in front of the fire, he looked, for the first time faintly vulnerable. He had changed into a brown and black tweed suit. But it was almost too well cut, and the neat brown shoes were too brilliantly polished. He would never make the real *Country Life* figure, and I made a mental note to have a word with him about it, before he went live on camera. God knows, he looked fit, and would need less attention from make-up that I always required.

"So, the *Radio Times*? Does that go to press early?"

The question was natural enough as professional interest but I thought I heard a special interest in the timing.

"It's best to get something as big as you scheduled," I said as we moved to sit down. Joe Bailey and Jane were busy flicking back through notes.

Joe Bailey's journalist ears were keen too. "You're interested in the timing for some special reason, Mr. Beaumont? You've got a new project for about then – haven't you?"

Max eyed Joe thoughtfully before he spoke.

"I think it's more or less known. I'm merging four newspapers to make one."

"That's your *East London News*, *West London* . . . " Jane Milward had done her homework too.

"We shall go into one daily. We're calling it *London Daily News* for prototype. I might drop the London if I can clear copyrights, and the lawyers are working on that. It will go everywhere south of Manchester of course, and I can print up there if we drop the London. That's as much as I'm saying now. Just don't peddle it too hard for the moment!"

"There seems to be a bit of unrest about where you *are* going to print it," I tried. We were getting to the direct questions now and having them answered. "A particular friend of mine – not one of your editors – seemed to think there was a new set-up for the production going up in Battersea? And the unions as usual will not play? I'd like to get that one straight, before we're in front of cameras, Max," I told him. "Those guys you saw just now are like a lot more we have on our side of the media. And if you've got more than the usual trouble with your half dozen unions – or however many it is – well, it could rub off. There are people who would go pale about that. Apart from which, those people behind the cameras, the sound booms, lights and the rest – well it's strange how they can make you look on the night! Whatever I do!"

"All that World Media are saying at the minute is all that I've said." Max was looking baleful.

Miss Milward made a note, and looked at him. At the now nonchalant face with the blue eyes. I could tell she was not immune to the Beaumont charm.

Boris brought in champagne, a half bottle. It just made four glasses.

"Well!" Joe Bailey said, taking his. "Good luck everybody! Let's get going, Mr. Beaumont. Is it all right to kick off again, Felix? Now the *sub-judice* stuff is over!"

"If it's all right with Mr. Beaumont."

"Now let's see then," Joe said. "Where are we?"

Physically we were exactly where we had been the midday before. Max Beaumont was seated again in the upright armchair in the half-alert, half-relaxed way he had probably sat on his horse.

"Mr. Beaumont was talking about going to school and a lady called Bloch," Miss Milward said, flicking through her notes. "In Berlin."

"Oh yes," Joe Bailey said. "That's it. I wonder Mr. Beaumont if you read, of course later, much about that time? Like Christopher Isherwood for instance?"

It was clever of Joe Bailey.

"His books hadn't been written then," Max Beaumont said easily. "About the time we were talking last. Of course I read them later on, but at that age I was much taken with *Emil and the Detectives* by Erich Kästner, and then I read a lot of Karl May with all his Red Indian stories, like *Old Sure-hand*, but told in a German way. If you understand me?"

Joe Bailey smiled gently. I could see he was coming in slowly.

"Was life really like Isherwood then? In Berlin at that time?" He was like a barrister, moving easily into a more searching phase of cross-examination as he asked the questions.

"You have me there," Max Beaumont said. "You must remember I was only coming up for nine as I went to school. My mother was increasingly under medical care for long stretches of time, my father talked to me in a way he would not have done otherwise. We were both lonely. Sometimes he had some friends in for part of the evening, or for dinner, mostly former military types and I was allowed to stay up. In a way unnoticed, but perhaps it was meant to be part of my education. On one such time they talked of Marlene Dietrich, who had been making her name at that time. Would that be what you mean? They had heard her in the night clubs, and I got an early impression that mother would not have approved. My father was always interested in new technical things, and we had had for some time a radio, but now he had a way of playing gramophone records with the radio, and in the evenings he would play Marlene Dietrich records and drink a bottle of wine. I was allowed to stay up and hear that wonderful, deep slow voice. But not to drink the wine."

"Did that affect you, later in life I mean?" Surprisingly it was Jane Milward, who was not strictly on the questioning line.

"I think I fell in love," Max Beaumont answered her so gently. "At the age of nine or ten, you can fall in love with a voice, or just a fantasy, you know. And go on doing it for quite a while. I was among many who fell for Marlene."

"What was she singing then?" I asked. "We might work one or two into the background." I nodded to Jane for noting.

Max Beaumont smiled, but never hesitated. "*Lola, lola. . . . meine kleine Pianola!*" "*Johnny, wenn du geburstag hast, Nur einmal . . .* I suppose a while before these she made *Blue Angel*. Any of you seen that? Actually an American – well he was Joseph von Sternberg – produced and directed it. That was the sticky, sweet side of Berlin, the rest, which doesn't even come through even with Isherwood that clearly, was not so seductive. That radiogramme when not playing the records, was telling news stories. The police had opened fire on the Nazi stormtroopers who fired back, and you could hear them yelling slogans as they raced through the streets. The race-war slogans. Germany awake! Judah perish! In the end, they marched to the Hindenburgpalast. Perhaps you know all this? Hindenburg gave in and Hitler became Chancellor.

"It was winter that year, when I started at school there was the Reichstag fire. I can't remember the exact date, but it must have been January or February, because Papa said the fire hoses were frozen. Were they really? We stood in the dark, all of us, including the servants, towards dawn it must have been, and the flames were funnelling up, and it seemed that all the fire-engine bells in the city were ringing all round us. A nine year old doesn't forget that kind of thing."

Joe Bailey adjusted his hornrimmed spectacles. "Can I ask this? When did you realise that being Jewish, or part Jewish was something? Was there a time when it didn't matter, and then it did? Do you think that belonging to that Jewish part of your family has influenced your life?"

Max Beaumont stared at Joe, and the mask that could slide over his face in seconds was there again. The lips thinned out, the eyes were fixed, and none of him moved at all.

"I don't feel Jewish as something special, or superior or different. And don't put that in your notebooks! My relations kept saying that we were just as German as anyone else! I think you might today if you were a soldier in the Israeli army; OK, I used to think about it quite a lot, yes."

He had realised being partly Jewish meant various things, when he went to school in Berlin in 1933, Max Beaumont said. Although a lot had been written and was still, much of it was new and surprising to younger generations today. His cousins had special days and ceremonies, and he, Max, had been to the Mitzvahs for the oldest ones. It seemed mainly concerned with eating. Because there were some things that his mother would not eat. In those days, when there were three staff working in the big kitchen, who knew that she was ill, and Papa talked very little about it, and fell in with whatever came to the table. He was more interested in his cellar, and tried to teach Max about the bottles and their different labels and years, and later Max said he wished he had paid more attention, although there had been plenty of time later to catch up.

But something did happen about this time, and it involved the servant Dieter, who had replaced poor Biene, and Max could recall his own feelings at the time. He experienced loneliness, of a kind which normally seeps into adolescence, but then he was maybe precocious, and probably priggish.

But in that big house, with both parents often away, he was genuinely alone. He had one of the first Schuco clockwork cars, a model replica of the racing Mercedes that had real steering, and wheels that could be taken off. It raced along the bare wooden floors of the long corridors, or the smooth, stone level of the passage leading to the kitchen area, where there were no carpets. These were the best places for the quick, silver-painted Schuco.

Dieter having stood for a moment, when he came round a corner in the passage, watched it finish its run as the motor wound down. As chauffeurs often did then, he wore black, shiny knee boots, similar to Max's own riding boots and looking down at Max, he carefully planted one boot on the small silver car and crushed it.

Then, he looked round, and as he passed the devastated nine year old he half leant down. Max could smell the acid polish on those black boots, so close to him the man stood. As he kneeled, there was also the smell of disinfectant soap the maids used to scrub the floors.

"*Little Jewish pig!*" Dieter hissed. Then his boots, clanking off along the flagged passage were the only sound.

"What did he say?" His father had stood by the new, big radio to which these days he seemed to be giving a lot more time, and he stared down at his son. "You are telling the truth?" The colour mounted slowly up his neck from the stiff white collar, and he put out a hand and held the top of Max's head, to look straight at him. Max had never known his father look like that, except perhaps the day Biene had been killed. Something in Father's eyes was frightening, and Max gave a little cry, and tried to move his head away. Father let go, and made Max tell him in more detail what had happened, and after he had done this and repeated again the words of Dieter, Papa sat down slowly in his big, straight-backed chair, and took Max not on his knee, but made him stand close against the chair.

"First you must make a promise, Max! Say it now! I will not ever tell Mama what Dieter said. Say it!" Max repeated the words.

"Can I have another Schuco, Papa?"

"You keep your promise and we will see!" said his father grimly, but he patted the back of Max's head. "Although perhaps we should make sure that Dieter is not around to do it again! But that is for me, and you will say nothing. Not to anyone. Understood . . .?"

What his father soon found out, as Max heard later, was that Dieter had become an early recruit to the Stormtroopers, and at that stage, kept his uniform in a suitcase, and put it on down at the police station. The new Chancellor, Hitler, had put a former flying-officer called Göring into the post of the Prussian Minister of the Interior. It was he who had thrown out non-Nazis, and replaced them with reliable stormtroopers like Dieter.

Colonel von Klieschen was not a fool. He knew how to assess power, changing situations, and above all was familiar with the word *realpolitik*. He left a considerable sum in Swiss banknotes and some loose change in his dressing room drawer. He did it again, and marked the notes. Not all were taken, only some.

Using his position with the bank, he brought in a department head from the *central kriminalamt*, rather than the local station. Most of the missing money was found in Dieter's room. The *kriminalpolizei*, whose manner was cool but correct, asked if he wished to make a charge. The Colonel said that in view of the man's time in his household he would not, but of course there would be no question of keeping him in employ. Nor would he pay him the usual notice of dismissal, and he would leave in the custody of the officers there and then. The Freiherr would require the police to record the matter, and emphasise to the miscreant that any return, or attempt to take retaliatory action, would result in immediate arrest.

At first Max received only a very brief word from his father that Dieter had gone. The other servants seemed shocked, but some of the older ones, discernibly relieved.

"That man is the enemy," Father said shortly.

After a short silence, Max asked: "What if he comes back to kill us?"

"It will be all right my son." Father stood in the big drawing room with the grey light coming through the tall windows, and Max stood also. "Sometimes I must help that school of yours with your education, in my own way. Do you remember a book I once showed you, with the soldiers downstairs? A famous general? Clausewitz! His principles are taught in every military and staff college in the world, although the German army is supposedly in disgrace. Well now, I will tell you his principles, and you will remember them. Because for some people it is difficult to understand that Clausewitz said, as principal number one: First safeguard your line of retreat!"

"Retreat? When soldiers go backwards, Papa? Away from the enemy!"

"Precisely! And people ask; how could a bold soldier make retreat the first thing to consider! So I will tell you, Max, and I think you will understand. It is always when you arrive somewhere, or are in a new position that the unexpected happens. Like when Dieter trod on your car. You did not hit him – he was bigger than you in any case – but instinctively you made your retreat to me, which was correct. Too often people think soldiers should plan always to advance. It is in most cases easier to advance, than to retreat. Retreats are not always defeat, they need not be. Not if you have thought it out, and planned it and know exactly what you will do to keep control. Do you see? Then you will fight again. And advance! After point number one of Clausewitz, if the unexpected does not happen, when you have made your retreat plan you can take point two: Consolidate your base! Then point three: Ensure your supplies! Only then can you advance!"

Although the whole matter was not spoken of, Max came to realise that what his father was thinking and expounding as a military man, was also something to do with the other half of both their lives. The bank of which Father was a director. There was more to come. Almost every day, they listened to the radio, or Max heard other stories from his Father, who spoke more and more openly to him.

A young manager of the bank had been jostled on the pavement by two stormtroopers who were in plain clothes, but wore the swastika armbands. He had attempted to move on, but they had closed in and knocked him to the ground. After that he was kicked in the face. Nobody in the street had intervened, in spite of the man's cries, and a car had pulled up and the young manager and his assailants had got in together and were driven off.

Nothing had been heard of him, and the bank and his desperate family's enquiries in all directions and at several high levels were met with feigned ignorance or bureaucratic indifference. Three weeks later he was released, thin, shaking, heavily bruised, describing in a whisper between broken lips and teeth the torture in a private stormtrooper prison. One of his arms was also broken.

It was his mother, now home again and propped up in bed, who told Max of others similar things, in a strangely flat toneless voice, things he knew uneasily that his Father would not have told him. He felt mystified and uncertain in the increasing sense of his duality.

"Papa will keep us safe!" he told his Mother, and held her hand, and she looked at him, the large eyes so dark in the tissue-paper white face. "Oh Max, yes! He will! Thank God we have him! That dreadful Herman Göring has said something." She fingered the bed sheet. "They are not afraid of arresting even Cabinet ministers if they are guilty of crimes! What crimes? They are arresting all kinds of people, Max, not just the dreadful communists. One of the bank's lawyers! And a journalist in Munich, and they say that they are Zionists and traitors – What does that mean? And there in Bavaria there is another police chief, a Herr Himmler. He has opened a correction institution."

"What is that, Mama?"

"Maxilein – you are so young, these are horrible things. I don't know! It seems especially that our people are being taken there." He knew well enough now what Mama meant, and watched her fingers, clenching and twisting, and he picked the hand away and held it close to his face, and felt the coldness of it, and breathed the scent of her skin and the familiar oversweet perfume. But he knew she was afraid, because he could smell that too.

The school in Bohlenstrasse, Max's first real mixing with the outside world was so different from the closed life in the big, pink house, and the private lessons with the Wurst. It was his main world now, in lots of ways. It seemed almost every day at first, that there were surprises, fears, and strange new knowledge in class, and in the playground.

The playground was at the back and to one side of the school building, and had a high wall round the road side. The surface was asphalt, which lent itself to hopscotch and ball games, and some of the girls skipped, and the very young ones sat round on seats that were like park benches, and played a sort of musical chairs or sang songs together. Two teachers were always in charge at playground time, and stood in the middle. They used whistles like policemen, but mostly they gossiped together.

Max with most of the boys of his own age, played Red - Indians, or threw a tennis ball. Football was not allowed. Such a private school was very female-dominated, by the women teachers and the ratio of girls to boys, most of the boys going on to Gymnasium, and the girls staying on to fourteen or fifteen.

Things happened in his life that were private and personal, things that no friends, or interviewers and would-be biographers would ever hear.

It was autumn, and there were leaves in the playground. A lot blew into one corner where there was a little wicket-fenced garden with shrubs, a triangle made by the fence and the backs of tall apartments.

Coming out to play one day, as they streamed up from the downstairs cloakroom where shoes were changed, Max heard his name called from behind, and slowed and looked round. Moving purposefully up the line of happy shouting and pushing juniors was one of the senior girls, now beckoning imperiously as she called his name, and unwillingly Max slowed. He was far too used to female command and supervision at home and at school.

She caught up with him, and together they moved away, under the trees along the wall. He knew her as Uta, one of the older girls, who in their last year helped when smaller children needed shoe laces tying or hands washing. Max felt her hand not so much on his shoulder, as tightening into his pullover, and heard her voice, thin and sharp.

"We will go and play together now, Max! You and I, that will be nice won't it? You haven't played with a big girl before

have you? Come, we will go this way! His heart sank because the voice was like the rest of Uta herself, sharp and thin, with her pale face and beady eyes on either side of a sharp nose. Max tried resistance, dragging against the claw hand on his pullover.

"I want to play with Rudi!"

"You always play with Rudi and the other silly boys! Now you can play with me! Komme!"

"Tomorrow!" Max begged. *"Today I must play with them, I promised to!"* He did not understand why, but he felt near to tears. They were moving away from the playground, and he could see the two bespectacled women teachers standing talking together, with games and screaming noise all around them. Why did they not look this way and see that he was an unwilling partner to the older Uta? It was the first time for Max that events moved with a pre-ordained, dream quality.

Now they had reached the end of the short line of over-hanging trees where a low and rickety gate led into a little shrubby triangle, and once through it, Uta moved swiftly and purposefully. A bench, one of a pair, half hidden in the shrubs, was dragged round, and still holding on to him she pulled Max behind it. Now they were screened from the playground altogether in the corner which smelt of damp earth and stray cats. No one came in there, because it was known as The Headmistresses' Garden, and anyway you could not skip, or run or throw balls in that little dank area. For Uta's purpose it was ideal.

"We will play mothers and fathers!" she snapped to him in her flat, commanding voice. And she crouched down, after carefully eyeing the playground beyond the shrubs, and then her pale features and beady eyes were looking up at Max's face, as he stood with his back pressed against the bench. *"Now you! Open your trousers and show me your pee-pee!"*

"I don't want to!" His voice was near a sob, as he grasped the bench slats.

"Take it out and show me!" The older girl snarled. *"Quickly!"*

He choked back a lump in his throat, as he felt her fingers slipping open the buttons of his school shorts, the way Maria had done it at home when he was smaller, when she helped

108

him to undress. But this was different, and quickly done, so that Uta had pulled the small organ out from the hole in his underpants, and was holding it in her hand, absorbed, staring, crouching there with her head just below his chin so that Max could smell the soap in her short dark hair, along with the dusty paint on the bench and the surrounding current bushes. He felt her fingertips pinching.

"You have not had the end cut off!" Now she held him between finger and thumb, and looked up accusingly.

Not hearing properly, Max misunderstood and his voice rose to a scream. "No, no you can't!" It was stifled suddenly by Uta's free hand clapping across his mouth . . .

"Keep quiet, you little beast!" Her face was now flushed, blotchy, and contorted. Reluctantly she let go and stuffed his clothes back together. "Why is it not cut off? You are a Jew! Why do you pretend not to be? They will kill all Jews, and quite right too! So don't think you will get away by telling anybody!"

Max, half in tears, shakingly did up his buttons, and Uta stood up, and looked cautiously over the nearest bush. Roughly she pulled him to one side, and away from the bench. She tossed her shingled head, and crouched again to glare menacingly at him, her face only inches from his.

"Now I will go! You will count twenty, and stay here! If you say anything – anything, do you hear me – I will say I caught you making pee-pee in the garden!"

She had gone. Miserably, Max counted, then pushed past the end of the bench, reaching the wicket gate, even as the sound of the big brass hand bell that was always rung by one of the teachers signified the end of playtime. Since that time and afterwards, he had never been able to tell.

For some days he had lingered, holding his Mother's hand at bedtime, but unable to bring himself to. To ask, to pour out his misery, the strange secret fear and the confused feelings. To tell his Father was unthinkable. Such a story would surely be punished. And above all, what about the cutting off?

In the playground he managed to avoid the tall peaky faced Uta, although she had tried again to corner him. By staying close with friends, other boys, hurrying and shouting to make a distraction, he kept out of her reach. Besides, on those really cold winter days, breaktime was cut down to half, and the

teachers stood at the doorway from the cloakroom to make
sure all were properly clothed with outdoor shoes, gloves,
coats, hats, and with scarves over ears and wound round their
heads too if they were long enough.

When he remembered Berlin, the city and the time as it was
that winter, Max saw it and experienced it in his mind like a
black and white film. Partly because there was always snow,
of course, and a biting, hard cold wind like the granite stone
square buildings, the bridges, and the shapes of the leafless
trees, so black. Even the big pink house, with its blue-slated
roof looked more grey in winter shadow, the pale, chilly light,
than its true colour.

One of the routines that started about that time was having
breakfast with his father, the Colonel, in the little first-floor
room that looked out over the trees in the *Tiergarten*. Then
together they would visit Mother, who had her tea tray and
fruit in bed.

"Goodbye my two men!" she said. "Work hard! But not
too hard, and come back to me soon!"

Father had a car from the bank still since the departure of
Dieter and it was a Mercedes, but a small black one, driven
by one of the bank drivers who wore a coat and a cloth cap,
which seemed a lot less smart that the uniform and boots of
Father's previous chauffeurs. Once when Max asked why this
was – and it was not within the driver's hearing, because he
was growing up now, and knew what was said and not said
in front of the servants – the Colonel had looked ahead for a
moment.

"There are too many uniforms about now, none of them
any good!" A quick downturn of his thin lips told Max, who
would liked to have asked more, that there was no point. Not
when his father spoke like that.

On such days, the car dropped Max at the corner of the
bridge. Only when it was snowing quite hard would he be
taken the extra distance to the school. In those winter
evenings now, he was allowed to listen sometimes to the
radio, the big new one in the drawing room. He sat in
the smallest and lowest of the armchairs. It was called
a *Mutterstuhl* and he only knew later what that meant,

because Mother said it was for feeding babies, and that it had belonged to *her* mother, who was dead, and had left it to her. Max was vaguely aware that it had to do with breast feeding, and sitting in that chair felt comforting. On the radio at five o'clock they told a children's story. Most of them seemed rather young to Max. He had grown out of the dreadful *Struwelpeter*, although occasionally he had dreams about the awful tailor and his thumbs being cut off, and this was all tangled up in some horrible way with the dreaded Uta, but there was still no one he could talk to about that.

"Tonight the Philharmonic is on the radio, and for that Max should stay up!" said his Mother.

"You would call it educational?" His Father liked to stand very straight in front of the fire, the big mantlepiece well above his head. There was a silver clock on the mantleshelf under a glass dome cover, with other ornaments and two candlesticks. If Max moved his head back or sideways from down on the Mutterstuhl, he could make it look as though Father was balancing a clock on his head.

"Sit still and don't fidget! If the boy gets into his night things then he can listen to the first part until the intermission! Sleep is important at his age, and school is his education, not for nodding off at his desk tomorrow!"

"Go and find Maria and tell her, Maxi," his Mother said. "Dressing gown and slippers tell her. And your bed shawl!"

On Saturdays when Uncle Paul and his family and two other relations, who also ran the bank with Father, came to lunch with their wives and children as usual, they all moved into the big room for coffee. After a brief discussion about it, the radio in its large cabinet, with the fretwork front and beneath a row of knobs, was turned on.

At first it seemed like a giant chorus, a thousand chanting voices raised in some hymn or martial chorus. But when that stopped, a single voice seemed to tear into the silence, high-pitched and on one note, the ranting words piling one after the other, until the thunder of the thousands who had fallen silent, broke like furious waves on a stony beach. And then the chanting started. *Sieg heil! Sieg heil! Sieg heil!* After which the jabbing, twisting, screaming voice of the orator began again.

111

Max felt his inside turning, half-excited, half-fearful, because when he turned to look at the grown-up faces, he knew that all this was upsetting them even more. He caught the eye of one of his girl cousins, sitting neatly with the younger children on cushions on the carpet. She was bored, and, knowing the adults were distracted, stuck out her tongue at him. Angrily Father moved across the floor with clipped strides.

"The corporal is getting above himself!" He twisted the knob and the ranting tirade was cut off in mid-flight. In the silence there were the sounds of mother comforting her sister-in-law, and the men standing up, moving uncomfortably, pulling at their own shirt cuffs, rubbing their fingers together. Uncle Paul stayed, balanced on the arm of the chair in which his wife sat. His face immobile, fixed on the fretworked front of the radio cabinet. Above his small, thin, black beard, the skin on his cheek bones and the bridge of his nose were, more than ever pale, a mother of pearl.

"Now he is saying openly what he will do with us!"

There was a tiny sound of crying from Max's younger aunt, the one called Danielle who came from Paris. She put the lavender-coloured cuff of her blouse across her eyes.

"What do *you* think, Otto? They dare not touch the banks! They depend on us for confidence abroad!" Uncle Paul said. "The dollars and the pounds and the rest – if they dry up? Then this lunatic and his gangster friends cannot survive! We shall be back in chaos again with the mark. Who is this man Schacht who is advising him? Should we go and see him? Banking is international! Alright, it is across national frontiers! We are Germans too, not swindlers!"

"I will find out Paul," Max's father said grimly. "You can leave it to me. I will invite General Lichter to dine – I have membership of the Eastern Command Club still. He knows everything, and he can advise me. I think for now – " and it was the same French again, with Father's heavy accent – *"Pas devant les enfants!"*

When, after much kissing on the cheeks, handshaking between the two, *dieners* and *knicks* from Max and his cousins, male and female, the rest of the family departed, a strange quiet settled on the big house. Father made calls with his new private telephone, and the bells could be heard, jangling and ringing through his study doors. When he came out he pulled on his big coat in the hall and sent for Maria, who had by now been promoted to housekeeper and senior. Partly, Max knew, because of Mother's ill health, and also, as Father had explained, as he was going to school and had a proper bedroom, he no longer required a nursery, or a schoolroom, and certainly not a nursemaid.

"Look after the Gräfin!" Father told her gruffly. He put the homburg hat over the grey bristles of his head.

"*Jawohl der Freiherr!*" Maria made a small bob.

"And you Max! Talk with your Mama! Make her happy. You can take your book to her room and read there. What are you reading?" He did not wait for the answer.

Maria opened the big front door. Outside it was already dark and there was rain on the bitingly cold East wind. At the bottom of the front steps the office car was waiting. Father stooped to enter the back, as the cloth-capped driver held open the door. Then the car moved away with its red rear lights blinking in the wet.

Not more than a few weeks later, perhaps in the school term after Christmas, Max remembered, his father made a sudden and silent entry into the big bedroom where he was with Mother, who sat up in a quilted dressing gown, blanket over her knees, by the small coal fire, while as part of his school work he read to her in English from the class book. There was a form, a sort of mark book that parents had to sign to say that the work had been done.

Father had entered and closed the bedroom door so silently that it was only then that his wife and son noticed that he was standing there, in the shadows cast by the reading lamp and the low flames of the fire. When he spoke, the abrupt, terse German words, had etched the memory into Max's mind.

"*Sie haben Paul genommen!*"

His Mother had stared silently at Father. Her hands went slowly up to her face so that only her eyes showed. Max was then sent from the room, ostensibly to tell Maria that Father would be having his evening meal with Mother in her room. Uncle Paul being taken? What could it mean? Taken to where? And by whom?

113

Father spent that evening in his study, and the telephone bell could be heard almost continuously. Various callers came from the bank. Max watched them in the hall, from where he sat at the top of the stairs. Some did not stay long enough to take off their coats. Others brought papers for Father and spoke to him respectfully as *Herr Direktor*, or *Der Freiherr* and, but having delivered the papers, also left quickly. There was something about their manner, some looking round curiously, some furtive, shuffling their feet.

"Where has Uncle Paul been taken?" He had come as usual to kiss his Mother goodnight. But although she kissed him, this evening two and three times, on the forehead and cheeks, she could not answer. She only shook her head and bit her lips, and twisted endlessly at the corner of the counterpane, closing her eyes so that Max saw only two small tears forming under the lashes.

"It will be all right!" he told her stoutly. "It will be all right, Mama!"

CHAPTER SIX

It was past eleven, and we had sat listening for two hours, while Max Beaumont felt his way through the memories of his childhood, and when he paused we remained watchful, and silent. I think this came more from an awareness of some effort involved for him in the recollections, than any graphic quality in the telling. I watched as he levered himself up from his chair, straightened his back, and took a quick look at his wristwatch. The immaculate cheviot suit fell into the lines and shape that Saville Row had intended.

"Eleven twenty-two!" he said, but the empathy he had created had not instantly disappeared, just as a part of Max had not yet come back from that early Berlin. Perhaps it was the sense of that which made Joe Bailey look at his notes, hesitating.

"Did your Uncle come back?"

"Yes, two days later. They had given him no food, and for a man who was no longer young, he was quite badly hurt. A broken collar-bone and extensive bruising where it could not be seen. And a broken finger."

"How would you know that?" I was surprised to hear the harshness of my own voice. "I mean, I got the impression you would not be told?"

"I wasn't. I learned later, years later, from one of my cousins. They were sent to Switzerland, taken by my father at my Uncle's request, and they stayed there."

"But the man himself, and the Bank?" I was rehearsing the sort of questions I might be asking in what was now less than a fortnight's time. The point was to know the sort of reactions, how far to go, when people had reasonable grounds for avoiding personal revelations.

Max Beaumont studied me. The still good-looking tanned

face, with the improbably ice-blue eyes, and it was as though our roles were reversed. Then, suddenly as quite often, he smiled, the disarming twisted-lip smile.

"They had got him to sign something. To say that the bank had been in the pay of foreign banks, undermining German currency for their own good – the usual thing the world was beginning to hear, churned out by Goebbels. Everybody know about Goebbels?"

"For pity's sake, Max!" I looked at him, almost angrily, but then I realised that he was in fact being polite. There were two, even three generations in between then and now.

"These are media people! They may be another generation, but they know. Was the bank taken over?"

"Eventually yes! A Jewish merchant bank like Schönberg and Klieschen was virtually expropriated. My Uncle Paul got away to Switzerland to join his sons, some others were not so fortunate. My father stayed on the Board, and later other confiscated banks were merged with it. I think he had a confused notion of duty, or perhaps the need to provide for my mother and for me. I was told afterwards, that even Paul urged him to stay, to look after what family interests he could. They could not believe the Nazis would last. Soon everything would be restored. My father was of an era that knew a military code of honour, and within those limits he was also an educated man. Have any of you read any German literature?" A sudden donnish snap in his voice brought us all upright.

"I'm afraid not, sir," Joe Bailey said, and Miss Milward shook her head.

"Some obvious stuff. I went to Oxford after demobilisation," I said, and felt oddly self-conscious.

Max Beaumont was reaching to a lower level of the small table beside his chair, a shelf that held just a few books.

"This was the last thing given to me by my father much later. An early edition of a book by another *Freiherr* – a fellow Baron! Except that it was already written two hundred years ago! *Umgang mit Menschen* by Adolphe Knigge. How to handle people, is a loose translation. Perhaps if the other Adolf had taken it on board, things might have been different." Max was cold and crisp. "Here's a piece I have often used!"

116

It was astonishing. Max Beaumont was about to read to us from some minor classic, translating as he went along.

I nodded quickly to Jane Milward. I knew as Max Beaumont started to read in his quick, clear, high voice, that her shorthand could take it.

"I despise the notion that one can make of people what one will! When one knows how to take advantage of their weak points. Only a scoundrel can and wants to do that, because he is the only one who doesn't care what means to use to attain his ends. The honest man cannot make anything of anyone, nor does he care to; while a man of strong principles does not allow himself to be manipulated." It was typical that Max Beaumont banged the pages of the book together noisily, with no show of self-consciousness. "That's all!"

"I'd like to have that typed!" I said hurriedly. "I can't get a grip on a single creed or statement like that so quickly. If its important to you Max, it's important to the programme."

"It was just a thought – that you might find it interesting!" He gave a cold, bright smile that went with the voice. "Most people would probably tell you I, for instance, could not possibly claim any such code of behaviour. But I do!"

Joe Bailey laughed shortly, but it was no way deprecatingly.

"I must earn my living now!" said Max. "It's been a bit like prisoner interrogation here too! And of course I was a journalist once, right at the very beginning, a hell of a long time ago! You're pretty good at it, Mr. Bailey – you and Miss Milward."

"I ought to be. It's still the way I earn my living," Joe Bailey answered.

There was a knock at the door of the library, which opened slowly to show the bespectacled face of Al Chemmy.

"Half eleven, Max! Car's waiting, and the guys at Park Lane are getting restless!"

Max stopped beside me on his way to the door.

"I can't say I'm enjoying this, Tolly! But then it's not your fault, and I'm sure it's useful – at least that's what Al Chemmy tells me!" He looked round. "You're welcome to stay on." Now there was the more friendly, lopsided grin again. "I guess you would like to sit around and have a Major Max session, isn't that right?"

The door to the library shut on Max Beaumont and his PRO. Joe Bailey dropped his notebook on the carpet, and leaned his head against the tall back of the couch. When he took off his glasses and closed his eyes, Joe's face looked quite different, blank and somehow younger.

Miss Milward was fumbling in a handbag, making room to put away the notebook with its ball-point pen fastened to it by a rubber band.

"Felix!" Joe said, "did you follow all that? I mean does it explain anything to you?"

"Bits of it," I said. "But I think you have to know more to add him up. Remember, I was fairly close to him that time after the war, in Germany, and he talked about it then."

Joe nodded, looking out of the big window with its distant view of Richmond Park. He and I had, after all, been through much of the same basic, professional maze, coming out at different times and places. We both knew, in our respective ways, the problems of the interview. Together we were listening and probing and getting impressions, searching for the mainline of Max Beaumont. The centre *leitmotiv* – and it was inevitable that the German word occurred – to make the personality come across clearly in a major television presentation. This was why all the preparatory work had to be done. To the viewers it would all appear a natural progression, spontaneous questions, expanded answers, close-ups giving a significant understanding of the man and the achievement. Then the whole back-up of camera work outside the studio, flashbacks of places and times.

For a moment I felt Joe Bailey and I were involved together, in a sort of common bond.

"Owen is going to have his time cut out to get some good background stuff," Jane was on the same line. "Shall I transpose my notes for you, Mr. Tolly? They'll be a copy of what Joe wants to keep, aside from his own."

"Thanks that'll be fine!" I glanced at where Max Beaumont had been sitting. "He's nervous about all this, isn't he? I wonder why?"

"Isn't that just the man himself?" Joe said. "He's a lot of things all put together, not always adding up."

"I don't entirely get it though," I fretted. "I have after all a longish reputation for these big set-pieces. I've worked on them for years, as you know. Actors and politicians and aristocrats and trade-union leaders, leading figures abroad and sporting champions at home." I wanted to add that in almost all ways, Max Beaumont was different from all of them.

"OK!" Joe said. "I know what you mean! So he's a tycoon? An international publishing and business tycoon known round the world. But is he? There is less known about Major Max in actual fact, by almost all of us – let alone the public. Look at that piece he read to us – the book given to him by his old Dad. Is that the language of ruthless business? He's trying to refute that he's ruthless. It's all too good to be true, after that line about safety belts when he was pulping people in Belgrave Square!"

Joe and I stared at each other, uneasily trying to identify with Max Beaumont.

"Look, I'll say it straight!" I tried. "Max is partly Jewish, partly very German, and yet more British by adoption and purpose than either of us! He's less streetwise than you or Owen, but he has a sort of single-minded driving quality, trained and tried. And only deep inside is the subtle genes stuff."

"I think it's nothing as simple as that." Joe looked at me flatly. "He has a lot to hide somehow – that's the impression I'm getting. In the past and," Joe paused and stabbed a finger at the empty chair where Max Beaumont had been sitting, "right now! At this present time! I hear a few very odd rumours about what is going on in Fleet Street. It's not just tank-tactics in Belgrave Square that's bringing Major Max in front of the cameras in my opinion, and I know Owen thinks much the same!"

"Well, Joe," I said. "you're the eyes and ears on the payroll! Use them. If when you've got something, we'll try it out on MB and see if he reacts. Come to think of it I'm due for more chat with Al Chemmy. I'll see what he's offering for vibes. But listen, remember that Max is not like you and me, not

119

at all! He has not had to worry about the same sort of things for a very long time."

Joe nodded, but it was more or less automatic. He was restless now.

"You're right!" he said. "I have got one or two problems. Who's going back to Lime Grove?"

"Mr. Tolly, where do we meet tomorrow?" Jane Milward wanted to know. "And how long will this go on would you say? Because I can keep up with Nightwatch too, if you or Owen can switch me some help. But I can't really do fifteen hours a day, and not over the weekend."

"Take my car, Joe" I told him. "The taxi is due outside. And if you would talk to Owen when you get back, perhaps Jane can get the rest of today off. And then some regular help for at least another week. I'll let you know where and when for tomorrow."

"And you?" Joe Bailey asked.

Privately and on my own account, I had thought of doing some side research and reference as it is called which meant staying put.

"I'm going to make a few phone calls from here," I said. "I'll be calling Germany and one or two other places so it may take a bit of time."

We left the library, and the other two moved through the hall with me, and we separated there. Boris the indoor man, appeared as though by some radar system. He was wearing his linen house jacket and as he went ahead, I saw him beaming with a flash of gold teeth at Jane.

"So now all working very hard for Mr. Beaumont, yes?"

I wondered how often, and to how many people, he had said that, as I walked with purpose, back through the hall and into the smaller of the two drawing rooms. Some sounds from in there had made me fairly certain I would find her. Dogs, if allowed indoors, stay with people, and I had glimpsed one of the wolf hounds round that door as the three of us had walked past.

Mrs. Beaumont was watering an impressive row of tropical plants that rose up across the high windows from a specially tiled ledge. She looked round, unperturbed, as though I had every right to be there, while the dog sniffed around my

120

ankles.

"Max loves these things! I think his Aunt Sybilla grew them when he was young. Have you come to Aunt Sybilla yet?"

"Indoor tropicals like that are very much the German or Swiss thing," I said. "So that could be it. We've heard about a number of aunts and uncles but not that one."

Deborah Beaumont looked at me thoughtfully for a moment. Whatever the rigours of the campaign, money had not been spared in helping to stave off the passing years for Debby Beaumont. In her smoke-blue cashmere wool dress, grey-blonde hair pulled back into a comb, she looked the epitome of all that is enviable – rich *and* slim.

When she smiled, no make-up cracked, and the lips without lipstick were genuine. And because she could see my appreciation that included credit for intelligence, she knew also that I wanted to talk, and so put the watering can down among the wispy barked tropicals.

"How's it all going?" she said. "I hope Max isn't saying anything he shouldn't?"

"So far it's fine," I said. Perhaps it had not been such a good idea, this drifting-in act, and I was not even sure what I had in mind.

"I'm good at thought reading." She smoothed down the sides of the blue cashmere dress. "Why don't we sit down? These rattan chairs creak like hell, so if either of us says anything we shouldn't we can pretend it was the chair. I guess you were thinking of pulling me in on the interviewing? At some time?" It was all the kind of dialogue that only those American females like Mrs. Beaumont handle so very well.

"We'd certainly like to," I told her. "I mean it would be odd if we didn't. But it would be up to Owen Owen actually as he is the producer. I think it might depend on anything that pointed hard in your direction for an answer. If you know what I mean."

She was thinking that over for a minute. The room we were in was warm. I suppose because the tropicals facing us along the window side needed a fair share of central heating. An aroma from the plants, with their strangely shaped deep green leaves, some with buds and tiny flower, was the scent of the jungle. There was also the more expensive kind, used

121

by Mrs. Beaumont. And both served as a sort of counter-point to her grey and blue coolness as we both sat there.

She picked up a piece of petit-point work stretched across a wooden ring, and the needle moved in, pulling with it a pale-green thread. I saw a slight movement of her wide, pale mouth that seemed to show she enjoyed what she was thinking about at that moment.

"Are you trying to work me out?" she asked without looking up. "I know you and Max have known each other a long time ago. Germany after the fighting, he said. But you're not really like him are you?"

"To find out who and what he is," I said, "is exactly why I'm here."

"I suppose you think Max is a type? The international publishing tycoon?"

"I wouldn't, but most people might." I hesitated. "It's already clear to me and people working with me, that he is all sorts of things that make it complicated. He read us a piece from a book his father gave him which is hardly a tract from the Harvard Business School. His father was old-school Prussian officer caste. I would hazard that Max's genes are military as much as money."

"Are you being polite or professional?"

"Well, I'll start by being both!"

She tilted the cloth in the cane ring, and dipped the needle again, and smiled. I liked it, even if it was not directed at me.

"You let him tell!" she waited. "Perhaps you think I follow a pattern too?"

"Being married to any big man can be tough," I said carefully. "There could be extra problems with Max."

When she did look up, with the needle and thread in mid-air, there was no smile.

"Look," I was going carefully. "When I was seeing Max almost every day, that was a long time ago, almost another world, and we were pretty young at the time. Max always played his own rules."

"If you call him Max, I don't see why you can't call me Debby! How long were you with him in Germany?"

I wondered quickly if there would be other questions coming as a natural progression. It occurred to me that

122

Mrs. Beaumont was capable of gently needling me like the stretched linen on her lap. I wanted her help for this programme, maybe one of my last big interviews, maybe *the* last. It mattered more than concepts about where loyalty lay, as between husbands and wives.

"On and off for a year or more. Looking back it was a very important time, I think for both of us, professionally and in lots of ways. Max had the problem of belonging to both the occupying army and Germany. If that means anything."

"Well, it does of course. You must understand that I'm not all American. My mother was English, my father was American. He was also part Jewish, and came over here for World War One."

"Was Max your first husband?"

She smiled at the directness. "No. But I was his first!"

I thought if Debby Beaumont could be indiscreet it would be intentional, with no help needed from me.

I think she picked up that train of thought too, because she weighed the pause, and then asked another question, rather as though it was her turn.

"Are you going to give Max a rough time?"

"Hardly," I said. "We've all borrowed a bit from John Freeman – take Robin Day or any of us. But you know your husband is unknown to the public in a curious way. There have been many small items about him, one main piece in a Sunday paper once, no biographies as yet. It's as though he has tried to keep out of the limelight. In spite of Al Chemmy."

"Poor Al! He's really a very straight guy. His job, as Max told me once, is to focus interest on the Empire not the Emperor. My husband is not a shy man – you must know that, but he is not a publicist. He believes his achievements speak for themselves, so there are others who seem to overshadow him."

"A nice wife's speech!" I said. "But help me to present the whole man. It's important to discover what moulded him, what motivates him, where and how the past shaped the present."

"I think I have always had that job too!" She stopped the movement with her hands, and leaned back in the rattan chair, which made all the small, expected noises.

123

"I haven't been around on the media circuit world-wide, without knowing that someone is always on the look-out for the dark side of the moon. In the way that he is a famous man, Max is very exposed. He has powerful competitors, and in the newspaper world they can be vicious."

"And what about – say the trade union world? In Fleet Street?" I ventured.

The needle resumed its intended calm movement. "What do you hear?"

"I don't. I am the three wise monkeys," I said.

"I think you know, Tolly! We understand each other. There are people who gossip to me about my husband. There are other wives, who had I suppose, to face the same problem, and the same sort of questions. Of course I don't like the idea, but I love the man. Now, I've said enough! Are you staying for lunch? I have the wives of two of Max's top men coming over, just salad and quiche you know, but a nice bottle of Gewurtztraminer. Would you like that? They might prove much more informative if you worked on them!"

"Please don't think I work like that!" I said. The invitation deserved more than a polite answer. "I would like to stay," I said in all truth. "But let me say this. Max, I count as a friend not a beetle for dissecting. I hope we can be together again on this programme. OK, it's my job, but it means more than just that."

I got up and took the hand that was offered, rather to help her get out of the creaking chair than for any formality. I had seen silver framed pictures on small tables.

"Those photographs. They would be nice to know about!"

"Children, weddings, the usual things! Max and I have two sons, long gone on their way, one married and in the States, the other in Australia. I have a daughter from the first time round. She's in the European thingummy in Brussels. Now, if you keep walking the way you came, you will flash up on Boris' screen and he or Rinski will let you out. Will you be back tomorrow? Or the team?"

"I don't know," I told her honestly. "We're a bit in Max's hands. We're on such a tight schedule. He's giving us time, when and where he can. We should be with him every day somehow, from now on, at the rate we're going."

124

Mrs. Beaumont smiled, then also sighed. "You'll probably see more of him than I shall!"

When Owen phoned and said we would meet in Park Lane with cameras at three, I wondered as the usual contract taxi took me up Park Lane and down the other side, what the atmosphere would be like up in the main UK boardroom of World Media. What sort of meeting were we to be shown? Was Max laying on a high-powered get together for the cameras that would be phoney? Owen had said we had no library shots of anything like that, only some black and white when he bought *The World*, and some CBS tape of troubles with strikers in New York, and helicoptering in to the White House when the Kennedys were there, which must have been one of Jackie's The Good and the Great parties, I reckoned. The Park Lane building was one of those Regency three-storey affairs, white painted outside, with fine ironwork balconies in front of bow windows. So Max Beaumont moved from an enviable home environment to an equally listed and elegant place to work in the UK. What did he have in New York or Chicago? Someone had told me that in the US he worked from a porticoed Old South headquarters, just outside Washington, complete with magnolias and cherry blossom – and of course, horses.

There were no Beeb trucks or vehicles parked under the small manicured trees, and a sergeant from the corps of commissionaires walked politely across the cobblestones.

"How long would you be here, sir? There is no visitors' parking."

"Don't worry. This taxi goes away!" I struggled to get out. "Are the BBC lot here or not yet?"

"All inside, sir! Vehicles moved away." The uniformed man led me to the elegant front door, which curiously it seemed to me, was locked, and opened by the sergeant with a flourishing, outsize key.

"Bit more security now after the Major's little do the other day!" the sergeant said. "If you'll just step through there, you'll get your buttonhole and then you can join the other gentlemen." He meant the usual security and lapel tab, with the microchip.

125

"They're all graded." It was fastened by a young man who had what I call an improbably old face. Also a Scottish accent. "That means you're Mr. Beaumont's!" He wore a designer black jacket and tight trousers, and kept close beside me up the curving staircase with its thin bannister rail.

"What do you do here?" I said. "As you know who I am!" Sometimes I play the TV role hard if I think it will get what I want. My escort reacted cheerfully. "Well, as it's you, Mr. Tolly, I'll tell you, I'm one of the Major's minders! He doesn't want police around you see, although they were offered."

"And what is the qualification for the job? Or is it just since the other day's affair?"

"Three years with Mr. Beaumont, seven with the SAS before that. Here you are, sir!" He opened a panelled door.

Inside Owen and the camera and lighting crew sprawled in various priceless armchairs. The room was full of cigarette smoke. Coffee cups and video camera gear were on the table. Owen got up and came and stood beside me.

"It seems this meeting is for real. I wanted to get these shots and get back, but although the lighting lads have their gear up, in there, we haven't got in yet. There are about fifteen of them. All Beaumont top brass, no strangers. But, damn them, we've been here half an hour! Waiting! That dynamo doll who runs his routines has been in a couple of times, and now I've told her we don't really care any more!" Owen Owen slackened the flowing blue tie round his striped shirt collar, and looked at me with exasperation.

"Liz Charlton!" I said. "Yes, I would think she might even tell *you* that."

"We must have some footage of Beaumont and the first fifteen in action!" Owen fretted.

The door at the other end of the ante-chamber was opened swiftly. Liz Charlton stepped out, short blonde hair and classic tweed skirt swirling. She always heard everything.

"Fifteen is Rugby isn't it – in Wales, Mr. Owen? Well the scrum is just breaking up! He has told me to bring you in! How long will you be, he wants to know? Because he can't hold all our people for more than ten more minutes really. They're all in hot seats. And three have to catch planes."

126

"The lighting boys have fixed the room," Owen snapped. He had pulled up his tie again, and now smoothed down the soft, heavy black hair. He put a hand on Miss Charlton's shoulder and for a second I wondered if he might end up catapulted to the carpet, but Liz Charlton put her arms by her side and smiled.

"Stanley checked the lights over too!" she said.

"Who the hell is Stanley?" I asked.

"The nice young man who brought you upstairs. That's his job," said Liz charmingly. "Now, there are some other ground rules which I have to tell you, so I must be quick! You wanted this for the programme?"

"Right!" I said. "It's a natural part of what we're trying to get across."

"Well Al Chemmy should have been out here to mother you all. But he's inside fending off some publicity uproar that's reported down at the *Flash* plant. And if *Flash* doesn't appear, that's a million pounds for one night's stoppage. The other people you'll see in the conference won't be named. Don't ask for them. You won't get them."

"Christ!" said Owen loudly. The crew who had been chatting or dozing in the chairs behind us sat up and stared. "What is this sweety-pie? MI5 or a commercial outfit that wants some expensive publicity?"

"Easy, Owen!" I told him.

"You can record what's being said, because Mr. Beaumont has handed round a script. The real business is finished," Liz said, pointedly.

"The real business is about the new set up at Battersea," I said brutally, the only way to treat this one I calculated.

Liz Charlton turned grey eyes away from the watch on her wrist, to give me a short, sad look. "Do you think I would tell you, Felix Tolly?"

"Tell me!" Owen said. "You can trust a working man!"

I suppose there is no reason why a boardroom should be different from any other place people get together to made decisions. I have seen them in many forms. A Palava hut of bamboo, the decision-makers cross-legged on stools. Downing Street, the White House, Krupps, Royal Dutch Shell, the Vatican. There were very few of these where you were allowed to bring cameras, lights and eavesdropping sound and camera equipment.

The board room of World Media came as a pleasant change. It was a large, high-ceilinged, green and white room, with a row of tall, soundproofed windows overlooking Park Lane. The dozen or so men and two women were standing, as though by pre-arrangement, a protocol, with Max himself in the middle.

But TV and radio technicians have an idea of their own importance, and together with a faint whiff of spearmint chewing gum from behind me, came the immediate whirring of a shoulder-held camera. The two lighting boys were already moving round, in their trainers, silent on the royal-blue thick pile carpet, checking. Then they stood by Owen. The sudden white glare of soda lights, caused some of the Beaumont Decision-Makers to turn away, and I noticed two of the men produce dark glasses and put them on. They all began to sit down again, so far without a word, but the silence was ominous and restless. Only Max remained standing, elegant, relaxed, smiling almost mockingly.

"Have you counted them in, Liz?"

"Yes, Mr. Beaumont."

Now he looked at me, and then slowly round his cabinet at the table. Max was an actor, in his case a natural one. Only more so when TV cameras were around.

"I hardly need to introduce World's top board to Felix Tolly I think! Not that his face would launch a thousand ships maybe, but it is known to millions – certainly a great many more than ours are. So we are honoured that the BBC has come to us!" I saw out of the corner of my eye, the second camera using zoom on Max as he remained standing, but we would not be using that sort of speech. He sat down in the pale-blue leather chair. It was the same as all the others, and in front of us the big smooth rosewood table was almost covered with papers, but I knew they were almost certainly innocuous.

Now Al Chemmy had risen. In contrast to his chairman's relaxed, affable manner, he looked solemn.

"Ladies and gentlemen, Mr. Tolly and Mr. Owen!" Al was saying. "This is what the company calls a Security Room,

128

and it is here that strictly confidential meetings are held between top executives of World Media. I am asked to tell you that anything you may see and hear is confidential and no notes must be taken. Only Mr. Beaumont will answer questions." Al sat down. It was getting like the White House.

Owen Owen, who had so far been silent, pointing with an irreverent finger at the direction and closeness he wanted his two cameras, chipped in.

"Can we go?" he said. "Run the thing for real?"

"OK!" Max Beaumont agreed. "We know this board meeting is symbolic for you, part of a scenario." Al Chemmy pressed a switch on the wall and behind Max Beaumont a large illuminated panel lit up, showing a black and white negative of what was obviously an architect's drawing.

Although I had seen more of him in the last two days than for many years, Max Beaumont looked well in his command of World Media. His blue shirt collar had the usual crispness, the soft grey suit, and the black and iron-grey hair, with those blue-chip eyes in the lightly tanned face, all gave him a debonair look.

A sort of buzz went up from the people round the table. The picture on the wall was not expected.

Max looked thoughtfully at it. "Now has anyone got a pointer?"

One of the two women, sitting near to him – she might have been forty or fifty, with heavy features and no make-up, her dark hair in a bob cut – held up a plastic ruler. Max took it from her, and smiled in a friendly way, and suddenly I knew instinctively what was going to come.

"There is an old principle that I have always found worth following!" He tapped the screen with the plastic ruler. "First safeguard your line of retreat! Maybe you know of it, some of you? It was handed down from a famous general, and it applies in business as in war. In the media these days, it sometimes gets hard to know which is which! Now that general, he was not one of your Harvard School men! His first point was – safeguard your base! That is what we are now doing! This is our new plant at Battersea, and most of you round this table are involved in that!"

"Max!" Owen said interrupting, "we don't want any censorship on this later!"

"We're flexible!" I said urgently, sensing a new tension among the board crowd. "We only want a quick scene of how you work. We can cut out sound! Probably will. Use our own voice over!"

Owen exchanged a warning look with me. He was Producer it said. Max Beaumont was not sticking to any prepared script, whatever the PR department had told him. The set-up at Battersea was obviously not new to this group, but was still very much under wraps, and Max was now choosing what would go on our programme for his own purpose.

"Here in the UK – and those of you who spend most of your time running World Media somewhere else will know – we have had one hell of a pasting from the unions in The Street for far too long! We are in negotiation with them now for the manning of this new, purpose built plant. Bob – what sort of progress are we making?"

The eyes of the people round the table moved silently, like Owen's finger directing the zoom lens, and went to a big man with a tired, crumpled face and heavy eyebrows, that looked out from under a shock of strong grey hair.

"Tell what you told us earlier, only make it three lines!" Max's usually careful vowels were harsh now.

"It's rough going!" The big man looked away from the lens. "We're getting some movement, not a lot. Neither Sogat nor the NGA want the change. The NUJ are split."

I guessed this Bob was Max's chief labour negotiator. Beside him, scratching on a note-pad, a small, almost insignificant man, his eyelids drooping, was Dennis Laycock. I knew him. He was chief executive of World UK. With faces on our film it would not take long for researchers to put names and functions to everyone. The man called Bob, with the tired negotiator's voice, went on. "The Electricians," he said, "Salt of the earth! Something different!"

There was the sound of appreciative sympathy round the table.

Max Beaumont used the plastic pointer.

"This floor is all composing terminals, direct to the one below, and under that is the machine room, as it is still being

130

called. On the south side are the road transport take-up bays. You can see the multiple exits to the side. Newsprint storage is taking up the whole of the ground space at the other end."

The two cameras had been rolling on with only the small motion of zoom adjustments. Now Owen held out both hands, fists closed, stopping vision and sound.

"Mr. Beaumont! If this is off the cuff for us – I just want to ask, what are you publishing at Battersea? Or going to?"

"Dennis, will you take that one?" said Max easily.

Dennis Laycock had been managing editor of *The World*, until he was moved to oversee the Beaumont UK publishing. I not only knew Dennis, but liked his style. Max would not pick a yes-man for a hot-seat.

"Present plans are for the merged papers, launched as a new title, riding on the back of the Group's London locals, it can ride straight in to give effective competition to London's only evening. Probably with editions spanning noon to midnight."

"Lookout Nightwatch, here we come!" Max Beaumont said, and this time the laughter was brief but unmistakably sycophantic.

He turned round, pointing the plastic ruler across the table. "How did it go in New York, Phil? We've gone through this one over there!"

"Tough, Max! You were there, you know! Tough, but we made it." The American hardly moved his mouth, and folded his arms.

It was time everyone was reminded of the influence, money and total audience commanded by the BBC.

"I've said no censorship, once we've recorded!" Owen took the lead at just that moment. "OK, all of you?"

"In Germany we had more trouble than in New York!" The other woman, a thin-faced, middle-aged blonde tilted her head away from the cameras. "Of course! We have pioneered most of the equipment!"

"Steady, Gerda baby!" I now heard Dennis Laycock's accent as more Australian than American, but Max Beaumont was back with his picture-board.

"Here are some figures!" The architect's plans were replaced by the touch of the switch and a two-column set of numbers shimmered faintly on the screen.

"I doubt we'll pick those up, Felix!" Owen whispered. "There's a lot of bounce from the lights. Let him do a bit more pointing, and we'll quit."

After only a minute or so more, Owen suddenly faded the lamps that had quietly been heating up the room, leaving the usual feeling that it was about to rain. Also the faint smell of UV and burned dust motes. Owen's Welsh lilt cut into the surprised silence.

"Just to thank you, Mr. Beaumont! And all of you! That'll do us!" He ran fingers through his hair. "We, at the Best Box Co., are grateful!"

I moved to get round to Max and shake hands as some sort of formal gesture in front of his people and had got as far as starting to say something, when the double doors opened again, and Liz Charlton now led in two white-jacketed men who looked like medics, but I saw one was carrying a tray of glasses, the other three bottles of already opened champagne carefully wrapped in their napkins.

"Nice work, Tolly!" Max Beaumont came round and shook my hand now. And from somewhere a flash of still camera made those strange blue eyes of his even more brilliant. I saw Al Chemmy gesturing to his own photographers who had followed the champagne, and the flash was repeated. Then Max Beaumont made a sign to Liz, and our lighting crew and camera boys were being served champagne first. Some of the board room VIPs moved away after a short word with Max, who watched them go, responding with a raised hand, or a nod. I remembered some were working on airport flight-time. Presently the Beeb technicians were trooping out, and Chemmy and Laycock were flanking Owen and myself.

"Nice workshop you have here, Mr. Beaumont!" Owen said. He nodded round, at no-one in particular. "Not the usual Times Furnishing or Grub Street perpendicular! That's not a print over there! Matisse isn't it? What's the other one?"

"Pissaro," I said, not to score, but to keep Owen within bounds. I might have known better.

"Why doesn't the Beeb give us a place like this, with the park outside the windows?" said Owen. What's the square-foot rental?" He emptied his glass, and twirled the stem.

Max did not even bother to look up. He was signing and reading a succession of papers that Liz Charlton was putting on the table in front of him. But I could tell from the way his pen paused that he had heard.

"Just over two hundred. Are you planning to use that, Mr. Owen?"

Owen Owen grinned. "Not all chairmen know that sort of detail!"

"Mr. Beaumont knows exactly that sort of thing!" Al Chemmy said heavily. "But if you don't mind my saying, it was a bit pushy to ask!"

Owen put down his empty glass. "The trouble with us Welsh," he said easily. "Is that we still have an invisible ball and chain round the leg. I'm on my way! Can I know when we get back to the Beaumont story?"

"I'll get it sorted out and let you know," I told Owen.

When Liz Charlton had left the room with him and Joe, there was a sense of unease. The four of us stood for a moment in the big open space by the windows.

"Is that guy going to carry on running this thing?" Chemmy wanted to know. "Because – if you'll allow me, Max – that worries me."

"How is that?" I asked him. "Let's get the aim right!"

"Well, getting the biggest possible audience in this country to see what sort of person Max Beaumont really is, and to like what they see!"

"I thought we were following up a news story that got your chief into the headlines the other day? Perhaps I've got it wrong?"

"We're not fooling you, Felix! So don't you pretend to us!" Dennis Laycock, put a tactful hand on Chemmy's arm. "There are bound to be angles. It's Al's job to look at all of them. Max here has never before put himself out as he is for you. As a person. I know! I tried to get it out of him when I was editing *The World*."

Max himself had been sitting, his face expressionless, only his eyes moved and the cleft of his jaw.

"Thank you gentlemen! That's it! I shall stay here for a while. Dennis, you have another meeting in the Fleet Street boardroom at six. Can I phone you?" It was of course a dismissal.

"Max" I said. "You have my numbers too"

I went downstairs and stood in Park Lane, and watched the relentless traffic tramping down to Hyde Park Corner. There were trees with golden, falling leaves that drifted down to lie around us on the cobbles. I spoke to the commissionaire about a taxi, but he smiled and pointed.

Liz Charlton had phoned, and a car was pulling into the forecourt, and the chauffeur was getting out to open the door for me.

"BBC Lime Grove" I told him.

"Thank you, Mr. Tolly!" It was TVP again.

At Lime Grove, Owen was nowhere in sight, but Jane Milward came looking for me with a red printed message slip. But before giving it to me she sat herself down on the chair only. We were back in the glass-walled cubby hole that was my office for Nightwatch.

"How did it go this morning?" Jane asked. I liked Jane, she was never pushy, but had her own kind of feminine prescience. One hopeless and failed marriage they said, and a young daughter to keep.

"Interesting," I said. "I want to see the film and sound."

"I'm going to have to move full-time onto this Beaumont job, Owen says. Which suits me, but makes it difficult to do continuity on Nightwatch." Jane still held the message. "He's put Susan Wakes onto the job – know her?"

"Susan's OK," I said. "Is she doing the Running Order for tonight?" I looked at my watch. "Did my wife call?"

"No to both." Jane looked at the message in her hand, and laid it on the desk. "This one is really for Shepherds Bush, I would have thought. But Owen said it was for you. Do you know Rita Henckmann from German TV?"

"Is that the ARD London Office?"

"What's that?"

"*Allgemeine Rundfunk Deutschland* they call it *Erste Fernseh* too – state owned. There's another in Mainz – *ZDF*."

134

Jane turned the small piece of paper round on the desk, so that her neat writing and the printed words, giving time, date and action required, faced towards me. I was wrong. The call had originated from Hamburg.

"What does she want?"

"She's coming to London tomorrow, and wants to sit in on the making of the Beaumont programme. At least she said her bosses want her to."

"Well apart from that, and you and I, let alone Max Beaumont, it's pretty unheard of for any other outfit to sit in on a current affairs programme preparation! There is a route I suppose. ARD in London, gets onto Shepherds Bush."

"She says they've done that, and everybody's happy."

"The usual calculating machine is at work on the foreign rights earnings," I said. "Of course, they're sure to show the programme over there."

"Her English is flawless, with an American accent if you know what I mean," Jane said. "She wants to know where it's all going on."

"It's unusual for anyone outside to come in at this stage," I fretted. "I mean usually they buy the finished product when they've seen the video."

Jane stayed sitting, looking down at the desk, and I noticed then that she had done something different with her hair, put it up with a comb, and the frill neck to her blouse was part of the same Victoriana bit, with an option to look buttoned up, or the other way. She bit her lip, then looked at me quickly.

"Max Beaumont has already said yes! I think she got at him first. Which you must admit is a bit fast!"

"You mean she actually made direct contact with Beaumont too? They don't waste time, the Germans, do they!"

"Max Beaumont is still very interested in something basic to him, beside power and money." Jane began to look a little pink. "This Lili Marlene was able to get to him through *Das Fenster*. She said so."

"*Das Fenster* is the magazine that Beaumont started in Germany after the war," I said. I know he's still close to them." I looked at the message slip again. "I'll still have to speak to Owen Owen. He's producing."

135

Jane left, and I started to make some notes about the Park Lane board meeting, and did not see Owen Owen at the glass door, tapping and entering simultaneously. He put the pink-coloured running order for Nightwatch on the desk.

"What's the trouble, Uncle? This is your last night on this stint! No programme tomorrow, Saturday! Which only leaves the Beaumont!"

"That's the trouble." I said. I looked at Owen's unlined face, the quirky thick lips in the blue stubbled jaw and the humorous dark eyes. "Uncle now, was it!"

"OK young man," I said. "Have you heard we've got a German TV dolly coming on the Beaumont job with us? Cleared herself personally with Max first."

"Liz Charlton just told me, she phoned." Now Owen looked moody and sat down on the desk. "I suppose she's one of these pale-faced kraut kids, ex-Washington, ex-Moscow, six languages and a judo black belt! The French have them too. You've met them I expect?" Owen was always ready to talk TV philosophy right up to bell time. "Our TV is all over Europe, even in front of American soap, and our programmes are probably top of the export league. But she must have something this one. How in hell did she get round Max? We can't stop her if he wants her around, Felix. Liz Charlton said the same, and the next session is his place, Richmond again!"

"How about Joe? Joe's important," I said. "And Jane, come to that. I think she's fallen under the Beaumont spell, by the way. Can they both make weekend duty?"

"Joe will, and if we need Jane and she's hooked, she'll come won't she?"

Owen standing again, looked at his watch, checking it with the studio wall clock. "I heard just now that *The World* is in dispute tonight, and most likely won't be out tomorrow. That goes for *Flash* as well, probably. I gather that Bob character we met had orders to put the boot in! If it spreads to Max's Sundays that's serious for him."

"I'll tell Jane to accept for tomorrow then," I said. "And that must be whether the Beaumont empire is in disarray or not!"

CHAPTER SEVEN

"Couldn't you just leave it all now to Owen Owen and Joe Bailey?" Chloe asked. She had been asleep when I had come in the previous night. Nightwatch and the usual professional post-mortem afterwards meant I had not got back to Barnes until well after midnight. Now I was sitting on the edge of the bed next morning, with the cup of tea Chloe had brought me.

"No," I said. "I'm the one that's got to do the action. And you know, Chloe, the whole thing hangs on the questions and the preparation. If it's sloppy, a million people push the other buttons. If I've heard Max Beaumont in the original, I know how much he'll give, and more to the point, what he won't! And what is going to be relevant and maybe dynamite! I need success again, darling! I can go on for quite a while yet. The whole of the Beeb is like quicksand these days. Or like a patient that too many doctors have worked on, and patched up, and prescribed for – or given electrical treatment to, or whatever they do for the palsy!"

Chloe was up, dressed and from the look of it, ready to go.

"You forget," I told her, "That I am one hundred and ten years older than you are!" I felt like it sitting there. "The Beeb is keen on early retirement these days, and nobody has put me up for a K yet!" I got off the bed now, and wandered round the bedroom. I did not like what I saw in the mirror. "I sometimes wonder if I shall even make it to pension if they push me out!"

"Why not get yourself a new dressing gown? While you wait?" Chloe said.

"This is an old friend! I won't dream of it!" I put my hands in the pockets, and found a miniature bottle of scotch. "I have very few in this world now!"

Chloe was moving towards the door.

137

"Jennifer and I are going to the garden centre. The phone-call list is in the study! There was one earlier last evening from a dragon voice who said she was assistant to the Downing Street Press Officer. Did they find you at Lime Grove?"

"No." I shook my head, and sat down on the bed again. "But that's not the K either. They don't come through the Press Office. That's Sandy – I wonder what he wants?"

I had known Sandy Baggs for as many years as his appointment, and a few before that, and contact with him was also part of the job. For both of us. With parents, like Owen Owen's who had the sense of humour that wished that name upon him, he had developed the dermatological impregnability – as Sandy himself called it – that had carried him from Fleet Street to the sunny side of a better street – his own version again. Chloe had written the phone number in her copper-plate hand, and I saw it must be home rather than Westminster. I poured the little bottle of scotch into what was left of the morning tea, and pushed the numbers.

"Nice of you to call!" Sandy's voice was the up-market end of the Scottish spectrum. It had been broader when he worked for the *Glasgow Herald*. "Are you at home?"

"Yes," I said. "Sorry I wasn't in when you called last night. If you chaps watched TV you'd have seen I was busy."

"Taken in the spirit intended! I'll come to the point," Sandy was saying. "I'm at Chelsea too."

"Very nice!"

"By which I mean there's no bugaboos here, Felix, and I trust none at your end. But I want to talk carefully. And off the record. OK?"

"OK," I replied. "We had a scrambler here but it got used for the eggs." That appeared to cause a long pause before Downing Street's PRO came on again.

"I'd like to have a quick meeting with you, but the fact is – well it's Saturday. And the Sundays are generally after me by this afternoon. Then your lot, and then the Monday Heavies. Part of you being busy is of course Max Beaumont. Right?"

"Top marks, Sandy. Who blabbed?"

"Don't be bloody ridiculous, Felix!" The accent neared Glasgow again. "I called Al Chemmy, Max Beaumont's front to people like me, and he confirmed, and offered

Owen the Owen whoever he is. But I know you!" Sandy gave a heavy sigh. "We also know the Director General, two or three controllers and who else?"

"You have the clout," I agreed. "What can I do?"

"There are people in high places who think it would be a good thing if Mr. Beaumont was presented in the kind of light that would fit in with present policies."

"Coming from you, that sounds like the Politburo!"

"Aye! The view is that Max is about to strike into the very vitals of the kind of thing that has been hamstringing this country for decades! If you show him up as a bloody foreigner, a yid, and an arrogant bugger at best, throwing thousands out of work, that would not help."

"I go for your loveable frankness, Sandy! Max is not to be played with. He's with Clausewitz. He thinks he's still in the war, guarding the flanks, only trusts his own people, doesn't like the remotest suggestion of interest in his business from any government department! What do you want me to do, Sandy?"

"Not me, Felix!" Sandy was reproachful. "I don't influence you any way at all! Just being helpful. The powers who pay me reckon Max Beaumont is deep into something that may settle a lot more. Whether you or Beaumont will feel the sword on the shoulder I very much doubt. He plays so bloody clever. One big daily backing the right, and the other the left! As I said – just trying to be helpful. Concentrate your mind a bit!" I thanked Sandy for calling, discarded the dressing gown, skipped a bath, and took a shower instead.

Shaved, brushed, combed and partially dressed for weekending at Richmond, I drifted into the little morning room where Mrs. Braxton had set coffee on the electric keep-hot, and the makings of toast. Also a croissant in the napkin. I buttered the croissant and thought carefully about the Sandy Baggs line. Of course it went on all the time. Guidance, direction, helpful leaks.

My thoughtful wife had put the cordless phone alongside the coffee pot before going out, and I reached for it just as it sounded off.

"Listen! I've got Joe with me!" It was Owen Owen. "We need a word rather urgently before this next session at

Richmond." There was a pause, the cordless phone playing whispers with its own static. "If we pick you up we could talk in the car. I've had Al Chemmy on the line, and Joe made a few calls last night. I suppose you know that neither of Beaumont's big dailies were printed last night?"

"Thanks." I had decided not to say anything about my call from Sandy Baggs. "I'll see you soon!"

I carried the cup of coffee over to the small writing desk where Chloe put the morning papers. The Corporation paid for this complete pile of newsprint, and I always marvelled at the British public's seemingly insatiable appetite for news, and whatever else accounted for several timber forests pulped each day. Not a new thought, but wry for anyone who had been dishing it out to them on the box only a few hours before. Not one of these Fleet Street creations could beat the programme I and others had created the night before, not for headlines nor visual. How long would they all last?

I could see that the pile of black and white stuff – a little colour here and there nowadays – was distinctly in shorter supply today. Although being a Saturday there were freebees, the magazines, and the egg-head weeklies also Beeb provided, lest I should miss a word. Which was also pretty daft, as the studio were at work every day clipping and reading and stitching together, following up lines and angles, researching and telephoning. So, no *The World* and no *Flash*. I wondered what that had cost Beaumont.

I glanced at the front pages of the others, and ranged quickly over the column heads. They made small, ungloating and careful reference to the industrial dispute affecting World Media.

I went back to the breakfast table, remembering the little note with Chloe's green-ink handwriting had still a third name and number to call. I looked at the little carriage clock on the writing desk. Owen and Joe would be twenty minutes. Then, I looked at the name again. Mrs Rita Henckman. I had forgotten about that one. While the number rang I wondered what she looked like.

It was the Carlton Tower Hotel that answered. I recalled in the odd, split-second way the brain works, which is perhaps encouraging and also terrifying, that this was where we had been told Max Beaumont liked to take people for lunch when not using his own premises. The operator was putting me through to an extension. The voice at the other end was clear but not crisp, just a shade husky. It occurred to me that my call might also be the alarm clock.

"Felix Tolly!" I said. "You called last night?"

"Oh, Mr Tolly! This is Rita Henckman, German television!"

It was not a musical voice, too precise, but with a certain usage of the mouth that comes across even on the telephone, because I suppose all men like to imagine a woman's looks when they hear but cannot see her. The advent of the viewing telephone is going to spoil a lot of things. I rather fancied Rita was sitting on the edge of the hotel bed in her nightie.

"I've heard about you," I said bluntly. "Are we missing something? How did you get onto Max Beaumont? We don't, at the BBC like other stations anywhere muscling in on our work."

"No, no! Please don't misunderstand me, Mr. Tolly, the angles are at our end." Her laughter was all genuine. "You must know where Mr. Beaumont came from! And what he did in West Germany after the war! And his press interests there today. The story of his life would interest a lot of German viewers!" I had begun to hear another inflexion now. There is nothing like microphone and radio training.

"Are you German yourself, Mrs. Henckman?" I said curtly. There was only a slight pause.

"Yes, I am sure you can hear how bad my English is!"

"But you have spent more time in the States than over here?"

"Yes." Pause again. "I was married to an American. And I spent seven years in Washington, working with our bureau there."

"You are not married now, Mrs. Henckman?" I was putting the voice and personality over hard, realising I could be misunderstood. "If I am going to introduce you to other people, I mean people working on this programme, well it helps to know. Is Henckman your maiden name for instance?"

"My husband was an American, although with a German family name, and I will tell you that he crashed in his own plane two years ago and was killed. Does that help?" The voice had gone flat, clipped, with an odd note.

Would I never learn that even a small probe needs to be ready for the unexpected? I covered by explaining that it was to avoid stubbing a toe on the unexpected that we were pre-running through the Beaumont story. It was appropriate enough.

"I'm sorry!"

"That's OK." Now she sounded almost bored. "His passenger was another woman. In some ways it made it easier. Now, Mr. Tolly, may I ask you something? You say you are running through the scenario with Mr. Beaumont before going in front of the cameras. I plan to join you for that? This is – how do you say it? A job of work for me! I want to give my editors – I think in Britain you call them something else, not sponsors, like in the USA – an advance idea of what we can expect. Are you asking Mr. Beaumont about his time in Germany after the war?"

"We haven't got that far," I told her. I was looking at the clock across the other side of the room. Owen and Joe would be around to collect me, any minute. "Look!" I told her. "It's never done in my experience. The BBC does not let any other programme join in a current affairs major presentation. The only person who can bring you in is Max Beaumont himself. The best way to him is through his public relations man."

The small laugh at the other end of the line was like ice cubes in a glass. "I have already spoken with Max personally. I had an introduction. He said you would not object. Do you object, Mr. Tolly?"

This confirmed, of course, what I already knew.

"We're with him again this morning, at his place at Richmond," I said reluctantly. "Are you welcome there? You'd better check." I had another thought. "Do you know where it is?"

"I can find out. So I think, Mr. Tolly, I will not anymore disturb your morning. I have a few people to see and things to do, and later, I join your session!"

142

Out of the morning-room window I could see the taxi swinging up to the front door, and I was walking with the cordless handpiece towards the door. "Mrs. Henckman I am sure you know how to get exactly what you want! But now I must say *auf Wiedersehen!*"

Her laughter was like the sound of a cocktail shaker as I rang off.

At Richmond, the fellow who was called Rinski, the outside man, opened the car door when we arrived, and virtually pulled me out.

"How is Mr. Beaumont this morning, Rinski?"

"Oh he is very good, sir!" When Mr. Beaumont goes for riding, they try to shoot him! We have lots people with guns! I think Mr. Beaumont is happy. He is alive yes?"

"Is that true?" Unsmilingly, Joe Bailey peered up the big stone stairs towards the front door. He adjusted his spectacles and looked round as though he expected a hand-grenade to be tossed from the laurels at any moment.

"I'm not surprised!" Owen Owen had the collar of his dusty melton overcoat turned up, the lump of black, overlong hair hanging on his forehead. "I thought that the horse-riding caper was asking for it, after what he did the other day. Too bloody easy to do a sniping job in this park wouldn't you say?" He feigned nonchalance, but moved quite quickly up the steps.

As we approached the front doors, only one half opened, and the inside man in his white coat stepped behind it, so that beyond him, I saw Max Beaumont's driver and former sergeant, the one I had met on Newswatch.

"OK, Boris! You can let this lot in!" he said. "Morning, Mr. Tolly! Gentlemen!" The door was closed and chained behind us. "If the other two could go on into the library, Mr. Tolly, the guv'nor would like to see you privately for a minute in the big room. This way, follow me!"

I left Owen and Joe being led away by Boris, and followed the broad shoulders and boxer's walk of former Sergeant Dasher. He opened the big white-painted door, and with much the same ceremony as the outside Rinski, pushed me in.

"Mr. Tolly, sir!"

Max Beaumont was standing unnecessarily theatrically in front of the burning logs and stone carving of the great fireplace. For a man who had lost a few millions overnight, and from what we had just heard, had been running the gauntlet in his own back yard, he looked uncommonly smooth. The tweeds had given way to a camel-coloured cashmere jacket, cream shirt and heavy foulard tie. The neat shoes twinkled at his feet, as did the cuff-links at his wrists.

Looking much more as though he had had a hard day's night was Al Chemmy, also warming his backside, to the right of Max Beaumont, his rumpled suit was a foil for his master. I stood still.

"I hear there was somebody anxious to hurry on your obituary this morning Max?"

"That's why I thought we might have a quick word with you before we join the others," Max said tersely. "How much can we keep it strictly off the record?"

"Only as much as you can do it yourself, on appeal." I had thought he would know that. "You have all the influence."

"Al here says the security people will put a D notice on it! That would apply to all the media."

Max Beaumont was in fact fairly tense. He smiled, but I fancied at something he was thinking about, behind opaque unsmiling blue eyes.

"Except the foreign press as you must know," I told him. "If they run anything, it gets hard to keep it quiet. What happened anyway? Your man Rinski said someone tried to shoot you? I think we ought to know. You see, Max," I explained, and I was suddenly weary of all the drama, "If this does get out, it has to go on TV news again, even as just a statement. Which smacks our programme about."

"Doesn't it act as a teaser?" said Al Chemmy. "Bring them on?"

"No it doesn't."

My camera-trained eye saw Max Beaumont's profile turn to Chemmy with slow, stone sharpness. "You Al, can tell the staff that if anybody speaks at all they're fired! The story is denied! It is an allegation! Not true!"

But Al wanted to tell someone, and he turned to me.

144

"Max was riding as usual, somewhere on the far side of those Penn Ponds. Know 'em? The two big bits of water in the middle of the Park." Al was making his thwarted press statement in measured tones. It was the voice of the fire chief or head of police, and as Al spoke, his hands went behind his back, and he looked ahead, rocking on his heels. "He was walking his horse at that point, and says a single shot, probably from over five hundred yards away, missed him over the top. By quite a margin, isn't that right?"

"What did the sheriff do then?" I asked rudely,

"Sorry, Max, but five hundred yards! If anybody wanted you, why not short range out of a bush? With a bazooka?"

"They might have hurt the horse!" Max could change style in seconds, there was no smile. He shrugged. "Perhaps it was the league against cruel sports? We were back here and on the telephone in about ten minutes. It was not very loud, that shot, and as I was in full canter a second later, whoever it was must have got out of the park gates quickly. There's not a lot of traffic on the Park roads at that hour, but the big jets come into Heathrow every two minutes. I didn't even hear the shot – only the air being parted. Do you know the sound, Tolly?" He looked at me with a droll expression and I knew why. "Like a party cracker being pulled!"

"Not my idea of a party!" Al Chemmy said. He shook his shoulders dramatically. "Keep alive, Boss, we need you! I'm off! I'll sell it to the staff, like you said, the story is that some punters were having a shot at the deer in the Park. Got that Tolly!"

"Brilliant!" I said, politely. "You seem to be piling up people who don't like you," I added, as the door closed on Al. "Joe Bailey has been telling me a good deal more about the Battersea project. I understand that chief executive, Bob what's-his-name, the labour negotiator – he moves around in a bullet-proof car with his own two minders?"

"Bob Ricksdorf. And Alistair McKenzie, *World*'s chief executive, you met him the other day too! He doesn't want to fall down just now either. A wheel came off his car on the motorway a couple of weeks ago. Would that be better than a bazooka for you?"

"OK. OK!" I said. "Now listen, Max, please! Joe Bailey and Owen – he is the producer of this show remember – they've got some pretty sharp questions in mind for this morning. I'll blow the whistle if it gets rough! I've had a couple of phone calls this morning, and if you and I didn't know each other from earlier times, I'm not sure I wouldn't be roughing it up too! I never know where I am with the controllers at the Beeb. I can be faded into oblivion. Not like you, the way we've just been talking, but without the right pension and the handshake. I'm too old to go to CBS or NBS anymore."

Max had started to move towards the other door, the one that led through to the library, with sudden impatience now, but he stopped his hand on the door handle. With him even the smallest things seemed measured, gestures calculated. It came naturally, like a cat walks along the top of a fence, and he spoke in the assured, elocution-taught voice.

"I can tell you this, Tolly old mate!" As people do when they have absorbed another language, Max liked to use colloquialisms. "You are strictly as old as you feel! Of the two of us, you have the advantage! You can go into any restaurant, theatre or shop, and the world knows your voice, your face! Beautiful women will stop you in the street!"

"You," I said pleasantly, "can go into any bank in the world, Tokyo, New York, Zurich, present your name and they will put it in sacks for you and carry it to the car!"

We stepped through into the big room with the handsome windows and book-lined walls, where Joe Bailey and Owen had found a set of dice. The little leather box was on the coffee table, and they were busy rolling them.

"Perhaps they have the real answer – in that game!" Max said, as both men got up.

"I'm sorry I kept you waiting." Max was not really sorry. He was only acknowledging protocol, telling the boardroom, the tank-crew or whoever, as he had all his life, to stand easy.

"Well, let's go!" He sat down, crossing his legs, looking down at the creased trousers. "Where were we?"

Owen Owen sat back on the settee opposite and studied him as though he was still playing liar-dice. Joe, at the other end, clip-board laid on the settee cushions between them, had taken off his spectacles and was slowly cleaning them, polishing with a little yellow cloth, and holding them up to the light from the windows. I shifted uneasily. I knew these two. They were not worried about their jobs, they were highly employable around half the world, and knew it.

"Jane isn't with us today," Owen said. "So no shorthand notes. I have her stuff up to date, in fact I was reading some of it through first thing. Joe might want to write down a few times and places, that's up to him." He nodded across the intervening space. "I notice you haven't got your own recorder for monitoring today?"

"Perhaps it's the hidden one?" Joe had put his glasses back on, and was leaning forward.

For a moment Max Beaumont looked from one to the other. The shrewd tanned face went taut and one of his hands stroked the arm of the chair.

"Are you boys happy?" he said. "Coffee? A glass of something?"

"There's just the four of us here," I said quickly. "Let me say that Max Beaumont has not exactly had a great night with the stoppage in Fleet Street, and it seems that riding out in the park, he narrowly missed being shot by some poaching deer shooter."

"That's OK, Tolly!" Max said evenly. "I understand writers and broadcasters perhaps, although I only employ a few hundred. My life is not even as creative as these two. I was saying to Tolly here, that no one would recognise me, walking along the pavement. I'm maybe the pilot of the plane. People don't see him. I decide where it goes, but it's the sum total of the parts that make it fly, lots of very complicated parts! There are navigators and engineers and cabin staff who keep everybody happy. I don't know whether you, Joe, or Owen can wind me up, to make me a character like Beaverbrook or Rothermere, or Axel Springer in Germany, or Hearst, the way he was, in his time, in the States."

"You don't act like any of those," Joe Bailey said slowly. "We can see you. What you did the other day to take out these two in Belgrave Square put you up front for once. Now we're following through."

"The way you spoke just then," Max's voice was a caress, "Could you be Jewish, Joe? For instance?"

"My father was Irish," Joe said. He packed the white ivory dice together in their little red leather case. "So where does that leave us?"

"It depends." Max Beaumont went on being pleasant. "Where and when. About 1938, it was enough to put you in a concentration camp on the one hand. Or perhaps last night, opening your front door, to the other side in Crumlin Road?"

"What happened in the park this morning?" Owen demanded. "Whose side was that?"

"*The Deer Shooter*, boyo!" Joe said sarcastically. "You heard! Take two! We're making a new film!"

"Look!" I said. "The job here is to get on with Max Beaumont's life! What makes him what he is. Where did he make the grade on the way, the mainspring, the motivation. That's what they're after!"

"The motivation is a date with destiny, and the instrument gauge is marked up in ruthlessness," Owen said. "Let's try that!"

"That's a fancy, disagreeable idea!" Max Beaumont told him shortly. "You can say what you like! But I'll decide what I say too!"

"How much money did you lose on the breakdown last night?" Joe asked.

"Breakdown? Well it wasn't a print breakdown. It was just plain blackmail, sabotage! These union people will bring the temple down. They've been at it for a long time."

"I spent some time in and around the Street yesterday," Joe said slowly. He stretched one arm out, along the back of the settee, and faced Max Beaumont, his big spectacles glinting. He looked like a boxer resting on the ropes. "Most of the people I talked to seemed to think you are an outsize shit!"

"An outsize *foreign* shit!" Max said, and now he looked almost happy.

"They say," went on Joe "that you are giving notice to quit to more than three thousand workers – Sogat people, NGA, NUJ, because they will not agree all sorts of tough new agreements, new machine methods, and are upsetting all the carefully worked out negotiating procedures. You have put Bob Ricksdorf, your chief labour negotiator, into fast-forward. He and Laycock your chief executive, are going around armed with bodyguards, like Chicago in the twenties! I've got an NUJ card!" Joe said. "Have had for years!"

"Then perhaps you could help me!" said Max tensely. "Persuade some of your friends – and I mean the journalists, not the machine room men, nor the unskilled louts of Sogat, that what they are being offered is the future! At better pay rates, if they will work the new systems that make it possible – systems the Americans and the newspapers in Germany are using, that print better papers, more economically and create jobs!" It was still the boxing ring, Max Beaumont, flexing his shoulders in the casual cashmere jacket, his eyes bright, the cleft in his dark and unshaven chin tucked well in.

I wanted to stop this abruptly. I did not want my programme screwed up. But Max was leaning forward talking quietly, very forcibly now.

"I will tell it the way it is! After forty years of publishing, here, the States, Europe, and mixing with TV now, well a polyglot like I am has to be careful to get the idiom right! OK? I spoke of bringing the temple down. Do any of you still read the Bible? It has a quote for everything! I always liked the bit that said: 'Muzzle not the oxen that treadeth out the corn!' Do you get that idea, Mr. Bailey? Your father probably did a fair day's work for a fair day's pay – oh yes I know the old Karl Marx and Keir Hardie bits too! They have come in useful at meetings with these characters who call themselves Fathers of the Chapel. Or Imperial Fathers! For years these people have even been warring among themselves. In the press rooms, for instance, the NGA machine managers and the Natsopa machine assistants. Other publishers have tried to buy them off, with more and more money. But the employers – they will not act in concert! Never have, never will! Go into The Street again, Mr. Bailey, with your card! See if the men will let you in to report on their restrictive practices. Like reserve stand-by workers paid for a night's work, who never come in. How the newsprint rolls break mysteriously. No journalist, not even the editor, is allowed to walk through the *World* composing room without their permission! Watch how clean copy is relogged into the computer, and pasted

149

onto the page, watched by no less than three overpaid men, supposedly correcting, and then see how many errors per column you can count next day! Joe, your old man would turn in his grave! And the pay rates these people are getting are far higher than coal-face workers in the pits! Until now, my top people in the States, Germany, and France as well, they were laughing at me for what goes on here! Now I have had enough!"

Max stopped speaking. I saw Joe was polishing his glasses which seemed to have misted up again.

"How many newspapers and magazines and other media do you actually own or are under your control? How many TV stations?" Joe asked.

"Lumped together? Which includes some pretty small radio channels in the States, Canada and Australia? Some hundreds!"

"You can't remotely know all the people who run these things. How do you know they're fairly treated and paid? That they're any good? That what they are churning out every day, every hour in words and sound and pictures are even what you'd approve of?"

"I don't, but I have a command structure. Staff commanders, and line. I pick the top. Some grew with the job, some didn't. I'll give you an example. And by the way, I'm not sure I like all these current words about areas and situations and taking things on board. There are always *only* people! Do you know my chief labour negotiator was himself a Union negotiator? A General Secretary in fact. Although I always thought that title sounded more Soviet than British. Yes – he crossed the floor as they say in the House of Commons."

"Poacher turned Keeper," said Owen, "is the way we would say it at home. Why do you think that you are the right person to have so much power? To directly affect the lives of so many people, and then, through their work, the views and opinions and information of many millions more?"

"*Quis custodiet ipos custodies* in short?" said Max.

"What is that?" Joe, looked from one to the other. "Latin was not part of my schooling!"

150

"Plato!" Owen told him with faint irritation. "Who spelled out all the options. Who is going to blow the whistle on God, is what it means!"

Max Beaumont eased back in his chair, still completely unruffled.

"I could give you the old answer. About the right time finding the right man, and to some extent I think that is often true. Churchill, Monty, Eisenhower – all in their different ways. It was in the way. You see, that was my education, the real one. And I didn't learn Latin either, Joe! I was taught in one of the most effective, patient, ruthless and efficient establishments to do one thing. Command! To organise, to administer, to control – call it what you like! With a view to winning! Not like the Germans, and to some extent the Americans, who have got to win and don't know how to lose. But you will *always* lose in real life. Some time, some how. So accept that, and know how to lose well – and then how to recover and win. Well, either you know that one, or you don't. Mind you, we Brits," and Max turned his face slowly to all three of us, with the quick crooked smile, "We have almost made a virtue out of losing! We need more winners like me!"

"Do you say that because you are only a paper Brit?" Owen murmured.

"Or a paper tiger? Or a paper tycoon?" Max retorted. "Look my friend, I had a tank squadron to command in the last weeks of the second world war, when I was twenty-one – and a major! I could make that armoured squadron move across any kind of country, like a football team, like you direct a big TV show! I could take it over, round, through any terrain, like cars on a race track. I can make a newspaper work, or put magazines and books into existence like a top chef runs a good restaurant! I can run the whole damn breathing, fighting, moving combination of people, plant, money, power and timing like an armoured division! OK? I was trained to do it, to lead from the front! Maybe it was there from the beginning, to be trained. But don't let anybody tell you that anyone can do it, because they can't! I have to know people, usually better than they know themselves. Know finance, so that I am never in the hands of the accountants and bankers. And enough technical stuff about machinery and electronics, so that I know who's bluffing and what decision could go wrong and how."

Max Beaumont stood up. It had been impressive. "Do any of you like poetry?" A sudden harsh note in his voice made us all sit up to attention.

"Poetry?" Owen said thickly. "What poetry, Mr. Beaumont?"

Max Beaumont cleared his throat, and I glanced at Joe Bailey who by now seemed to be slightly dazed. I realised, and could hardly believe that, Max was about to recite. He had cleared his throat and now rendered.

> *"If you can keep your head when all about you*
> *Are losing theirs and blaming it on you*
> *If you can trust yourself when all men doubt you*
> *Yet make allowance for their doubting too.*
>
> *If you can dream and not make dreams your master*
> *If you can think and not make thoughts your aim*
> *If you can meet with triumph and disaster*
> *   and treat those two impostors both the same.*

"Of course, what Kipling didn't know, was that nowadays there would be no more respect for that sort of thing. Or is it self respect anyway? But there's some real backbone in that poem!" He stopped, rather as though he thought at least one of us would make some sort of appropriate comment. But no one spoke.

"I haven't read Kipling for quite some time," Owen said at last.

Max Beaumont's smile this time was like frost in the sunshine.

"It is just a candle in the darkness!" he said. "I really don't think I've ever had this situation before – to bare my breast for the pen that is mightier than the sword. Or is it a TV aerial?"

At that moment the door in the panelling at the side of us opened, and Liz Charlton stood in the doorway.

"I don't like to do this." she said, "but the Empire is in a fairly restless state Mr. Beaumont! I will bring in the morning Bollinger for you, and you will answer three fax, four telex and make one phone call for me in the next room. Mrs. Beaumont says all is set for the ladies' lunch, but there is a Miss Henckman – " she glanced at me – "Have I got it right? And should she be with the lunch or the work-session?"

"That's this German TV staffer I told you about," I said to Owen. "At least she got through to me on the phone, but I haven't met her. She told me she had an OK to join us from you, Max?"

"My number two let the call through to Mr. Beaumont," Liz agreed. Standing there she made a splendid silhouette in the doorway.

"She used an introduction from people on *Das Fenster*," Max Beaumont said almost evasively. He got up moving towards Liz. "I'll be back, and we'll carry on with the help of a glass of the eye-brightener!"

When the door closed on Max Beaumont and Liz Charlton, Joe Bailey took off his glasses which always made his face look sad, and somehow bare. Owen stuck his legs out straight in front of him until they almost touched the chair where the head of World Media had been sitting.

"Felix!" he said. "We never have outsiders in on presentation for a current affairs show. Ever have anything like this before?"

"No!" I said. "But if she's personally invited by Max as his property, what can we say?"

"What about Beaumont and women?" Joe said. "Are you going to probe that, Felix? Nobody has ever really proved if he went off the rails. Didn't you say you were with his wife a day or so ago? What is she like? And take that smashing girl Friday of his! Could you stand having something like that around you, almost day and night?"

"Listen, Joe!" Owen stayed languid, stretched out. "Can't you spot the obvious?"

"Meaning what?"

"Liz doesn't play! You can always tell! They make great secretaries for people like Max B!"

153

Before Joe could answer, Boris entered the library with an open bottle of Bollinger and glasses on a silver tray. He poured, leaving us to help ourselves to the glasses, without speaking a word.

"Good luck fellows, and don't make dreams your master!" Joe Bailey said flatly.

"What's the score when he comes back?" Owen sitting up now, looked at me, fretting. "I've never met anything quite like this before! There's got to be some main thing in his life. Some *leitmotiv* – is that the word?"

"It'll do," I said. I knew he was weighing up what Max Beaumont had just been saying, trying to find the central feature in Max Beaumont's life, that when properly brought out and analysed would explain him as an individual, make sense of the whole character.

"You know," Owen said. "I have a sort of reputation for these productions, and you have for handling the big people, Felix! Of course the thing is, that nobody is really talking about Max's origins. Is it because it's not fashionable? In race-equality terms?"

"If all men count with you, but none too much!" Joe slowly recited. He looked thoughtfully into his glass. "What about all this stuff?" He nodded at the champagne. "Is that the Prussian cavalry? Or the Jewish banking bit? He's not the Perrier water, bottom-line-calculating type. Look at this room! The pictures, the furniture, the books – somebody's actually read them. The Savile Row clothes and the shoes – notice the shoes? Lace-up brogues, polished to see your face in them! Foulard ties, Jermyn Street shirts. It adds up to a charade! More English than the English!"

"But that's just it! That's not acting, he's himself!" Owen said.

We stared at each other in silence after that, joined by a brief moment of professional unity, each one trying to identify himself with Max Beaumont.

"Look!" I said. "We're all trying to put him together like an identikit. Partly seeing what we'd like to be ourselves, and what we'd rather forget, and even how we think the world sees us. That's always the problem with objectivity. Isn't that true?"

"Possibly, I'm slow getting round to him," Owen said. "If you get to a certain position with money and power, what TV or the Trade Unions or anybody can do to you, doesn't really matter. It's as simple as that!"

"You mean if life has been a kind of play-act from when you were very young?" Joe said thoughtfully. "And you've had to study life, like learning lines, and roles and audiences. And triumph and disaster! Until maybe you're permanently stranded between Dachau, Clausewitz, Kipling and Sandhurst. Is that it? Nobody could really be like that!"

"Well, I can only say that he isn't like you and me, Joe!" Owen reached across to the champagne bottle and tipped some more into his glass.

Hand-made doors, that open onto soft carpeted floors are almost silent, and it was as though Max Beaumont was with us again by levitation. He moved noiselessly and was there in the chair. He leaned on his elbow and smiled round at us.

Joe was right, I thought. If you were the lead, the star, the one for whom the whom the whole play had been written, life on that stage became real.

Owen got up with another glass which he carefully filled.

"Why don't you have this, sir!" He would never have dreamed of making such a gesture or speaking to Max Beaumont like that a day ago.

155

CHAPTER EIGHT

It occurred to him, Max Beaumont said, that all his recalling of early days only started to have significance from when he came to England, although perhaps even that was not so, and the Jesuit theory about having a child until it was seven, after which anybody could have it for the rest of life was the real truth.

He had heard his Uncle Paul say something like that, when the whole subject of staying or going had first come up, although he could hardly be Jesuit. He heard his Uncle call the situation dangerously uncertain. And there was the grim fact that they were talking, and he was allowed to listen.

He only knew later, about people ageing suddenly, and at that time, in the big gloomy *wohnzimmer* of the house by the Tiergarten, Uncle Paul was plainly very tired, and his small figure in the black suit more gnomelike, his face always pale, now also permanently sad. By comparison his father had resorted to the clipped, Prussian accented tone, but this was something that Max knew meant his father also was disturbed.

His cousins, the two sons of Uncle Paul were not there. Suddenly a week ago, they had left for Switzerland. Something was happening at the bank. The new regime, under this man Hitler, had unbelievably taken over, on the pretext that the Jewish banks had been undermining the financial stability of the Reich.

"You will be all right, Otto," Uncle Paul had said flatly, almost with indifference, as he struggled into his fur-collared coat in the hall. "You are not one of us. But with the boy, it is different!" He had put his hand on Max's head and turned his face up towards him. "*Baruch Adenoi!*" he had said.

156

It was the last time Max saw Uncle Paul.

Max and his father were to go by ship from Hamburg to London. It was the big steam ship, a proper ship his father said. He and Mama had made the journey once before. On banking business, his father said. But for some reason he looked away, and seemed embarrassed by it. But for Max, the whole thing sounded quite dreadful. He was to stay with his mother's younger sister, an aunt whom he had never met. *Tante Sybilla* was a Schönberg. She would improve his English, and had said she would be happy to have Max, as she lived alone, unmarried. Perhaps it would only be for a short time, but probably now it was best. Later he would come back. When Mama was in better health, and things were cleared up at the Bank, and everyone could see what was really happening with these new madmen who were running the country.

When he left school a week later, the other boys of his class were envious. Berlin was a dump compared with a really big city, one of them agreed, and in London there was even a King, who sat on a golden throne with a crown on his head. But two of the older boys sneered, and one of them had taken him by the jacket collar and shaken him, before Max could break free. It was good and proper that he was "being chucked out". And that was what should happen to all the rest of his kind – this was what their fathers had said.

When Max repeated this at home, his own father had abruptly turned away, looking out of the windows of the big room, saying nothing.

Worst was the goodbye to Mama, who was once again in bed, propped up by many pillows, and she had held both his hands, and it seemed at though she did not want to let him go. She had cried and Papa had patted both their hands on the bedclothes and said: *"Es ist für das beste!"* Almost as bad was saying goodbye to Miska, who lay curled up on the far end of Mother's bed, mostly because he seemed indifferent to Max's going.

The journey itself started by train, on one of those bitter, cold March days when Berlin seemed a grey, shadowy city. Hamburg was bleary with fog. Ships hooted and sirens sounded, and when they went aboard Father had said, as they stood together by the deckrail, that the sounds were like dinosaurs trapped in a swamp, and Max had shivered at the notion. Looking up at Papa's clamped jaw, he had remembered the idea of the dinosaurs and the look on his father's face, recalling both together, whenever afterwards, he heard the melancholy blast of ships sirens anywhere else in the world.

In London they stayed at the Royal Court at Sloane Square, which, he was told, was the hotel his parents had stayed at before, when Mama had first visited her sister in England. It was conveniently near to Aunt Sybilla, who lived on King's Road, Chelsea, and the first time they went to her house, one of a row recently built beyond the town hall.

They walked, and Father talked. He pointed out that the cars and buses, as well as the still considerable horse traffic, as in Berlin, were on the left side of the road. This was not only very illogical, like a lot of things, as Max would find in England, but also dangerous. He would make sure that Aunt Sybilla realised this, and Max must have someone with him always when he went out.

That King's Road walk Max remembered clearly for a long time. He thought people were staring at him, because his clothes were different. His ankle boots and knickerbockers were certainly not the same as the shorts and bare dirty knees of two boys who made rude noises at him from the other side of some railings. They had fled when his father half raised the silver headed cane he always carried.

"Hold your shoulders back when you walk Max!" said his father. "And now, in the street we will talk English! Which is no difficulty for you, and then people will not stare! See how the trees in that square are looking? It is much warmer here than in Berlin."

"Can we please speak in German with Aunt Sybilla?" Max had asked. He never got an answer, because at that moment Father had stepped off the kerb, looking the wrong way, and was nearly knocked down by a strange, tall black cab, that was open in the front, so the driver had turned and shouted at them. Father had raised his hat.

158

"Remember to be a gentleman in England, Max! At all times. Taxi drivers are not gentlemen, but most especially in this country, it is important!" He had been sufficiently shaken to have gone back to speaking in German, except for the word Gentlemen, and Max had pondered over this.

A few moments later they passed what was obviously, from the smell and iron railings, and the same word spelt out in black letters on a white enamel sign, a public convenience. Max stopped.

"Can we go there?" He spoke slowly, nodding. "I need to pee-pee badly, Papa! It is for us, it says so!"

"You can wait until we get there!" His father said brusquely. "Come, it is not far now, just a short way!"

"Oh Papa, what will it be like, living with Aunt Sybilla?" Father strode along, Max trotting to keep up. "Is her house like our house?"

"No, but you will be all right there, and Mama will feel happy that you are with her! And you must be a credit to us!"

Mother had shown him a surprisingly large photograph before he left Berlin, one which he had not seen before, and she told him that it was Sybilla, her sister, when she was in New York where she had been working. Max had studied the thin, intelligent face, with the large, limpid dark eyes, and the full, turned down mouth, and instinctively recognised the likeness.

"She will be lucky to have you, even if it is perhaps only for a short while! You will be good for her," Mother had said, and sighed. "My poor sister! She has in some ways had a sad life, but in other ways far luckier than I. But she has not had any children of her own, so she will spoil you I think. But don't tell Papa!"

In the King's Road, Father halted, and turned at a blue-painted wooden door, with a brass letter box and numbers. He pushed a small, round brass button, and the sound of the bell inside could be heard out in the street. There was a cake shop next to the blue door, with rows of small iced buns, and big round cakes, pink, chocolate and orange in the window. There was some steam on the glass and the warm rich smell of baking from the kitchen at the back, was

159

comforting and nostalgic, reminding Max of cafés in Berlin, open to the street. They had the same smell.

"Is it Aunt Sybilla's shop?"

His father laughed, just as the door was opened by a buxom young woman in a grubby green overall, and a tangle of carroty red hair tied up on top with a black ribbon. He knew at once that this was not his aunt. The maids at home were always crisply smart in black and white, with the little starched caps on their heads. Max stood close to father and stared, and for the first time he heard English with another accent, broad and melodic.

"'Tis the young fella himself then!" She made no move to let them in, standing looking past them both, peering into the street in both directions, in the timeless manner of the Irish on a doorstep. Only then did she step back.

"You'll be Miss Sybilla's brother-in-law!" she said in a familiar way, nodding to Father. "She's expecting you both. She's above!" In the tiny hall, when the door closed, it was dark and she led on up the tall flight of stairs to a floor above, with the warm smell of the cake shop still following them. But now the Irish maid was leading the way into a longer hall, Father following, hat and stick in hand, unbuttoning his coat. Max was still listening to her words, putting the sounds and meaning together because, somehow, and it seemed odd, the sentence construction was familiar, more like German, with the beginning tumbling out at the end.

Aunt Sybilla came out from a front room in the upper hall. Dressed in a trimly cut black suit with a white blouse; she was almost more like the Berlin maids, but also Max noticed what of course no maid at home would wear, pendant coral earrings, and a coral studded bracelet.

She stretched out both thin hands in his direction, and Max had automatically dipped his head, heels together, stiffly making the *küss die hand* and a *diener*. And he heard her laugh, a cool musical sound, that he had not heard from his mother for a very long time. He watched Papa bestow quick kisses on both cheeks of this strange lady and he felt embarrassed. All three of them were being watched also by the carroty head, which was now tilted on one side.

160

"Would I be takin' the coats please miss!"

The coats, hat and stick were borne away to a large cupboard in the hall, and Sybilla led the way to where daylight spilled through large sash windows in a front room, and the Colonel walking stiffly, now spoke in German, and Max could hear the awkward formality, even though he used the familiar *du*. Then Aunt Sybilla laughed, and with a little scoop, took Max's hand, and her own felt cool and smaller than his.

"Shall we speak English now? You are like a native, Otto, I have heard you! And how about Max here? That is what he has come for isn't it?" And, because he had been listening anxiously, Max again heard another, different accent to this new language – the variation Sybilla had acquired in New York, and they had sat down, still rather formally in that front room.

In everyone's life are certain rooms to which memory can return, as though it was visited only days ago, and Max could recall every detail and also his feelings of that moment. The sofa and two straight back chairs, a club fender with its dark-red, cracked leather seats and brass rails in front of the small, slow burning coal-fire. An antique desk and chair on one side, a corner cupboard on the other, and as the room was combined for dining and sitting, a round table with wheelback chairs stood between the two quite large windows that were framed by thin unlined chintz curtains.

When he did recall it all so much later, that room often seemed more of a real home than Berlin. But now it was different, foreign and strange, and the insecurity was something as tangible as the dull smell of the burning coal-fire, or Aunt Sybilla's scent as she sat on the sofa beside him. But she touched his hand again, as though she knew how he was feeling.

"Has this boy got no things with him?" Her thin aquiline face looked from father to son. "I didn't see a grip or a bag! Or did you leave it below? By the door?"

"Have no worry dear sister-in-law, they are on their way!" Max's father sat upright, legs crossed in the creased trousers, pale yellow button-down spats, showing over his shoes. "His

161

trunk and bag are coming from the hotel by taxi-cab. Is right? Is taxi or cab?"

"Taxi," said Aunt Sybilla briefly. "It depends how English you want to be. Well, I suppose you couldn't carry that much along the pavement. But did you not want to ride with it?"

"For the boy's first day, it is good to walk! We have been sitting on boats and trains. And for me too, it is worth the distance from Sloane Square to see a little something of London again."

Father and Sybilla had gone on talking in a desultory way. Messages and affection conveyed from various family names in Germany. Somehow, Max could tell that the present situation as it affected himself and the reason for his being there was being avoided. Sentences were started, and then turned to something else.

Presently the doorbell rang again, and the luggage arrived, and the big trunk was brought upstairs by the taxi driver and the Irish maid, and father left the room to pay the man. In that first moment of their being alone, his aunt looked directly at Max with her dark-brown eyes, the heavy lids, and arched eyebrows making them seem almost too large for her thin face, and then she grinned. Suddenly, unexpectedly, like a schoolgirl, and had put both her hands together, fingertips pressing tightly.

"Max!" she cried softly. "That is a nice name! Will you be happy here do you think? We have a lot to do, you and I, to make it right!"

Then father was back in the room with them, and presently some coffee and cups arrived on a tray.

"This is Mary!" Aunt Sybilla made the introduction with one limp hand, as though neither party had met before, as she arranged the cups for father and herself.

"Mary is from Ireland and is a treasure beyond treasures! Max you can run along with Mary now you know each other, and go upstairs and see your room! Mary, you can give him some of that bottle of pop I got. I guess you don't like coffee yet, Max? Then your father and I have a few things to talk about and we'll give you a call. I have taken the rest of the day away from the office."

162

Mary, who had a much larger, stronger hand than Aunt Sybilla's took Max out through the door, closing it behind them.

"Now young fella!" she said. "If we get a lot of the stuff out of this box of yours, that'll make it light enough to carry it upstairs, the both of us!"

Max began to feel important. He had been given keys to the trunk, and the things said by this new maid, he could understand. In a strange way she was familiar, even to a quite different scent to the expensive kind used by Aunt Sybilla, and more like the Berlin maids when they came close to you, and it was work, and bed and warmth and some other quality that made for closeness.

"I drink coffee!" he said, slowly and while he turned the little key in the trunk lock. "I drink it with milk, yes?"

"Do ye's then?" She looked at him, with pretend solemn respect. "And who'd have thought it? Well we'll start upstairs with this lot between us! Together they carried armfuls of clothes out of the trunk up the next flight of narrow, wooden stairs, and along a passage.

"Is pop also lemon?" said Max.

"It's what your aunt calls it, for sure! And there's the royal bedchamber!" With one foot she pushed open the door, taking two more steps to dump the load of Max's belongings onto the iron-frame bed. Max did the same, with his own load. And suddenly there was a lump in his throat at the sight of so many familiar things, a pullover, riding clothes, books, all seemed to be accusing him of this monstrous upheaval, just when he needed their reassurance.

"Now what is it? You'll not be crying then, a big fella like you? Here!" She wrapped a large arm round his head and forcibly pulled it into the bosom of the green overall, so that Max fought for breath. As quickly, she thrust him away dramatically.

"You're better now! Is it ten then? And is it Maxiwilliam?"

"No!" Indignation restored courage. "You will call me Max! Can I go back to my father?"

"Quite the young gentleman for manners I'll say that!" Mary looked at him. "We'll make one more journey and bring up the empty box, for I'll not be doing that alone!

Now your aunty, she's in the bedroom next to you see? And then there's the bathroom, and there's stairs up to the roof garden, and me own bedroom at the end of the passage. So now you know it all!"

"What is it upstairs?" Max asked, politely. He rubbed his eyes.

"A flat roof. With a few tubs and plants and that! Your aunt says you can play up there when it's fine because there's a fence all round. But you're not to lean out of the window here!" She beckoned him over to the bedroom window, which had an upholstered box seat below it, and she parted the muslin curtain. Max looked out. Below was the street, busy with horse carts, open top buses, and cars of intriguing and unknown make. Now Mary was nudging him, and pointing across to the other side of the road.

"D'ye see over there, the place with the sign over? 'Farr's school of Dancin'! I'm over there in the dance hall, when I have my evening! Nice and handy it is! Perhaps ye'll be coming with me – a fine big young fella for your age!" She cackled briefly, and looked at him, her head on one side. "Are ye feelin' better now?"

Father, Max and Aunt Sybilla returned to the Royal Court Hotel for an evening meal. They spoke in English, which the Colonel at times obviously found irksome.

"*Verdamtes salz! Es geht nicht!*" He shook the salt cellar. "What will you do to improve his English, Sybilla? Private lessons? Every day?"

Max found his pie with cabbage and strange tasting potatoes unattractive. How long was he to stay then? Nobody seemed to say. "I know why you stay in this hotel of course!" his aunt was saying. "But you could do better, Colonel!"

Father turned his long pale face to one side, to see if anyone had heard, and spoke in a low voice. "Are they against us still? The last time here it was not easy! Like now, we did not speak German in public!"

"Oh heck!" Aunt Sybilla said. She looked at Max. "There's a new generation coming now! In New York it's no problem. I sometimes think the English are so bad at languages they wouldn't know if we were from Mars! Have you had enough

Max? We'll try and find you an ice cream. Somehow they don't seem to have caught up with knickerbocker glory here yet!"

His father left to go back next day, but came once more to see Max at the King's Road house. He was formal, concealing emotion. Max clung to his hand with both his own for a moment. Suddenly his father kissed him, quickly on the side of his cheek. Then the door opened and shut and he was gone.

Aunt Sybilla said Max should come into the front room, and sit with her a bit and talk about things. In the afternoon they would go to the natural history museum where, she said, there were all sorts of wild animals. Stuffed, of course. There were whales too, as big as houses.

"Do you like being called Max, or Maximilian?"

"Mary wants to call me Maxi-William! Is it a joke?"

Aunt Sybilla looked at him carefully. "Some people call her Dairy Mary. But perhaps you wouldn't –" She stopped. "We will stick to Max."

"In Berlin we have a zoo! Real animals!" Max said. But it made him suddenly near tears. Father going back all the way to Berlin and the big house, and mother still lying in bed, and Miska. Would she miss him too? The room they sat in was smaller than any of the rooms at home. And although the sunlight came through the two tall windows, and made patterns on the blue carpet and the board wooden planks of the floor, the old grandfather clock in the alcove made a noise like indigestion, and with a dull, thunking sound struck all the notes of noon. How could he ever feel he belonged here? Even speak like other people, make friends?

"It is too soon for you to go to school," Aunt Sybilla was saying. "The next term starts in September, and that gives us a chance to really polish up a bit. You can go to the public library, which I use, and I will show you. You must read, Max! All the things you can, especially English history. Now, we are very lucky because across the road there is a Mr. Pillock who teaches English to foreigners and to children who are lazy about nouns and verbs and such things! So I have arranged that during the week, you will go there for one hour in the morning and one in the afternoon, and

165

Mr. Pillock will give you homework to do by yourself. Do you like your room, Max?"

Max nodded. He watched carefully as she stood up, smoothing down her skirt, walking over to a bow-fronted cupboard, fixed in the corner. When its doors were opened the whole inside showed a pretty egg-shell blue colour, and on the shelves were glasses and bottles of all kinds. Sybilla half turned her head like a bird does, to look at him again, her lips twisted in a way he would recognise in later years, was much as his own smile.

"As the sun is over the yardarm, dear – that is an expression the English and Americans use, and I wouldn't want to explain it right now – I am going to have a drink! And it is called a Dry Martini. Somehow, I don't remember your parents and the rest of the family drinking very much at all, do they?"

"Father drinks wine," Max said solemnly, forgetting and relapsing into German. "I have tried it, but I do not like it!"

When he looked back on those first weeks in London, Max Beaumont could remember them in a sharp focus, because at that age most youngsters are freshly impressionable. He also had all the precociousness of an only child, brought up with adults, and subjected to his German schooling.

For instance, Aunt Sybilla had made a curious remark, one evening when she saw that Mr. Pillock had put a gold star sticker on a page of his homework book.

"It is not the Star of David!" She had said, with her special smile. "But you are Jewish. Which means you will have to be more clever than the rest! Did your mother ever tell you that?" And then she had sipped one of her Dry Martinis. "How Odd that God should Choose the Jews! Say that after me Max!"

He had done so almost impatiently, standing by the grandfather clock, waiting for it to strike again, and to tell her that he understood how it worked, with its bob weights descending and rotating the cog wheels. "I am half Jewish! Also German!" He paused, changing the subject with easy sophistication.

"What do you do in your office, *Tante Sybille?*"

166

She explained that since leaving Germany after the end of the Great War, she had gone to a finishing school in Switzerland. There she had improved English and French, and left as soon as possible, for another branch of the family who were in New York, where she had been first a banking secretary, then working for *The New York Times*. When the paper needed a research girl for the London Bureau she got the job on the strength of what were considered her European connections. Later she had changed again, when an enterprising Mr. Stefan Laurent started up a new magazine called *Lilliput*. He also had plans for a magazine like the *Berliner Illustrierte*, she told Max, but it was a secret. Aunt Sybilla was very happy with her work she said, and for a woman, was well paid.

"Not like America, but good for England! I know about money," she said, "from banking, and because I am one hundred percent a Jewish kid!" This was when she laughed, her rare laughter, and then looked away. "Money, Max!" she said, "is like a pocket handkerchief, that's all! It's damn awkward if you suddenly need it, and it isn't there! Now you should know it is your father who is paying for you to be with me, and for your weekly pocket money, and to start riding again – if you did well in the first term at school, he said!"

Sybilla had finished her evening dry Martini. "Why don't you go down to the library now, Max? You remember where it is? Remember the lady in charge? Miss Murchison! Remind her who you are, and read some of the magazines and take out a new book. Then be back by six thirty for supper. OK?"

Max was happy to go to the library. It was something he could not explain, but with its hard polished floor and the books in so many rows, and the faint smell of board and paper and book bindings, it was at once familiar and exciting, rather similar to father's study. Also the smell of orderliness was almost German.

The children's library was pretty well empty when he got there. He had missed Karl May and *Old Surehand* and the others, and was happy when Miss Murchison suggested *Two Little Savages* by Ernest Thomas Seaton. Here were Red Indians again, and he felt a strong sense of unity with them. This seemed a better book than anything he had read in

Berlin, and because his father had taught him, he looked in the front and saw that it was an American book. Or course they would know best of all about the Red Indians.

"Can I sit here and start to read a bit now?" he asked.

"Why yes dear, of course," the librarian said. "Use any of the tables."

She could not know that she was talking to the future Max Beaumont, or that she was helping him take his first steps along a number of warpaths, the culmination of which would be the publishing of millions of words, that would, in turn, occupy thousands of librarians all over the world.

It occurred to Max Beaumont, in explaining those early days of transition, from German childhood to English, and the quickly growing-up into adolescence, that it was almost impossible to pass on what it meant, to change nationalities. At that age it was hard not to think so often of how food was different from home, and so were the sounds and sights and people's faces and voices. The advertisement posters which seemed to be everywhere in the streets and on the buses, told him that he was a foreigner in a strange land. He wanted to speak German to Aunt Sybilla, and to begin with often did. She answered him in English.

For the first month or two, there was the Sunday phone call from Berlin. In the hall of the King's Road flat there was a little dark corner by the stairs, with a table on which stood the telephone. It was like a black, ebonite bedside lamp, with the hearing part the shape of a small black bottle, hanging from two prongs on the side. When Aunt Sybilla had finished talking into it, and remained sitting in the cane chair, Max would sit on the bottom step of the staircase beside her, and listen to the tiny, far-away voices that were Father and Mother in Berlin. It was regarded as a wonder enough then, and it was almost impossible to remember the difficulty of telephoning even Europe then. Aunt Sybilla said it was time that the European countries learned a few things from America, where telephoning over a few thousand miles was already easier and quicker.

"Why did you come over here, and not stay there then?" Max asked her, with his usual directness, and she had looked at him, her slim hands quietly turning the necklace at her throat.

"Funny, Max!" she said. "I did not want to become an American." Perhaps later you will understand. I have a Swiss passport. Also American. But of course I am not Swiss, nor American. So what am I?" He was to remember this particular conversation, fifty years before such considerations were more relevant.

"I would like to live in Berlin again!" Max tried to smile at Aunt Sybilla when he said it, but somehow he couldn't. Mother had cried on the last telephone call, as she nearly always did, and his father had sounded like his own gramophone records, when something went wrong with the winding up of the machine.

His aunt had put the slim cool hands quickly round his face again, kissing him twice on the forehead. He knew it was considered. Instinctively he could tell such things. Then she slid her hands down his shoulders, hugging him close to the black silk of her dress and her taut, trim figure that was so different from Mama's ample warmth and comfort. So was the taste, when she kissed Max on the mouth. The scent of Aunt Sybilla was different too. It came out of a bottle, which he had seen, when he sat on the edge of her bed, and watched her squirting the little fat rubber bulb to make the spray. When he asked to, she had allowed him to do it, spraying carefully the back of her tilted neck, under the short-cut hair, and also on her wrists.

Once a week the two of them went to the cinema, usually in King's Road. This helped his knowledge of the language, Aunt Sybilla said. Either with her, or Irish Mary he discovered the world of Laurel and Hardy, and a funny man with a banjo and another different accent called George Formby. Mary giggled, and said some of the songs were not really for boys of his age to know about. But she wouldn't tell him why. Then the film of his beloved *Emil and the Detectives* was on, and another from Germany called *Mädchen in Uniform*. He saw this with Aunty Sybilla, and although the speech was in German, with English subtitles, she became subdued in the dark cinema beside him, and when they came out of the dark stuffiness with all the other people, and walked back along the pavements, it was late, and Aunt Sybilla held his hand. He could not see her face clearly, even in the pools of street lighting, but Max thought she had cried over the film.

Watching the street lamp-lighter at his work was a constant fascination any evening. He rode a bicycle and carried a long pole, with which he touched the lamps along the street and they flared into bright cold light. Another character who became part of his new world, usually only to be seen at weekends, was the muffin man, who rang a hand bell, rather like the blue overall milk boys in Berlin. But the muffin man carried on his head things called crumpets on a tray which had a white cloth over it. Max was sent downstairs to the street with money for him, and the crumpets were put in a paper bag and born back in triumph to the kitchen if Mary was to cook them, or far more exciting, to the living room, with a brass fork in front of Aunt Sybilla's coal fire.

It was on one of those crumpet toasting Sunday afternoons, with her face unusually warm and pink from the fire, she had stroked his head as he knelt holding the brass fork to the red coals.

"It will be time for school next week, Max! Your English is good enough now, and Mr. Pillock is absolutely confident you will manage. I understand there are one or two other boys from different countries there anyway. India and really foreign places!"

She had got up from the brass fender, leaving Max silent while he buttered his crumpet with the old kitchen knife. She opened the corner cupboard nearby.

"OK, so it's sundown at this time of year! Which means I can fix a drink! A dry Martini. I need some ice cubes and as Dairy Mary is having her evening off I shall get them."

There was a way his aunt had of moving across the floor that was strangely fascinating, and Max watched, slowly eating his crumpet. It was as though she was gliding, with small steps across a dance floor. His keen ears could hear the tiny squeaking sound of silk stockings rubbing together and the rustle of other fabrics as she moved out of the room.

When she returned, the ice and the drink were shaken and rattled in a silver elliptical pot, then poured into a triangle-shaped glass with a small piece of lemon peel in it.

The glass misted instantly with the ice cold fluid. She coiled up in her armchair.

"I want to go home," Max said. "To Berlin!"

"You are old enough to know that things are difficult in Berlin, and all Germany for that matter. Bad things are happening. Your cousins in Switzerland are staying there. The Nazis and Mr. Hitler are doing very nasty things to Jewish people. We are lucky to be out of it!"

"I am German!" Max told her. And stared into the red coals of the fire, where faces and castles and animals formed and moved and went away, and there was another sort of hot, burning feeling too at the back of his eyes. Aunt Sybilla, bent forward. "You are already such a big man! You can have a sip of my drink, there, try it! Then you will feel better!"

It tasted like the scent in the little bottle in her bedroom, and he scrambled up to his feet pulling a face as the taste worked down his throat.

"Like medicine!"

"A sort of medicine," Aunt Sybilla agreed. "Now come and sit beside me and listen, because there are one or two important things to say. When you go to school, which is now in only a week, it will be helpful if we have a school name for you. A sort of pretend name. Do you see what I mean?"

Max shook his head, and watched as she drank quietly from the wide-mouthed Martini glass.

"It is not easy to be a foreigner and most certainly not in England. I was lucky to start in America, where people have many different names, and it is normal there. But that was when I changed my own name, Max. Of course I was married first anyway. All ladies change their names to their husband's when they are married."

"I know! It is the same in Germany," said Max. Then he asked. "Where is he? My uncle?"

"Your poor uncle, my poor husband he is dead," Aunt Sybilla said flatly. "He hit another man for saying something stupid, and the other man hit him on the head with a bottle, and presently he was dead. The other man said he had done it to defend himself. Even so, he went to prison. But our name was a German name too. I did not want to use it when my husband was dead. I went back to my own family name –

171

that is your mother's name too, before *she* was married. Do you know what that is Max?"

"It is *Schönberg*!" Max said slowly. "It is Uncle Paul's name, and it is on the door of the bank too, on the metal plate there!"

"Not any more, because the Nazis have changed that!" Aunt Sybilla said bitterly. ("You see, it is part of the problem Max! I have changed my name round, perhaps because I lived in Switzerland for so long, where they speak French as well, and I made a beautiful new name out of Schönberg! It means the same thing. You cannot make Beautiful Mountain a name in English. Beaumont! If you like it, you can have it too! I chose it because in a way it is not entirely French either. There are lots of Beaumonts in England, going back to William the Conqueror. Wasn't 1066 in Mr. Pillock's lessons for you? And there are real advantages! If occasionally I express myself strangely in English, I admit to a Swiss education! You can do the same Max! It helps, believe me! You can keep Max, and your middle name can be shortened to Dan. I have thought it all out you see!"

"I wish I was a Red Indian. Then I could be called Beautiful Mountain!"

"And Beaumont?" Aunt Sybilla sounded for once, impatient.

"Is it to be a secret? Just for us? So that nobody else knows?"

"It will be much easier for you to explain to the other boys. You are living with your aunt, and we have the same name. So, now that is settled, you will have to have your new school clothes marked with your name, and I must get Mary to sew the things in."

"Will I like this school?" Max asked. "With only boys and uniforms?"

"You are starting in the junior form, it won't be so bad. Your father thought you might go to boarding school living away from here, and I said no. I have heard too much about English boarding schools. I can take you each day on the bus from here, which goes to Fleet Street where I work. Your City of London School is only a block away on the river!"

172

Max stood close to her chair. He was silent. Then suddenly he kissed her. "I am glad we have the same name!" he declared, but he said it in German.

It was no good pretending that the first day of starting as a new boy was anything that Max looked forward to. What he experienced there became, as he later knew, a base for a lifetime of attitudes and feelings about important things. Power over others for one. When you had a great deal of it, you looked around to see how the underdogs were faring. Humbug and expediency were two words in English, or any other tongue, as he later told editors and executives that were responsible for most of the nastier problems faced by the human race.

Of course today the City of London school is a thoroughly enlightened, worthy and modern educational establishment, and he had personally met any number of younger men who had been there in recent time, who seemed refreshingly relaxed, unusually intelligent and pleasantly confident.

On that first day, he had left his boiled egg, with the spoon sticking in it, and told Mary who sat with him in the kitchen, that he was too unwell to go to school. Aunt Sybilla, who always took her own cup of coffee and a piece of toast in her bedroom was called. Still fastening a string of amber beads round her neck, she looked at Mary's battered alarm clock on the kitchen dresser, and told him to stick out his tongue and say "ah". She put a cool hand quickly on his forehead.

"I'm afraid it's something called schoolitis!" she said. "You can make that egg into a sandwich, Mary! Put it in a packet for his satchel. Now, Max, you might get a chance to eat it later, or on the bus with me. And cheer up! Because you look fine in that grey blazer and your black and red tie! Where's your new cap?"

"Ye can travel on the outside of the bus!" Mary said. "That'll give ye an appetite! And clear his head for the work, will it not, Mrs. Beaumont?"

There were open top buses in those long-ago times, and they took one of the pirate buses as they were called with its brown and yellow livery, cutting in on the red buses in what was to be the last of that sort of free enterprise for a while.

Firmly Aunt Sybilla took him to the school side entrance where the other boys were streaming in, look-alikes in little round caps and grey flannel shorts and jackets. She had the good sense not to kiss him there and then, but put an unexpected half crown in his hand and said it was for the tuck shop as well as his bus fare home. He was to come back to Chelsea on his own. The tuck shop she said was where, in boys schools, you could buy extra food.

"Pies and chocolate and things like that!" she said, vaguely.

There was a prefect, in the cloakroom entrance, a much older boy who wore long trousers. The windows were barred and there were rows of lockers and a smell of latrines and damp concrete. The new boys, all like grey mice, milled about and looked unhappy. There was no tuck shop.

"Come on you lot," said the prefect loudly. "Stop snivelling! Get yourself a locker and put your caps and comics and buns in them!" With a rolled up newspaper he made a swipe at the nearest boy, and pointed up the unlit concrete staircase.

"Corridor up there! Turn right, classroom number three on the door! If you can count that is! In there by nine o'clock which is three minutes, standing by your desk. Standing! OK? Till the master comes in, and says you can sit down. Mr. Stacey he is! There'll be a few of you won't want to sit down by tomorrow, with Mr. Stacey!"

They had clattered past the prefect and up the stairs, pushing and shoving, all elbows and bare knees. Max looked anxiously for one of the real foreigners he had been promised, a coloured face or a turban. He had started recently to read a boys paper, *The Magnet* in which a turbanned Ram Jan Singh attended a mythical and exciting school with Billy Bunter and others. Now there were only pale faces, some almost grey, like their uniforms, others red, excited, and many with half-closed eyes miserable from lack of sleep. They jostled along the cold corridor with its tile floor and dark-green dado walls. There was a scramble for desks in the classroom. Everyone wanted to be at the back. Max ended up in the second row. He sat down quickly as did some of the others, then remembered and stood up again. The desks were ugly, battered things, dark-stained, carved and scratched on their lids with many initials, half-started words, others that

174

had been scratched out and some inked in. In a hole on the top edge of each desk was the inkwell in a small china pot with a hole. In a scooped-out section was a brand new dip pen with a steel nib and plain wooden shaft.

Mr. Stacey made his entrance. He looked to Max the personification of Mephistopheles, in a black and white engraving that hung on a dark passage wall in Uncle Paul's house. The black gown, half-wrapped about him, seemed to float him across the wooden floorboards. Two peaks of hair, like small stub horns, and narrowed eyes completed the effect. He stopped in front of his own desk, mounted on a small dais.

"Good morning! When each day I say good morning, you will say Good Morning Sir! Say it now! Any boy I spot not saying it will write out Good Morning one hundred times!"

The chorused chant rang out. Then there was silence and Mr. Stacey looked carefully along the rows that faced him. "There is roll call each morning! That means I read out your names. You will sit not where you like – and I can tell where the dolts are in this class already from where you are sitting! In alphabetical order! So I can remember your names easily! After that I may move you around. Especially any boy at the back, who thinks he can fool about where I cannot see him! And boys who are so stupid that they have not been listening to what I say. They will sit right up in the front row. Now! I have here a cricket bat, and in the summer term you will play cricket! But I use my cricket bat all the year round! And it leans against my desk to be used on particularly stupid boys who are disobedient, insubordinate or ill-mannered!" The eyebrows, whiskery and pointed, came down over the narrowed eyes, and ranged along the rows of small faces. He stabbed a sudden forefinger at a boy in the front row. "You! What's your name?"

"Kerno, sir!" Kerno was a chubby figure with a round, red face and a mop of untidy black, greasy hair. He seemed to have had some difficulty knotting his new school tie, and began to pull at it with both hands.

"What did I just say, Kerno?" Mr. Stacey undoubtedly knew that the more spirited boys were at the back of the class, and the less astute had been forced to the front. They would all learn, in due course, the meaning of Sods Law. Kerno looked doubtful.

"I dunno sir! About cricket, sir!"

"Come out and stand in front of your desk!"

Kerno extricated himself slowly, and in a lumpy uneven way.

"Now!" said the master easily "You may turn round and face the class. You see, you have not been listening to a word I said, have you Kerno?"

The example that was being made was not lost, and as all eyes were now on the mottling face of Kerno it could be seen that he was already grasping the dilemma of how to answer.

"Bend over your desk, boy!" The master's one hand was already pressing him down, the other had produced the cricket bat from somewhere behind the black gown. He wielded it single handed so that the descending bat came down three times with an unpleasant thudding sound on Kerno's tightly stretched flannel-covered rear.

"You may sit down!" the master said, breathing heavily. He put the cricket bat against his own desk with careful nonchalance, and Kerno returned to the other side of his, and lifting the lid could be heard behind it snuffling and blubbing.

Max thought that Kerno was possibly the bravest person he had ever known. Not to be compared with his father as a soldier, or little Biene who had been beaten and kicked to death in a deadlier version of what they had all just witnessed. He felt inside, as he sat there, that first day at school in England, as though he had a large stone somewhere in his stomach.

"When I call the roll you will move! Quietly and quickly without spilling the inkwells. The names starting with A will sit in front, beginning next to Kerno, who will stay where he is. Then Bs and so on. I presume you can all spell your names?"

Max remembered his just in time. He also thought that probably that classroom and Mr. Stacey might in some extraordinary way go on for ever. In that room, with its windows constructed in such a way that they were too high to look out, the rest of the world did not exist. Sitting at those scarred desks Mr. Stacey taught arithmetic, English

176

grammar, history and geography. Sometimes there was no escaping his flat, rasping voice for all of a morning or afternoon. There were five-minute breaks in between lessons, when the class was ordered out into the corridor and the master disappeared, with the other figures in black gowns. Their pupils also clustered round their classroom doors, and the game was to try and eat a sweet, or pinch or hurt any possible victim without attracting the attention of the two or three prefects who patrolled the corridor.

They were too young as yet for a science class, but there was Art. This was in another classroom, appropriately badly lit, presided over by a cadaverous art master, whose chief requirement from the class was total silence. In Max's mind for many years, when people spoke of art, was the image of a Roman helmet. This object, a costume drama copy, complete with chin strap and stiff red plume, stood on a stand at the head of the room. The boys had to draw it in pencil on a single sheet of paper, issued at each art lesson. The tall gloomy art master kept them applied to the task by slowly stalking the rows of desks, carrying his own chosen implement, a long wooden pointer. At the end of the lesson he set one boy to collect the drawings. Next week the Roman helmet was still there. By the end of the term Max could have drawn it in his sleep.

French was also taught in another classroom, in the basement, almost as though that was a proper relegation for anything as contemptible as a foreign language. The French master was small, yellow-faced and shrunk into his gown. He pounded the blackboard with his chalk, frequently breaking it into pieces, and screeched his strange syllables and vowels to the class. At first he had given Max special attention.

"Beaumont! Vous êtes Francaise?"

"Sir?"

"Imbecile! Vous comprenez Francaise?" He advanced down the line of desks towards Max. The teacher believed in the tried principle of sticking with the chosen tongue. It was not only the British who believed that if they shouted loud and long enough the natives would grasp it.

"Votre nom! – C'est Francais?"

Max eyed him cautiously. The small black-gowned figure now stood above him. With his beaky nose and yellow eyes he looked like a crow. He even shifted his weight from foot to foot like a waiting bird.

"Your father is French?"

"No sir!" Aunt Sybilla's formula was the only one to use. "Some of my family are from Switzerland, sir!"

"Ah! La Suisse!"

"I think they are from the German part, sir."

"Les Suisses parlent trois langues! Can you say that boy?"

Max tried and failed. The French teacher's *aide choisir* was an old plimsole. Max felt the sole of the rubber and canvas shoe against his ear, smarting and ringing through his head, as he failed again to reproduce the right noises. The crow was back at the blackboard, breaking chalk, stabbing out the words.

"*Les Suisses parlent trois langues! Je Parle Francais! Tu Parles, Il Parle.*" It went on. "*Ouvrez vos livres! Prenez les plumes!*" They had to write it out on the lined pages, ten times.

The classrooms were nothing to the sense of real terror and persecution that prevailed in the playground. It was a sense that was to haunt Max, with an intensity that turned him, and some of the younger boys, into small grey animals, developing early protective, evasive qualities, fearful, quick and isolated in their misery.

It was in the playground that gangs of boys from the older classes ran dens, from which they sallied out, and dragged their victims back for versions of unpleasantness that made the half hour of school break for the smaller boys a time of stomach turning fear. They had to be pushed out through the cloakroom doors into the expanse of grey asphalt by the prefects.

"Out you go! Stop snivelling – 'course it isn't cold! Run about then! You! Answer back, and you'll get lines!"

Max feared especially the gang who lurked in the long building that was the urinals in the far corner of the playground. Which denied any question of using them for their intended purpose, itself another misery. Then there were the third formers, who were the Fives Court mob, already into furtive smoking at the back of the concrete fives

178

courts, a strange, ancient game played with a heavy glove and ball. Another gang had a select little cage, made by the locked and gated entrance and passage into the playground.

Max kept moving round one of the big square pillars that supported the covered part of the playground, outside the cloakroom entrances, where all the boys stood packed closely together if it was raining. Then there was surreptitious arm twisting and stomach punching, not to be seen by the bland, indifferent prefects and the masters who were well away in the common room, with tea and biscuits.

By sliding round one of the big square pillars and keeping eyes in all directions, you could escape the random prowling press gangs who made their rapid sweeps through the playground. But eventually they caught him.

They had dragged him by the wrists, through the little knots of hop-scotchers, marble players and other groups of older boys, better able to offer single or united defence. And how often in life, so Max noticed afterwards, nobody hurried to intervene. In the grubby, white-tiled entrance where gates made the cage, the smell of urine, wet concrete and cigarette smoke compounded a special memory. There were about ten boys, some interested, others bored, shouting and jostling with each other, some pale faces, some burly, or spotted. They already had one other captive, a boy who must have been from the form above Max, and they had his trousers and underpants down round his ankles, and he was crying. They were teasing him, lifting his shirt, while one of them with an open penknife threatened him.

"You've had it cut already! So why not a bit more eh?" The boy was crying, tugging frantically against the hands holding his arms. He started choking as though he might be sick.

"What about this one? He's a yid too isn't he?" Max felt one of his arms being twisted up his back, and cried out at the shooting pains in the shoulder, and he thought his elbow might break. "Open your pants quick – let's have a look at you!" One hand was released, and the twisting pain reduced. "Take it out and let's have a look!" But like Uta in that other faraway Berlin playground, they were disappointed.

179

"He's no yid!" one of the spotty faces said. "He's a Hun anyway. My brother heard him tell old Frenchie!"

"Lost the war didn't you eh?" The biggest of the bullies said, slowly. "Probably come over here to be a spy when he's grown up!" His hand reached out and took hold of Max's hair and pulled. Tears of anguish and pain filled Max's eyes. They were still twisting his arms behind his back, when from somewhere outside the trap of the entrance alleyway, they could all hear the playground bells ringing for return to class. Carelessly, as though nothing had happened, his tormentors stopped at the signal, and began to move out of the playground. There was always a punishment for those late back from the breaktime.

Miserably Max and the other boy, who should have been united by their shared plight, avoided each others eyes and ran out, adjusting their clothes, rubbing hurt arms and heads.

"They'll try and get us again, you see!" the other said shakily. "I'm going to tell my mother! My Dad does nothing – says we ought to look after ourselves!"

Max had neither Mother nor Father to tell. Although in class he managed to keep out of the way of the cricket bat, and only occasionally caught Monsieur's gymshoe on the back of the head, the playground remained a nightmare place the first autumn and winter terms. Caught once by the fives-court gang, and taken to their den, they bent his fingers back, one at a time, telling him that he would not be able to write again, and would get punished for that too. He was so hurt and miserable that he felt a wet flood of warmth down his legs, and realised why, even as the bigger boys holding him saw what it was, and their laughter and jeering drove him to desperation, and kicking and punching he broke free.

With his gym towel and shorts from his locker he cleaned up, but nothing could quickly remove the smell of his own urine, and back in class he had to endure the hidden taunts, and surreptitious charade from the nearest desks. This attracted the attention of Mr. Stacey who stalked slowly down the lines until he stopped by Max's desk and sniffed the air. The rest of the class busied themselves, writing with scratchy nibs and clinking pens in the inkwells.

"If any boy has need to go – real need, and not just monkeying!" pronounced the master, "they have only to hold up their hand! I shall punish any boy who messes himself out of laziness or deliberately. You're not in the nappy class now you know!" This produced a classroom of sniggers and having achieved that, the master appeared satisfied, and strode back to his dais.

CHAPTER NINE

It was Irish Mary who probably did most to help him, she had taken his hand that evening, and he had yelped at the hurt fingers. It was she too who looked after his clothes and the washing, and could well have put some notions together. Max did his homework at her kitchen table.

"Are they after you at school is it? Let me have a look at that hand!"

Aunt Sybilla came home just before his bedtime most nights, but sometimes she had what Mary called "one of her gentleman friends" who took her out again, almost at once, for dinner.

On Mary's two evenings off a week, his aunt would make some special dish, and open a bottle of wine. She showed Max how to use a corkscrew, and he was proud and happy when Aunt Sybilla said: "Open a bottle of the red wine in the front room, Max!"

That evening, when she called him into the same front room and asked him about school, he found it difficult to answer. Although they went together on the bus each day, sitting upstairs at his request, he never felt like talking about the school. Aunt Sybilla had a small attaché case from which she read papers and printed things, and Max was often desperately trying to remember dates or arithmetic tables that were to be recited that day.

Sometimes, as Fleet Street and the Law Courts came in sight he felt a horrible panic and nausea. She had looked sideways at him, her pale, thin face, with the big eyes unsmiling.

"It can't be at all easy for you I realise, Max! Nobody wants to go to school, or to the office either I can tell you! Look, soon it will be Christmas and the holidays!"

"I want to go home now!" Max meant Berlin, but in many ways Berlin was fading in his memory, overlaid by the strangeness and demands of his new life so acutely, that he felt unsure where he belonged.

Every Sunday morning as routine, Aunt Sybilla made a place for him at her table in the front room, and he wrote a letter to his parents. Each week there was a letter from Berlin, and once his mother had sent some not very clear photographs of herself in the conservatory, overlooking the Tiergarten, in some sort of special chair, with a rug over her knees. There was another of Miska the dog. This made Max snuffle, and Aunt Sybilla said that she would get it framed for him, and took it away and put it in her handbag. For Christmas, Father wrote, he would come over for two or three days, and stay at the hotel again, and he would bring presents. It was rather doubted whether Mother could come. Father's letters were always in German.

Max and Aunt Sybilla sat on two sides of the brass fender, the fire between them.

"What does it mean?" Max asked. "Not to be as she should?"

"Exactly as you have translated!" Sybilla said. She sounded, on this subject, as on some others, coolly distant.

"It really is a difficult language, English! I must read to you. We will read poetry and things! Do you know a good poem for boys? It is by Mr. Kipling, and it is called *If.*" She could recite some of the lines.

"If you can wait and not be tired by waiting.
Or being lied about don't deal in lies –
Or being hated don't give way to hating"

Max had listened, his face solemn. "That is a poem I would like to learn!"

"Your father gave me quite a job!" she said at last, warming her hands at the fire. "To bring you up over here!" From the opposite fender, Max with sure instinct, wondered what was coming. "Dairy Mary tells me you are being attacked by the other boys. Is that true? They are

183

hurting you? Cannot you hurt them back? Don't boys fight to protect themselves? Can't teachers stop it?" Max shook his head, and they both stared at each other across a gap of incomprehension.

"*Ich möchte nach hause! Ich habe so fürhtbar heimweh! Ich möchte wieder meine Mutti sehen!*" When Max broke into his mother tongue, crying of his homesickness, it had an effect he had noticed before. His aunt withdrew, like a snail into its shell, defensive against psychological fears of her own.

"It is a good school, Max! All little boys behave – well, they are horrid, except you of course! Do you want me to speak to your headmaster and the others?"

"Can I not go back to Berlin now, *Tante Sybilla?*"

"Max, I have to tell you something you will not like, and that I have known about for weeks. Your cousins telephoned from Switzerland. Their father, your Uncle Paul, my older brother, they have arrested him and taken him to a KZ. Do you know what that is? It is one of those concentration camps. They have taken other people from the bank too! It is all too terrible! You cannot go back now!"

"Have they taken Father? Mother?" Max heard his own voice like someone elses, strangely far away.

"No, your father is not a Jew! Your mother – who is my sister – she is an invalid, she does not go out, they are not interested."

Max stunned, just stared at her, then ran up to his room.

The result presently was that Aunt Sybilla's concern about him became strictly practical.

Max was to attend McPherson's Gymnasium to learn boxing, and in that way he would gain confidence, protect himself and not be picked on because he was a foreigner.

"Do I have to go?" again Max asked.

"You can try!" And Aunt Sybilla, with her smiling thin face, the quick smoothing down of her black silk dress was also again effective, unmoving, reasonable.

"What is a Hun?" Max asked her.

She was silent for a moment, and her hands went still. "It is a nasty word for a German! When you know how to Max, you hit anyone who calls you that!"

184

McPherson's Gymnasium was on the first floor of a red-brick block of flats beside Burton Court and the little park where Dairy Mary sometimes took him at weekends as it was only a short walk along the King's Road. One of the attractions of going there was to see the Chelsea Pensioners, who wore red or navy-blue coats and tall peaked hats and on their chests rows of medals. They reminded Max of the soldiers in Father's study, and he often stood watching them moving along the pavement outside the railings of Burton Court. Across the road, from the Chelsea Pensioners, was McPherson's Gymnasium.

McPherson was a burly Scot with greying hair, an India-rubber face and a brusque but kindly manner. He turned Max over to a younger version of himself, while Aunt Sybilla on their first visit disappeared into his office which was in a corner of the big, wooden-floored gym, always bright with light from tall, frosted windows. Max got into shorts and a vest in the changing room. Sybilla before she left, gave him a book of tickets. One was to be given up each time he came.

The young instructor was one of several. Some boxed in a real ring, with ropes and canvas floor at one end. A pair of boxing gloves to fit Max were taken out of a rack in a little side room and he felt a new, odd quickening of his spirit.

"You call me Charly, see!" Briskly the gloves were laced on. "Not done this before 'ave you?" Max shook his head. "No, well we ain't gonta 'urt you see? Just get you fightin' fit that's all! Ever 'eard of Jimmy Wilde? No? That's 'im in the photo there! Bantam weight – 'e used to train 'ere. There's Carnera – real heavy he is!" The man was looking at Max appraisingly.

"I s'pose you'll end up welter, I'd say. Now . . ." They had moved to one end of the gym. "I'm puttin' on my gloves see? I sit on this bench, to be about your height, and you hold your fists up like this – like I'm doin'! That's right! That 'and half across your face – that's it! Lookin' out over the top. The other one comin' forward ready to hit me – that's your left! Then we'll change it about!" Although Charly's patter went on, his mouth didn't seem to move. "Now don't get jumpy son! I'm not going to hit you back. All I do later, is to show you where I could've done! Right? 'Cos you've got to move about. Move your guard! Change around! Move away now. Yes walk away! Ten paces. OK? Now turn round, and come towards me, moving your feet, but always keep your left in front. Not walking! Sort of quick step – never change your feet, and keep on your toes. That's right! That's it! See how quick that brings you in? And now you take a bang at my face! GO ON! Yes! With that left! Now! You can't hurt me, see! Where's my glove? Right up there to meet it wasn't it? Off you go again, don't look behind, just dance away like! Come in again and let's have a big one! Smack! That's it!"

In all sorts of places, later in life, Max Beaumont could hear Charly's voice, his encouragement, hear the squeaky sound of his own plimsolls, twisting, slithering across the floor, and the hard smack of the leather boxing gloves. And always there was the smell of those gloves, the leather close to his face. And when proper bouts started, the spit and sweat that rubbed off on the leather, and Charly himself who smelled of sweat and a kind of animal fitness.

Over the weeks Charly taught Max boxing in the way Herr Mocher and Frau Bloch had taught him about horses and riding, and because they all loved their sport and craft, the love rubbed off too.

Charly had small tight features, with blue eyes, not unlike Max's own. They looked out from under his lowered brow warily, over the gloves.

"C'mon Maxi boy! 'it me nose! Oops y' done it! Now me guts! That's it! Never lower than that, or the ref will 'ave you! Listen to me! Turn sideways, see." His bulgy, gloved hands turned Max's shoulders gently – "Now tuck your chin in, lead out with that left – see what I mean? You're all protected now! You don't make any sort of target!"

Sometimes he had other instructors, all of them kind, easy, strong men, who roughed up his hair, and clumped him across the shoulder. They showed him the photographs of the champions again, and explained how it was your legs that got weak first. They explained how to use the time between rounds in the ring to get your breathing steady, to wash out your mouth with the water but never to drink it, to use the ropes for steadying, turning on, bouncing back.

Colonel Otto von Klieschen did not come that Christmas, and Max was sad and his spirits dropped. He had planned that his father would meet Charly, and together they would show him the boxing.

Father had telephoned that Mother was not well enough to leave. He sent a letter from Switzerland with money for Max to buy a present for himself and Aunt Sybilla. There were four big white five-pound notes, a Christmas card of silk of birds and flowers from his mother, and a sealed letter for Aunt Sybilla.

"I shall keep half the money for you, Max, and we will spend it on things you need. Your father is not happy, and he has decided to leave the bank – perhaps you can understand why. I can read you some of his letter. He will certainly come here some time in the new year he says. And they like the Christmas cards we sent. Now we are going to have our Christmas time here and be happy! Your Papa is not too keen on telephoning to England he says in his letter. It is of course expensive."

Max looked at her, and his blue eyes had the new, wary look like Charly's.

"And because there are other people who like to listen also!"

She stared at him, surprised. It was a level stare because Max nowadays seemed to be standing higher. He was growing unmistakenly taller.

"How do you know that?"

"I heard you say so! When you were speaking on the telephone to the cousins in Switzerland." Max paused. He looked down at Aunt Sybilla's small red shoes tucked against the brass fender rail. "You must have forgotten I also speak German I think!"

"Your father said you were to keep up your riding if it could be done," Aunt Sybilla said, "but really I think with McPhersons that is enough at the moment."

After that Christmas a new loneliness would enter into Max in the early mornings, when he woke, perhaps at five or six o'clock. Sadness and homesickness combined to make him creep along the corridor and turn the handle of Aunt Sybilla's

187

door. She must have been half awake herself, for she called out sleepily in a whisper "Is that you Max?"

The room was in curtained half darkness, as he took the oldest route for consolation. Holding up his pyjama trousers with one hand, he slipped into the small double bed beside Aunt Sybilla. Slowly she turned, silently, breathing only a little faster, and Max's own eyes were squeezed shut, with some quickening sense of excitement. It was the warmth, the shared cover, the softness and shape of another body in the thin covering of her nightie. Her bare arm came round his shoulders. It was the simple, atavistic comfort to the male of any age, a woman's body in bed.'

That was how it started. Afterwards he would creep often into that bed, for here at last was real security, a special happiness. And strangely, Aunt Sybilla lying quite still caused Max the first stiffening of his own flesh against hers, without knowing what it was about.

It was Dairy Mary who seemed to understand that horses meant something special to him. It was when he was having tea at the kitchen table, while Mary ironed. She used two flat irons, and while one heated on the stove she worked swiftly with the other, moving it over the garments until it cooled, when she would spit briefly on its underside to confirm the temperature had gone, and exchange it for the hot one.

"If I had a horse I would pack up my things and gallop away with you Mary, and never go to school again!" Max said buttering away at his bread. "Will you buy me a horse, Mary? And I will take you with me! We could ride a big one together!"

"Is it that bad – the school I mean?" She sounded sarcastic, but she put her head on one side as always, and the carroty hair flopped over, and her red-cheeked face leaned over the ironing board towards him. "I've heard tell about some of the things they do at the boys schools, and I know! There was a convent school my sister went to at home. That was bad enough with the girls! They were pulling her hairs out, one by one, so that it didn't show! And nobody believing her!"

For a moment Max thought he would tell Dairy Mary about the misery and nightmare of it all. Perhaps she knew

188

intuitively, for like Maria had done, she came and pressed his head against her apron, then as abruptly pushed his shoulders away with her big, work-roughened hands.

"Perhaps it's your aunt you should be telling it to! But she won't be back till late as usual, and there's something we can do as might cheer you up!" She looked at the battered, metal alarm clock on the kitchen dresser, and began to untie her apron. "Horses is it? Do you know the Mills stables yet, then?"

She put on her old tweed coat, and together they went downstairs to the street door, and out into the dusk of King's Road.

"You can do your schoolwork and all, because we'll not be gone that long!" They were hurrying to the corner now, and crossing the road by what was then King's Cinema, and turning into Church Street. It was not a direction Max had taken before, and as he hurried along, holding her hand, Mary explained.

"There's the Phillips Paper Mills, on the other side of the river – do you remember me saying so, when we went along the embankment then?" This was when she had taken Max to look at the Thames, and to Battersea Park. "The big place, with the barges in the water! Where they collect up all the waste paper. Well, it's done with the horses and carts! Now you'll see where the horses go at night!" The real explanation of their breathless expedition was then revealed. "I've a friend there, and the time's about right for seeing them come in! It's to put the horses away for the night, do you see?"

A big archway opened into a great cobbled yard. It was the sort of yard common to old coaching inns, and as they drew in, Max inhaled again the special smell that is the world of horses' stables, hay and dung. And back came the Grünewald, Ritmeister Mocher and Frau Bloch, with the jingle of harness, the horses' heads in rows of loose boxes and the other sounds. Hooves on cobbles, buckets, and the splashing water.

Max and Mary stood to one side under one of the lamps that lit the yard that evening. The arched entrance behind them was soon filled with the clang and stamp of heavy horses, and the rumble of metal-rimmed cartwheels, as a

189

pair of greys came in, at the end of the day, the tired driver and ostler already sliding down from their seats. Other men appeared, and slowly, carefully, the great horses with huge straining legs backed the heavy dray under the shelter of overhanging bays where there were more of the same carts.

The horses were released from their shafts, the leather and brass harness and heavy collars were removed, and then, with only ropes to guide them, Max standing by Mary, watched amazed as the driver and his mate led them up a great wooden ramp. The huge grey rumps and great shaggy feet stamped upwards, disappearing into the darkness of stables above.

"They've earned their rest, poor things!" Mary said. She clutched her coat round herself saying. "Me Dad had a couple like that as did most of the work on the farm! He said he'd never have one of them tractors at all!"

Max became aware that they had been joined by a stocky, youngish man with a cap, worn in a jaunty way. He also had on an old leather waistcoat, and stable boots, and when he spoke it was in the same accent as Mary.

"Hello then! And who's the new boyfriend, would it be?" And although he gave Max a friendly glance in the poor light from the lamp above them, it was clear that his real interest was for Mary. Max could see his look stayed briefly with Mary's face, then moved slowly down to the open top of the old tweed coat. She seemed slow to put it together with both hands, and tossed her hair.

"It's my friend that I was telling you!" she said to Max, and then to the man, "This is the young fellow, and him mad keen on the horses! Now Mick here, he's looking after some of them, so you might come down here when you want to, and look. Might he not, Mick?"

"You could come more often ye'self too!" the man replied.

In many ways life on the King's Road then, as now, was full of surprises. For Max, a very special shop was Laffeaty, the shop window filled with bicycles, train sets, model aeroplanes, gliders, meccano, roller skates and air guns. A small echo of Schlummers. Behind the plate glass against which Max pressed his nose, was a treasure cave and one day he spotted

190

his old Schuco racing car, the same silver colour, real rubber tyres and working steering wheel. He saved carefully, until again he could hold that true friend in his hand, and lying on the floor, set it off across the boards of his room where it raced away, disappearing under the bed, or bumping into the skirting board.

There was another shop that Aunt Sybilla and Mary both went to, which was the draper and haberdasher, who sold ribbons, and laces, and bolts of cloth and reels of cotton. All of no great interest to Max, except for the overhead paying system which he would have liked to stand and watch all afternoon. It was really an overhead railway, with great wooden balls that could be split in half. Into these the shop assistant put your money and a piece of paper, and the ball was then hoisted up into a trackway on the ceiling, and went bowling solemnly down the shop, round the corner and out of sight. Soon it would come back on another track, so that there was no risk of collision with the other balls, all solemnly rolling their money round to the collecting point. The assistant would take it up, open the two halves like an Easter egg, extract any change and a receipt, and hand them to the customer.

Another term was starting at school, and Max knew now the name of his chief tormentor, a boy who was two whole forms above the second form that Max was in. He was called Bolsover.

Sometimes when Aunt Sybilla kissed him goodbye in Fleet Street, Max would still try to hold onto her hand. Bolsover he knew would lurk on the way to the gates of the school, hanging by the doors of the newspaper warehouses with their great rolls of newsprint in Bouverie Street. He and one or two of his gang could sometimes be spotted in time to avoid them. But at other times they would catch the smaller boys and start a bout of arm twisting right there in the street, or chase the desperate runaways with frightening threats of what was to come, later in the playground.

Max walked carefully, looking. Oil fuel made rainbows in the puddle water, and there was a strong taint of printer's ink in the air and smells of etching acid, and the big newsprint rolls. It always seemed to be half dark in Bouverie Street, by

191

the back entrances to the old *News Chronicle* machine room, and there were plenty of places to lurk.

Bolsover must have been waiting behind one of the warehouse entrance pillars because he suddenly appeared and got into step with Max as they turned the corner.

"Hello it's the Hun! Morning, Hun!"

"Hello, Bolsover" Max answered placatingly, because you never knew Bolsover's mood, and sometimes he could, especially if he was on his own, be satisfied with just being frightening.

"I'm going to come and look for you today!" said Bolsover.

When Max thought back, he could see Bolsover, the stocky active thirteen year old, with the red face and grinning teeth, already outgrowing his grey shorts and flannel jacket, his grubby school cap and red and black tie fastened in a greasy knot. But Bolsover turned, having seen a friend on the other side of the street. "Don't think you'll get away today, Hun!"

Max spent a miserable morning, and when it was time to go outside, he hung together with some of his own form mates, hoping that perhaps even Bolsover might be deterred by numbers. But then suddenly Max felt something flick against his head and turned. Bolsover was behind him, and there were two more of the bigger boys with him, and they were all grinning.

"You're not only a Hun, you're a doggy-woggy Hun!"

Max stared. Bolsover was holding out a leather dog collar, already attached to a lead. It was the lead that had been flicked at him. "I'm going to put this round your neck and take you for a walk, doggy! Don't you kids think he'd like that? Why don't you try and bite me, doggy?"

Max could only remember, as in later situations, that he was standing alone, in more or less the centre of a circle, because already it was clear that nobody was going to help him. It was just about possible that if he did nothing, and did not move at first, he could suddenly turn and plunge away, and Bolsover would grab the nearest other victim rather than give chase with the dog lead. And maybe that was what would have happened, if Bolsover had not flicked the lead again, and this time caught Max in the face.

192

He was aware of the slight pain of the leather, flicked across his face, but at the same time it was as though everything else inside him stopped. He heard one of the bigger boys tell Bolsover not to use the thing like that. And probably Bolsover had not really meant to, because his arm was by his side now, and the dog collar dangling on the playground.

Max had not really known, until that moment, that he had been born with the athlete's co-ordinating hand and eye. He recalled only that inside he went chill and very still, and that he was no more aware of sounds or the faces round him, only of Bolsover, taller than he was, and older. He did not know until that minute that he was going to strike him, and somehow when he did he was even surprised, but knew at once too, that he must hit hard again, which was what they taught you in McPherson's Gymnasium.

He had not planned it, but he heard Bolsover give a scream of pain, as he landed his punch on that critical point above Bolsover's trouser belt, Bolsover doubling up, his hands moving to cover the hurt when Max struck the same place again.

Probably you were born with an instinct for fighting, whether you were Prussian or Jewish, and he was both, and all he knew now from his short training was that Bolsover was off balance and winded, and he was at him before there was a possibility of recovery. He did not kick. And what else was it they had said he might not do? Bite? But he knew enough to go on driving short, stabbing blows into Bolsover's solar-plexus as they both went down, rolling on the black grit of the school yard.

He could hear them urging him to give it to Bolsover again, and then suddenly the bigger boy was sick, vomiting as he lay on the ground, and crying at the same time. Max was cool enough to stop and get up, and then to realise in a strange, distant way, as though in a dream, that he had better move away quickly, through the crowd, because there were prefects coming, and what was called fighting was punishable by a headmaster's caning.

By the time the school bell rang, he had dusted the dirt off his hands and knees, which were faintly scratched, and brushed down his clothes, and found the clean handkerchief that Dairy Mary put in his pocket, which cleaned the small amount of blood off those scratches.

When he got home that evening it was Mary who looked him over. Having had brothers herself, she asked him to tell why he had been what she called brawling. And after she had told him what the word meant, she had dragged from him the rest of it, including what must surely happen now, when his opponent recovered.

The next day Bolsover was not at school, but it seemed his parents had complained, and the form master told Max that he was to report to the headmaster when Bolsover returned, and they would both be caned. That led Max to leave the kitchen breakfast table the next day, and go and find Aunt Sybilla, drinking her small cup of black coffee while reading the newspaper headlines, and state that he was not in any circumstances going back to school.

It was fortunate that Dairy Mary came in at that moment with more toast, and told all that she had learned, adding her own embellishments. So that when Aunt Sybilla had also got up and dressed, her face quite pale, she put a hand under Max's chin and spoke in her quiet voice, the one that never seemed emotionally roused.

"Maxi – is this all true? The cricket bat? The gangs – and all this going on so long, without you telling me? And are you sure about this caning? I had no idea they did such things to children in this country. Nobody told me about it at the school, when I first went there for you!"

In that moment all three of them just stood there, and then Aunt Sybilla glanced quickly at her wrist watch.

"You will stay here this morning! I will have to go to the office first, and then I will go down and see this headmaster of yours! Probably I will telephone you then, and we will see." She paused, finishing her coffee. Then she said. "Why did you go on hitting this other boy when he was down?"

"If I hadn't, he might have gone on fighting," Max said coldly.

Thereafter, he had worked on his school books in Mary's little sitting room, lying on the rug in front of the gas fire, a position he preferred to sitting at the table. By the end of the morning his Aunt had not telephoned.

"And how can you write like that?" Mary said, on one of her visits between her room and the kitchen. "Or do you take ye're weight on your elbows?" At which she had given a curious, cackling laugh, and Max had rolled onto his side to look up at her. And she, looking down at him, was fumbling with a hand inside her blouse to pull up a bra strap, an adjustment he had seen her do before, so that he stared now, openly curious, and for a moment she stood and stared back, and that silent exchange was yet another beginning.

In the afternoon Aunt Sybilla sent a message that they should go to the Natural History Museum at South Kensington. Max was inclined to favour the Science Museum next door, but Mary liked all the stuffed animals which she regarded with amazement, and things like whales and dinosaurs with awe. After that they spent some time in the butterfly room, where Max loved to pull open and shut the many mahogany cabinet drawers containing the small perfection, the colours and design, the frail wings, of the butterflies that fascinated him.

"Those big monsters," he told Dairy Mary, who sat nearby on a bench. "They didn't live any more, after a few million years! But these little flying things they still do! Some even live on those plants on our roof garden!"

"I've seen them," Mary said peaceably. But she looked at him with curiousity. "That's a queer thought indeed, for a young fellow it is! What brought that to your mind?"

Not understanding her, he had put out his hands, and suddenly had held onto each side of Mary's ample bosom, pressing gently through the jacket of her suit. She looked at his hands, but made no effort to remove them. Instead she ruffled his hair.

"It's all to the glory of God!" she declared, getting up.

Aunt Sybilla had returned early, and called for Max. He came slowly into the little hall where she was putting her coat away, and she turned to him. Although the light in the hall was dim, he could see her dark eyes were bright, and her thin face twitched.

"I have seen that so-called headmaster of yours! You will not be going back to school, Max! I have withdrawn you. I think that's what they say." She looked along the hall, noticing that Mary had quietly opened the kitchen door wider. "I think I dislike that man more than anybody I have met for a long time! He tried it on about female emotion, and I gave it to him! He didn't like it, not one bit! He wrapped himself in that awful black cape thing. And his face! I asked him if education meant hitting people smaller than yourself, and he talked absurd English rubbish about discipline! I had no idea such things went on! I wish I had known before we started." Aunt Sybilla was quite out of breath. "Is that you, Mary? Max will not be going to school for a while! And I shall have to depend on you to help me. And Mr. Pillock across the road. I telephoned him, and he says he can do French and arithmetic."

"We had the cane at school, girls and boys!" Mary was openly standing in the kitchen door now, and looking prim. "Girls on the hand, and the boys on the backside it would be, and no great harm done at that!"

"Well that's your opinion, Mary! And it may or may not have reached your brain!" snapped Aunt Sybilla. "You wouldn't kick the clock if it told the wrong time would you?"

"I might at that now!" said Mary spiritedly. But she retired, closing the door to the kitchen, and Aunt Sybilla told Max to come into the front room.

"The other thing," she said. "Is that your Papa is coming over here? It seems he has problems that he can't talk about on the telephone, and besides the line is so bad. But now he is going to be here in a few days, and then we can decide what to do."

Max wanted to say again that he would like to go back to Berlin with his father, but he realised this sounded ungracious and even unloving, because he was still getting over his deep amazement at Aunt Sybilla's courage in speaking to the dreaded headmaster, and the unbelievable relief of realising he had never to face the horrors of that sort of school ever again.

"Now I have a headache," Aunt Sybilla said. "And you could find my bottle of aspirin by my bed!" She had turned to the cupboard with the pale-blue lining. "I am going to take them with a Dry Martini! I see I have opened a bottle of white wine which is far too sweet for me, but if you like you could have half a glass, Max. I am ashamed to say, I did not know what a brave boy you have been!"

When his father came over, Max had definitely intended to beg for return together to Berlin. He had often wondered what might have happened had he done so, and at the time he could not really identify his feelings. Only a great deal later, and on many occasions, had he recognised how critical that time in his life had been.

To start with, he knew that somehow they – both he and Father – had changed. This time his father had flown to London by aeroplane, an early Lufthansa flight to Croydon airport, which in itself seemed unreal somehow. Tied up with this novel manner of arrival, the Colonel seemed unreal and remote too, as though he had just materialised, with no recognisable link with Max's own past, but as a new and different person, appearing literally out of thin air. In Aunt Sybilla's home in King's Road he now looked unfamiliar and out of place. It was Max's first experience of what the passage of time and distance can do to all relationships.

On the first evening the three of them had an unhappy dinner, it was so formal, again at the Sloane Square hotel where the Colonel was staying. Max wondered if his father had been told about his change of name, and did not approve. But he did not like to ask. Would this explain why he also did not feel as he used to, with Father? These were strange uncomfortable thoughts. The conversation was difficult for the adults, because both had questions to ask and information that both wanted, but were guarded because Max sat between them. Sometimes his father spoke in German, and although all three understood perfectly, Aunt Sybilla for some reason was distant, and spoke back in English. Max too, suddenly found the other language heavy. It seemed to make his father humourless and slow to understand. Where was the old Papa, and why could Mama not have come too, on the quick and easy aeroplane?

"You should remember that your mother is very far from well." It was as though Father could listen in to his thoughts, although he was looking at his sister-in-law as he spoke. Then he put his big hand over Max's smaller one, which at that moment was playing with the bread roll, and maybe it was to stop that. But he put his monocle back in his eye, in the old way, and screwed a fixed smile on his face. "Mama could in no way stand the strain of travelling here, by any sort of method!"

Nothing was the same in Berlin, Father said. The new government had made things particularly difficult for him personally because of his position in the bank. His face was stiff, more like a mask, when he spoke of what he called the other side of the family being in a very unfortunate position. Also how difficult it was for him to maintain the big house, finances were a problem, there were some sad and even unbelievable stories going about. You did not know whether to trust the newspapers or the radio anymore. Personally he was able to read the Swiss papers which arrived daily in his new office, and he explained that he had a directorship with a big insurance company. Whether to trust the English and American newspapers was another matter. Although he could read them well enough, the new people at the top in Germany said they were full of lies, because once more the world was against Germany and her legitimate aims. He glanced round over his shoulder as he spoke.

This seemed to make Aunt Sybilla cross. Max wondered what she meant when she asked Papa if he thought the Gestapo were at the next table.

"They can be anywhere," he had retorted, and changed the subject.

The following day he and Aunt Sybilla went out together, without saying where they were going.

Max, lying on the floor of Dairy Mary's room made slow translations from the French homework set by Mr. Pillock. They went to visit the stables in Church Street in the afternoon.

When they returned there was tea served in the front room, and father and Aunt Sybilla sat on the brass fender seats and put their cups on the mantlepiece.

"*Komm doch mal hier!*" Max's father put an arm round him, and as he had never done before, gave him a small hug. "I think it is still best Maximilian that you go on with your learning here! Sybilla says I should talk English with you, and maybe that is right. Perhaps one day all the world will talk one language, and I think it will be English."

"Can I stop learning French then?" Max asked. He felt lonely, as only the young can, when they both laughed.

"*Touché!*" said his Aunt. "Listen Max! Your Papa found out that there is a new school, just started, and run by a German professor and his wife. They are of course refugees from Hitler, and had their own school in Berlin."

"Then they are Jewish," Max said. There was a short silence.

"Yes," his father said shortly. "Of course."

"It will be quite different," Aunt Sybilla went on, speaking quickly. "For one thing it is a co-ed school – boys and girls. And women teachers as well. There will be no bullying, Max, no cricket bats. There are big gardens with lessons out of doors. No uniforms, a swimming pool! Half the children are from Germany or *suddetendeutsch*, so you will not be called a Hun anymore."

"Yes, in Germany it is not good." It was as though Papa was speaking to himself, looking into the red coals of the fire. "They bait the Jewish youngsters, Sybilla!" He was angry now. "*Jude raus*! You hear it in the street!"

"You can be a weekly boarder at the school, Max," his aunt cut in. "You will like that I think! Then come back here at weekends, when I have proper time to be with you. And Max, you are grown up enough to understand – Papa is paying for this school not me, so it is to him that you can be grateful. Nobody is too young not to know about the realities of money. It is important! You are having enough difficulty getting money over here, Otto!"

Max held onto his Father's hand and wished he was not angry about whatever it was, and kept holding it, until they saw him off at the front door.

"You can both see me to the airport tomorrow!" Father said suddenly as he stood on the pavement under the street light, a tall, thin, erect shape, seeming himself rather like the lamp post, in his buttoned-up grey coat and homburg hat. "I

199

will call for you in the taxi. You will find it interesting, Sybilla – perhaps soon everybody will fly by aeroplane."

And then he was gone, stalking away at military pace along the King's Road.

They had gone out to Croydon airport, and seen him disappear into the Lufthansa Focker that looked like an overlarge dragonfly made of corrugated silver.

Max had waved until it was out of sight, standing on the platform of the old, square-shaped control tower, and wished then very badly, that he could have been inside the aeroplane too – flying still seemed like some sort of magic – back to Berlin, to the big pink-coloured house, to the sight and sounds and familiarity of it all. *Mutti*, Miska the dog and riding in the Grünewald. That father should be going back without him made a sort of cramp in his whole body. He held Aunt Sybilla's hand as they descended the stairs from the observation terrace.

"Why can't I go back?"

Disconcerted perhaps by the strange new business of air travel, and things her brother-in-law had spoken about, Aunt Sybilla's answer lacked any remaining discretion.

"It is dangerous now, Maxi!"

Max Beaumont's words came to a stop – for no connective reason, not in the way you make it happen for camera, or script or any of the professional reasons.

His descriptions of his family, the change from Germany to England had inadequacies and gaps about it. Even so, when he stopped speaking, I felt personally I had seen some of the things that had shaped the years that followed. Right then he seemed to me more real than any of the others who were present in the Richmond library. Perhaps they were thinking that too, what it might mean to be born with not one, but two or three lots of genes, backgrounds and loyalties – shaping, forming and so providing, motivations and ambitions.

Owen Owen had an expression of faceless caution that I had not seen before, a look of shared experience. A particularly Welsh prescience, I thought, more suitable for the moving end to a choral rendition or the injustices of the Rugby field. Joe Bailey had again taken off his spectacles and was polishing them, but his face was turned, gazing short-sightedly at Max Beaumont as though he was himself still standing on that old airport spectators' platform.

It was Owen who spoke, flatly and without emotion.

"Your father," he said. "And your mother too. You don't have to answer this of course – and I'm jumping on a bit I suppose – I got the feeling just now, that after that time, you didn't see them again? I do hope, you understand I only want to get the sequences right." He stopped. I knew the answer. Max had told me of course, all that time ago in Germany after the war, but no detail.

"If they stayed in Berlin," Owen went on, "Well, they could hardly escape the British bombing raids. Berlin was flat. Did you have to face that at some time? That this country that you adopted, or adapted you, eventually, killed your parents?"

"Not the bombs, Mr. Owen!" Max Beaumont's light tan-coloured face was almost as expressionless as Owen's, but the blue eyes were different, seeing something a long way off.

"My father had some escapes from the bombing I heard about later. You are right though, I did not see him again. Nor my mother. Does the name Claus Graf von Stauffenberg mean anything to you? He placed the bomb in a briefcase under the table of Hitler's HQ. Hitler was injured but survived. The Gestapo rounded up many people. They took my father for harbouring two of the younger officers who were involved. Like them, although another generation, he had long realised that Hitler was not only a dangerous megalomaniac, but the personification of evil, and that would ruin Germany.

"Stauffenberg was shot in the courtyard of the German War Ministry. Some of those, including my father, although a former army officer, they hanged after interrogation and drumhead trials. Do you know how? They were hung outside the court in the yard after the trial, with piano wire. And they took film of it to show Hitler. Now, thank you for asking – I never saw them again. My mother? The Nazis had dealt with her much earlier, which perhaps also explains my father's end. Her illness and dementia required hospital treatment, and during the war the Nazis had a euthanasia programme for people like my mother, who was Jewish and could not be cured. They killed over ten thousand that way. Two of those Nazi doctors were on trial in Frankfurt not long ago. All right, they were old men by now, but they got jail sentences of four years each."

He rose to his feet suddenly. Nobody else moved, and none of us cared to look at his face.

"Only twelve thirty-two!" Max said carefully. "I thought it was much later than that!" Somehow it seemed to prove something, like the theories of time and relativity.

The door to the study opened, after a brief knock and quickly he turned. It was Liz Charlton. She stood for a moment, tall and trim, her eyes quickly taking in all of us.

"A bad moment?" She put her head on one side.

It was, of course, a bloody awful moment. Only Max Beaumont was outwardly at least, composed.

"OK, so you asked! Now it's over. The Stauffenberg story is in the history books. But perhaps you havn't read them? Why should you?" Max Beaumont's voice was still careful elocution, and that was all. But he smiled, and now he put a hand on my shoulder. "What has lovely Liz got for us?"

"The working lunch you were to have in here, has been changed by Mrs. Beaumont! Mrs. Tolly is here with three of the main board directors, two with wives. Mr. Chemmy, Miss Milward, and a new young lady from Germany. You know about her, she says. But it's not totally unworking," said Liz Charlton as we all moved towards the door. "Bob and Dennis would like some quick approvals. They're waiting in the front room."

"How the hell did my wife get in on this?" I asked her. I knew only too well how American wives like Mrs. Beaumont could turn a planned sandwich into Breakfast at Tiffanys.

In the big drawing room Chloe came over, and the glass of champagne in her hand was almost like a Beaumont club tie. She kissed my cheek. "I got a phone call. She said there would be other wives!"

Deborah Beaumont came over to us, and I thought again that by and large she looked pretty good, comparing favourably with some of the younger women. Her face had that special fine-drawn quality of expensive care, even in the bright light of midday.

"Tolly! That is still right isn't it? Where are we now?" I knew what she meant.

"Pushing on fast" I said. "Adolescence!"

"Well, I'm glad you're keeping him out of that new place! It's like a fortress! I've seen it and I don't like it," Mrs. Beaumont said. "Barbed wire, floodlights – you can't get in or out without passes and the airport search!" She looked round, but we were being left tactfully alone. "There are other special people helping too. But I don't know everything! Max can be very secretive. One or two people involved in this new project are not really what they seem, I think – the ones from the States and Germany. We must get into lunch right now – Max wants to be clear and back on your thing the way it was first planned! I think you've met most of Max's directors who are here – the wives can introduce themselves."

The lunch table was a sparkling affair of flowers, crystal, silver, and almost as many white-coated servants, as guests, I thought.

"Joe Bailey has been telling me how it's going," Chloe said before we were separated. "He reckons you'll be here another two sessions! That's why Mrs. B. sent the invitation for me to come. She said I might not see you all week!"

I was being steered by the elegant Liz Charlton, who had come alongside, and was escorting me to the other side of the table where Max Beaumont was flanked by Jane Milward, with a new hairstyle and even more fetching semi-see-through blouse, the same pink as her face when Max, plainly recognising another conquest, was bantering with her about missing the morning session.

"I thought if your male colleagues were busy this afternoon you and I might be taking the afternoon shift alone?" I heard, as I was seated next to Max Beaumont's other lunch companion. I knew who it was, even before I made my introduction. I wondered too, how she had wangled that place.

"You must be Rita Henckman!" I said, as we both began at the avocados now in front of us. "We talked the other day. I'm Felix Tolly!" I didn't know why, but some quality about the representative from ARD made me certain that

203

this good-looking young woman was not going to be remotely interested in me, as soon as Max was available.

She did not reply, shaking long, straight dark-brown hair to one side, and turning a tanned, classic fashion-magazine face towards me, the dark eyes appraising, carefully. It was a strong, slim, fine-boned face devoid of make-up. I noticed she wore no jewellery and a man's white linen shirt showed under an expensive black leather baggy sleeved thing. Where the cuffs were turned back, her hands were curiously strong looking, also with no nail varnish. To complete the picture I was picking up on the air a thin, sharp, expensive perfume.

"What sort of get together is this?" It was still the Euro-American voice I had heard on the phone.

"A working lunch at the court of King Beaumont. Were you invited, or did you just gatecrash this too?"

"I was asked by Mr. Beaumont to sit beside him." She seemed immune to even direct reproof. "You remember you agreed I come to join the run-in – you are calling it that? When I telephoned here this morning there was no great problem. I came because Mr. Beaumont invited me! Why do you call him King?"

"You will see the ceiling swathed in an imitation tent or marquee effect, and it made me think of King Arthur. Do you know the legend?"

"He sought the Holy Grail of course!"

She, so clever. Bored by me, but I had the feeling nevertheless this Rita was nervous. On my other side I had the lean-faced man I knew as Bob, who was Max's chief labour negotiator, and as I bent over so that we could each receive a ready made dish of a baked potato with cream and caviar and the kind of gammon that Americans like for breakfast, he grinned. "You're right! I'm interested! The last three weeks I've had no regular meals and less regular sleep!" His vowels and consonants were transatlantic too, and for a moment I felt tired of them all, the toughness, and wariness. People watching each other, to see if they were safe, or made money, or got on TV or wore the right clothes.

"I'm Bob Rickdorf – just in case you forgot, and why not? We met at Park Lane!"

"What's new at Battersea?" I ventured. He shrugged.

"Right now there's five thousand print workers and others we're firing on Monday if they don't like the new look at Battersea. Which it doesn't look as if they will. That's Sogat, NUJ, NGA – the lot!"

"Have you got the EETPU playing?"

"That's what's making it possible!" Rickdorf pushed the potato round his plate.

"Because if you hadn't," I told him, "I might as well go home too! The Electricians would shut the Beeb down then, if we put Max Beaumont on the box."

"Don't worry boy. We're sound! So is Big Beau! And listen – you give him a square deal! He's a great guy. No poking into his private world with the surprise pop-up question."

I looked at Bob Rickdorf, resentful, of this. The tough, tramped-out sentences and the universal accent that went with something very like sycophantic threats. Obviously the men round the throne could not all be of the same elegant, cosmopolitan stamp as the man at the top. And his personnel director, who could operate in Fleet Street, New York and where else, would have to be a tough operator. Bob Rickdorf's face was etched with tired lines. The long and wolf-like face leaned closer across the arm of his dining chair.

"Being lied about don't deal in lies, was the bit I meant friend!"

"Does Max quote Kipling to you all?"

Rickdorf, like some others, including my wife I noticed, had now lit a cigarette, his food half finished. There was fruit and cheese, but also coffee cups clattering in front of us.

"If Max Beaumont is going to be the subject of hostility from Trade Unions, the Labour Party and the rest of Fleet Street," I said, "Is it the wrong time to profile him in depth on TV perhaps?"

"I think that is in fact exactly the idea. Don't think I'm telling you your job will you?" Rickdorf now looked concerned. "This is for Al Chemmy, not me. But there are people at the BBC who don't like the Press these days. Or the entrepreneurial world of any kind. Now listen. Don't look

205

where he's sitting now, but with what. Get me? It would be easy to damage the old man on the box, Mr. Tolly!"

"Listen Bob!" I said, and meant it. "I've known him earlier as a fairly close friend, about as long ago as you've been born! I knew about Max and women very early, if that's what you mean."

"I mean I would never forgive you, if you put anything out that would hurt that very special little American lady over there!" Bob Rickdorf stubbed his cigarette. "She knows, always has done. OK? But it's more than just you and your take-him-apart team. Who is the German glamour next to Max on your other side for instance?"

I turned instinctively to find Rita Henckman had obviously stopped conversation with Max Beaumont, and now the tawny coloured face was turned my way, half hidden by the long dark hair, the thin lips shaped in a Gioconda smile.

"Such a strange lunch party, Mr. Tolly! So many interesting things talked about! You see I can lip-read, Mr. Tolly – not very far away, but enough. I learned to when I was in a place where one could not speak aloud. Your friend is one of *World*'s top people I think? He would be pleased to know we have been talking about Max's philosophy, and I asked him if he could ever like Germans. And he said that German women in particular had always fascinated him!" Now her voice dropped until it was hardly more than a surprisingly bitter whisper. "I must tell Max how protective all you people are!"

Abruptly I pushed back my chair, and got up, having no wish at all to be shuttlecock between German television and Max Beaumont's personnel hatchet man.

Max was on his feet too, helping Jane Milward, a hand on her arm, her flushed face under her new hair-do, wearing a soppy expression that said she would personally re-write our entire script as a soap version of Love As A Many Splendoured Thing.

People milled about, looking at watches, kissing cheeks, shaking hands and performing other post-luncheon rites, and I found Chloe had conjured herself beside me, and I was one of those being kissed.

"Listen darling, I must go! Fun to see you in the midst of it all, not that you looked so happy once or twice. God – he's a charmer that man! He must have been a knockout when he was younger. I've been watching him."

"Like us all," I said.

"You're a funny one, Felix Tolly! You're as good as any of them here, better probably too, by a long chalk! But if I'm not mistaken, there's not much I do like round this lot. Power and money, and good looks, men and women. But also double-crossing, double-talk, treachery even. I can smell it you know, I always can! So you take care! When do I meet you this evening?"

I could see the chubby figure of Al Chemmy, beckoning full armed at me.

"We've the tickets for the Haymarket tonight, don't forget! I don't want to miss that!" Chloe cautioned, and meant it.

"Nor you shall," I told her.

Chloe moved away, joining those leaving the room, and I took a quick look round at Boris and other minions clearing the long table as I walked into the ante-room. Max Beaumont was already sitting with three or four of his people, including Bob Rickdorf. They were talking tersely and in shorthand jargon. Liz Charlton slid constant signature books in front of him, being fed in turn by another secretary. A young man with a sheaf of documents, released them methodically for initialling. Somehow I felt sure he was German and a moment later heard some stilted English that might confirm it. But Beaumont looked up at him, and spoke English.

"It will all depend on your people – you know that don't you? Well, tell them again tonight, when you get back!"

The man could run his international circus from the back of a lorry I didn't doubt, but it would not get our job forward, and I had promised Chloe about the theatre.

Now Al Chemmy had come over to me, and looked important, taking my elbow.

"Sorry Felix – about the lunch and now this! Max has got a lot on his plate! Your people are back in the library – I corralled them off there with the coffee. I gather that kid from German ARD or whatever they call themselves – she's OK, eh? Your people have cleared her to sit in?"

"No," I said. "She got to your boss first. I don't know how long she'll stay, but it's unusual and Owen Owen is being diplomatic enough not to object so far."

Solemn-faced Al looked round cautiously. Here it comes again, I thought.

"The boss is onto her, and you've got to take care of him, Felix! Like some of us have been doing these many years. OK? He's *very* careful, sure, but there are too many enemies. And he's in the middle of the rumour and zoom-lens business, and once or twice it's been touch and go."

"Don't tell me, Al" I said. "I've got the message."

"I'm sorry for running on business time with these fellows!" Max said, still signing as Al and I came and stood nearby.

"Thanks!" I said. "I don't eat caviar every day!"

"Maybe you should work for Soviet TV!" Max Beaumont suggested. "D'you remember when we went out to make that programme offer to them, Dennis?"

"Personally I like the baked potato – I'm fussy!" Bob Rickdorf said.

"You're a country boy, like me!" Al Chemmy said.

"So where were you raised, Al?" Bob Rickdorf asked.

"A place called Diss, in Norfolk."

"Some of the best steaks I ever had were in a pub there. The place was called some sort of farm animal," Max Beaumont said.

"The Black Bull, sir," Al told him. "They still have good steaks at the Bull."

"Was that it?" Max Beaumont was looking across at his own reflection in an ornate looking glass that balanced over the mantlepiece. He moved a hand to his tie, and adjusted the lapel of his coat. "Let's buy some pubs like the Bull!"

There was laughter and the conversation moved in a sort of familiar pattern. We were in any executive dining room, or waiting for another board meeting to start, when you talked about mainly nothing, and thought about the agenda and what lay beyond.

"Are those interrogators of yours ready, Tolly?" Max Beaumont said, and he got up, and moved restlessly to the window.

208

"They're waiting for you in the library!" Al Chemmy was saying, and it seemed to me that the other men just quickly faded away. There were no farewells or salutations.

Max stepped out across the big room, so straight-backed and brisk that Al Chemmy seemed to roll after him like an old ship, and I suddenly caught sight of my own rounded shoulders in the hazed glass mirror and thought maybe it was time I changed to less heavy spectacles, and perhaps put some colour into that mane of professorial grey hair.

In the Library the scene was still the same, except that Rita Henckman was with us, rather obviously keeping herself apart. She was on Max Beaumont's side of the dividing table on which she had put her own tape-recorder and was waiting, the lynx-eyes almost closed.

"You had changed schools," Joe Bailey was looking at Jane Milward's notebook. "What exactly did you do then, that was important to you personally?"

There was careful silence, and I saw Max Beaumont's face go into the old mocking mould, the Jewish humour balancing the teutonic look. There was light in the bright chip-blue eyes, but he stuck out the still firm chin with its marked cleft.

"I played Red Indians mostly," he said. "Which may have saved my life later. And learned about sex. It was a co-educational school you remember."

CHAPTER TEN

What was called Progressive Co-education in England in the late thirties was considered avant guard, Max Beaumont said. His father was not entirely in favour and thought it likely to make boys into sissies and the girls into tomboys, after a certain age.

"I spoke to the headmaster about it," Aunt Sybilla had told Max. She smiled. "He said you might perhaps break your heart more than once before you were fifteen, but was this such a bad thing?"

He never would tell anyone a lot about his experiences of that time, at the Richmond co-ed school. It was not only at school, because the sharing of the bed with Aunt Sybilla seemed to be all part of life at that time. Although he knew in a way, that it was a babyish thing to do, it had become accepted by both of them, and became unspoken understanding. Indeed so unspoken, that all the time he was with her, in the darkened warmth and comfort of her room and her bed, neither of them spoke a word. Mostly they both slept, or certainly she appeared to Max to sleep, until the small silver bell of her alarm clock sounded.

The first time this roused her, she told Max that he must go back to his room, and that Dairy Mary would be bringing her cup of coffee in five minutes. She added that if Mary went into his room to wake him, as she usually did, and found he was not there, she would certainly be frightened and probably scream, and think he had run away or fallen out of the window.

Max had gone back to his room and crouched in his pyjamas on his own bed, thinking. There was the warmth and shape of Aunt Sybilla's body, and the touch of the thin black nightdress, sleeveless, and rucked up, so that his own two feet sometimes touched the bareness of her calves. They turned over together, so that he stayed close against Aunt Sybilla's back, breathing the specially sweet scent that seemed to be in her short dark hair on the pillow, only inches from his face. His hands wandered and found her breasts, which were small and firm, and they stayed there, it seemed a natural thing to hold them, so that at first, in this new found security and sensuality his fears were allayed, and he slept. Then if he should turn, sometimes he could feel the quick movement as she followed, and her breasts against his back and her thighs too, warm against him, through his woollen pyjamas. He could hear, close behind him, a soft quick sigh escape on the pillow. Max had known for some time that Aunt Sybilla had her admirers and perhaps lovers, the knowledge of the difference was one of the many things you learned at the new school, and he was learning fast. Sometimes, not very often, she would stay away from the flat for a night, Max knew, although he was not there during the week. Dairy Mary told him, but otherwise kept discreet confidence. There was of course, Mick at the Phillips Paper Mills stables. Max could imagine Mary might benefit from having the King's Road maisonette to herself.

At Richmond Hill School there was astonishingly no pressure at all to attend classes. Max made a fine Indian encampment in a copse in the grounds. He was happy to be shown by the crafts master how to make a wigwam from pictures in books. An old tent was cut up and reformed. Some branches were stripped and made the framework. He was shown how to make stencils to pattern the wigwam by the art mistress, who might have been ten years older than he was, and who found his tumbling black curls, lean jaw and sky-blue eyes worthy of special time and effort.

Progressive Co-education in England was still feeling its way, as the German headmaster and his wife were surprised to find, for the English staff of both sexes were not the steady, unimaginative people they had been told, and with teenage girls and boys, it became clear that the female and male staff were interested in not only the special principles of the educational system.

211

As the art mistress held a stencil to the canvas, and Max stippled in red ochre and blue, their fingers touched, and he became aware of the magic of the unspoken and the Message that is Not the Word. A thin column of smoke rose from his Indian fire, and the sharp smell of the ochre paint seemed a counter point to the warm scent of the art mistress's long dark hair that brushed against his cheek as they worked intently on the patterning.

"You could make a totem pole!" she said standing up.

Still crouching by the bottom edge of the wigwam where he was stencilling, Max looked up, and could see above her bare knees, under the short woollen skirt. "You know what they were, I suppose?" She did not move, although noticing his gaze.

"Tall carvings – things that told about the tribe, different heads and faces!" Max said. Slowly he raised his eyes.

"They were phallic symbols of course!" She looked at him smiling, mysteriously. "Do you know what that is, Max?"

He was silent, already given to a pride that would not admit to inferiority of knowledge.

"It is a penis symbol!" the teacher said softly. "The token of male supremacy, or the claim to it, by the North American Indians of course. Which is why in fact their civilisation was not all that civilised."

Twenty years on, Max would remember, and wonder if she had that act underway. Now he said:

"Could you show me how to make one?"

"You would have to do it as a class study. I will do some drawings. But you must come into art class, Max, otherwise I cannot help."

This was always the way. They used natural curiosity and whatever motives came about, to lure them into classrooms, to learn skills and disciplines.

In the art class he met Rachael, who having agreed to see the Indian camp one afternoon, crouched by the ring of stones in which Max burned the fire, and later showed him how to twist water pastry round sticks and put jam on them. She had a pale, thin face with small, quick eyes, a greenish colour. She also had a long, heavy braid of red hair that hung down the back of her short sleeve, yellow, aertex shirt in a thick pigtail.

212

"Will you be my squaw?" Max asked her.

"Does that mean we sleep in the wigwam?" she asked.

"We ought to," Max said slowly. He watched her face.

He knew – and guessed that she did too, that this was the special meaning. There were other words for it too, love words and the bad words that the other boys used and told him about. Did she know that? The green eyes in the pale, thin face slid away, looking down, into the cooking fire.

"They'd come and find us!" Rachael said. "You know how they keep the dorms apart. And a teacher sleeps with us girls!" She giggled suddenly. "I mean in the same rooms. What does co-education mean? Why can't we sleep in each others' beds? I asked Dr. Steinz once." Rachael stared at him, crouching, almost whispering. "When he had one of his private talks with three of us girls because we were all in one bed, and he said it was stupid and might make us grow up peculiar! That's what he said, but he didn't explain!"

Max put some more sticks on the little fire which gave off sparks, and the thin spiral of smoke rose wavily into the silver birch that hung over their heads. Rachael had moved because of the sparks, crouching still with her legs apart, so that he could see her knickers, which were also a pale-green colour, like her eyes. She knew that he had seen them, he could tell, and the warmth from the fire, the tiny crackle of the burning sticks, the smell of the wood smoke, and damp undergrowth and trees, made for a special closeness, a green enclosure. Behind them, the foided back opening of the wigwam made its darkened interior mysterious, waiting, his first experience of the tension of potential.

"I'd do it!" Rachael said at last. She looked round and back at him, so that the fat, auburn pigtail swung across her shoulder.

"So would I." Max plucked a blade of grass and chewed the end of it. But they didn't.

Max learned the bit about the broken hearts. As he moved into his teens, his good looks, the lean sallow face with the always improbable combination of bright blue eyes and thick, curled black hair did their damage. With the fickleness of youth, it seemed girls could be hurt easily.

213

Then he found he could be too, and learned early the probable truth of the theory that there was usually one who loved and one who was loved.

There was Sonia, the tall shapely fourteen year old who had joined the school a year after Max, and who, like so many of the children, had mystery and unexplained sadness in her background, that showed in her rather Slav features. Sonia's appearance was more dramatic than most, with dark tumbling hair to her shoulders, a mouth with lips that were naturally almost purple in colour, and seemed to be always pouting, except when she smiled, in a theatrical way that made a circle of perfect, small white teeth. Then the thin eyelashes rose, and her large, dark eyes seemed to have little gold lights in them.

It was school drama that brought her and Max together, because her English was not yet so good, and she, moved down a grade, was cast opposite Max in a class preparing for Romeo and Juliet.

"Where for art though Romeo?" Sonia mocked him in her accented and sultry tones, whenever she met him in the corridors or outside in the gardens. And Max fell heavily, and knew the knee-weakening, overwhelming passion that made him suddenly short of breath when he saw her at a distance, so that he dreamed impossible dreams, and planned hopeless plans. Once she had left a pencil forgotten, by a book on her table, and he had taken it, a pale-blue stub, with a brass holder for a little red India rubber. It became his most precious possession, and he kept it all the time in the pocket of the long grey trousers that the boys of his age were allowed to wear.

It was the pencil that led to his first love letters, although hardly that, they were little three-and four-word notes on torn scraps of paper, passed surreptitiously in class, and of course read on the way by others, which made it even more exciting.

"I have your pencil."

"Give it back."

"I will keep it for ever."

"Why?" And then the inevitable.

"I love you."

Sonia wore silver bracelets on her stick-thin wrists, and made gestures that caused them to clink and slide together, and in the school craft class Max created, with much effort and patience, a woven silver and brass wire bracelet. It was, when finished, a rather gypsy thing, with red and green beads strung into it.

He decided to give it to her right away, and found her in the school bicycle shed. For one moment he thought she would hand it back. But she didn't. Instead he saw in the half gloom of the bicycle shed, the strange, sad expression on her face that was something he did not understand. She slipped the coiled bracelet over her fingers and onto her wrist to join the others, lifting her arm so that they jingled and fell back. Then quickly and easily, because she was as tall as he, she kissed him, with the soft, full lips, so warmly on his own. He watched, overwhelmed, as she wheeled her machine out, and then without looking round she had gone, and he was left, cast motionless in the dim light of the bicycle shed, with the light patterning its dusty floor and the oily metal smell of the bicycles.

After that Max was love-sick. The near hopeless, all-possessing, celibate passion of a thirteen year old. Some of the other boys teased him about it. But in that sort of school, all were vulnerable, even the teachers. They married each other. Quite respectably, tactfully doing it in the school holidays so that the following term only one or the other, but never both, returned to work.

The heart-break came when term ended, and Sonia went off with her father, a mysterious figure who wore a homburg hat and a black cloak. He was reputed to be a theatrical impresario, and was going to work in Hollywood, taking his glamorous daughter with him. She simply did not turn up one day, and nobody knew why.

"You're not yourself at all!" Dairy Mary said, when he came back. "Here's holiday time, and if I remember it used to be a great relief at that! Now out with it! What's the matter? I make your favourite tea – sausages and mash is it, and you sitting there with two left on the plate! Are you going all right?"

"Going where? Max had asked suspiciously.

"To the lavatory of course!" said Mary impatiently. She came and stood close beside him, close enough for the feature that made for the nickname, as Max had since also

215

learned at school, to brush against his face, the starch of a new, clean overall crackling faintly, and she took hold of his head between her strong hands.

"You're a big fellow now and as tall as I am! Will you stick out your tongue to look at!"

Max's tongue came out all too readily, and for that Mary released one hand and reapplied it quite hard to the side of his head again.

"Not like that! You're not for the doctor, not yet I'd say! Are you crossed in love perhaps? Is that it?" Clever, romantic, Irish, earthy Dairy Mary. His blush gave the answer.

"What's crossed?" he mumbled.

"Has she taken another then darlin'!" cried Mary, now all interest. "Of course your Aunt, so busy with her gentlemen friends she wouldn't notice, but you can tell me!" Her face was pink with animation now, the carrot-coloured hair flopping as she tossed it back impatiently.

Increasingly those holiday times threw them on each other for company, with Aunt Sybilla still at work each day, it was Mary he saw most. Once a week Aunt Sybilla paid for Max to go with Mary to the King's Cinema across the road, or to the Classic, past the town hall. He liked best still, the funny films, but then, as a first love affair with an image, the beautiful, teenage, bell-voiced Deanna Durbin.

Mary had taken his hand and held it, at first when there were unexpected exciting bits or frightening ones, and for this Max was subsequently grateful. There were chances to get away at school later, and to go to the local cinema, which was the courting couch of those days, when the billowing wet-mouthed music came from the great organ that rose and fell before the screen, accompanied by the slow fading of the lights, and in between the usherettes selling chocolates and drinks and ice creams. When he first asked the daughter of the French teacher if she would come with him after school, it was specifically to hold her hand in the Richmond movie theatre that he had in mind. It was showing Charlie Chaplin in "Modern Times", which everyone knew was an important film to see, as well as funny. And though she was allowed to come with him, and they walked almost without talking to the cinema, he realised that the hand holding bit might

216

lead to a rejection, the thought of which was unnerving. And then when the lights went out, because he had done it so often, he took her hand with a smooth confidence that was later reported to the other girls by the French teacher's daughter. And Max found that an enhanced reputation of some sort went with it.

The cinema also provided another important ingredient of life in those days, the black and white news reel which, Max Beaumont said, was somehow more important than today's TV news systems.

"It was quite different, and I suppose that sounds crazy, especially to you people, and no way for a multi-channel proprietor to be speaking either! So we'll ex that out."

"When something is rare or would you say a treat," Jane Milward said, "well it's bound to be important!"

Max rewarded her with his handsome, lazy grin, then the blue eyes ranged from her across to the German girl, who was sitting by herself. He was the only one who had had much chance to talk with her, and the rest of us could only offer professional acceptance of this newcomer on sufferance. In what had, after all, become a strangely close and personal relationship with Max Beaumont for us all. At least that was the way I sensed it, and I think he did too, because now he looked at me and said:

"Tolly, because our *Deutsche Fernseh* representative ought to know, it was on those newsreels that I first saw Hitler, and I mean actually saw, moving and talking! He was made real to me, through the newsreels. With those great mobs, the swastikas, the saluting and chanting and the uniforms. Do you know what *Kristalnacht* was, Frau Henckman?"

The girl looked down, holding the cassette recorder in her lap, and I realised that she was really not even Jane Milward's age. Perhaps twenty something, although it was getting increasingly hard to tell these days. She had the small, strong, tawny-coloured face that many German and Italian girls seem to have. She could have been Jewish too, which might be for Max intriguing, except that it was statistically unlikely. How many were left after the holocaust?

217

"I don't really know!" The faintly guttural American accent I had first heard when she telephoned. "I'm really sorry! I suppose I should know."

"Well let's not get too sensitive!" said Joe. He twitched his shoulders. "I have no great idea either! How does it relate to you, Mr. Beaumont?"

I rather wished Joe hadn't put it that way. But as always, Max seemed to be unperturbed. It was curious, this inscrutability, the only sign was a fractional narrowing of his eyes, which would go kind of opaque for a moment.

"It was the ninth of November 1938. A protesting Jewish student had shot the German ambassador in Paris." He was speaking himself now as though it was a news bulletin. "That was all the Nazis needed – they rounded up hundreds of thousands of Jews in Germany. The majority went to the concentration camps we now all know about. The brownshirts and the SS beat up people, burnt synagogues and smashed Jewish shop windows, the streets were full of splintered glass –"

"Thus *Kristalnacht*!" I said, just to help everybody.

Even so there was a sort of hiccup in the proceedings.

"What did it do directly to you?" It was Owen persisting now, and he was making sure I was going to decide how much the answer was important.

"To me? Well, shall I say my aunt got more news of it than most, through her job, the news agencies, contacts she had in Switzerland and New York. Whole families of people she knew, relations of mine too – just disappeared. It was days before my father spoke to us both, and he was strangely distant, unlike his usual style. Hesitant, and saying only that he had removed my mother from the hospital. But he spoke to my aunt for some time, and afterwards," said Max, "she had spoken to him."

"Your father says now it is quite clear that for some time you cannot go back to Germany. He does not know for how long." What she did not tell him, was that the Colonel had said there was going to be another war. Another one for his generation he had put it. "Your Papa thinks we should both move to America. There are some of the family in banking there."

"I don't want to go to America! I want to stay here with you!"

"In that case your father and I have had to take another decision. Perhaps you will like it, or maybe not, but I think you must be helpful!" Aunt Sybilla was agitated and miserable. Although it was well before noon, she made for the corner cupboard, with it's beautiful eggshell-blue interior, and filled one of the triangular shaped glasses. But she didn't ask Max to fetch ice, just stood there, sipping, holding the glass with both hands, and looking at him over the rim.

"Your father wants you to have the protection of another passport, Max!"

"Isn't the one I've got good enough? Where is it anyway?"

"I have it, of course. It is German! Your father wants you to go to the States, and eventually get an American passport. If not, we try for an English one. You can get naturalisation papers. You have been resident long enough now. Max! I have got two passports. I told you, because long ago I gave up my German one for Swiss. Then I got an American one, after I married there."

Max had never seen Aunt Sybilla seem so emotional and disturbed, and sitting on the sofa, watching her carefully, he saw that both hands on the stem of the glass were shaking.

"Max – terrible things are happening in Germany! There is the war in Spain, where your father says the Germans are training for more. God! The Colonel ought to know I think! Then Mussolini has taken Albania, and the Japanese are bombing and killing thousands in China." On Aunt Sybilla's cheeks under her eyes, the moisture was shining now, and Max shifted unhappily. He looked, for want of anywhere else, at his aunt's neat patent leather shoes with their silver buckles and high heels. To see adults cry was a great embarrassment.

"I know," he said. "I have seen on the newsreel at the cinema. How do I get nationalised then *Tante Sybilla?*" He said.

"Listen, Max dear, listen carefully!" She smiled bravely and emptied her glass. "It will be fairly quick and easy in your case. For one thing I have an MP – that's a member of parliament, you know don't you? He is a good friend of mine, and will sign papers for us. But, there is more than that I have to tell you. Oh, it didn't seem to matter before, Max! You were in fact born in this country, here in London! That will help, because it is on your birth certificate which Otto has sent to me!" Aunt Sybilla had sat beside him now, her slim shoulders were rounded, and she clasped her hands round her knees. Max stared, uncomprehendingly.

"But I was born in Berlin! I was I know!" he shouted. At last equally, if not more, disturbed than she was. But she shook her head.

"It's quite simple really. Your parents were over here, for your mother to see me really, because I was ill. Just after I came back from New York, the time my husband was killed. I would not return to Germany for various reasons I won't go into."

"Uncle Paul?" Max became quickly cold. The emotions of other people, as well as his own, were something he could not stand for long.

"Not your Uncle Paul. His father," Sybilla looked strained, then she went on. "How do you know such things? It's all rather a long time ago."

"Cousins," Max said briefly. "Your part of the family seem to talk a lot. Whisper! whisper! But go on, go on!" Now he was shouting again. "Where was I born? How then?"

"Your poor Mama was pregnant, you were not due for a month, but London was our best place and chance to meet, and your military father did not consider it a risk then, and they stayed at the Royal Court Hotel, as always. Well, you were premature! The North Sea I should think. My dear sister went into Queen Charlotte's, and after a week had a Caesarean. Not much fun then, nor I suppose at any time. How can I say, never having had any!" She looked at Max. "You were back in Berlin in a fortnight! You had a British birth certificate, but of course your father got a German one as well. I just saw you as a bundle, with your blue eyes, and already quite a lot of that family hair."

Max looked at her dispassionately. "Is a Caesarean when they cut a slit and pull you out?"

It was Sybilla's turn to look distant. "Obviously you know! Yes, except that it's not you that gets cut open it's the mother, and after that there was some sort of general septicaemia."

But Max was not really listening.

"If there is a war," he said. "Whose side will I be on?"

"Who said anything about war?" said his aunt, desperately.

"My Father," Max reminded her coldly.

He liked that story, Max Beaumont said, because it showed how all sorts of things shape our lives, and we often know only half of them, and then perhaps not the important ones.

"That question you asked was answered rather soon." Joe Bailey was looking down at his clip-board. "But how did it feel, changing over? I guess Felix you'll ask that probably?"

"I might," I said, but I could see Max Beaumont was looking at Joe.

"I suppose nobody else here has – what was it you said, Mr. Bailey? Changed over? For a moment you made me feel something wierd, like a sex change."

"It might even have felt like that," Joe Bailey said coolly. "That's the point! I've often thought I'd like to have another interesting nationality myself, maybe Chinese, or something with a long-term future. Owen here, he's dual anyway, and Jane – she was born in Cheltenham and what could be more gilt-edged than that?"

"Oh Joe, do shut up!" Jane was saying, and then I realised that instead of waiting for me to reveal the fascinating fact that Tolly came from my remote Scandinavian ancestors, the others were all looking as though by some instinctive joint curiosity at the girl called Rita from German TV. Why these moments occur, one seldom knows, but the atmosphere was suddenly, out of nowhere, tense and waiting. She had not noticed because her attention was still fixed on Max Beaumont, with a lack of expression, also like his, that I have seen on the faces of world master-chess players. Then she turned and saw the others, and her face changed.

"I do not know what previous generations did!" It snapped whatever the build-up was. "I would like to be a citizen of the world!" And she shrugged, and made another little gesture, almost of irritation, at even the emotion in that statement, swinging her hair to one side, and then back again. She could, I thought then, be a tiresome handful.

221

Back there in the library, we seemed to have run into a hiatus, and because I knew that really everybody was there to help me, I moved to push things back on the tracks.

"So you got your British citizenship, and Neville Chamberlain got his piece of paper for peace in our time. Things I can remember too, Max, began to show it wasn't going to be like that! Gas masks for everybody, air-raid shelters, ration books just in case! All that stuff."

"When war actually started, I was still in Chelsea, I remember writing a letter, I don't doubt over-dramatic, it was to my parents. A sort of *Schatten der Zukunft* piece," Max Beaumont said.

"What's that?" Joe Bailey pounced again.

"Events casting their shadow before!" Rita Henckman drawled, and looked away from Max Beaumont, and scornfully at Joe.

You could of course find that very cliché appropriate to his first job, Max Beaumont pointed out, and it was, anyway, obtained through Aunt Sybilla and Stephan Lorant on *Picture Post*. The red-bordered cover of that weekly magazine could be seen in every household of that time, like a TV set today. Its influence and persistence, helped change the minds of people and politicians, from appeasement to collective and resolute action. When the Germans later were threatening to invade, it even showed how to make firebombs and throw them at tanks! Heady stuff for a fifteen year old.

Max visited the photo libraries in Fleet Street, took corrected proofs down to the printers who were in the basement, and came to know more intimately the oily smell of printing machinery, and the acid tang of printing ink and raw paper. He also felt extraordinarily grown up. With his first pay packet, he bought Aunt Sybilla a half of Gordon's gin in its little square bottle – that sort of drink was already getting hard to buy – for the dry Martinis.

She in turn bought him his first grown-up suit, dark-grey flannel and a modest blue woollen tie, and about once a week they had lunch together. Because in the suit and with his height, the well-known pubs in Fleet Street like the Cheddar Cheese let him in. He drank his first beer and disliked it.

It was the week before the Germans invaded Holland and Belgium, that Max was offered a better paid job on a daily newspaper and took it. Aunt Sybilla had already changed to working with the BBC. Translating she had said. He had learned she was involved in broadcasting to what was called The Enemy. This phrase gave them both strange, uneasy feelings. Max Beaumont was now a British citizen. It had all gone forward in surprisingly short order and easily enough at his age.

A much delayed letter had arrived via Switzerland from his father, addressed to both Max and his aunt. It was short, almost scribbled, in black ink, and spoke of Two Countries and Peoples so truly like each other, so tragically at war again, and begged Max to Remember His Beginnings, but above all to think clearly, to be honest in purpose, and to do what he felt to be his duty at all times. Honour with courage were the prime duties for anyone.

"It is rather a German letter," Aunt Sybilla said sadly. "He says nothing about your Mother.

"My father is German," Max had said stiffly.

"And your mother is Jewish! As I am. And you too! Which is why you are here!"

"I want to get a bicycle," Max told her.

"Why do you want one?"

"So that I can be a messenger for the Home Guard!"

"Oh my God!" she had said. "I can't stop you!"

On her new job, Aunt Sybilla was away more often in the evening. Max had supper in the kitchen, eating whatever ration coupons allowed, unless an off-the-ration rabbit or piece of whale steak came from Mary's shopping forays. She was in no way amused by the start of the war and its problems, least of all because Mick from the stables had volunteered for the army. She and Max ate, facing each other over the oil-cloth cover of the kitchen table, the hideous, black-out calico blind pulled down over the kitchen window. Above the table hung the opaque goldfish-bowl light.

Mary grew less dismal as she drank and refilled her glass from a fat, flat bottle.

"Australian it is!" she said. "Red wine from all that way, and full of iron and other goodness they say! The doctor said I was anaemic, and would you believe it!" She picked her teeth thoughtfully, and looked at him. Then emptied the glass, tossing it back, and giggled, showing her widely separated teeth between the red lips, and tossing her carroty tumbled hair from one side to the other. "How would you think that feller could just go off to be a soldier without so much as askin'?"

"Anaemic means thin!" Max said. "You don't look like that to me, Mary!"

She glanced down at herself, with the almost automatic guesture of slipping a thumb into her blouse front, hauling on the bra strap.

Max followed the movement, and Mary stared at him, mockingly, and leaned back in her kitchen chair.

"And how would you know that my fine Mr. Beautiful Beaumont?"

"Of course I know, I can see!"

"You've had more than an idea of your aunty's little titties, I'd say. From what I know of the shape of her bed all these years! Isn't that so?"

Max stared back at her, breathing a little faster, lost for response, but already developing the instinct that was a sort of readiness, there and then, almost like the boxing.

Mary picked up the flask-shaped bottle and tipped some of the red wine into his empty water glass, and the rest into her own.

"Try that!" she said.

And then suddenly, she slipped two front buttons undone on her blouse, and eased a magnificently heavy and rounded breast from one side of her bra so that it seemed to rise between them like some glorious great moon. Round and pale, but certainly not remote, the soft warm skin showed gentle blue veins and the jutting pinkness of the slit teat and the fat aureole. As suddenly as it appeared it was gone, as Mary pulled the blouse neck together with eyelash lowering slowness.

Then those eyes were flashing at him again, and her red face was aglow, grinning triumphantly. "There! Have y'ever seen the like of that then? Dairy Mary is it? Oh, I know! Your aunt's a fine woman in her way, and I dare say I'll miss her!

224

But she's no respect for the likes of me! And there's Mick, him saying I've the finest pair of tits the good Lord created, and gone for a soldier! So what's the use of it all?"

Max drank the sweet wine slowly, looking at the face opposite him, which had now turned sad and bleary. Then he said it.

"Show me the other one!"

Mary rose unsteadily. "I've another bottle in me room. You can come in and lie by the fire – like you used to that way when you did your schoolwork. Just leave the dishes, I'll do them later!"

They moved through the open door into her little bed-sitting room, where in the past he had spent so many evenings.

There was only the bed, and one old leather armchair in which Mary sat, and with the blackout curtains drawn, and only the reading light on by the bed, it was snug.

Now Max lay full length on the little rug in front of the old familiar fire, its flames in the gas mantles hissing, orange and blue. It was in this same position that he read or did homework, but now he just lay with his head held on his hands. From here, where he was below her, he saw that Mary was leaning back in the old chair, her eyes closed. Was she going to sleep? But now it was suddenly clear he could see more than that. As his gaze ran from the turned in shoes up the heavy tan stockings, Mary was being careless with her skirt. For the first time that he could remember it was pulled well up above her knees.

As he watched, silent, enrapt, she moved again, the hem of the worn, dark-red, velvet skirt moving further up, and apart, as she widened her legs, and he could see the tops of those thick stockings with the suspenders and metal clasps stretched in the shadowy paleness against bare thighs.

Now, they were both waiting and watching. Mary through her eyelashes, studying his face, and the boy at her feet also feigning a kind of sleep, as he raised himself on one elbow to see more. The more she intentionally showed was visible even in the shadows, for Dairy Mary had no knickers on, and it was quite different from Rachael by the Indian camp fire, when he had remained in just the right position to see between her small legs. Because now in all that was in view of

225

Mary, there was deliberate assertiveness, and with it a certainty of the irresistibility of the oldest magnet in the world. It made his hands reach out, and he sat up, and wriggled forward, wanting to touch those stockings and thighs, feeling along the warmth and smoothness of the passage way they made to the mystery in between.

"Do you like it then? What you see!" The unexpected hoarse whisper was only slightly louder than the stuttering gas fire behind him. When he heard his own voice, it was strained and he was breathing fast, but not without control. Control was always everything.

"What do we do?"

She put a hand on his head. Not peaceably now, because she entwined her fingers in his thick, dark hair, and her voice was heavy and quick and commanding.

"Show me your thing. Quickly! I've seen it before, but you was smaller! It's big now I know." For Max it was a flashback again, to the Berlin school playground, with the older Trudi, the demand was the same.

She drew him by the hair to the single bed, with its grubby counterpane, and as she fell upon it, dragged him on top of her, so that their faces were together, and her eyes seemed to be hugely enlarged, and her hair, smelling of soap. She pushed away from him, rolling him to the wall.

"Open ye're flies, boy! Here! Let me take it out! That's right! D'you see, you're not a boy much longer, for it's a fine thing! And me at the right time of the month, and ready for it! There back on top of me again! In you go, quick as you like! Never mind your trousers – they're not in the way! D'you feel it?" She was rising and falling under him on the flat hard bed with its hair mattress, and he was holding her, his hands on her shoulders, then the tops of her arms, as she pulled up the front of her blouse, struggled to free again the splendid, lurking breasts, so big were they, so generous and reassuring. Quite different from Aunt Sybilla's small pear-shapes under the bedclothes, as Mary had surmised. How extraordinary that women could be so different in such an important matter! And here was Dairy Mary with her hot, red face, cheek to cheek against his own, and her eyes wide open as he felt the turmoil explosion come suddenly

226

without control, and then she was tightening on him, begging fiercely.

"Keep it moving! Yes, that way!" Wildly rocking she was now babbling without restraint, "Oh now! The blessed virgin! It's me too!"

And because it was the first time and shared, it was not like doing it alone, and being angry with himself afterwards. So why the sadness, as he kissed her thick neck, and the ear found under her tumbled hair, and when she heaved, he was rolled over, and suddenly falling, thumping to the floor. He lay there for a moment, feeling the floor's hardness, confused and ridiculous, his bottom bare, against the wood. Until a big, red kindly hand came down and found his, and took it and squeezed, and they both continued to lie there at different levels.

Mary's face, not so close now, so that she looked more like herself, was peering down at him.

"Are yes alright then, the man? Was it like you thought? Tell Mary!" There was nothing he could tell her. Although years later he would have liked to. And in less than a week Mary had gone.

"It's too bad!" Aunt Sybilla had said, in the quiet, controlled voice that more and more she used for all conversations, as though she was still in the broadcasting studio. "Will you miss her, Max?"

He thought carefully. "I suppose so, yes!"

Aunt Sybilla looked at him with the deep, dark eyes, and the thin, sallow face that smiled rarely now. "I suppose you will. She helped to take care of you for a few years in lots of ways."

Did she know, Max wondered uneasily. You could never tell with Aunt Sybilla.

"Why did she leave?" he asked.

"Money. At least, that must be one thing. She will earn twenty pounds a week in Ulster, in the Sunderland aircraft works she says. Also her boyfriend is training in barracks over there. She needs to be with him she says, for if he was to get killed she could still bear his child. Really, these Catholics are extraordinary!"

* * *

227

"There's one thing I was going to ask." Owen Owen pulled at his dark chin with one hand, which told me he was a bit embarrassed. Unusual for Owen.

"I don't know, Felix, whether you're going to get into things like this, but I was wondering if you might ask Mr. Beaumont what it meant to him being brought up, in his formative years, by two women? I seem to have put that pretty clumsily, maybe you can do better?"

Max Beaumont looked quizzically amused. I knew more than the other four probably guessed, that there was part of an iceberg of Max Beaumont under the water, that we were never going to be shown. And Owen Owen, clever, perceiving, Welsh Owen was beginning to realise that too. The two women present here and now, were both watching him curiously, in the way that women do with their faces turned sideways.

"It couldn't be otherwise could it? Of course, you're right. A lot of young men of my generation, and I met them fairly soon after the time we're talking about, were brought up largely by men." Easily rather than evasively Max started to expound. "That was the prep-school and public-school kind, who mostly made up the officers in the British army, and it seemed to me, that as a result they lacked a kind of reaction to a lot of things, Mr. Owen! They were afraid of feelings for one. Women are capable of being just as aggressive as men, determined to get their own way, often more successfully, because they have that feeling for other people that is more perceptual. A lot of young English males were taught, or made to think, that feelings, sensitivity, imagination, call it what you like, undermine real character! You can always tell, at least I think you can, if a man has been firstly, allowed to be a child and loved as such. *And* then allowed to be a man, and loved as such! Women do both, better. Have you read Jung on the subject?" Listening, I saw again the early, easy grace of the man, as he parried and answered the question. I saw the preserved, if no longer devastating good looks that were there when I first knew him. And truly it was in large part, a feline charm. Now, in what the ad. boys would call his mature years, he was like a well preserved older tiger, flexed and resilient, and with the big cat quality of reserve power.

228

It was the German girl, Rita Henckman, who now got her wires crossed. She seemed to move about, sinuously, in her chair. "Is it that you do not like women then, Mr. Beaumont? Is that what is being said?"

"I like all women, my dear Rita, from nine to ninety! At all ages, I find them fascinating! There are lots of them working for me all over the world. Would you like to be one of them?"

"I do not think you would pay me as much as German television!"

"It would depend on what you were doing for me!"

I was grateful to Joe Bailey, who moved in swiftly to track away from this suave and dangerous line of dialogue.

"Was riding that bicycle in the air raids interesting?"

The transition was so perfectly done by Joe, but it made me uneasy that Max was answered as though women and bicycles were all good, equal topics.

"The German air raids started in that autumn of 1940, after their failure in the Battle of Britain. And when it seemed as though this country might be invaded, did you know that Churchill had posters printed saying 'Why not Take one With you!' He meant it too! Kill an invading German soldier! And people would have done. They were never used, those posters. But I saw one, because *Picture Post* had it. Do you like that idea, Rita?"

Joe Bailey was pressing on grimly, and had no intention of sharing questions and answers with unwanted media guests.

"If you were in the air raids, it made you hate the Germans? How did you feel?"

The girl from German TV reacted too, as if she had done this bit before, her eyes narrow under drooped lids, and the full dark lips seemed to carry more than a trace of contempt as she looked at both men.

"A lot of people have sacrificed themselves like that! The Germans did it, against the Russians! Did you not hear of that? It was done to the Americans in Vietnam! And in Palestine!"

"I didn't mean it that way," Joe said patiently. His voice was kinder than the girl deserved. "I would like to fill in how Max Beaumont felt when the war really started for him. It sort of identifies the time, and history and character, that Mr. Tolly has to bring out in questions."

Max Beaumont smiled at Joe in a bright, hard sort of way. "The idea that I might get killed by some of my former countrymen, who were up there in the sky? It's a good question, Mr. Bailey!"

"I try to keep them that way," said Joe.

"I can give you a quick picture, Mr. Bailey, of my first encounter with the war, let's say, when I was a cub reporter, just starting to earn your sort of living! I was coming back from a job at Chatham in Kent. I had started up the road thinking I might get a hitch back to London. People were more friendly in those days about hitch-hikers."

I looked to see how Joe had taken it. He was listening, looking at Max and then at Jane to see if she was writing.

"I had walked about a mile, that warm dusty, autumn afternoon of 1940, but there wasn't a car in sight. So when I thought I heard sounds along the road behind and getting closer, I turned to look, and then, such ignorance, realised I was witnessing the drifting descent of a storm of empty brass cartridge cases, raining down from that peaceful, warm blue sky. And when I looked, actually, not so peaceful, because up there, so very high, what looked like hundreds of silver minnow fish, drifting, all in the same direction, and now I heard for the first time the sound of war over England. Airplanes, diving, rolling, climbing, and the tiny, far away growling snatch of the machine guns, a quick sound, like matches make, struck against the box. And in the same way, there were sudden bright flares of red bursting out up there, and the planes fell so very slowly, those tiny silver shapes, trailing long straight lines of smoke like charcoal brush lines against that blue sky."

"This was aerial dog-fighting on the grand scale, the start of the Battle of Britain," Max said. "Then when the German air force resorted to heavy bombing by night, London and other cities, in that winter of 1940 and 1941, I was in that, as were millions of other civilians. The Blitz. Sometimes sent out in a lull, riding my bicycle in the dark, with no lights, through the rubble strewn roads, lifting it over fire hoses and round bigger blockages where whole buildings had fallen into the street, ambulances and fire engines working in the light of the flames, with people shouting and digging in the debris. The all-clear sirens would eventually go, and then maybe ten minutes later, or even as the first thin light of dawn came over stricken London, that banshee wailing of the warning started again. Usually it was German reconnaissance planes, coming to take photographs."

There was one morning, Max said, when he had walked to work in Fleet Street, because no wheeled transport could get through, and from halfway down, the roadway was choked. Rubble and snaking firehoses, blown-up vehicles, paving stones and broken glass. And hanging over all, the heavy, sour stench of burning and dirt and explosive in the air. At the end of The Street, and of course he meant Fleet Street, and he would never forget the sight, at Ludgate Circus, the short railway bridge that crossed the road below St. Pauls was hit, with a whole railway train, engine carriages and the lot, dangling down into the street with half the bridge gone.

Maybe they could understand Max Beaumont said, that in that moment he was back in Berlin, with the trains in the basement, and he remembered leaning against some sandbags in Fleet Street, and well he didn't like to say he was crying, because it was a mixture of feeling sick misery and anger, and fear too. Where and how could all this end? Would the Germans march into the ruins of London? Would they take him prisoner? And Aunt Sybilla too for that matter, and put them into the same concentration camps to which Uncle Paul and the others had gone?

He felt a big firm hand take his shoulder, and still in the grip of this nightmare, tried fiercely to wrench away. Then he saw it was a big, red-faced London bobby in blue uniform, but with a torn jacket, rubber knee boots and a tin helmet.

"What's the matter son? Got 'urt 'ave you?"

"No. I'm just tired I think!" Which was also true.

"That's two of us," the policeman said. "Got an identity card 'ave you? Let's 'ave a look."

Max pulled the grey card in its plastic holder out of his jacket pocket, and after looking at it briefly, the bobby gave it back.

231

"Chelsea eh? Bit of a way from home aren't you?"

"I'm going to work!" Max told him fiercely. "I work here! In Fleet Street! I've got a press card too! Do you want to see that?"

The policeman laughed. "Off you go!" he said. "But with that black on your hands and all over your face now, have a clean up from one of the fire 'oses first! There's plenty leaking about! You can 'ave Fleet Street, son – what's left of it!" These words, Max Beaumont pointed out kindly to us, if either of them had known it, also had what cliché writers call a vein of prophecy. And all this was just to give anybody who wasn't around then, an idea of what the London Blitz was like – at least to a seventeen year old. Now the next step was getting near.

"I shall be called up soon!" he told Aunt Sybilla. "But I'm going to volunteer. In three months now, I can!"

"Surely they're not taking kids like you!" She had put her cup down in its saucer with a shaky hand.

"If I volunteer I can choose what I do! Is that a good enough reason?"

"I suppose you want to join the Air Force, and be one of the Few, owed so much by so many!" she said.

"You forget – I am already one of the Chosen, the Bible says. Or half of me is! Which is one reason why I want to get into the Army to fight."

"Why not the Air Force?"

"I might have to bomb Berlin! Had you thought of that?" Max said. And then he pushed back his chair, and moved quickly, round the table, because Aunt Sybilla had started, silently and slowly, to really cry this time, open-eyed, her thin face tired and creased.

That summer the news of the war was changing. In the desert it was the tanks that formed the spearhead of the attack against Rommel. In June Hitler invaded Russia, and it was obvious that the German armoured columns were making the pace once again. In their first attack on Poland there had been stories of the gallant Poles, hopeless in a lost world of their own, attacking tanks with cavalry regiments on horses. But the Russians had tanks, and their defending counter attacks were also with armoured regiments.

232

So, Max pointed out, and it was just for the record, tank troops were the élite, and later there was Monty, wearing a black beret that showed what he thought. Of course, today it was red berets, and the SAS who had inherited the mantle of élitism, and no one should forget the green berets of the original commandos, who really were perhaps the toughest and most resourceful of all. But for Max Beaumont on that day in 1941, when he rode the usual bus with Aunt Sybilla up to Fleet Street, everything else was going to be different from then on, because as he had told her, he would ride as far as Sloane Square, and get off there as he had heard that there was a real battle tank on exhibition in the square of the Duke of York Barracks.

What he did not tell her, was that also in the Barracks was an army recruiting office. And with certainty for him, as a volunteer, it was horses and cavalry in their modern form, descendants of those lancers, dragoons, cuirassiers, hussars, and grenadiers of the miniture metal army in the study, for which he was destined.

He walked past the sentries at the gates, pointing to the plain white-painted sign of the Recruiting Office. The colour sergeant, with the peaked cap, glittering brass buttons and dark sash, was more avuncular and kindly to Max than any bearer of three stripes and a crown would be after that for quite some time.

He took Max into the office where a captain sat, hatless, informal behind a trestle table. The sergeant stamped and saluted and Max was invited to sit down. The captain wanted his birth certificate. Not unprepared, Max was able to give it to him, the red printed British one, not the other one that his father had in Germany. Nor did he offer his naturalisation papers, which he calculated were nobody's business at that point. Later perhaps, more would have to be revealed.

The officer jotted down details on a form. He returned the certificate. He looked at Max carefully with pink-rimmed eyes set in a pale, pinched face. Max, being taller and sitting up, could see that he was balding, a little round patch in the fair hair as the captain bent forward to write.

"You have an unusual name, Mr. Beaumont? French ancestry perhaps?"

"I don't really know."

"As a recruit you will call officers sir, you know. So you might as well start now. Just sign this form here will you, and I shall witness it!"

Max signed with the pen he was given, and the officer fumbled in a canvas haversack, and pulled out a small paperbag of the kind banks use to hold coins. From it he extracted a bright silver coin, and pushed it across the table top with his forefinger.

"Just take that will you?"

"What is it – sir?" Max picked it up curiously.

"A shilling! The King's shilling! You have taken the King's shilling and you are sworn in! We don't go through the other rigmarole, but that is still part of the volunteer drill. You will find lots of tradition goes on in the army!" The officer stood up, and Max did too. He looked at the coin in the palm of his hand.

"Can I spend it?"

"If you want to. Lots of you young men who come in here blow it on a beer! Others say they'll keep it as a souvenir. It's yours – do what you like. You are free to go now. Did you decide in which arm you want to serve?"

"With the tanks! Sir!" Max said.

The buff brown envelope came through the letter box in King's Road just three weeks later. It enclosed a rail warrant and ordered Max to report to 30 Primary Training Wing, Bovington, Dorset.

I looked at Max Beaumont sitting there in the library as he reached that point, and knew that his mind was not really with us. There was almost a physical change in him as though he was adjusting himself from one physical environment to another. His eyes had hardened, and the lines round his mouth tightened, and everything he was telling seemed of curiously new importance. He was explaining, but it was as though it did not really matter whether we understood or not.

"You were a Trooper when you went to Bovington not a Private. I never liked the idea of being a private soldier. There's nothing private about soldiering, and at its worst, there's none of the kind of privacy that most men need to

234

even keep sane. Has anyone been to Bovington, or know it at all?"

Jane Milward said she had, and for some reason she blushed when she said this, and when he grinned, it implied they shared some piece of intimacy. It was extraordinary how he did it with all of them, young, old, plain, ravishing, of any extraction of nationality. I had once seen Max Beaumont at a Film Ball, distract the attention of a well-known actress who was talking with Humphrey Bogart, which surely says something.

"I went to see T.E. Lawrence's cottage," Jane was saying. "It's at the end of that lonely road that leads through Bovington. I thought it would be somehow exciting and romantic, after I'd seen Peter O'Toole in the film you know."

"I do know." Perhaps in his mind, Max was on that road again. "There's a loneliness up on that sweep of tank-training country that is unique. In the winter I arrived there it was like a harsh black and white photo, and with the wind biting across the Bovington parade square, it seemed like the end of the world."

CHAPTER ELEVEN

He was, by any standards, still very young that winter of 1941, Max Beaumont conceded, and it was difficult to look back and try to identify his feelings about those first weeks, the shock of being turned from a young civilian into a soldier. They were a mixed lot, those who arrived to share the tar-blackened barrack hut with him, forty of them, sleeping on two-tier wooden bunks. The windows had to be kept as clean as laboratory optics, the wood floor scrubbed white, and the barrack room table scraped with old razor blades, to satisfy the corporal who slept in his own room, guarding the door. He could still smell that hut, any time, a mixture of Carbolic and metal polish, and the bedding straw in the palliasses that made a lumpy mattress under grey army blankets. The worst moment was when he had to make a parcel of his civilian clothes and the army sent them home. It seemed as though part of himself was taken away, never to be returned, and he was not trying to be affected, he hoped we'd understand, and he recalled these things for anybody who had not been through it.

The other recruits were a very mixed bunch, all volunteers, some straight from a few well-known public schools, the rest from everywhere and anywhere, builders apprentices, shop workers, stable lads, mechanics. It was a good thing, Max Beaumont said, that he had also started work, because he knew what it took to earn a weekly wage, and made him acceptable all round.

It had occurred to me more than once, while Max Beaumont was working through these reminiscences, that certainly everything about his early years, his upbringing and background, must have been of inestimable value in the adjustments he had to make. He had been an only child.

Then during his first years in England, he lived in the care of two women, developing a strong heterosexuality, and his very mixed school experiences had early taught him some basic rules of self preservation. Starting work early would have sharpened inherited characteristics and perception, turning to advantage all that made him Anglo-German-Jewish.

If a young soldier wanted to get on in the Armoured Corps Primary Training Wing, Max said, it was a good thing to start with no preconceived ideas. A few simple loyalties, and no side, that might have to be knocked out of him. Rich boys had a harder time than poor ones. It was an advantage for a new, young tank trooper to have been used to eating plain English food, to hard manual labour, sleeping in a cold room, and not complaining. There was no privacy. You washed and shaved in cold water. It seemed like all that he had read of the Crimea and the Great War. In fact he was right. The barrack huts were from 1914–18, and at this level of the army, not a lot had changed.

There were no lockers for possessions. Every day all that you had been issued, blankets, mess tins, gym kit, spare boots, extra uniform items, underwear, even toothbrush and razor, had to be laid out in a precise pattern for inspection. If there was any flaw, retribution was swift and often seemingly unjust. Extra fatigues and drills were routine. When you had a rifle that you knew was as clean as tired eyes and fingers could make it, you were told it was filthy. In addition, told you had not stood close enough to the razor, and in reacting then as you did, you were dangerously near committing Dumb Insolence and Silent Contempt. All this, as you stood to attention on the open square in that winter's bitter wind. While other squads marched and counter-marched to the wailing harsh screams of the drill sergeants, and the crash of boots in unison. Turn! Stamp-stamp-stamp! At the end of the square, the flag of the Royal Armoured Corps on its tall mast stood out stiffly in the wind, a splash of red and yellow against a steel-grey sky.

"The sound of the trumpet call at both ends of the day were the loneliest sound I had ever heard," Max Beaumont said. "Reveille was before daylight, and the stars were still out. Last Post, at the end of the day, so sad and mournful, and fit only for the graveside.

"Have you ever shaved in cold water, Mr Owen? Or tried the taste of tea out of a metal bucket poured into a mess tin just licked clean of porridge? It smells like hot pee – if you'll forgive me!"

"I use an electric razor," Owen said off-handedly. "But I know what you mean. I sail boats, day and night watch – I've had tea like that."

"Well," said Max Beaumont, "to show how life has changed, if you'll push that button, Jane, that one by your end of the sofa, then we might get a cup of decent tea." He glanced across at Rita Henckman next to me, and spoke in German.

"Oder Möchtest Du Lieber Cafe, vieleicht?"

She nodded, just the merest inclination of head in response, her eyelids drooping like a china doll, but she said nothing, and I wondered if she was going to be around much longer, because in my experience, once the foreign TV lot had got a feel of what a programme or a feature was like, they pushed off, and the rights department took over if their report was favourable. I was more interested, having picked it up, in the "intimate" *Du* that Max had used. To be charitable, it could be that he was more up to date with current German usage than I was. A lot of the new generation now went straight into the familiar *Du* like our wonderful English language permits all the time. Rita Henckman had passed the age when *Du* as between an adult and a child, was routine, and as if she knew this, she leaned over towards me, the unbuttoned leather jacket open, and asked me to pass an ash tray from the nearby table. All that was adult and feminine, protruded briefly, from her white shirt front.

"If we are to have a cup of coffee, I would like a cigarette! I can smoke I guess? Thank you!"

When Boris had brought the tray with tea and coffee, and Jane had poured, and cups were handed round, Max shifted in his chair, sipping his tea while we waited. Then he moved forward slightly, resting on the arms of his chair, and

238

held his cup with both hands. I saw the knuckles whiten slightly as he began to speak again.

"I have often thought of the talk I would give if I was running that RAC Primary Training outfit – what I would tell those young troopers about the training, which became more specialised, and relentless, and demanding, and was never explained. Not in real terms, that would have made sense!

"To fight a tank, as an officer, you had to be a trained driver, a gunner and a radio operator as well as tank commander. How else could you tell the crew what to do? The failure rate was quite high. The real fear all the way through, was that you might be busted – RTU they called it. Returned to unit! But at no time could we have any idea what we were being got ready for! Have you ever gone without food for twenty-four hours or more? Perhaps you know how you feel when you haven't slept for three days and nights? When you hear and see things that aren't there? Remember when you had a really bad stomach? Diarrhoea, headache! Look back at that time you got caught in real rain, a winter storm, cold as well as wet, for hours – days sometimes – you couldn't change clothes! Owen, the off-shore sailor knows that bit! Think of the most bloody awful noise you've ever known! Perhaps like standing on the underground platform when a train goes through at speed, and there's the shock wave, too. That's only faintly like one small shell going well overhead. Did you ever get really scared? A near-miss car accident, so your brain fused, and you struggled to breath and you've seen somebody you were fond of, in a road accident in a nasty mess? Listen! Lump all that together! Now judge a distance – two hundred yards or two thousand? Remember the one-way streets round Hammersmith, recite five strange phone numbers, get the direction you're facing! Now give confidence to all of us in this room – all shit scared! That's what we were being trained for!"

It was, all in all, quite a performance, and when Max Beaumont stopped speaking, I wondered if he would be able to put it together again if I asked him to in the studio.

"It isn't fashionable to talk about it like that!" he was saying quietly. "It isn't the usual cinema version. But you

239

don't forget." Certainly he had not got over the exhaustion of those first weeks of training, and at times during the first fighting in Normandy and after, he had often wondered if it would have been better to have been told about the miserable realities, the humiliating small things in some precise, steady army language.

There was nothing that could prepare you for the reality of battle, reality that meant the action, all the technicalities, maps, weapons, timing, judgement. Time, place and weather too. The heat and dust of France and Belgium in the summer of forty-four were one thing, and the crippling, unbelievable wet-cold ice and snow of Holland that winter, was another.

Of course, there were instructors at the Junior Leaders Regiment who had seen front-line service, mostly in the desert. Two or three of the officers were wounded, one had a patch over one eye, and wore the military cross alongside his eighth army desert-service ribbon. Another at the gunnery school had a distinct limp, and it was rumoured had an artificial leg, but nobody liked to ask. Most of all, there seemed no way to ever ask that key question: "What's it *really* like sir?" What was it like when you were wounded? The information was never proferred, it was a closed subject.

The RAC Junior Leaders was a war-time, élite training regiment, formed to turn out tank commander NCOs and Officers. Max Beaumont had gone there from the primary training with a good report – unknown to him. Several of the others did not, and were posted off, usually to infantry regiments, because the basic principles of infantry was already part of that first three months, and it was rammed home that every tank soldier must be prepared to fight on his feet if his tank was shot from under him. Certainly he had seen it happen, Max Beaumont said. You did not just take it for granted that you drove around in a tank. As he learned, he realised that much was in common with his beloved Red Indians. Even the process that went into attack and defence methods were just the same as in McPherson's gymnasium. You presented as little target as possible, you feinted, you gave ground, you wheeled round and when you moved went in quickly. Some other things were familiar. The tracer, fired from a Bren gun at night, made patterns like he had seen in the sky over London. Learning to strip that Bren machine gun, and put it together, while lying on the ground beside it, and in the end blindfolded, seemed not very different from some of the repairs he had done on his motor-cycle. Only in the army it had to be done as a drill, counted, by numbers, so that you could do it automatically with one hand. "Because you've been hit in the other arm, see?" said the instructor, shortly.

The homesickness that had been almost debilitating at first began to go, when he had written to Aunt Sybilla almost every day at first. She had replied as frequently. One letter he had kept, from the many that had been preserved by her. It had dark, unspoken implication between the lines, that spared neither of them. It was about the gas-chamber.

As part of gaining confidence in their equipment, Max and his troop was marched to a miserable weed-grown piece of wasteland. They were to sit on benches inside the concrete bunker there, and the door would be closed. A quantity of the real thing, phosgene gas, would be released into the chamber. With gas masks on and shown to work, the instructor would knock on the thick observation window. It was an order for the masks to be taken off, and anyone who did not take off their mask would be on the serious charge of disobeying a direct order. They would then know why all ranks in the army had gas masks.

When they stumbled and fell out of the chamber, weeping and half blinded, retching, lungs feeling as though filled with barbed wire, most of them lay on the rough ground, or sat slumped up against the outside of the concrete chamber, eyes closed, heads pounding.

The army does not like walking-wounded lying around, and after a few minutes, the gas masks were back in their packs and each small detachment was fallen in and marched away.

"At the double!" shouted the corporal. "Get that stuff out of your lungs!"

"None of the others, I think, felt involved like I did," Max Beaumont wrote to Aunt Sybilla. "As we took off our masks, and that gas seeped up from the tablets, we sat there, miserably beginning to choke, and I thought of them. We had heard about it already by then. The ones we knew, and all the others. Was it like that, with no way out? And for a moment, I thought I must get through that door, and I sat, and because there were tears streaming from all the others eyes, I looked no different."

The training got tougher, and more specialised, and you could never really explain to anyone outside, what went on, or was happening inside, to yourself. The RAC Fifty-eighth Junior Leaders Regiment's one and only function was to turn out tank commanders who could win wars. Montgomery had decreed that the British army was to comprise soldiers who had "a fit brain in a fit body", and in the same spirit if you were to command tanks you had got to be a trained driver, gunner and radio operator. You also learned to run in boots, carrying forty pounds of equipment and a steel helmet and rifle, and you changed from PT kit to parade battle dress, and into denim overalls, and back into drill gear, and then round again. You learned to forget nothing, no single detail. To polish *behind* your cap badge, and the soles of your boots, and for every default there was penalty and punishment. Extra guard duties, so that you became so tired you fell asleep in the technical classrooms and were punished again. One minute late for anything was a crime. There was a precise height at which knees were lifted when marking time, arms had to be swung to shoulder height. Officers were saluted for six paces exactly, before the arm was brought smartly to the side and the head turned. It mattered. It mattered all the time. For ever afterwards it would matter. For *remembering* horse-shoe nails, was how battles were won and not lost.

When they at last got near to the thing that it was all about, real battle tanks, they had no preconception of what it could mean, but there was a sort of date-with-destiny about it. They had seen the dust plumes, far away on those bleak hills beyond the camp, and occasionally much closer, a Covenanter or Crusader had come clattering and rumbling through the Bovington lines, at the regulation five miles an hour on its way to the workshops down the hill, the faces of the black-bereted crew caked with dust, as they peered from turret and driver's hatches. The heavy, growling roar of the

242

engines revved and eased as the metal track plates squealed over the sprockets. They were like hugely dangerous metal monsters, and Max and the others stood and watched in silent awe. They would soon look like that. They were going to learn to control, and turn and goad those monsters, fire the long, fingering guns from the strangely delicately moving, restless turrets.

They learned to drive trucks first. Small ones, big ones, alone and in convoy, by day, and by night. Every morning, paraded by their vehicles in crews of three, they found some fault had been set up, nothing would start until it had been found. Simple things, a battery lead that looked connected but was not, petrol turned off, plug leads detached. Then more complicated. The last crew to locate and rectify the trouble was, of course, automatically on fatigues. The first tracked vehicles were the open, fast little Bren-gun carriers, steered with two sticks, locking alternately or both tracks, like tanks. You turned them round too fast, and they lost a track. This taught you how to replace track-plates, pins, sprockets and tensioners, and in the classrooms, with their models and diagrams, the bits and pieces were explained. Transmissions, suspensions, gear boxes, carburettors, dynamos, distributors, starters, lighting systems, lubrication. Then there were written test papers.

"If you thought that as a tank commander you would ever have clean hands you know now you won't!" the chief instructor said.

Was it the model trains, the Schuco or the bicycle? Nonchalantly, Max Beaumont said it seemed he was a natural with machinery, and written tests bothered some of the others, but not him.

Then, out from the tank park each day they went in the real thing, cruiser tanks, out onto the tank training grounds, that blasted heath, a deformed moon-landscape, with every feature that could test your driving ability with forty tons on tracks, at up to fifty miles an hour.

You had to realise that everything on a tank was heavy. To sit inside the bare, metallic driving compartment with its close, flaking, silver paintwork, staring through the rubber flanged periscope, or jacking up the squat seat to peer out

243

above the hull, you grasped the two stubby control sticks that were like bicycle handlebars, and instruction came through the earphones of the headset clamped to your head. Pressing the starter button for the grinding scream of the start-up motor brought on the thundering heavy rumble of the hugely powerful engines. Max soon found those engines could be blipped like a sports car, while he watched the flicking, trembling needles that showed revs, temperatures and pressures.

He learned how to claw up seemingly impossible slopes, balancing the tank like a circus elephant on the ridge, then lower it gently down the other side. Away then, making those engines bellow up through the gears, moving the lever between his knees, until the heavy armour was crossing terrain flat out. Then you struck an unexpected pit or fault, and the crash of bottoming suspension and the swearing of the instructor in the headphones mingled with pained cries from other pupils in the turret.

"It's no use knocking out your own side when you're being paid to kill the enemy, Beaumont!" The instructor said.

It was interesting that the gunnery course instructors, with their ballistics and fuses, ranges and persistent safety drills, were different types from the NCOs who taught tank driving and maintenance. For one thing, they explained, there was little purpose in just farting about in a tank and talking on the radio, because that was not going to kill any Germans or Italians or for that matter Japanese. The guns were the point of the whole thing.

They had a great invention called the pellet range. This reproduced shooting from a tank's main gun, but saved the cost of real shells, by mounting an air rifle inside the gun barrel. The turret of a tank was set up in an indoor shooting range, and in front was a long sand tray, simulating a battle area, with small model houses, trees, a road with a truck convoy, a badly concealed anti-tank gun and toy infantry hiding near a wood. There were small wooden tanks, that moved jerkily, and unexpectedly into sight.

"You load the pellet gun!" said the sergeant, reaching through the open framework of the mock turret. "Here's your ten rounds – put 'em down there in that tin lid, right?

244

Now when you pull the spade grip trigger, the gun will fire! When you twist it right the turret will traverse right, and left for left? Is that clear?" There was always an obligatory reply.

"Yes, Sergeant!"

"Now, Commander!"

"Sergeant?"

"You give the orders, depending on what you see! Everyone listen now, because this is how you work as tank commander and gunner, and I shall tell you only once!"

"Two pounder! That's to tell the gunner which weapon you want him to use, see? If you want the co-ax machine gun, say so! Then you give your distance. There's going to be lots of training to get distance judging outside, but in here there's distances marked out on the sides of the range, see them? You shout it out! You will have intercom for the real thing, but we can all hear without that now, so give the range, and tell the gunner what it is he's looking for through the cross-wires. Ant is anti-tank gun, see? And Hornet – that's an enemy tank! And make it clear and no messing! No squeaky voices, like some troopers I know what got their balls kicked off!"

Easily, naturally, Max Beaumont had proven as much a crack-shot on the pellet range, as at distance judging, and equally on the tank ranges at Lulworth Cove, where they fired the real guns. These were the two-pounders, and later the six-pounders of the British tanks, which had been made to answer the Germans deadly and vastly superior eighty-eight millimetre. At Lulworth, Max learned to load the turret bin-racks, with the heavy pointed shells, some armour piercing, some high explosive, coloured-coded and marked accordingly. For an air burst, to go off above ground, especially useful to kill an anti-tank gun crew, you could set a screw fuse.

Inside the turret he pressed his right eye against the soft rubber telescopic sight, watching the dancing cross-wires, elevated or depressed the gun, swinging the turret round with the spade grip, and combined trigger. The noise was disorientating. A heavy blast within the tight confinement of the turret as the whole tank lurched on its tracks. The flash of light flared beyond the cross-wires of the sights. Then on the target a sheet of red and yellow flame, as an aged truck or tank hull, a thousand yards down the range, was engulfed in fire and smoke. The slam of the heavy gun breech returning, and the clang of the empty shell case falling onto the metal floor of the turret, or sometimes into a canvas collecting bag, was a useful alarm bell to return reeling senses to alertness again, to the reek of hot metal and pungent cordite, unforgettable smells and fumes. Things sometimes happened that didn't seem so funny, because you were being marked and watched and moved like a chess piece all the time.

It was at the gunnery school that Max knew the fear of certain failure. The final skill involved firing the big gun from a moving tank at a moving target, and he sat in the turret of an outdated Valentine tank, while down the range a motor with a cable pulled a heap of shot-up metal as target. As the driver turned the Valentine round in tight circles, he had the two-pounder on it through the cross-wire sight, while the sergeant instructor acting as commander, above him in the turret top, called the fire orders.

"One thousand, hornet moving right, a.p. fire!"

A.P. was armour piercing and the loader had slammed the shell into the breech, while Max had the spade grip traverse hard over to the right. He felt his right leg being pulled suddenly into the metal-work of the turret cage in front of him as his overall trouser caught on something. By his own traversing action he was being dragged into the cage, so that his fist tightened round the trigger grip in automatic reaction. The shattering crash, that filled the turret with smoke, came as the two-pounder shell left the barrel.

According to the enquiry afterwards, Max's shell had screamed over the roof of the gunnery-school officers mess in the valley below with its customary noise, like an express train. It was near enough to midday, for a number of officers in the mess bar to spill gin and tonic over themselves, fellow officers and the mess carpet. While up on the range, with the expletives of the gunnery instructor in his ears, Max was being escorted under close arrest to the guard room.

He learned once again, the army's remorseless code of responsibility. It was the sergeant instructor in command and in charge, who was on court martial. He was reduced

246

to corporal and posted to regiment. Max had not even a chance to apologise. He had a week of sweeping leaves, extra guard duties, and more basic military principle from his squadron leader.

"You could be returned to unit! Your instructor has been. You would be posted, to a regiment as a trooper! But that would be thinking of you, not of the country! You are a trained tank driver, your gunnery training is finished and you have experience of armoured corps work as a leader! This has all cost the country thousands of pounds. We know that in learning to drive a tank you have, like all troopers, probably already broken several hundred pounds worth of machinery! Now get out! Get on, show us you're worth it! One more like that and it's RTU!"

On the radio operators course the theme came from a thin, watery-eyed sergeant back from the desert-rats with plastic-looking skin on one side of his face. One day, in a Nissen hut instruction room he changed the subject abruptly.

"Maybe you lot would like to know why I don't ease up on the bloody morse! I'll tell you why I and the rest of the instructors in this dump keep going for you! Pushing you, making it tough! It's not for you we care! Its for the ones who'll be dependent on you – all you lot from here will be officers or NCOs. So you've got to be good, see? Bloody good! The lives of other blokes are depending on what you can do with the radio!"

Physically, Max knew he was fitter, tougher, leaner and harder than he had ever been, as he moved on to the final phase. Tanks moving across country, changing formation from line ahead to arrow head or abreast formation, covering each other, as they leap-frogged forward, hugging positions whenever it was possible to get hull down, or turret down, hidden behind high ground.

Curiously, there were only two of his troop from that time that he remembered. One he recalled was burly, thick-lipped and with gleaming brown eyes. Jon Rondhem was his name. He looked like a Panda bear because on those final exercises every man's face was a coated, matt dust mask, with the white shape of goggles left behind, when they were lifted up to the black berets. In one of the barrack huts he had shared bunks with this burly, fair-haired trooper, who took the bottom bed because he said you got away with inspections better if you had the bottom.

"You wouldn't have thought of that would you? Beaubum, or whatever your name is!" His panda-like pink tongue came through his thick lips. "Sounds to me as though you're a Frenchy Jew boy! Well that's OK with me, Beaubum! Because I'm a Serth-Efrican Jewboy see? My Dad sells gold in Johannesburg! When this lot's over, I'm gonna be a millionaire! What's your dad do, Beaubum?"

"He's a banker."

"Well if you get to be a banker you buy my gold! OK?"

The other remembered face was quite different, pale, gentle and horse-like. "Andrew – please don't call me Andy!" – was the son of a vicar from Winchester, and had long pale eyelashes, but also a calculating expression that changed to a beatific smile when something went wrong.

Both of them were sent with Max to WOSB – the war-office selection board – as potential officers. Before that there were interviews and talks with the training officers, and the commanding officer himself.

A key question would always be: "Why do you want to be an officer?" It was deceptively dangerous. There were those who answered with the old-fashioned response, that they wished to better themselves. Or that they wanted to become officers because their fathers had been officers. Anyone who answered that they wanted to sleep in sheets or the chance of better food, or even to be recognised as a superior kind of soldier was certain to get no further.

For Max the question had come during a long wait on an exercise, when he had been studying the map, sitting in the front of his Bren carrier. He was surprised to find the Captain of the Royal Tank Regiment, who was one of their instructors back from the desert fighting, the one with his stiff-legged walk, leaning beside him on the carrier hull. Again Max saw beside the desert star ribbon, the MC. He had a countryman's plain weather-beaten face, and a small corn-coloured moustache that looked as though it had been stuck to his upper lip as an afterthought, some kind of joke. In fact he was rarely seen to smile at all. For a while the Captain steadied himself against the carrier, as he used binoculars, and when he lowered these, leaving them to hang round his neck on the strap, he had unexpectedly asked:

"If you were given the chance to apply for a commission, Beaumont, would you?"

Max had turned round to look at him. Under instruction there was no need to stand up, which otherwise would have been routine, and he sat, holding the steering sticks of the carrier.

"Yes, sir, I would!"

"Why would you want to be an officer?"

He had answered without thinking. "My father was an officer, sir! I'm better if I'm responsible for other people! I need to command to get the best out of myself and help others, if that makes sense, sir!"

"It might do," said the Captain, and took himself off.

Max found himself at Winchester WOSB, in a squad of ten, with some candidates who were older and included a corporal in the Scots Guards, a commando sergeant, and a sergeant major from the army pay corps. In spite of the differences in age, background and service experience they shared a common ordeal for the next three days. This was the ultimate test. Had you got what it took to make an officer? Everything in Max strove to keep steady, to maintain a cool, thought-out approach.

There were tests, written and oral, they shared meals with the examining officers, who seemed to be watching how they handled a knife and fork, there were assault courses with individual and team challenges, and tactical exercises out in the field with imaginary situations presented for response.

"You are in command of the group here!" Max was told on an empty hillside. "You have standard infantry weapons and a two-inch mortar. Enemy parachute troops, probably not more than two dozen, have seized that railway bridge, and are expecting reinforcement within the hour. Run your O Group!"

Maybe he made it seem a big thing, the way he explained it, Max Beaumont said, but effective O Groups had meant a lot ever since. O stood for Orders, and it could be for a small handful of people, or the kind of thing Monty had done for

D-Day, with three hundred high-brass following his pointer across a blackboard at that secret HQ in Hammersmith. The formula was the same, and maybe for TV we would find it as useful a way of making decisions that lead to action as he had.

First you had Information, because without Information, every scrap of it, you could get nowhere. Enemy troops first. Who? How many? Where? Then Information Own Troops. And that meant who was on your left, right and upwards. Next, Intention, and that was probably the most important bit of the whole thing, and you kept it very short and to the point, so that no one could forget. We *will* take the village, seize the bridge, hold the high ground. Or come to that, take over the bank, buy the TV station or start the colour supplement, and the important thing is that everyone should know exactly that real objective, because afterwards it would all get very noisy and confusing, and you had to keep that main intention firmly in mind.

Of course he ought not to forget Method, and you spelt that out by saying who did what, and where the centre line was, and there was Administration at the end, and Inter-Communication, because unless that worked, and the codes and signals were clear, you got chaos. All he could say was that it was a system that was effective in really bad conditions, such as Harvard Business School never dreamt of.

Max Beaumont got up, and I was glad that he did, as I had been going to do the same, because if there was to be the promised evening of theatre-going, I had to leave. And for a moment we both stood, and looked at each other, and I knew that he still stood straighter and looked fitter and younger than I did, and maybe it was all to do with successful "O" Groups.

The others got up more slowly. The two women actually stayed sitting, Jane reading back silently from her notebook, and Rita Henckman with her still face, and half-closed eyes, looking edgy and restless. She it was who spoke before anyone else.

"Why do we have to stop now?"

"I've got to break, because Liz has signalled there is some urgent development around the Sunday papers. Tolly you and I must have a private session before this show hits the road! Is that still an expression? I get so out of date." He had returned from the past, and was once more the cool wielder of power of a far greater order than anything Sandhurst had groomed him for.

"Signal?" Joe Bailey, brow wrinkled, peered over his spectacles, Joe who missed very little. "Does Liz do telepathy? I didn't see her put her head round the door? Or did a buzzer go?"

Max Beaumont looked at him. Not in any way perturbed by the inquisitiveness of Joe's questioning. It was merely a slight sharpening of the chiselled, aquiline profile, in Joe's direction.

"Correct! You saw nothing and heard nothing, Mr Bailey! Not telepathy. There are so many clever tricks with microchips now, and our printing union friends do not like any of them! I have a silent vibrating pager in my pocket, OK?"

Rinski, normally the outside man, as Mrs. Beaumont called him, came to show us out. With his dark-blue chin and unsmiling eyes he looked me over as he opened the double-bolted front door.

"Are you coming back, Mr. Tolly?"

"To-morrow!" I told him.

"Mrs. Tolly's waiting for you, sir!"

"The taxi-cab you mean," I said. "There will be another one for the others."

"Mrs. Tolly showed up on the monitor quarter of an hour ago, sir!"

"What?" I must have looked startled.

"That's alright, sir! We've got a TV programme here too! On production all the time it is! Monitoring cameras round the house! I saw Mrs. Tolly arrive and park under the trees over there!" He pointed, and I could see the Volvo now, with Chloe winding down the driver's window.

"Thanks, Rinski!" After looking round, Max Beaumont was nowhere I could see. I started down the broad stone stairway and across the gravel drive.

251

Chloe pulled me across for a kiss as I got in, and turned the ignition key. We moved out between the gate pillars, and as we did, I just spotted a figure with the two guard dogs, pulling back behind the rhododendrons.

Chloe always stared straight ahead when she was driving, the way the school had taught her all those years ago, but she lit a cigarette while steering. Now I was able to look at her, and I saw her face was made-up and ready for the theatre outing.

"They just go out riding three or four as a party, and dressed the same, so that nobody would know who's who! That Liz Charlton told me. There are more people watching over Max B. than you think." I spoke, because we could share thoughts.

"Thank God we don't have to live like that!" she said, and meant it.

"Look, if you threaten to sack five thousand people, and with them are a lot of the most militant kinds of trouble-makers in the country, don't you take all sorts of precautions? More like in France or the States? The way I hear, there has been what amounts to sabotage and accidents in the Beaumont plants for a long time. It's one of the reasons Max Beaumont wants someone he trusts to give him a good image!" I said. "The programme is billed for Thursday. We just made the *Radio Times* cover. If there is trouble Down at t'Mill, he'll need good viewing figures!"

"I don't think Max is the only person heading for trouble," Chloe said. She still looked ahead and I still watched her, but this time one hand did come off the steering wheel to touch mine.

"OK, I've made a few enemies over the years!" I said lightly. "In the Fleet Air Arm we didn't get the training the armoured boys did, but I expect I could collect a flak jacket from the Beeb!"

"I think it's the Beeb who could be drawing a bead on you, darling! Which isn't very funny. But I'll tell you, and risk spoiling our evening, because I think you ought to know. Jerry Potts phoned this afternoon."

"Social call?" I said.

252

"No, not social call," Chloe said. We had stopped at traffic lights and now she looked at me and I could see she was anxious.

"Darling, he says you'll probably get a call from the Assistant DG. About what he calls the developing situation around Max Beaumont." She puffed hard on her cigarette as the lights changed.

"We shall be out this evening, so that means to-morrow!" I said. "Then I could be at church! Then walking the dog."

"Felix be serious!"

Back at the house there was time to have a drink and I poured a small one for Chloe too.

Jerry Potts I had known for twenty years, he was senior editor, News and Current Affairs and had been with the Beeb for twenty or more loyal years. He and his wife Barbara were the Edinburgh Scots-come-south kind. Four kids, certainly grown-up now. I decided I would have to give Jerry a quick call, whatever it was about.

Chloe had changed already, into a blue and white silk dress. My oldest offspring, Jennifer, was with her mother on the verandah, also dressed by *Harpers and Queen*, I thought.

"Can I have a drink, Daddy?"

"I don't see why not. What's that dog tied up with?"

"It's the ribbon I didn't want. I liked this blue one better!"

"Not to the theatre with the aged parents?"

"Colin! Actually his birthday. He's the boy you said was bright," Jennifer added helpfully. "He wants to become a Tory prime minister, that's why I chose the blue!"

"What's a drink?" I said shortly.

For some reason I had a sudden mental recall of Max's Aunt Sybilla, and the blue-lined drinks cupboard that taught how Dry Martinis were made. How early did they start now? I suppose my daughter probably hit the hard stuff regularly.

"Gin and tonic please!"

"The future prime minister driving I hope?" I said. I fetched Jennifer her drink, and put a splash of Courvoisier in an expensive glass from the study's private cellar for myself, and dialled Jerry Potts at home.

"Jerry!" I said. "How's the Bush? Seething with gunpowder and plot I hear. More important how is Barbie?"

"Right now I've no real idea." Jerry had the level voice of a Scot educated at an expensive English school. "She's in Edinburgh with the two boys, probably in the castle doing a sword dance with a pure malt or an impure friend!" There was a short silence between us. I could hear Jerry clear his throat and knew that he was unhappy.

"Felix! I talked a wee bit with Chloe, but I guess she's left it to me, and you'll know well enough that it's the sort of leak I wouldn't pass on to anyone. I'm after all only – what would it be? Ten years younger than you are?"

"A Junior," I said. "Let's have it."

"The Assistant Director General himself. I don't know whether the Governors are onto him, but he's likely to be onto you Felix. It's considered hot, your Max Beaumont programme. There's Gitsen saying he's not been happy about it for some time. He's no friend."

"I once told him at a dinner party that he didn't understand the political role of television!"

"That would be when you were the darling of the age, Felix old sunshine! Now you're little bit older, can you afford to tell Channel Controllers?"

The Courvoisier took a clammy hold and I drained the heavy glass tumbler.

"So what's in the air?"

"Its more a case of what's going to be allowed to go on the air when you get Max Beaumont running live next week! I don't need to tell you that it could be Beaumont is about to blast Fleet Street apart with this move to Battersea! The unions have only just realised that he's got them across a barrel, with his new all electronic set-up. It seems it can be operated by a handful of journalists and electricians!"

"Listen Jerry!" I said wearily. "That's not news, it's been that way in the States and Germany for some time."

"OK. Let's put it this way. There are people, but only some of the people, who think Beaumont is the first to be blowing an overdue whistle on what has been a dirty game for far too long. There are others who put him in the rogues gallery of unacceptable faces of capitalism. What are you going to show him as? Felix! There are a lot of National Union of Journalist card-holders in the Beeb! If

254

you whitewash Beaumont when all their mates in The Street are out of work what might happen then?"

"I think journalists are in the end intelligent enough to know what it's all about," I said.

"People are suggesting that this is a typically clever move of Beaumont's, to get himself favourably portrayed at just this time by an old friend!"

"Jerry you grieve me!" I said. "Is that my way? The producer – you know Owen Owen – and two of the Night-watch team as well as myself are on real depth preparation, and we're not yet finished. The big stuff is still to come. Far more thoroughly than I would normally do, because I don't really know the man, nor does the rest of the world. Nobody has had a chance to find what really shaped Max Beaumont!"

"Felix – they're saying you're an *old* friend of his. It needs one of the young, bright, see-all-sides babies! I just thought you'd like to know!"

"They can't cancel me now!" I knew that was not true. It had been done. "I'm printed as scheduled in the *Radio Times*! We've had two thirty-second advance flashes on the box last week!"

"Like I said!" Jerry had done his bit. "Give my love to Chloe!"

"Thanks pal!" I said, and meant it. "Do you know what Clausewitz said? First safeguard your line of retreat!"

"Well whoever he was, he had the right idea!"

"Give my best to Barbie!"

I put down the phone as though it had some nasty disease.

The way things were turning out, that evening was the best possible thing that could have happened, because I had more or less forgotten, something that I needed, and was going to need in a big way. My Face Is My Fortune bit. I thought of what Jerry Potts had said. In my shaving mirror these days, I saw a pale, watchful face with a large pair of spectacles, grey hair, still plenty there, but the wrong colour, and a mouth and jaw that have become – could it be slack? Maybe from earning my living by talking.

We took our seats in the dress circle of the National. It is then that you notice that one is being noticed. It sort of runs along the rows, as they wait for the curtain to go up, because there is always some rinse-haired matron who has read the programme and started her first chocolate and had time to look around.

"There's Felix Tolly, in the front row! With that good-looking woman, obviously much younger! Wonder if she's his wife?" And the low excited murmur goes along the rows, behind and around. During which I move the bow tie, and look around, as though I too was searching for friends, and Chloe who can hear it all and loves it, reads me the cast from the programme.

Fame is not even a many splendoured thing because it is not real in any of its versions. I will not claim modesty, nor many other virtues, but I know that on that particular evening I was glad to be Felix Tolly, veteran newscaster, interviewer and TV celebrity, note *not* Personality! They come two a penny. The irony was that Max Beaumont could have walked onto that stage as the curtain went up, and I doubt if anyone would have known who he was.

Afterwards, at the Caprice it was the same, although there I daresay Max would have had a few tables to nod to, and people who would come over. The Caprice with its good food and enviable reputation is also glitz and showbiz. It is not my favourite for a quiet evening, but it passes on an expense account for TV trade, and Chloe likes the pink tablecloths and the way they do her favourite langouste. The People who do come over to our table, in the way that is more Beverly Hills than London, greet her by name. Which is nice, if your fortune is not your own face, but your husband's.

I was still feeling good, a kind of quiet restored sense of the rightfulness of things, when we got back to the house.

Until the phone rang. It had to be someone on TV time. The study clock said nearly one in the morning.

"Two things," said Owen Owen without preamble. "It's been another innings with Max Beaumont after you left, and he went off in the end with the German girl, to take her down to the new plant where they're expecting trouble to start tonight. Joe and I think she's not averse, if I may put it that way. We weren't asked, and Jane is even miffed."

256

"Owen," I said. "It's getting a bit late tonight for these games. For me."

"Not my real reason for calling, Felix. Earlier on, Graham Gitsen was looking for you. He says it's urgent he speaks with you over this weekend. He asked me how far we were with the controversial Beaumont feature. His description. Somehow I didn't like it, Felix."

"What the hell's going on, Owen?" I asked him.

"Politics I think," Owen said bleakly. "Listen! I've dumped the notes and tapes of the session you missed at your place. They should be there somewhere. Max Beaumont won't give us any more time until to-morrow afternoon. Jane asked to be let off, part of what I was telling you about, I think."

"Don't call us, we'll call you," I said.

"Not original, but understood," Owen cleared the line.

On Sunday mornings, Chloe always brought coffee to the bedroom for me, and her own Earl Grey tea. For this ceremony she wore a rose-petal silk gown, and settled into one of the bedroom armchairs to re-read the theatre programme. She had already weighed me down with the pile of Sunday papers that the good Beeb paid for, but could not force me to read. Usually I sat up throwing onto the floor the ones with the headlines I disliked, and reading the front pages of the others, like Churchill during the war.

The straws in the wind this particular morning were that there was no colour supplement with Max Beaumont's *Sunday World*, and his pop tabloid *Weekend* was only thirty-six pages instead of fifty something. All his friendly contemporaries ran varying degrees of comradely stuff on the impending confrontation between him and the Fleet Street unions as time ran out on his proposals for them to switch to Battersea. It seemed that already part of *The World*'s production had gone electronic at the new plant, and a large part of the distribution had been achieved by private road haulage, to get round union blacking at the major wholesalers.

I reckoned it was easier for Churchill, as he sat up in bed in the famous siren suit. There was censorship then, and a Ministry of Information, and he had only to pick up the scrambler telephone and he would be told the truth, the whole truth, even the depressing truth about any battlefront. So that when my phone rang so far-too-early, I hid behind a newspaper, which was to tell Chloe that I was much too famous to pick it up myself at such an hour.

"Who is it?"

"Graham Gitsen!"

I counted to ten and took the instrument from her. "Felix Tolly!"

"I must apologise for a rather early call on Sunday!" Gitsen was not only too early, he was too urbane, too up, too shaved, too dressed and devious. "I hope I haven't disturbed you? The point is, I've been asked by the ADG to have a word with you. He left for New York last night you know." The flat, level, clearly enunciating voice. It would have been nice, for instance, if he had mentioned who he was. Perhaps living the life of Max Beaumont was bad for me.

"And to whom am I speaking?" It was surely deserved. But he knew I knew.

"You must have been told! Graham Gitsen here! I think we need to have a word about the Beaumont situation, because you are, shall we say, masterminding this one, although I haven't heard it said that you are executive producer. Owen Owen is Producer, and will have to be considered as that."

I continued to listen to the words coming through the ear piece, like a xylophone being struck on one bar. I had had enough, I decided, as something snapped.

"What the hell is all this?" I snarled. The ensuing short silence was Management dealing with Difficult Talent. Gitsen sighed, audibly.

"A talk," Gitsen explained. "Because I don't think we want this on the phone, Felix, and that is why I am going to suggest that I drop in at your place, so that we can have a quick review of things. I'm sorry, but we don't think it ought to wait until tomorrow. Barnes isn't it? I'm on my way to Epsom for a round of golf, so I can come your way, quite easily!"

Gitsen arrived at half past ten, which gave me time to get ready. He parked his BMW outside the front door, and this enabled me to meet him on the porch, where I suggested it might disturb the Sunday household routine less if we went straight round to the garden-house and had our talk there.

I had met Gitsen before of course, and he had changed little. He walked across the back lawn beside me, a short, stiffly upright figure, wearing those rather awful aids to golfing, the baggy, overcheck trousers, in purple and green, topped by a pale yellow cardigan and shower-proof jacket. I did not ask him about his handicap, nor make any observation on the suitability of the weather for the sport of golf. I wanted to get this over.

We reached the big, wooden garden-house, and sat down on two of the cushioned seats that faced out across the small silver birch copse and the pond. The summer-house smelled pleasantly of kindly nature and the seasons of the year.

In the manner of a man who has some unpleasant task ahead, Gitsen looked momentarily nonplussed. I made no move to be helpful, and now that I came to look at him again, I decided that his small neat face, well-shaven but with the blue-shaded jaw, and the rimless spectacles gave him a put-together appearance. When he spoke there was no real movement of his mouth.

"The fact is, there's a good deal of worry about this Beaumont programme, Felix! He has last night given notice to more than five thousand staff, including journalists. You've seen this morning's papers I suppose?"

"I have," I said. "I think the notices apply to the machine and distribution staff. Very few of the journalists."

"It's all getting very dangerous, and potentially explosive – typically Beaumont," Gitsen said. "The Corporation has to be politically so careful – more than ever these days. The other thing to consider, and I'm sure you have it in mind, Felix, we employ a large number of people who are National Union of Journalist members. Now!" He held up an arbitrator's hand. "What happens if this thing spreads? As it's bound to! It could bring out our own people, and have TV and radio badly affected! Beaumont is not the most tactful person, and the unions are telling us that he

259

is totally intractable and unreasonable and they have the distinct impression that he is no longer open to negotiation. Something they have never met before!"

"Look Graham," I said. "I know a good bit about Fleet Street too! I've worked in and around it as much as anywhere else, most of my life. It is the prime example of what the world has in recent years called the British sickness! Scandalous overmanning, unbelievable restrictive practices, top of the league pay levels – far above coal-face working miners levels for instance – and with no relationship to work, hours or skills. OK – some managements share some of the blame, as usual! The newspapers have never stuck together, and have let things go from bad to worse under what has amounted to blackmail. Now Max Beaumont, using technical innovations, and aided by no-strike contracts with the electricians, plus help from the rest of his empire in the States and parts of Europe has the courage to fight! He talks in a way, as though a lot of business life was still a military operation, and perhaps it is. He has said that for too long the unions always had the ultimate weapon, and now he has got it! He will produce papers at this new high-tech plant without them if need be – just a relative handful of journalists and members of the EETPU."

"That's not the point! Not all the electricians like it!" Gitsen moved about uncomfortably on the hard wooden bench. "In the Corporation we have to keep more in touch with these things than you, Felix! Try to think what happens if our electrical people walk out! I was asked to sound out your attitude to the overall situation and I must say I think your siding with Beaumont could be very dangerous! It's a politically explosive situation!" Graham Gitsen repeated. His voice did not rise, and I realised I liked this less than if it had.

"Why do you say political?" I tried.

"Well surely that's obvious! You know this government's attitude to unions? They will welcome Beaumont's action. But I'm sure we cannot afford to. Or should even present him in a favourable light! The thing is really, to get to the point – you have been a long-standing friend of his, and the whole question of bias in a major programme of this sort, at just this time, is not something the Corporation wants. We have suffered for it too often in the past!"

"You can't cancel me now," I said coldly. "It's in all the printed schedules. We've run the usual teasers. Beaumont has always been a largely unknown figure to millions of people, and apart from the sensation the other day, the current situation makes him even more newsworthy. How can you avoid suffering being accused of bias, censorship, trade union pressures and a few other things? That's happened too!"

"It must always be our position to see all sides!" Gitsen's manner was as though he was reading from the Corporation Charter. "A lot of people think you will be far more sympathetic to Beaumont – than for instance, Roger Bullen!"

"Roger Bullen?" I said. And I knew instantly now how the chess pieces were being set out.

"It might be better to have him handle a programme like this, and change it to a balanced, all round consideration of all sides, including Beaumont with others! Not one man's life story. Nothing has been decided yet," Gitsen said. "It's a question of several things we are looking at. It might be a better way than cancelling altogether, which could be an alternative."

"I'll tell you this!" I said. "If you move someone else to work on this programme, I shall tell him why I'm not doing it! And tell a lot of other people too!"

Gitsen looked sad. What had gone before had been stalking. Now he slipped the bolt. But his voice was still the steady epitomy of the reasonable man.

"We were looking at your extended contract, Felix, the ADG very recently. Because you are of course still getting major exposure and assignment beyond the Corporation's usual retirement age. That has to depend on review, and that is on-going. What the book calls continuous review, and that in turn depends on whether you still have employable abilities, whether you are adaptable enough to go along with guide lines, a department determined policy and other things."

The time had come to end this game in the summer-house and send Graham Gitsen to try the tactics of golf. I got up. I

261

might not be Max Beaumont, trained in the harsh practice of annihilation. But I had not been able to live near the top of TV's curious dung heap, nor had confirmation the previous night that my audience was still there, without knowing that Gitsen need to be put off his stroke.

"You must go and knock the little white balls about!" I told him, as we stepped out across the grass. "And I will consult with my conscience about your advice, Graham. And as that is a fairly hardened organ, I daresay the noise will be heard at Portland Place and a few other places. I do hope none of it will reach you before you reach the eighteenth!"

The white BMW had left, even as I saw there was another car, a sizeable Mercedes parked in front of the garage block, as I went back into the house.

"Where is my wife?" I asked Leone, the older of the two au pairs.

"She is in the salon with another lady, but you are to go in! They have coffee for you too!" Leone said.

It was Mrs. Beaumont, sitting in what was normally regarded as my chair, looking as composed as though she would like to be there for the rest of the day. She wore a cashmere pullover with tan-coloured trousers, and the over-red mouth smiled genuinely in my direction, as she waved a hand and a wristful of gold jewellery at me.

"I didn't drop in. I told your wife I wanted to see where you both lived, when we had lunch! And she asked me over! Max has been gone all night, and he is still not home. I rang after breakfast, and heard you were busy, so it seemed a good time. It seems that German TV girl is interviewing him." The smile went quite pointedly as Debby Beaumont looked straight at me.

"Do you want coffee dear?" Chloe was fussing about now in an unfamiliar sort of way.

"No, thanks! What with one thing and another I think an early-day Scotch is what I have in mind!"

I went to the sideboard. Rita Henckman was not yet on my list, but I could see Mrs. Beaumont and I might. have problems to share. "I have just been, if I am not mistaken, morally threatened," I said as I poured from the decanter. "Does it sound as though I shall be seeing Max this afternoon? As planned?"

I did not propose to sit with the two of them. I figured Chloe would tell me what passed between them, if it was any of my business. Now I wanted to get to the telephone. That Mrs. Beaumont had come over to visit Chloe was unexpected, but it was a budding friendship that could do without me I felt.

"Chloe dear, you and Felix must enjoy such a calm life here!" Mrs. Beaumont was saying. "You see, Max never stops, and after all there is not much in years between the two of them."

"I am going to be in the study," I said politely. "I have to catch up with the Max Beaumont story, and the notes and tapes are in there." I paused at the door, "I shouldn't worry over much about German TV!" I said. "We can get rid of her in two minutes!" Prophecy again, of course.

CHAPTER TWELVE

Sitting in the study I plugged in the recorder Owen had left, and looked at Jane Milward's notebook with a paperclip marker, and Joe's separate pages from his clipboard. Joe seemed to like the yellow, lined paper which marshalled his quick clear hand in straight furrows. I found myself now, considering Max Beaumont not as a person, a friend, but as a piece of work, a study, even an experiment, and then the first words on Owen's tape had Max's voice-back, telling how he felt too.

"This is the damn strangest deal I've been through ever I think! Having orders to sit here and talk – well it amounts to orders! Let's go on! I'll keep on talking!" He did. I could close my eyes and Max was there again. "There was no greater thing in his life than going to Sandhurst. You could not possibly explain that. Not comprehensibly to outsiders." The phrases wound on with measured emphasis. Sandhurst was an Officer Cadet Training Unit for armoured units only, and there was a distinction, history and panache that belonged only to Sandhurst. The place was not a boys' school nor a university. It had always been, and still was, a professional institution that turned out leaders who could fight. You even had to go to a pre-OCTU to get ready for it. A preliminary canter before the race proper, and it was like Max Beaumont to make that comparison, and he recalled pretty clearly what the Commanding Officer said to Max's troop when they paraded, at pre-OCTU.

"Now that you are here you have finished your other rank existence! In addition to extensive work, you will have a great deal of PT. This is essential! When a battle is over, an officer has to look after his tired men – in fact start the day all over again, before he gets any sleep himself. His Squadron Leader may easily send for him with new orders for the next day. Attack, or counter-attack goes in at dawn. So an officer has to be much more fit than his men. If you are untidy or slack, other ranks will want to know how you have come to be selected for a commission and may take a dim view of all officers as a class."

The first thing Max had noticed in the new existence was that the barrack room had spring beds, polished floors, individual lockers, and space, and it was a big moment when the corporal who showed then the dining hall called the cadets "Sir". Even more interesting was to find at that first meal that they were waited on at table by girls of the ATS.

About that time he had had a short leave pass and gone back to Aunt Sybilla in the King's Road, which had become under the Blitz almost a different world. There were few shops open, most with boarded up fronts. There were sandbags piled in front of doorways and over cellar openings, with white daubs to mark corners and edges of the pavements in the blackout. From Paultons Square there flew a barrage balloon.

Aunt Sybilla was now living in the one front room, that had lost most of the glass in the two windows and was partly boarded up, so that electric light was needed all the time. She had moved her bed in there, and suggested Max sleep in Dairy Mary's old room behind the kitchen.

She had told him that he too looked different.

"It's that awful haircut partly! And the way you stand, and move. Those old clothes of yours don't fit you really do they? I'm afraid I can't spare any coupons for you and I really don't know what you could buy anyway."

"I shall wear my uniform," Max told her. "I don't feel comfortable in these things. But I have got some coupons to give you – for food rations!"

He did not tell Aunt Sybilla that she looked very changed. There was an exaggerated blackness round her eyes, which were yellowed and dull, and her mouth had become a thin line. He noticed how grubby everything was, and even Aunt Sybilla's clothes seemed dowdy.

"I never thought to see you turned into a soldier, Max," she said. "I don't know what I can offer you for fun, which I'm sure you need. I seem to have so little time even to keep this place clean, there is so much dust from the bombing, it gets everywhere. Of course, I'm still working on the BBC Foreign programme."

They were both sitting at the table, having finished tea, which had included the last of a rather fine chocolate cake.

"It was in a food parcel from the States, our relations over there seem to be doing a lot better than we are. Now that they are in the war, there are lots of their people in uniform over here too. I go evenings to one of their clubs to help. They're very polite those GIs I must say, and their uniforms seem to be altogether smarter and better cut than yours, dear. Why is that?"

In the end they went out to a little restaurant that Aunt Sybilla knew. It was one of the curiosities of war-time rationing that no coupons were required in restaurants.

Max felt an unhappy mixture of guilt and relief when those three days were over, and he returned to the Blackdown pre-OCTU. He was straight away put to learning how to take a motorbike up almost vertical hills, through rivers, over boulders and across ravines. There were six of them in each squad under a sergeant instructor, a pack of helmeted and goggled figures, their Enfield bikes growling and surging in formation as they made for the trial grounds.

What did this teach you? Well, you knew what it meant to drive through the seat of your pants, Max explained. How to judge terrain, not as the infantry did, but for a vehicle. With only two wheels you paid at once for any mistake and you got to know exactly what an internal combustion engine would and would not do, which prepared you for tanks, those most complicated of cross-country machines. A note on Joe Bailey's yellow paper was interesting. It was just a thought, Max Beaumont said, since the other day, and he passed it on for what it was worth, because life was all cause and effect. But when he saw a motorcycle anytime, he gave it more than a cursory look, and when he looked at that particular motorcycle and its riders in Belgrave Square that day, he knew with instant certainty that they were behaving strangely.

You could take it or leave it, but that was just one of the legacies of wartime training, and there were others of course, more from later on, and they got over-layered in the mind, and every so often things would come up, and you did something automatically, because that was what it had done to you.

When Joe Bailey asked whether that was what seemed to matter, being disciplined into a state of almost robot conformity, and Max Beaumont had told him what the Squadron Leader said on the last kit inspection before Sandhurst, Joe had noted it down.

"It isn't a matter of great importance whether you show a mug the right way up, or webbing equipment is not quite up to standard, or you leave bolts and magazines in rifles – which is actually, a more serious matter. But it *is* important that while you are under training you learn attention to detail! Time after time I am told by you cadets that you were in a hurry, or that you forgot, or something. The time may come when you'll forget something much more important than a mug or a buckle, and a fearful price will be paid for it!" It was the same lesson, being taught and absorbed, forever, amen.

At Sandhurst, as an incentive to remind you of this, should you have erred, you might have to double round the perimeter road in full battle order, with packs, steel helmet and rifle. On a sweltering hot summer day this stretched physical endurance to the limit, and drove iron bitterness into the soul and you had to drive and goad yourself and for Max it was still the same poem, to *force your heart and nerve and sinew to serve their turn, long after they are done*! Dear, tired, dowdy Aunt Sybilla had been right, and he wrote to tell her so.

When he first saw the white stone Georgian elevations of Sandhurst, the great Palladian entrance of the Old Buildings, with its columns and broad steps, Max felt a strange, almost predestined association with the place. Was it possibly the long Prussian line of soldiering that would always be part of him? This had long been a school for British officer cadets, now to include him, in its shaping and moulding. It was all very well to laugh at things like that, if you didn't know how much genes counted, in reconnecting where you belonged.

In the Royal Military College, each cadets' rooms had only two beds, there was a servant to look after them, old retired soldiers, who as batmen cleaned belts, gaiters and rifle slings. Meals were in a dining hall, with table-cloths and glasses, and you no longer had to bring your own knife, fork, spoon and mug. There were more civilian servants to wait at table and ATS girls at the hot-plates.

And then there was the gold Royal Military College cap badge to mount on the black berets, and that special moment, when back in their rooms, they undid the neck of their battledress blouses and wore collars and ties.

A large, full-length mirror in the main entrance hall had in gold letters over it, words that had clearly stayed with Max Beaumont over the intervening years: *Are you a credit to your regiment*?

In front of those noble Georgian elevations Max learned other things. The punishing 160 light-infantry paces a minute, with rifles at the slope, until it felt as though his legs and arms were breaking. There were lectures and PT, battle-drill, map reading, night patrols and compass reading in the dark, forced marches doing one hundred yards in quick time, and one hundred doubling, carrying platoon weapons, Bren guns, mortars and shells as well as rifles.

In the darkness, albeit the lanes near Camberley were black and white with moonlight, a tall, lean Welsh Guards sergeant spoke to the cadets, as they lay with their feet up on their packs by the roadside. Nearly all the instructors had seen active service somewhere, and he had been in the second phase of North Africa.

"You'll be thinking you're alright in the tanks! None of this! Would any of you have heard of the hill four-o-three? Aye, well nor had we! The Yanks had been pushed off it by the Jerries, and we had just landed from the ships see? So we did what you're doing now, because there was no lorries see? Officers too, aye at the double march! Thirty-three miles! It was in the dark too, the only time it was cool out there, and then we went in, no stop! Over the start line with bayonets. Showed the Jerries and the Yanks how the British army does it see?"

On a week's final in Wales at the battle school, where live ammunition was used, the small, wiry infantry Captain who met them, explained the course.

"You will fire live ammo, mortars and Brens! You will do night exercises, crossing water in rubber boats under real fire. You will be taught how to use plastic explosives, fuses, the lot! You will sleep rough and you are bound to get wet – this is Wales! The school is allowed two per cent casualties."

Max was shown how the plastic lumps and the firework fuses, if placed cleverly, could make a ten-ton rock jump. The instructors were like laconic burglars.

"Take the tow from me – blow on it to keep a glow! Now put it on the fuse and turn carefully away! That's when you're most likely to fall – don't look ahead, look where you're going – steady, you've got time to get behind that next rock. BUT WALK. Don't run!" It was the same rule on the hand-grenade range. If a grenade failed to explode, it was always an officer's duty to blow it up placing a fuse. WALK there, walk back.

Otherwise, they doubled everywhere. By day, and by night. In attacks on empty and battered buildings, practising street-fighting in the little flint and slate villages, commandeered by the War Office. They climbed to the top of Snowdon up the back way, at night, when it was snowing, and Max found himself labouring upwards with half a dozen others. Two of them Canadians. Several of these, former NCOs, were in his troop, and by any measure they were tough, smart soldiers. As they clung to an outcrop, panting and heaving for breath, the snow wetting their faces, the Canadian with snow on his moustache, who was nearest to Max, pulled something out from his pack.

"Just like back home this, bud!" It was a bottle, the size the Canadian called a fifth, and the rye whisky burned a torch trail down Max's throat, making him cough and splutter. Then they climbed on, with the mounting noise of the wind in the dark and snow that stung their faces.

Back at Sandhurst they worked on the notorious Monkey Hill, with its high rope bridge, the cat walk, thirty feet above the ground, the vertical rope that swung across a wide divide. Max Beaumont said, that it might be a strange confession to

269

hear, but he had a secret password, something to hold onto courage, and he knew others had secret words to overcome fear, he had heard the tense whispers.

That the whole person that was Max Beaumont now, was a metamorphosis, was becoming clear. The Junior Leaders' Regiment, pre-OCTU, Sandhurst, had all added up, and made him rigorously, aggressively alive. He loved the stress, the demands, the mental and physical agility, as they stretched his endurance to new limits. The all demanding training at Sandhurst grew more intensive, and left little time for thinking or reflecting about anything else. Now once again, Max was with the tanks. They seemed like old friends. Churchills and Covenanters for driving and maintenance, gunnery with the six-pounder and the mounted machine guns, Besas and Brownings. The radio course stepped up operating skills and security on the air.

"You will keep all communication down to the absolute minimum." The humourless, instructing officer was taut-faced. "Why? Because all the time the bastards are listening in! Searching the frequencies, building up a picture of whether your troop, regiment or division is on the move. The Germans are very good at it. If you use any special words, or Christian names, they can even tell from previous contact how you are likely to move. No, I am not exaggerating! Why do you call up with, '*Hullo* Charley Baker Three!' And not drop the hullo? Simple again. If someone is not quick, they could miss the first part of the code sign. That is why we have *Roger* for Received and Understood, and the response to an order which is *Wilco*, meaning *will comply*! *Over*, is a word that means a response is expected. *Out* means no more is coming, nor required! Our Yankee chums say *Roger and Out*, one word too many, one more bit of help to the enemy ears!"

Cadets changed to different coloured shoulder lanyards, yellow for driving, green for gunnery. If you survived that, there was the increasing seniority of white for the wireless wing, and finally the red lanyard of collective training. Even by then, there was still the harassing uneasiness that something could go wrong, that all the time your card

270

was being marked, and you could be failed – returned to unit.

The assault course was now longer, three miles in battle kit, running in boots, up the steep hills, and through water to make sure you had soaking wet feet, the dozen or so PT sergeants, in their black overalls and gym shoes, ran alongside, encouraging, exhorting and throwing down thunderflashes, and the plastic percussion grenades that were allowed.

It was when he was labouring up one of those small hills, slowed to a panting, lung-rending haul, half-blinded by the sweat in his eyes, that Max heard an instructor trotting alongside. His admonitions were not the official ones.

"Come on cadets! Come on the cream! Get on the salt of the earth!"

In front was one of the Canadians, a big, burly ex-sergeant himself, and as the thunderflash exploded between his feet, he stopped, lurched sideways and swung a vicious back hander at the taunting instructor.

"Get the fuck out of my way you bastard!"

In a second the black-overalled instructor was leaping on his shoulders to bring him to the ground, with two others sprinting to the scene.

The Canadian cadet had seen service in North Africa with operation Torch, and had been a tank commander. Provocation was pleaded and failed, and when the troop filed into the white-washed lecture room for the weekly troop officer's lecture, they heard the small, 17th/21st Lancers captain, with the MC ribbon and the ugly stitched scar on one side of his face, speak quietly, in his flat, unemotional voice.

"The Commandant had no choice on this! What happened on the assault course was that a potential officer showed clearly that he could not keep control of himself under duress, claiming in defence that he was provoked." The captain lent on his elbows on the lecture desk and looked round the silent rows of his listeners. "A lot of provoking things happen in war! As an officer you cannot control other ranks if you cannot control yourself, that is absolutely

271

basic. Does anyone know a certain line from Kipling's *If*?"

There was an uneasy stirring along the benches. You remained seated when answering in these lecture classes, and Max Beaumont stayed put.

"If you can keep your head when all about you! Sir!"

"That's the one." The captain shuffled some papers in front of him, material for his weekly troop officers' talk. They had been getting steadily more advanced, more wide-ranging. History, mixed with recent strategy in Russia and Italy, and from battles of ancient Rome, the Middle Ages to the Boer and Crimean wars.

"Clausewitz to start with today," said the Captain. "Anybody know anything about Clausewitz?"

It was almost the next line from *If*, Max realised. The one about not looking too good, nor talking too wise, and Max had hesitated. But at Sandhurst they wanted to know what you knew, and you took the risk.

"Five main principles, sir! Number one being to safeguard your line of retreat!"

"Right, stop right there, Beaumont." The captain remained unsmiling. "We will debate that rather strange proposition, but perhaps I might hear from someone other than Beaumont this morning!"

In spite of such moments, Max Beaumont did not get the belt of honour when his troop passed out on the parade square. It was won by his friend, the one who wanted to be called Andrew, the son of a vicar who had the saintly, killer's face. Less than a year later he was killed himself, early on in the battle of Caen.

Jane Milward's notes when I took those up, were interspersed with production. Two stuck in my mind – cursory quickhand that she would type out properly if needed. One said:

Best of him is full face. Straight, clever, good looks. Not soft. Profile, almost evil, quickly then gone.

Looks like Karajan. Upper lip, jaw, intolerance lines. Not telling us everything, by any means. No women? Times he smiles, to himself a memory. Then gone.

272

I put the tape-recorder and notes into my bag, and went to find Chloe.

Sandhurst receding, I was beginning to fret again. I saw that summer-house scene in the garden, when I looked out of the window, and Gitsen's baleful stare and smooth voice came back. I had nothing against Roger Bullen, who was a likeable young up-and-comer, who had cut his teeth on Northern Ireland TV before moving to News and Current Affairs. But his future was not going to include delivering my come-uppance.

"I see your surprise visitor has gone! Now for lunch?"

On Sundays people turned up, and Chloe was always happy to make food for half a dozen or more, so I was surprised.

"Listen! I want to talk with you quickly now, before you have to go!" she said.

"About Debby Beaumont?"

"Well I know, it was sort of cottage visiting, and of course, she is much older than I am, and they are fabulously rich. And she has that American, sort of all embracing whatever! You know, condescending kindly! But what is special about this programme on her husband? You've done hundreds of them before."

"It might be my last for one thing," I said.

"Well, I thought she had looked in because I had asked her to, in the silly way one does, but she got round rather quickly to the programme and how much it mattered to have Max presented in a favourable light."

"I've had all that bit," I said wearily.

"Darling, listen!" Chloe lit a cigarette and puffed out nervously. "I like Debby Beaumont. She's been married to him for thirty years, but not his only woman, either before, or – and this is what it was all about. All the time they've been together! Honestly, Felix! I know women can be like that too, but why tell me?"

"To get to me," I said. "They all think I wouldn't understand. I don't see other women anymore, of course! I know I've got to get some better glasses, and maybe I'd look more yummy with contact lenses. Is that my sandwich?

Could I have a Scotch and soda?"

Chloe moved to the drinks cupboard, but went on talking. "She says he has a sort of Casanova complex! Something to do with his Jewish bit too, some Semitic male thing. She is scared, in a dignified sort of way, that you and the others will somehow stumble onto something and quiz him until it comes out."

The telephone rang, and I left my working lunch sandwich, but I was able to take the rest of the whisky and soda along. It was Al Chemmy's private secretary and she was brisk and to the point.

"Mr. Tolly? You will be at Richmond this afternoon with Mr. Beaumont? Right, well a number of things may make it a bumpy ride – that's Mr. Chemmy not me, and he will be very glad to know you will definitely be there. Mr. Beaumont has a Sunday that is like most people's Mondays, but he is determined to sit in that library with you and Mr. Owen from three p.m. onwards he says!"

"OK!" I told her, and took in half the scotch and soda. "Let Mr. Beaumont know I shall be on parade!"

Max took no notice of my entry, looking out of the window at the broad expanse of cloud and sunlight over Richmond Park. I saw then the profile, the way Jane Milward had noted it. The aquiline and arrogance, and I felt for half a second that I didn't give a damn whether Max Beaumont came on the box under my patronage or anybody elses. He had on a sand-coloured suede jacket that buttoned right up to a high white shirt collar, and he still looked as straight and cool as doubtless he had been on that day of the passing out parade at Sandhurst.

Owen was the only other person there, and Liz Charlton quietly closed the door on the three of us.

"I'm glad to have you two alone," Max Beaumont said as we settled down in the familiar places in the library. "This is a hell of a time to be talking with all that lot going on at Battersea! I might get jumpy if needled I warn you!"

"Let's talk of War and Sad Kings," Owen Owen quoted. "You are a sad king inside aren't you?"

"No needling," I said.

"Far from it," Max Beaumont's charming, crooked smile was turned on automatically, but I could see he was tired. "Men with a great deal of power and money seem often to lose the essence of what life is all about. I have met a large number of them. Mostly they grow fat, and even look shabby, these billionaires. They haven't time to read books, or sit with scientists, or attractive women or academics. They don't know how to keep fit, and claim they haven't the time to ski, or swim, or ride the beautiful horses they might buy. If you look at their clothes you wonder if they even know the skill and patience of Savile Row, or the difference between Chablis or Chardonnay, or why a Renoir is preferable to a Rubens! You *can* enjoy a *Sole Meunière* and enjoy your own soul! My father was better with Biblical quotations than those Jewish banking relations! What shall it profit a man if he gaineth the whole world, but loseth his soul? And the last time I heard him say that was when we listened to Hitler bawling 'Today Germany – Tomorrow the whole world!' "

For the start of a new round, it was, I thought, quite a small tour de force by Max, in his way.

"Then if you are not a Sad King, what about Love not War?" said Owen.

"You don't remember the songs?" Max Beaumont said sadly. "*It's still the same old story, the fight for love and glory! The other night dear as I lay dreaming! A Nightingale sang in Berkeley Square!*"

"Oh my God!" said Owen, scribbling on a piece of paper. "I'll check if we can get them for background snatches."

Max was smiling.

"See if you can get the march they played the day of the passing out parade! *'It wasn't the tanks that won the war it was my boy Willy!'*

"The actual day you got your commission at Sandhurst was deliberately made something you would never forget," Max Beaumont said. "There was the slow march, almost like goose-stepping," he admitted. The high sky and the clouds shadowed, lit, then faded the wide expanse of the Sandhurst parade ground and the ranks of khaki and black-bereted

275

cadets, wheeled and counter-marched to the band music and the last of the screaming drill sergeants, until finally the adjutant actually rode his white charger up the broad steps as the high point of the ceremony, between the white pillars, and was gone from sight. Immaculately in step, the newly gazetted second lieutenants marched up the steps too, into a new life.

Max had looked coolly at himself in that mirror later, for the last time. The tailored service dress, the Sam Browne belt and cross straps, difficult to acquire, but you had to have one. The person who had helped him was the officer in the Royal Richmond Dragoons whose name Max had happened to see on an Order notice for another troop.

Some cadets like Andrew, had uncles and older nephews already in the Blues and Royals. Others knew the Guards, who had their own Armoured Division. The big South African, Jan Rondhem, was going to join an armoured brigade from his own country, already operational in Italy.

Max had felt once again lonely, the pains of rootlessness. The signature at the bottom of the Order, ranked a major from an unfamiliar regiment, but a familiar location. Max asked for an interview.

"Why do you want to join the Royal Richmonds?" The Major sitting in the usual bare whitewashed office asked shortly. His face was thin, pale, and when he breathed he made a faint whistling noise, that might have been his teeth, or the straw-coloured drooping moustache. But Max saw the DSO and bar, with the Desert Star, the stiffness with which one arm moved, and his eyes fixed on the black beret that carried a gleaming gold Richmond Royal stag and hunting horn in a crested circle. He knew the answer was not to say that he thought this regimental badge the most elegant he had yet seen. The Major had a folder on the empty scrubbed table between them, and he kept a finger in it.

"I was educated at Richmond, sir! I spent happier years there than other places. It is difficult to form a sense of belonging," he hesitated. "I think the strength of the British army is its regiments, and that you feel you belong."

The Major had opened the buff folder slowly.

"That wasn't the only place you were educated?"

"No sir. City of London!"

"And –?"

Max was, as the army call it, sitting to attention. He could not have suddenly stiffened, but a sudden chill moved up his spine.

"Berlin, I think," the Major spoke in a courteous drawl, and looked up at Max from his study of the folder.

"I was born in London, sir!"

"So I see! By the way, don't sit there peeing in your pants! You are a fully gilt-edged British citizen, certified by the Home Office. But someone who loves you, once wrote to the War box, and suggested it should preclude your doing military service for the country of your choice. What would be her motive would you say?"

"Love," said Max coldly. "My aunt, sir!"

"Women, old boy, always difficult! Now the details I have here suggest that you might, for various reasons, dislike the present bunch of Jerries more than most? Also, there's a military lineage that would have impressed Napoleon and Blücher, so why not let it go at that?"

"Sir! Does all this sort of stuff follow me around forever?" Max's cry was genuine. The whole subject of his origins and background had never once before been mentioned. The simplest details were shown in his army paybook.

"In the army – yes! The War box is not as slow as people think!" The Major's thin face smiled. "I am prepared to put you forward to the Regiment, Beaumont! And there is, in your favour, another point. There is a recent signal out, that all units should if possible have available not only one Intelligence officer at HQ, but active officers, as back up if possible, able to speak and understand German! Does that fit? Can you still?"

"It was my mother tongue!" Max wondered how he could ask, not yet having encompassed the British and their foreign language reticence.

The Major glanced down at a piece of paper. "What is *Schutzstaffelsonderdienstgruppe?*" he said slowly. His accent was appalling.

"A special task force, sir, one of the SS regiments I would say!"

The Major let this fall into the absolute silence of the small, bare-walled room for a few moments. Then he leant across the desk.

"How do you feel about fighting and killing your own people, Beaumont! Quite straight with me! No nonsense!"

Tough, hardened and totally trained as they had made him, nineteen-year-old Max Beaumont felt nothing. His answer was intense.

"They are not my people! Nazis! And all the Germans who are with them chose *my* people as their first enemy! They have killed and tortured and attacked them – first in Germany then everywhere else the Nazi army goes!"

"How do I know you can keep cool about it?" The Major leaned back, stiff, unsmiling, and Max Beaumont looked back at him, with his own eyes the pale colour of glaciers, and now he said nothing.

"I see, well, that's alright then!" The Major seemed to relax. "There's one more thing actually I'd like to ask you Beaumont, and it's a thing you must tell me honestly, if you know what I mean. Do you think the German army is as good as the British? Or better?"

"You have actually fought them! I don't know, sir! Now the Russians and the Americans are in it too." Max was cautious. "The Germans can't win, but they seem to have taken on the world! Who else could do that?"

"I'll tell you then, what I've seen, because I take your point. A lot of people are counting them as supermen, rather as you say. I shall not be in it again and when you leave here, you will! When it came to a straight fight, the very best of the German army, the Sixth, under perhaps their best General, Rommel, we licked them! Inch by inch, to a finish! No Russians, no Americans! Alright, with some of our own kind, from South Africa and Australia. And now we are better equipped, better experienced and trained! You will be fighting them! And you will show them again!"

It was the sort of piece that Max himself was later to din into troops, over and again.

"The big show is getting ready!" the Major was saying briskly. "Do you know what the Richmond's role is? I'll tell you. We're training as flail tanks! You've probably heard about them. They were first tried in the desert, called scorpions. They have all the weapons of ordinary tanks and will fight in the usual armoured role if called upon. But they knock mines out. The regiment is part of a division of so-called Funnies! For the D-Day landing! With flails, Beaumont, you must realise, you are pretty well out in front of everybody else!"

CHAPTER THIRTEEN

"The Royal Richmond Dragoons," I said. "We must get this, Max. On the eve of D-Day. What did flail tanks really have to do? I've seen tanks in combat on film, the Israeli-Egyptian war for instance. But flails?"

"Do you think people now want to know what a flail tank was?" Max looked at me quizzically, almost mockingly.

"The thing is," said Owen laconically, "You've got to be asked about the war, and what you did, OK? So you got an MC. You may have to explain to half the viewers what MC means! But yes, I think we ought to know what sort of tanks you were fighting in.

"What happened when you joined your regiment?" I said. "Let's start there!"

"They were up in Norfolk, a place called Thetford. The outfit was lagered in some woods."

"Again, what does that mean?" Owen asked.

"Tanks parked as an armoured wall, and supply trucks, and soft stuff with fuel and ammo and rations in the middle. It's a copy of the way the Boers did it with their wagons, so that you protect the vulnerable vehicles with the fighting ones. The tanks were American Shermans, and I had never been in one before." Max Beaumont was oddly tense, and I realised that it was not only the World Media situation that must be on his mind, but being asked to get back in those Shermans in effect, could even be needling if anything was.

"I don't do this often!" he said apologetically. "But I'm going to have a smoke if nobody minds! Thanks – in that box there!" He lit the cigarette slowly with the table lighter. "Shermans were quite a revelation. They were roomy inside, with a crew of five. Commander, gunner, radio operator and down in front, driver and co-driver. And I'll tell you, it was the difference of a big Yankee car, a Chevvy truck if you like! The British Convenanters and Crusaders were fast, but cramped and touchy, like a two seater sports car. I had learned about technical things, how they work and who got it right and who didn't and I've never lost that, whether it's print, computers, facsimile transmission, your kind of TV equipment or just a fork-lift truck! The inside of a Sherman turret was white painted. Now why hadn't somebody thought of that before? It made it all seem clean and bright, and the gun was a big seventy-five. The breech inside still took up space, and shells filled the racks all round, and there was a co-ax mounted Browning, and another for that co-driver, and we talked to each other through intercom. The radio was the British nineteen set, in two parts, one for talking with your own troop of tanks, the other on net to squadron command. A tank is packed with gear. There is just room to do what you have to, whether you are driver or gunner or commander. But the Shermans were reliable, a bit high in profile – not so good." Max looked at the glowing tip of his cigarette and then over it, and directly at us. "The Germans called them Tommy Cookers! When they were hit, they brewed up at once!" The cigarette stayed upright between his fingers, a thin line of blue smoke rising and dissipating.

"The flails were a British idea. They saved sappers the slow dangerous game of clearing mines by detectors and by hand. On the front of each tank were two big arms jutting out, and between them a heavy roller hung with chains with small cannon-ball weights on the end. When the arms were lowered and the roller rotated, the chains flogged round and beat the ground, setting off the mines. I had to learn quickly what it was all about. There was a whole division of special equipment tanks, the Seventy-Ninth, under General Hobart. There were floating-swimming tanks, and others with whole bridges on top of them that they could throw over ditches or streams, and things called vaccines which were huge bundles of timber wired together, as big as a house, which could be pitched into an anti-tank ditch by an explosive charge. There were flame throwers called crocodiles. All getting ready for the D-Day invasion."

"Half the world's interested in high tec. to-day." Owen was scribbling notes. "When this bloody flail thing went rumbling round, beating up everything, how could the driver see to go anywhere?"

"Have you got some pictures still. What was it like?"

"The box is always bringing some war into everyone's living room," I said. "Tell us!"

Max Beaumont was silent for a minute, drawing on that cigarette, looking at us, and then over our heads, outside the windows where the light had changed, with rain clouds in the sky, making it darker in the room.

"I will tell you two – sometimes I am inside those damn things again! Suddenly and without warning I can hear and smell and see them. You're right! The drivers could not see when we were flailing, three to a troop. The lead tank had a compass, and the turrets were traversed to the rear, the guns pointing backwards. The commander up above, looking through his periscope, talked on the radio to the driver of the tank behind him, to get his left tank track in the leading tank's right track mark! The same with the second and third tanks. The speed had to be kept identical, the language in the earphones was to the point. 'Charlie two, touch left! Left! More left! Right! OK! Hold that!' When I hear a truck driver being helped by his mate to park, I am back there again! The noise of the engines inside the hull, outside the metal tracks, and the screech of sprockets. Nothing to the noise of those flail chains! They sent earth and mud high above us in a thick wavering curtain of black debris, and as the mines began to go off, usually mixed anti-tank and personnel mines, the explosions were as though we had created our own shell barrage and were moving slowly through it! You could smell the earth and explosive even inside, the reek of engine fuel, everything rocking! Tanks are warships on land. And then, as you cleared the mine field, you pulled away and you could see other armour, that had been waiting, stream through the path you had made. Infantry in carriers, or running, crouching behind. Speed, speed! Push on! When you switched to the other part of the radio for command instructions, the air was alive with the language and crackle of a brigade on the move." Max Beaumont had slowed, to

282

the elocuted accents that were his normal light drawl. "Quite interesting in a way!" He moved his head round jerkily, gently stubbing out the cigarette in the ashtray beside him.

"Later, the Germans had what you might call funny ideas of their own, like burying sea-mines in the middle of an ordinary mine field, and I've seen those in Holland, after Arnhem. They throw tanks in the air like Dinky Toys! Do you remember Dinky Toys, Tolly? Now there goes that green I see!" Max Beaumont was sitting so that he could see the light over his door. "I hoped the battle of Battersea might lull a bit this afternoon. I wonder what Liz has got?" Quickly he rose from his chair and in a few strides was through the door, closing it behind him.

Owen Owen looked at me, and pushed a hand through the heavy hair on his forehead.

"Do you feel the way I do?" Owen asked.

"I don't know," I replied. "How do you feel?"

"As though I was in those God-awful tanks!" Owen Owen said. "I wish it didn't confuse me! Sometimes he sounds like a boys magazine. A kind of continuous line from Kipling to killing."

"Or getting killed," I said. We were different generations.

"Check!" said Owen. "So he wasn't! And we've got to find how he feels about that. Generally a big guilt complex. I've talked with some of the Falklands lot, and in Beaumont's war he was fighting Germans – partly his own people. And they were murdering and gassing and eliminating his other half! How about that for concentrating the mind wonderfully?"

"He's certainly concentrating now – just about all the time I would say. You can hear it. He was given a single-minded Holy Grail training like some old-time Crusader, and then he gets more power than is good for anyone. Forty-tonners that can blast things off the face of the earth, men saluting and calling him Sir before he's even twenty! And a permit to kill on a scale that makes 007 look like a country doctor! After which he used the same approach to become a civilian Field Marshal. But unlike Dwight Eisenhower, his former boss, this guy's articulate, intellectual and has actually read most if not all the books in this room! There's a flaw somewhere, Owen, I wish I could find it!"

"Let's get it right." Owen jerked himself up onto his feet, and looked round. "Just what is a leader?"

I got up too, and went over to the bookshelves, and finding what I wanted, the *Concise Oxford Dictionary*, handed it over to Owen.

"Look it up," I said.

Owen turned over the pages slowly, while I waited for Max Beaumont to come back in.

"Well!" said Owen. "I'll make a note of this for Jane to quote in the read-off for you! Here's the Oxford version: Direction given by one going to the front, example, encourage by doing things, deserved influence! There's more of course, but that'll do!" Owen closed the book and sighed and looked at the empty armchair where Max Beaumont had been sitting.

The library door opened again, but it was Liz Charlton who entered, trim in a black and white check two-piece suit, her hair held high behind her head by an ebony comb. For a moment she looked at us, unsmiling.

"What's black and white and read all over?" Owen said, smirking.

"Surely we have more advanced riddles than that in the BBC Mr. Owen?" Liz said. "Although I must agree, the newspaper business does seem to get more like a Christmas cracker riddle every hour at the moment! The latest is that Mr. Beaumont wants to go down to Battersea, and they won't let him! As a result I have to keep an office full of people here and this is headquarters at the moment."

"You mean he hasn't been into the new set up since the trouble blew up?" I was not being tactful.

Liz still stood holding the handle of the half-open door. "He went in last night. Not in the usual vehicle, but in one of these armoured vans, marked as though it was computer stuff." She looked at us both, and there was no doubt as we looked back at her, that Liz Charlton was all things that look all right to all men. "There was another passenger with him. I thought you might have known?"

"She's keen that kid." Owen got it in one. "Less interested in what we're putting together than the Brits in trouble, any time! Strikes, violence, democracy collapses! Who gave her permission to see inside the new Colditz?"

"The Chief himself," Liz said shortly. "As I say, she went in with him. There is tight security, has to be! But this one he arranged himself."

"I suppose we ought to see the set up." Owen looked at me. "Do we get a camera in there?"

"Mr. Beaumont is the person to speak to on that," Liz said rather quickly. "It could cause problems. It seems anything can go wrong at the moment. There are people working inside who don't want their faces on the box. Do you know how they are getting staff in to work through the pickets? With the help of hundreds of police! Mounted, riot shields, the lot! There are thousands of militants, flying pickets, renta-mob and the rest, as well as genuine protesters and workers surrounding the place now, and someone who was there last night told me it was like the storming of the Bastille! Burning torches, singing the red flag – the lot. I don't want to see any of our people strung up on lampposts!"

"Nor any of ours!" Owen said.

"Please arrange security passes and whatever else, Liz!" I said. "If I'm still involved, I shall have to go in and see it for myself. To know where Max Beaumont fits in, and what effect he has on the situation, and vice versa."

"I'll see to it." Liz Charlton was gone, shutting the door.

"Nerves, nerves, everybody!" Owen said. "Damn that German girl!"

When Max returned, coming in silently, the red light going on over the door above his head, it was as though there had been no interval, except we were all left standing, Owen holding the book in his hand.

"Liz told me you were having trouble, with spelling she thought?" Max looked his most innocent.

"Your Liz Charlton has just told us how things are on the river bank!" I said. "It doesn't sound good. When can we get down there with you? And by the way," I chose my next words carefully. "Why the priority visit for German TV?" Max's eyelids now almost closed, and he slid across the carpet towards his chair and sitting down gave a small, careful shrug.

"You weren't around, for one thing! She telephoned me. I agreed to pick her up, and take her myself. She wouldn't have got security clearance and a pass otherwise. The way we're having to operate there now, damn it, I can't even get in myself it seems! My directors are telling me to keep away!" He was not answering the question. "Do you realise, I can't trust ordinary telephone, fax or some of the people who work for us? I have to use private radio to my top executives! And travel about in different cars, disguised! Some car was blown up this morning I'm told. Fortunately nobody was in it."

The door opened once again, in spite of the red light and the man called Boris, wearing an off-duty striped waistcoat entered carrying a silver tray with glasses and the familiar green bottle with the gold foil top.

"The eye-brightener!" said Max. "I think you can probably do with it as much as I can. He waited until the glasses had been filled, and Boris handed round on the tray and left us again. "I went into battle for the first time on D-Day. And now it seems there is some sort of pitched battle going on in my own back yard as it were, and they are not even letting me attend!" He raised his glass, watching the bubbles rise, his face suddenly like a small boy.

"It was shortly after D-Day that I got rather involved in a special relationship with champagne," he said slowly. "Perhaps that's why I like to have it around. Remind me to tell you!"

All three of us drank, and were silent.

Before D-Day there was sudden leave, just forty-eight hours. All the regiments knew it was the last but it could not be called embarkation leave, officially. For second lieutenant Max Beaumont, it meant a train back to London and a phone call to confirm that Rachael, who had proved such an amenable squaw in those days of Indian summer, could get out of her duties, now as a Wren telephonist at the Admiralty section at Teddington.

"Richmond Park would be a good place," Max said. "We can both get in there in uniform."

Richmond Park was full of American troops, and their Nissen huts and more elaborate buildings, but nobody had tried to stop Max and Rachael when they went in through the

286

Roehampton Gate, which was the nearest to where Rachael's parents had their home.

They sat under one of the great oaks and looked across the Penn Ponds. Rachael was changed beyond anything he could remember, and he must have too, because she had told him so. In their uniforms, both felt young and beautiful and special.

"I'm only a rating," she said, and giggled. "You're an officer!" It seemed to matter to her. On a previous leave he had stolen Rachael, blatantly and openly from a boy they had both known at the Richmond school, who was in the unglamorous merchant navy.

"Do you know, an American army corporal gets more pay than I do?" Max said.

"Don't be Jewish, Max! I know we both are, but it isn't money that counts!" And Max felt then a sudden closeness to Rachael. They had known each other a long time.

"They have these Jeeps, look, there's one of them there!" she said quickly. "I wish we had them! They're super little buggies. Daddy says when they were first stationed in the park, they went out in those things, shooting at the deer. They can go all over the grass and anywhere!"

"Not anywhere like a tank can!" Max said. "They're the King's deer anyway. A hundred years ago they would have been hung – the Americans I mean!"

"Do you remember when you played Red Indians, and tried to shoot things with a bow and arrow, and you tied me up!" She snuggled close to him and giggled again.

When they got back to her parents house, she let them in with her latch-key, which somehow seemed both intimate and independent, and then in the kitchen they both took off their uniform jackets, his service dress jacket with its proud shoulder pip and brass buttons, and her trim, waisted navy-blue top. It was Max's first sight of her in the Wren's stiff collared, white shirt and he noticed at once how much Rachael had altered in other desirable ways, her shirt front filled out so pertly, and how she lit a cigarette, and when she put it down in an ashtray by the stove, the end was red from lipstick.

"What are you looking at?" she asked, putting plates to warm. "I suppose you're hungry?"

"I am," Max said. He put an arm round her waist and pulled her to him, sideways, and kissed her on the cheek. It was somehow expected, and they both felt better. He enjoyed a faint smell of geraniums on her skin. Or was it in her hair? She was looking at him, mock solemnly, eyes wide, wagging a finger.

"One of the girls said that all men look at your bosom first, then your legs then your face. Is that true?"

"All at once," said Max. "I mean all five!" And then they laughed, and kissed again, longer and more seriously this time, a sort of testing. And when she had picked up her cigarette again, and started beating eggs to make their supper omelette, he had taken out a handkerchief to remove the lipstick he knew was on his mouth. Girls in those days seemed to wear a lot more make-up.

"You can have some sherry!" Rachael said. "It's all we've got, and you can pour us both a glass. You'll find it in the glass-fronted cupboard in the hall. Daddy and Mummy won't be back until long after we're gone."

After the brief supper they sat on the sofa in the large dimly lit and rather over-stuffed drawing room with the black-out blinds down, and the electric fire on. Rachael put her blonde head on his shoulder, and somehow Max knew instinctively that she was thinking that was how the film stars did it, and also that there was expectation, and he brought his arm round her, his finger tips finding the shape under the shirt front.

She swung round, and put her feet up, still with the little black lace-up shoes on, and was pulling Max down and beside her, so that their faces were so close that he could see only that her eyes were closed, and she had parted her lips and was breathing quickly, her breath still sweet with sherry. He knew this was the moment, when he was expected to do something, things that were talked about in the barrack rooms with crude directness. But it was not like the time it had happened so easily with Dairy Mary.

He undid her shirt buttons, leaning on one elbow. It was all awkward, and surely not like it should be, because he could only reach one breast which refused to come out of the tight-fitting bra, so he pulled up her skirt hem instead, looking at the black wool stockings and the band of pale flesh where the top of

288

her legs disappeared into firmly elasticated navy-blue knickers. Was he supposed to rip them off her? Was this the moment to take one of the two French letters he had in his trouser pocket, and try to fit it on? He was not going to get much help from Rachael, who seemed to have gone into a sort of trance. For a moment Max felt a quick annoyance with her, it should all be easier than this, more clear cut, all consuming passion with everything literally slotting together. He began to kiss her on the mouth again, and now she responded closely, clinging, pulling him, with difficulty, until he was lying on top of her, feeling the new shape of his own rising interest between them. And then suddenly, the kisses stopped and Rachael tried to sit up.

"I've got to go! You know I've got to go! And you musn't keep me!"

Slowly Max shifted his weight and sat up blinking in the red light of the electric fire, and saw her face properly as though for the first time. Her make-up was in a mess, she had pulled aside her tie and in the open shirt neck one nipple now showed over the bra edge, like a small pink flowering cherry. He tried quickly to kiss it, but she wouldn't let him.

On the whole, it had been a failure of course, though Rachael phoned him from her camp call-box next day, and referred to it as their "making love".

Max found other possibilities in those waiting weeks, when the entire regiment, guarded behind barbed wire, felt the strain of tension and boredom. There had been only one leave pass for officers and other ranks alike. So there were carefully organised trips to local cinemas and ENSA shows. It was ATS drivers who motored the small vans in which officers travelled out of the camp.

One called Peg had a saintly, almost child-like face, with a small upturned nose and short blonde hair under the regulation cap which she usually took off when driving. But her green eyes and bright, painted cheek bones belied the saintly look, and she had not wasted time when Max had sat in the cramped passenger seat beside her.

"What's your name?"

"Beaumont," he told her. The army made you used to only one name. He glanced at her, sideways. The engine was still

running as they waited in a gateway entrance to a field where a football match was the attraction.

"Silly, the other one! They said it was Max, is that right? I fancied you right off, like most of the others. Bit of alright you are – with those eyes and curls and all!" She put a hand seemingly carelessly on his thigh that was nearest to her, and leaned over. "Give us a kiss, luv. Not too stuck-up are we?"

It was his first experience of service from the other side, and from someone who knew how to call the shots, as Peg did. It was also the first time that he melted to the Yorkshire pudding warmth and saltiness of those earthy vowels, and the ubiquitous Luv. The small hand moved swiftly, scratchily, like a kitten, over his khaki trousers and came to rest in the crotch.

"You open my buttons – just the top two there, don't worry about tie. An' I'll do yours, like that, 'cos I can feel it's nice and big but we can't take it out here." She had leaned close, touching and probing. "Go on – don't be a silly boy! Look down and see them, you'll like it, they're nice and big too! Give'them a feel cos' that's what I need, see!"

Max looked round, there was no one near. He reacted increasingly purposefully, suddenly aware of something in him that lusted with this kindred spirit, irrespective of rank or any risk. It was another discovery about himself, the special appeal in the Pegs and the Dairy Marys and their kind, that was to last all his life. Different from the subtle, beautiful high fliers that would always be there too. But often closer, in some different, shared quality they had, a need that lurked always near the surface, instantly recognizable.

After that the meetings with "Pokeable Peg", her own name for herself, that had at first shocked the aesthetic but sex-hungry Max, became frequent. She had used the quip about herself, when he had spoken quietly almost out of breath, searching in the half darkness to see her face.

"God, you really like it don't you!"

"Don't most girls?"

"No, I don't think so."

"Some of the boys don't do it like you do either!"

"I can't get those rubbers on except when you do it!"

"Can't take the risks sweetheart – not that it would be with you I suppose. Almost a virgin aren't you?"

290

"Not now," Max had said.

The system was simple. Behind some workshop Nissen huts was a painted metal waste-bin. If Peg was free she would leave a small rolled up piece of blue paper behind the bin. It gave a time for meeting, which had to be a brief period after supper and before the trumpet sounded Last Post. At that time of the year it was still barely twilight, but Peg had got a copied key to a disused store shack, and there, amid old radio sets, carboys and ancient batteries they made love on a rolled out hair mattress. Of course it was risky. As well as the guard patrols there were other people who might have the same idea. When Max suggested this, Peg was vague and seemed unworried.

Before long Max discovered why. All his life he never talked about intimacy to anyone. There was even a curious, personal taboo which he never really understood, about exulting over it privately, to himself. But he found other men were not the same. When some of the younger officers were together off duty, in small groups, they talked, and there were those who boasted. One of them, a small, handsome dark-haired fellow with a moustache, who came from Leicestershire, and in many ways seemed older than the rest, talking of fox-hunting and parties. As he drawled out enough of his conquests, while they sat, packed in his bedroom, sharing his bottle of Scotch, Max recognised with a sick misery that was like a kick in the stomach, that pokeable Peg was not an exclusive property.

Before he could think what to do or say about it, she was no longer there, and no rolled up blue paper for nearly a week.

"Peg? She got posted didn't she? At least you could call it that!" One of the other girls in the transport line told him. "Driving a staff car she is now, Humber Snipe! She was asked for by one of the Staff colonels up at Aldershot, and the Wing let her go. OK Handsome? Don't look so blue – there's more birds in the pie! At least that's what my Dad taught me!" She was Welsh that one, and the lilting accent had a mocking tone to add to the look she gave him.

Max had his ration of Passes Out, that made possible a visit to a restaurant if you booked a taxi, and signed the mess book, and were back at a stated time.

There was a little shuttered restaurant, unusual in that it was not far from the camp in the next village, really a small town, dead after dark, and the place never seemed to be very full. But they served one main course, a splendid grilled steak with chips and peas. No questions were asked, but it was not whale or horse. You could never be sure of in London. An elderly man and his wife ran the place, he did the cooking and she helped. Waiting on the few tables, lit by candles, was a tall, slim woman who seemed to Max to be almost middle-aged, although she was probably not more than thirty. She had dark hair fastened in a pony tail, wore ebony drop earrings, and spoke with a tired voice, scarcely moving the thin, mobile lips. He could hear an accent, but could not place it easily. On the chance of guessing right he tried French, and the tired face tautened for a moment, unsure, then lit up, in the candle-light as she was bending over the table, eyes bright, white teeth, the head on one side.

Madeleine became his next one. Nervy, lonely, experienced wife of a Free French airman, who had gone down on a bombing raid. They said he was P.O.W. But if he was, said Madeleine, why did he not send the usual messages? She lived with her sister in a shared flat over the High Street. Her sister was not married, and was in the French forces stationed at Aldershot. It was an easygoing arrangement. When he could get out, they could use the flat, if the sister was not there. Max improved his French, his knowledge of more subtle and bizarre ways of making love, and yet as always as he learned, part of him stayed watchful.

Bizarre was Madeleine's favourite word. It was her explanation of some of their love-making together among other things. She was hard up, and loved the few feminine clothes and perfumes that were to be had on the black market. This meant money. He had put nearly all his pay into a bank account in London. Now he passed some on. In books he had read long before, there was reference to French women who were demi-monde. In a way it simplified things. Purse-strings for passion was preferable to parsimony and prurience. They all knew that none of it was going to last long.

CHAPTER FOURTEEN

There were a lot of things that could be told about the
Normandy invasion, and most of them had been said, and
written and broadcast, Max Beaumont agreed. If what they
wanted to know was how he felt and behaved, and what he
thought on that famous D-Day, it was not so damn easy to
recall. Scared? He was, and he knew most of the men were.
But it was different from later when he was sometimes nearly
sick with it, and yes, if he had to talk about it really he was.
Because this was the first time and most of them had no real
idea. What was it that Franklin D. Roosevelt had said? We
have nothing to fear but fear itself! Because that was the
truth of it, and the cold, still bit inside you was about that,
and whether you might crack up in front of the men.

They were sick all right. Seasick, nearly all of them, in spite
of the hydrobromide handed out, which gave you a headache
as well. And then you wondered why everything was at
sea for so many hours, and whether that was necessary.
That 6th of June, long before first light, did not seem
like the start of a summer day at all. A lot later he had
heard of a statement made by Rear Admiral Sir Philip
Vian who commanded the assembling convoys, agreeing
that the weather was unexpectedly severe for the launching
of an operation of this type. And he wished he could have
heard it then, because he would have told it to the tank
crews on board the LCT assault craft, and they would have
been amused. Anything helped. It was the fact that they did
all know that this was the invasion of Europe, and at that
time to be on a big show, something special, well, it was
a morale booster, it had to count. It was going to win the
war wasn't it? Not like some of those lousy drawn-out little
messes later, when a lot of people got killed and hurt all for

some unknown village or a map reference. But there was always what was called "the big picture" – and the reality of the job itself. The British army which sailed for Normandy was the reality of a pledge given to France and the rest of Europe at the time when Britain had stood alone. Churchill had said: "Remember, we will never stop, never weary and never give in, and that our whole people and Empire have vowed themselves to the task of cleansing Europe from the Nazi pestilence, and saving the world from the new Dark Ages." That Max could remember by heart. That surely was the war that was his war.

Lieutenant Max Beaumont, now commanding three troops, A Squadron, Royal Richmond Dragoons, felt the tossing of the sea had been going on for ever. It was not at all the same as the motion of a tank. It was possible to see that they were part of a vast armada spread on that grey sea out in that grey dawn. It helped to look at his mapboard, which made it all so planned. Organised for the assault was Thirty Corps, 7th Armoured and the 50th and 51st division for landing on Gold Beach. That code name had stuck in Max Beaumont's mind long afterwards. At the time of that dawn, with thousands of others he strained reddened eyes that stung with salt and tiredness towards the scarcely visible coast. The desire to get there was almost unbearable, an urge to get it over. Would they last the day? He could think of even that. If they got ashore, there were snipers and German *panzerfausts*, a simple bazooka drainpipe that could pierce a tank hull.

All the time he watched, seeing on all sides that the grey tumbling waters were full of vessels, in their shape and movement straining, like his own spirit, for the shore.

Like an orchestra launches a play, suddenly the Royal Navy began their bombardment, and it was as though the whole world dissolved in the most shattering sound any of them had ever heard. Salvoes of thunder were going overhead, and now the coastline could be seen as red and white fire, with black cloud mounting above, adding to where the fires started by bombers the night before had long been flickering in that grey light.

His sergeant, Stan Sturman, one of the few who was a desert war veteran, stocky, and with a face that never seemed to be free of the dirt and dust of tanks, sat with him on the turret top.

"That's giving the lads a lift, sir! Better than Alamein that is!" He gave Max a sideways look in the half light. "You look all right sir, not sick then?"

The Richmonds were the sort of regiment where the officers were still saluted and properly addressed. Not like some of the Hussars and Lancers, whose commanding officer was laconically called Colonel and tank drivers had Christian names.

A naval rating in woollen hat and duffle coat was shouting to them from below, through a tin megaphone.

"Captain's compliments, sir! Five minutes order for landing! He'd rather you was ready in case we muck about!"

"Tell Corporal Harris, Sergeant Sturman! Keep on that B set the whole time. We've no squadron command and I'm hoping we get some order from local command when we hit the beach! If we're not closed down, just watch what I do if the radio fails!"

Max had taken over this troop only two weeks before, in circumstances none of them wanted to remember. The previous commander, senior to him only by months, had stepped the wrong way from behind his parked tank on one of the last exercises, and an ammunition lorry too close and without lights had crushed him against another tank. The regiment had paraded for the funeral. It was not regarded as a helpful omen. The Colonel had sent for Max the next day.

"I had hoped to keep you in HQ squadron as 2 i/c to the I.O. You'll take Three troop because Major Anderson has asked for you. Count yourself lucky! You've got a good troop there, and a fine Squadron Leader. Note that bit Beaumont! I don't want ribbons! I want survivors getting to Berlin! You know the flail job well enough now, and we may not often work as a regiment. A lot of the time we go in as troop or squadron, and inevitably in front. If you're under local command with other outfits that means you've got to show them what sort of regiment we are! Anything to say?"

It was still the time for the great game, the straight back, the fixed gaze, the Sandhurst salute. There was only one reply.

"Thank you very much, sir!"

Now down in the turret, with only his head showing above the cupola top, for reassurance Max felt the thirty-eight pistol in its holster at his belt. Looking down inside the turret he saw Nobby Clark his gunner had against orders shielded the small red glow of a cigarette in his hand.

"Make that a last puff, Clark! I don't want my legs on fire with the Navy rocking us!" He turned again to stare against wind and spray. It was no good using binoculars. But what was that distance? God, they were so far out! A thousand yards? Closing quickly. He was of course lead tank. All of the Shermans were sealed. Up to turret level. Waterproofing gave them a chance, depending on the shore, and all the crews knew that if the depth details were wrong, there was little hope of the driver and co-driver escaping. All of the crews had been told to pee against the tanks before mounting, and one or two had still been retching quietly, saying nothing, before finally slipping quietly into the familiar hulls.

"Driver start up, prepare to move! Gunner you've got A.P. up the spout? Gun control, and co-driver!" Max's command gave gunner and co-driver permission to shoot without further orders if targets presented. A klaxon sounded, yelping above the noise and smoke of the tank engines, and a green light went on as the LCT stopped with a lurch that made Max think for a moment they had been hit. The bow ramp began to move slowly downwards. In front now was a strip of broken dark water, and beyond a beach, smoke covered, a mess of metal girders and beyond soaring red and white tracer fire. Figures were lying on the sand, but moving now, and already an amphibious tank was far up the beach, firing monotonously, regularly, the turret swinging.

"Driver advance! Go! Go!" Max heard the scream of his own voice in the headphones. The naval shells were thundering high overhead again, and suddenly Max Beaumont noticed something strange and sweet and beautiful because it was so unexpectedly familiar. It was a smell, not the acrid smoke and gunfire and engine fumes, but the smell of the seaside! Sand and salt water. For a second, bucket and spade and shrimp net, sand castles. Then the Sherman rolled, as the driver pulled one stick and then the other, to clear the brakes of water, and Max felt a sudden elation.

"All stations Charlie Three! We're there! I'm blowing now! You're OK for depth! Come on fast! Fan out, go left of me Charlie Two!" Switching over to intercom then. "OK Smudger blow waterproof! How's she handling on this stuff?"

"Feels a bit wet in here, sir! And the going shitty underneath!" Driver Smudger Smith sounded hoarse. "Don't ask me to turn yet, sir!" The waterproofing blew. Strips and binding, bits and pieces blasted by the cord explosive whirled into the air. Then suddenly in front was a metallic clang, like a giant bell, and with a shattering roar the tank up the beach disappeared in a sheet of flame. The shock of reverberating air thundered back towards them. There was nothing but a black oily cloud with a red light in the centre.

The rubber covered earphones that clasped his head crackled briefly, and he knew it was Sergeant Sturman although there was no prefix. "88 from the left sir!"

They must get off this beach fast. He saw the Sergeant's tank behind him fire the smoke mortars on the turret side, but the grey billowing cover moved quickly in the wind, and the thing was to move towards the dunes. Battered looking buildings of a village lay beyond, some on fire, but the houses still had their faded seaside colours, almost surrealistic in the light of dawn creeping into the sky.

All three tanks were jinking, twisting, climbing so agonisingly slowly, towards the skyline. Now Max saw figures in front moving, outline shapes in tin hats, singly and in bunches, running and throwing themselves onto the ground. What seemed extraordinary was that there were others, already on the beach. No one had made clear about what units might be in front of the flails. There had been the understanding that underwater defenses would be removed in the night, depending on the tide and beach. He did not want to look at the still figures, crumpled shapes, and a black frogman crouched by a blown-off wheel, his hands holding his head were wet red.

"I thought we were first!" Too late Max realised he was still switched to intercom.

Above the heavy growling of the Sherman's familiar engine he heard the stuttering fire of his co-driver's Browning, and Bren guns from both sides. Then, for the first time another sound, the German Spandaus. Their startling fire-rate answering back was like ripping calico. Where was that 88? Salvo after salvo of naval six-inch shells travelling overhead from the ships way out at sea should have dealt with that, but the sound was awe-inspiring, even coming from the right direction. It was like an endless tube train going at speed through the station, and the bombardment seemed to make the air tremble continuously.

The tank had stopped, and into the earphones came the croak of the driver again.

"Officer wants to speak to you, sir!"

Max raised himself quickly on the commander's saddle seat. A tin-hatted, tall figure was standing beside the tank, a lean-faced Grenadier Guards Major, wearing on his well creased battle dress blouse, the armband of a beach master. In one hand he held a plastic covered clipboard, in the other a portable megaphone. He looked up calmly at the Sherman as though they were all on Salisbury Plain.

"We need three separate lanes flogged off this beach old boy! The minefields are to the right of the last house!" The metallic sound of the megaphone was as though a robot was talking. "You'll see the white markers where the commandos are firing now! Crack along will you, because the Dorsets are coming in behind you now, and we can't all hang about!" He lurched off into the smoke even as mortar shells started dropping sporadically towards the water's edge. For a moment Max glanced back, saw the sea was full of large landing craft standing off-shore, with smaller assault boats swirling in foam and the rusty broken girders of the breached underwater obstacles.

Then he was mouthing into his rubber mike, the familiar words of command, and the tank was lurching forward, Smudger changing gear briskly as the engine revs rose, and he saw the other two, turrets weaving slowly, guns pointing and elevating, advancing in the staggered formation they had rehearsed so often. Max realised that in all the time of preparation, everything had been focussed on that landing, the beach-head obsession. He knew that orders would come through from his squadron as the other tanks landed, and there would be direction and command from the assault battalion which was only a small part of 231 Brigade.

It was one thing to know the units, to remember the codewords, to glance for reassurance at his own mapboard, lined and crossed with coloured chinagraph markings, but of course no commander in the first wave of the landing could grasp the whole picture of the operation. Yet instinctively he was one of those individuals born with a seventh sense of tactics. It was a remote but definite gift, a sense of battle. It had nothing to do with a bump of self-preservation, which was something entirely different, and you either had it or you did not. Now he had closed down, and could see nothing but the men crouching by the white markers, and two more tanks that were DDs, the amphibious Shermans, like the one that had blown up. They were hull-down in the dunes, only their turrets moving, and the dust and grit was on the skin of his face, working into his eyes. With that instinctive sense Max could feel the whole attack coming in, as though he personally was moving the divisions, landing reserves, transport, artillery, supplies. Attack was the order of the day and attack was in the air and in his blood, but it was as though he had two sides, the personal, immediate, and the feel of the battle, impersonal, ineluctable.

His troop was functioning, already beginning to sense its capabilities for the real thing, and as his driver worked the tank forward Max knew when he held back each lever in his hands, braking one track, slewing the hull round.

He pushed open the cupola flaps. A commando captain, his head heavy with their own style of helmet, laced with netting, was signalling that he wanted to mount up to the turret. The tank stopped, and Max pulled a rubber earphone aside to hear him.

"There's the minefield! The wire's down on this side, and they've taken the signs down on their own!" the captain was yelling and pointing. "If you can clear till no more go off, we'll get through! Can you work all three? The swimming tanks will give you covering fire, and Jerry's had a real pounding over there from the Navy!" The commando's eyes were narrow, reddened slits, and his face blackened with dirt, and dried blood on his chin. He dropped down again without waiting for reply, and ran crouching over to his own men who had Bren guns and at least one mortar trained across the sandy land ahead, empty but for clumps of dune grass.

Max glanced leftwards, where Sergeant Sturman and Corporal Harris had halted, turrets already swinging, their guns to the rear. And then he too was swinging round as his gunner turned the spade grip, and he heard the cranking sound of the flail drum being engaged by Smudger Smith. Don't hang about. Never sit still!

"Charlie Three! I'm on bearings for this! That's the way they want it, and keep it tidy!"

The responses came through the earphones as Max pulled the divided cupola lids over his head, turning the periscope sideways to watch Charlie Two some fifty yards away, knowing that Smudger would have taken a compass bearing for a straight line across the minefield. How wide was it? What sort of mines? And where was that eighty-eight, and some others, waiting for just this moment? Then there was only the tremendous sound of the beating flail chains, the cold wind coming through the turret as the engine roared at high revs as fountains of sand rose, and then the explosions as the mines began to go off, and the Sherman rolled and shook and lurched forward again each time, like a ship drives into a heavy sea.

He saw that his radio operator, Simpson, had his head on his arm, hiding his face, leaning forward against the radio, and he put down a hand, to touch the black-bereted head. Max was using radio to steer the tank behind, but as the man raised his face, grey coloured with red eyes, and dribbling mouth, Max mouthed to him as well, in the lip-reading talk of tank men.

"Soon be there! I'm going to want that A set in a few minutes, Simpson! You'll be all right! This is it – we're OK!" What else in God's name could you say? He could see the hunched back and shoulders of the gunner, whose face was pressed into his sighting scope with its cross-wires. With the gun traversed to the rear there would be no targets, but at least he could see out. "Touch right, OK, still OK! Left!"

Through his own periscope to the rear he saw his other tanks, and unmistakable enemy shell fire, probably meant for further back where the infantry would be grouping. It was high explosive and not armour piercing and Max knew that one of them would have to land virtually on top of the tank to do any harm. One fell short, and sent bits of shrapnel rattling against the side, hardly to be heard above the uproar of the exploding mines and the flailing. Max hit his head on the turret, he felt his heart beating and his stomach churning and for a moment thought he might be sick. Then the driver was on the intercom.

"Sir! There's no more, sir, no more mines and we've done three hundred yards on the clock! What now?"

"Stop flailing, find any cover you can see! I don't want any blown tracks now! Gunner traverse front! I'll give you targets! Simpson try to get Two and Three on, and see what they report!" That would give the radio op. something to do. Max swung his periscope round with the turret, seeking any sign of enemy near or far, then impatiently unbolted and threw back the heavy metal lids of the cupola, and hooking his earphones on a bracket, crammed the bowl-like helmet, designed for tank crews, onto his head. It was intended that all crew would wear them in action, but the black beret was familiar, better for everything. Except snipers.

There was less Navy shelling going overhead now, behind them the chewed up dirt trail through the minefield was filling with crouching, running infantry, and where the other two flails had stopped, there were the amphibious DD tanks belting through, swirling into positions that were like his own, partly hull down behind the small amounts of undulating ground ahead. There was a metalled road only a few yards ahead, with waving dune grass on the verges, and Max spoke briefly to his own tanks to cross it and take up positions in line with the DD Shermans. They had begun firing now. Max could see where, in front of a long line of poplar trees, there was black smoke and fire from trucks, and two shot-up German MK IV tanks, with far away figures moving, grouping, disappearing.

"There's dead ones, sir!" It was the co-driver muttering in his headset, "Three of them, just in front!"

They lay huddled, grey shapes, two with their legs a red mess, one had no head, and the grey coal-scuttle helmet lay twenty feet away, where something that had once been a belt-fed machine gun emplacement was a tangled mess.

The sight of those dead and mutilated left Max strangely unmoved. It was abstract, they were not people, they were not remotely his people. They were enemy, and he felt his mind closing tightly like a clenched fist.

"Swing back along the track!" ordered Max. The infantry still coming through the minefield gap included carriers and even two or three loaded trucks, rolling heavily. These were targets, and he did not propose to sit with them.

"Charlie Three! Signals!" It was Squadron HQ, faint, crackly, calling on the A set for the first time, and Max heard Simpson repeat the call sign.

"Stay where you are, and support all elements making for Bluebell!" Max pulled up his mapboard. It was one of the myriad code signs. He saw it was a high-ground feature beyond the poplar-tree road. "One and Two are moving round behind Daisy!" The tinny, radio voice that was the Squadron Leader sounded strained. "We dealt with that eighty-eight! It was in a bunker on the edge of the village, so you should be OK, but keep away from buildings! Leave those to the sloggers!"

Max swung his tank fast into position in a cloud of sand dust, just ahead of the other two, so that his troop were in broad arrowhead formation, all, stopping to shoot the 75mm guns with high explosive at the ridge, a thousand yards away, towards which the infantry, in a ragged formation of platoons and sections, were advancing through a cornfield, hung with smoke like morning mist. They had their own machine gun fire, as well as support by Max's troop and other armour. He became conscious of a strange uneasiness, as though it was someone else giving instructions to Clarke to bring the gun to bear. Using binoculars, that would not focus quickly enough he suddenly felt rigid and cold. Now he could see. At the far end of the ridge, under trees on the left, they were unnetting camouflage, and a moment later he knew what it was, even as the first 88 shell scored directly, drilling through the side of Corporal Harris's tank. In seconds that seemed to stand still he saw like some obscene unreality, the black jagged hole, and in the smoke, still without flame, two figures like rag dolls seemed to pitch out of the top of the tank, one of them on fire, hitting the ground and rolling over and over.

In his own reeking, fume-filled turret, the gunner was firing, the breech clanging back, like some berserk anvil.

"D'you see him? Take your time, put it in his middle! Jock get spraying in front! Keep their heads down! *Fire!*"

The co-driver's Browning was chattering already, and a second latter Clarke fired, and as the smoke cleared, red and white flame flashed from the end of the ridge.

"Driver reverse! Get off this!" Max found something clogging his throat, choking him, before he could go on.

"Charlie Two, two are you there?" He got back on the B set again, switching from intercom. There was stupid intercom talk on the air already, as other tanks thought they were switched to internal and were actually transmitting. Machine gun fire was splitting the air as the German troops on the ridge saw the flaming target of the shattered flail on the dunes. The unnerving rate of firing of those Spandaus, more like an electric sewing machine than the answering Bren guns' solid tapping, but the infantry were advancing fast. Dropping too, as he could see, through binoculars. Mortar fire from that poplar tree line was bringing down the steady, moving line of the Dorsets.

Sergeant Sturman was on the air on the A set, reporting the destruction of Charlie Three and of the eighty-eight on the ridge. Dazed, Max realised he should have done that himself, and then knew that Squadron HQ would not even question why, and was glad Sturman knew what to do. Simpson was tapping his knee, to get him back onto intercom.

"You're hull down now, sir! I'll just stop 'ere." It was the driver again." "Sir, it was Corporal Harris got out! And two more I see, and they've got something out to them now, it came up from behind!"

Max, swinging round his periscope, saw briefly that it was a tracked carrier, with its Red Cross marking, reversing out of sight, behind the stricken Sherman, which was blazing fiercely.

By night-fall on that first day, the Squadron Leader called his troop commanders for an O group. They were only three miles inland. Bayeux had not been taken. The squadron numbers were down to nine with three tanks lost. For the first time Max was almost too tired to move. He was not hungry. He was not sure if people were really speaking to him or not. There was constant bombardment and small arms fire, flares, and then darkness in the sky. They tucked the tanks into an orchard by a shattered French farmhouse, where in the field nearby lay dead cows, obscenely bloated, with their legs in the air.

The men made hot tea and broke into the K rations, cardboard boxes of tinned foods, chocolate and cigarettes. There was going to be very little sleep, with the threat of German infantry patrols. Turrets were to be manned all night.

Someone asked what news there was of the Americans on the right flank. Had they done better?

"They've had it rough, I heard from Brigade. Omaha beach." The Squadron Leader sat with his back against the outside wall of the ruined farmhouse. As he dragged on a cigarette, the glow showed his face smudged with dirt and his eyes closed to pinpoints with the dust. "Lucky buggers had beer dropped to them! Those Mustang fighters have suspended extra fuel tanks for long range, and they dropped them onto the beach later, from zero feet and that's what was in them!"

"Tell that to the RAF!" someone said. It was good for the only laughter that night. They had also heard that the medical corps half-track carrying Corporal Harris and the other survivor of Charlie Three had been wiped out by a stray shell on the way to the beach evacuation station.

"I can see I am getting quite beyond the point," Max Beaumont smiled frostily. "Talking about the fighting war is a curious business. If you were really in the thick of it you seem to forget a lot. I have always met a certain kind, who can say: But you must have known Tubby Clubbers, he was your Corps commander! Or surely that was when the Hampshires were landing? Or the 154th Highland were on your left! I cannot recall these things. The Fog of War was real for me. Only things that were close to me, that involved some special situation, images that pierce that fog. Some stand out, and I can tell you those – perhaps it was two or three days after the landing, when I first saw a Tiger tank. And thank God I was not near to it! They weighed fifty-eight tons you know, that is the sort of fact that does stay in my sort of brain. The Tiger was the Mark 6 German panzer – they had a King Tiger later, that weighed seventy tons! I only saw one of them in Holland, with a hole in the roof – it was rocket firing Typhoon planes that were the only things that could stop them. They were so heavy there were hardly any bridges they could cross. Now the Panther, that was a tank! That had a long 75 that could penetrate anything at two thousand yards, and it only weighed forty-five tons.

"Where did you see that first Tiger?" Owen spoke quietly. "Is that the kind of thing you might ask, Felix?"

"It was a place called Villers-Bocage, not far from where we had made it that first night," Max Beaumont said. "I can remember that place because we seemed to spend for ever around there, and we went through that town with other armour and infantry as the Germans pulled back to hold Bayeux.

"I had my troop of two, now joined by another, that had lost two, and we were back in some woods, about a mile from a road. The motorised infantry were waiting on the verge with some cruiser tanks, perhaps a squadron. This lone Tiger came lumbering unexpectedly out of some trees, not far from the road, and immediately opened fire on the infantry half-tracks. That was what I first heard, and got him in the binoculars. There was no way we could take him on at that range, and that Tiger went on, parallel with that road, brewing up one vehicle after another, the bastard! And then those tanks, poor sods! The Tiger destroyed them like a shooting gallery. I watched one Cromwell tank firing at him, and I could see the six-pounder shells bouncing off the side of that Tiger, even when they closed in to just a few yards!" Max Beaumont was looking down at the carpet, toeing it softly with his polished shoe. Owen and I waited, silently. Somehow it didn't seem the time for questions.

"Bayeux was taken next morning. Ironic when you think of the ten sixty-six tapestry. But Caen was a different thing. It became the biggest tank battle on the Western Front. Not to be compared with Stalingrad probably, but at its height involving twelve armoured divisions, including the crack German 12th, 21st and Panzer Lehr divisions. You see I can remember that, for instance! Goodwood was the codename for that one, and I suppose it amused the Staff chaps who were horsey. That battle went on for days, and led to the famous Falaise Gap, which closed on the Germans like pincers, with so much stuff captured and whole divisions surrendered, we thought for a little while that the Germans might be finished, and the war over. All the German stuff was good you know! Like their tanks. Their hand-grenades were blue-coloured things, like a tin of beans, but on wooden handles – they were a lot easier to throw than our Mills Bombs. Their helmets and boots too. It's little things like that which count. Try to get back into a pair of British army lace-up boots in the dark, if you've been optimist enough to take them off for the night. You could kick into German jackboots in two seconds!"

"Isn't it still like that with most things the Germans and the Japs produce today?" Owen said. It seemed a sad but real comment.

"Give me another personal picture!" I urged Max, and I took off my spectacles and polished them. Was it that fog of war? I felt I could not see Max's face now as he talked on, but I realised the light had faded outside the big windows as though it might rain, and inside he had not yet put on lights.

"The Poles," Max Beaumont was saying. "That was at Falaise. All right you want it personal, and you see, I had a special thing going for the Poles – I'm talking about the First Polish Armoured Division. In that short time when I first joined the Richmonds, some Polish tank officers came over to see what flails did, so that they would know about them. They were mostly small fellows, quiet, even over a drink in the mess. But I had a special feeling about them which I don't mind admitting, because nothing else reminded me more of those soldiers in my father's study. Their badges with the Polish eagle, and as I say, they were quiet, tough

306

types, but with a sort of elegant gallantry. In those flat, Polish voices they told of how they had marched out from the Russians, with their General Anders, for hundreds of miles. Somehow they were history," said Max. He shrugged. "They could drink too! They had been stationed in Scotland a long time, but I don't think even Scots could beat those Poles when it came to the whisky.

"We were in reserve on high ground, to give supporting fire if anything came up for flails, when the big thrust started before Falaise and I could see them around the start line through the binoculars. I had heard they were going in with the Canadians, after American daylight bombers had softened up the German defences, which as far as they knew did not include mines for us.

"The Polish armoured boys went in steadily at first, but then like cavalry! This was their first big action, and all sorts of pennants and carefully preserved regimental colours went up on the turrets. One of the Canadian infantry officers told me after, that they were singing before engine start up, quietly in unison, slow Polish battle songs. Those cruiser tanks do fifty flat out, and they carved through the 12th SS and kept going. Trouble was they didn't seem to know what a bomb line was, or maybe the Americans didn't, because a lot of those romantic, gallant Poles got on the wrong side of the bomb line and were wiped out by the bombing."

For a moment I thought Max was getting up to make the point that there would never be anything good to say about war, because he had shifted unhappily in his chair. But he suddenly smiled.

"I nearly forgot about the champagne!"

"I don't think I could drink any right now," I said.

"You're not being offered any!" Max said sharply. "It was the story I promised to tell you. Right there, in that carnage of the German army, there were fields of abandoned trucks and guns and stuff, and when we moved forward again, some of our friends from the commandos could be seen carrying cardboard cases. We were halted under trees, waiting for orders, and one of the tank crew came up and told me that there was a German army store in a barn, and most of it was champagne. Was it just for the commandos? Of course it wasn't! There is no better repository for two dozen or so Bollinger, than the inside of a tank turret!' Max Beaumont's pleasure at the recollection of this fact was real. "The shells are carried all the way round inside, and a seventy-five shell is about the same size as a bottle of the old eye-brightener!

"Well, we weren't exactly short on ammo. but there were some empty spaces in the racks. People said afterwards that some of the troop had dumped shells to make space. The whole situation was so different from anything we'd ever been prepared for by training. There was so much Jerry stuff and our own, lying about, after even a small show, and apart from prizes like Luger pistols, we were picking up things that might come in useful all the time. We'd already learned to weld spare track plates onto the turret and parts of the hull. The airborne's silk parachutes were a prize – they *were* silk then! The women at home hadn't seen silk for years, and the paratroops had left them hung up in trees, or stuffed under the hedges, and pushed on.

"That champagne story didn't end all that happily. We were moving up, and there was a call for flails later the same afternoon, and we were hanging about to clear a way for a flank attack by Guards Armoured. My driver took a cut round a blocked road by going through a hedge, banged the front end into a ditch and pulled one of our tracks off. It happened all the time. Who should turn up, but the regimental second-in-command, who had a ferret look about him at all times, small eyes and a clipped moustache. He got out of his scout car, battledress smartly creased, no overalls for him, and started nosing around. I dare say that although we'd had only a moderate amount of the stuff to drink, one or two of the bottles had already broken, and the turret smelt like an expensive party. He put me under open arrest. It would have been close arrest, as he pointed out, but there were no other officers around, for escort."

"I may report cowardice in the face of the enemy! I find it extraordinarily suspicious that you have become unfit for combat! Your crew are all on a charge!"

He motored off to find the other tanks of the squadron, and we unloaded all the bottles onto one of the supply trucks in the dark that evening." Max nodded at us, as though this explained everything. "It's been Bollinger ever since Falaise!"

It was after Caen that the Allied armies began to move fast. Out of the Bocage country, with its deep hedge-lined lanes, small fields and limited vision, the Americans under Patton began to cover distances of fifty miles in a day. The British moving over territory less open, swung up north towards Brussels. By a pre-arranged plan, made up by Eisenhower at short notice, it gave the Free French and the US 4th Infantry Division the privilege of liberating Paris.

Flail tanks were not in demand. The Royal Richmonds came together as a regiment for the first time, in a village near Evreux, not far from the Seine river, and indeed not far from Paris either. For tanks and soft vehicles there was much needed maintenance. For the troops, laundry, and proper billets. Football was organised, there was washing in hot water and unbelievably, visits to a field cinema unit.

Max had been sent for by the Colonel.

"I've got a job for you young, Beaubum!" The old name had been picked up by the regiment, but the Colonel's use of it showed this was not going to be an unhappy matter, like the brief unpleasant interview that had followed the champagne-for-shells. "With a name like that, you can't sit on your arse here! Have you those papers, Gerald?"

The adjutant gave him two cyclostyled sheets. The Colonel was just over thirty, with an MC and bar beside the desert star on his battledress blouse. The adjutant was not much older than Max. Both the others, although they had rested now for three days, looked several years on. It was in their eyes and the creases that pulled round the Colonel's mouth.

"You speak the language, right? Denis as regimental I.O. should get this job, but as you know the M.O.s sent him back with some sort of blood poisoning. Did you see him before he went?"

"We had a chat about the Hitler Youth, sir. There are quite a lot of them with that Panzer Lehr lot."

"His hands are swollen up like dirty great gloves. Now I come to think of it, Gerald, you can get the M.O. on for a piece in Orders tomorrow. All troops will pay close attention to hand cleanliness! Not wash in petrol! There's dirt and disease everywhere, and all they keep on reminding us about is V.D! All I can say is never mind their pricks what about their hands? I can't run an armoured regiment with no hands can I?"

Max and the adjutant knew the Colonel was acting. It was the form, A tough, partly coarse line, affected by the more intelligent ones as a sort of barrier. Informal, but no nonsense. Feelings were out. Feelings made grown men cry when they had to be told about families killed in air raids at home, or that a leg would have to be amputated.

"Wilco, sir!" The adjutant scribbled on his field pad.

"You will go and interrogate prisoners, Beaubum! Tank crews especially!" The Colonel lifted his tired eyes from the sheets of paper.

"This bumf is from Thirty Corps, but it's American origin. It seems the Yanks have got any number of them in their cages up the road to Paris, and before they're shifted off, units in the area are invited to send Intelligence Officers for closer knowledge of the enemy and method of – well blah blah! It all goes on! I can't give you this, because it's classified. Gerald you will signal them on the line they give, and you will give Mister Beaumont a paper authorising him, and a map ref. Don't go overboard about it, Beaubum! Just break a few of their fucking arms, and come back and tell us what you find out. You can push off as soon as Gerald has it fixed up, but don't be away for more than a day. It says you've got to bring your own rations, I see. OK?"

"What do I travel in, sir?" Max asked respectfully.

"Well, you can't have the only jeep, that's for sure, which is what I suppose you'd like!" The Colonel turned to Gerald.

"Daimler Scout car?" said the adjutant. "Good for two."

"Sir!" said Max Beaumont. "Instead of the scout car driver can I have Sergeant Sturman? It would be good if he came with me I think, because I'm pretty sure some of those Germans speak some English. It would do a lot of good if Sturman came back and could tell the NCOs and tank crews about enemy low morale and bad supplies, which is what I rather think we'll find. Plus any technical stuff. They'd take it from him better than just a driver."

310

The Commanding Officer seemed to be looking at the pips on Max's shoulders.

"Not a bad idea! I don't see why not? Anything against it, Gerald?"

"Max'll have to sign for the scoutcar of course," said the adjutant. "I believe the Yanks are quite keen on them!"

Max got up, saluted properly and went to find Sergeant Sturman.

"We're going to Paris. OK? The other job is the real reason, but we'll never get a better chance. You're driving the Daimler. Make sure there's enough jerry cans of fuel in the back. What'll those things do, if they're pushed?"

"Fifty." Sergeant Sturman looked puzzled. "Why Paris sir?"

"Have you ever been to Paris?" Max knew that the Sergeant, a former Durham miner had certainly not. "You'll never see anything in this bloody show otherwise, except shit and K rations."

Sergeant Sturman got the idea. "That's spreading gloom and despondency, sir. Paris, ooh la la! 'Ere I come! What about the Jerry prisoners then?"

"You just stick with me, and we'll do what we have to. You should be able to talk with any of them that have English. And Sergeant!"

"Sir?"

"Bring some cigarettes!"

Half an hour later they were on the road, leaving a somewhat surly scoutcar driver in the transport lines, telling Sergeant Sturman to bring his Daimler back as good as he got it, and that meant clean.

The prisoner of war cages were in the American V Corps area, some twenty miles west of the Paris outskirts. Along the road there had been plenty of interest. To assist convoys of troops and supplies to move without the hazards of map-reading, signs of all sorts were increasingly nailed to trees and buildings. The TOP HAT symbol had been the way to follow their own Thirty Corps, into the forward zone. There were other American army signs. For hazardous verges, seen in all areas, the one that for Max had another, totally different image, was SOFT SHOULDERS. There they were, in his mind, pale and gleaming in a backless evening dress, shimmering, elusive, scented, beautiful. Another world away. He would have mentioned the idea to Sergeant Sturman but doubted if shoulders in Durham were like that.

Following directions they swung into a large dirt area that was a vast army vehicle park, bulldozers, huge lorries, mobile cranes, jeeps. All the products of wartime Detroit were there.

Both men dismounted, stretching after the cramped ride, and Sergeant Sturman removed the distributor head from the engine and padlocked the door.

Ahead of them, down a muddy track, they saw huge rolls of barbed wire mounted ten feet high in all directions. There were more cages beyond the first one. Behind the wire were rows of brown-coloured tents in endless lines, and outside, patrolling GI's with slung guns strolled in pairs. At the entrance, box-like buildings, later to be the portakabins of every building site, were marked with US Army Provost signs.

"Christ look at them Yanks!" Sergeant Sturman grunted as they tramped along towards them. "They know how to do it properly! Should have seen them round us at home, sir! Them uniforms made the girls a push-over! Niggers some of them too!"

"You were in the desert, Sergeant – did you see any of the Indian regiments? The Gurkhas were there. Were they niggers?"

"All niggers!" Sergeant Sturman was unrepentant. "Them Gurkhas they were a lot, I tell you! They weren't after Lugers, sir, they was after ears! Frightened the lot of us, as much as bloody Jerry!"

Round the main group of the portable command boxes there was more barbed wire, and armed guards in white helmets. One of them escorted the two British inside a box hut to a trestle table, behind which sat a fat master-sergeant. He took Max's papers without formality, looked at them, and gave them to a soldier to copy details onto their own paper.

"OK Mister! You and the sergeant is it? Cap'n Fellburg'll take you in for interrogating! Soldier! Take these men along to Cap'n in number three!"

312

By the time they got there, Captain Fellburg was outside box number three, saluting away a Major and a Captain of the Canadian Black Watch. Max saluted the Canadian Major, who returned it crisply. The American Captain who seemed to have grown tired of the whole thing, nodded and smiled wanly. He was a tall, pale-faced young man, and wore issue steel spectacles and a small forage cap.

"You guys got your papers? Right! We've had a lot of response to this thing, and there's been all sorts in here – even US outfits I hardly knew! Richmond Rangers?" He saw their faces, then looked down at the papers. "Nope, Dragoons! That's right! Tanks that would be!" The Captain was now stalking along with them in his tall rubber-soled lace-ups. "The way it goes is this. I can let you have an interrogation session for half an hour! You could see about three German tank officers, or enlisted men if you prefer, in that time."

He pointed to a tent, still inside the administration compound and they stopped. "There's a chair and table in there – the prisoner can sit too if you want that. He comes under escort, who stay, and take him away. Okay? Sorry we can't give you more time, but the whole deal had us on the hop when Allied HQ thought it up! We want the whole goddam lot closed and out! Do you or the serge speak German?"

"I do," Max said. "I thought Sergeant Sturman might be able to talk to some of the prisoners and get some information on his own."

"Can't do it!" said the lanky Captain shortly. "It's not that way. They're a rough lot in those lines, especially the SS. They could grab a man for hostage. I'm not saying they would. But we've had some. Most of them are glad to be out of it. They're all on short rations of course, and maybe you know, that keeps most guys quiet!"

He led the way in through the tent flap. It was airless under the brown canvas. Inside the floor was earth, with a piece of duck-board leading to a trestle table and two hard back chairs facing across it.

Two of the US Military Police with their white helmets and armbands, and short carbines slung on their shoulders came to the entrance. They stood, faces flat and expressionless, although one was plainly chewing gum.

313

"These men will help you, Lieutenant" said Captain Fellburg. "The sergeant will have to stand by. If you have any cigarettes we don't object to you softening the bastards."

"Get's 'em to come in easy!" observed the man who was chewing.

The Captain, preparing to leave, gave Max a keen look.

"We don't get too many from your army, Mister. That speak the language I mean. You sure you don't need any help? My folk came from Bavaria way back!"

"*Sehr freundlich aber wirklich nicht nötig!*" Max was polite.

"*Scheint der Fall zu sein!*" Captain Fellburg said sardonically. "OK escorts? You got it? The lieutenant wants Panzer officers! You're quite right Mister, you don't get much out of the crews! When you leave, I'll give you all our routine intelligence paper. General background stuff we've prepared to save time. OK? See you on the way out then!"

He left with one of the helmeted policemen.

In the presence of the other one who stayed, Lieutenant Max Beaumont and Sergeant Sturman were silent. There was something unexpectedly condescending about our American allies, Max thought. Not unfriendly, but from the first escorting soldier, the master sergeant and now in the bearing and manner of the two MPs at the tent flap doors, there was a quality that in Kings Regs. was called Silent Contempt. He knew, even without catching his eye, that Sergeant Sturman was feeling it too.

"What's the guns you got there?" The guard who was still with them wanted to know.

"Webster thirty-eight revolvers." Max told him shortly.

"Any good? Got any Lugers? I'll buy 'em! For dollars!"

Sergeant Sturman coughed softly. "You could buy my gun, soldier!" He spoke in his gravelly North-country accent, wiping a hand across his mouth. "But you see it's only been loaned to me by the King of England, see! And I don't think he'd like that!"

The American was in no way sure how to take this. He laughed, a dry humourless cackle.

The entrance to the tent darkened, as the other guard appeared with the first prisoner, who stood to attention by

314

the table. The guard had a clip-board now, and he read out from it.

"Says he's from the First SS. Major – can't read the son of a bitch's name, sir!"

Max wondered what the enemy, in the person of the tall, cropped haired, pale-faced man who stood woodenly staring over his head thought to that if he understood. Max sat down and opened his field notebook on the table. He spoke in German. "What is your name Major?"

"Tienemann!" The Major still stood like a private on parade, and showed no surprise at being spoken to in his own language. Max reflected that he had probably already been questioned by fluent US "I" Corps people, like Captain Fellburg.

"You can sit down if you want to! We have not much time, and I want to ask you some quick questions. As you can see, we are British tank soldiers, we are interested in technical things."

Max said this to encourage a more co-operative response. He knew well enough the routine of name, rank and number only response, and this one looked as though he would be that kind. Max was also aware of a curious reaction in himself, something that was making him want to gaze away from the white-faced stiff figure opposite him. He fumbled for a moment, taking the pencil with its little metal point guard out of his battledress pocket. This was the first member of the German army he had been close to, near enough to touch, someone to speak with, a person. They were the enemy who had tried to kill him, who had killed his own men, who had murdered his relations. He did not then know a lot of things, yet to happen. The SS First Panzer under General Peiper had not yet murdered the American prisoners at Malmedy. After that not very many *Panzer* prisoners were taken by the American army.

"I will stand!" The Major spoke in English, scornfully. He continued to look ahead.

Max felt a sudden high pressure in his head. It ran round the edge of his beret.

"You will sit!" The words spat out. "That is an order! And you will speak in German. That is an order too!"

315

"*Jawohl!*" The German pulled back the chair and now for the first time gazed level eyed at him. He folded his arms.

"You say you are Major Tienemann of First SS? You have the black trousers but some sort of infantry jacket? Where are your insignia? Rank? Regiment badges?"

"They have taken them! All as souvenirs! Every badge. And my jacket. Also my Iron Cross, Lieutenant! First class and bars! My wrist watch, and rings." He shrugged. "To be expected you will say. But I did not think the Americans would be like the Russians!"

"You are going to have a lot of time to think about a lot of things," Max said. "And the German army? What do they do?"

"I do not know. I have had too much fighting to see prisoners! That is for infantry."

So Max was to learn that endless story. It was the first of many times that Germans would not know, were not involved, never responsible for the hideous, small things and the horrendous, unbelievable ones.

"What was your unit?"

"Panther Battalion, First SS." The tired yellowed eyes in the pallid face with its stubbled chin, for a moment were bright. Max reached for the packet of Senior Service in his trouser pocket and put them on the table.

It was totally ridiculous, but that moment of pride, if that was what he had seen, halted some notion of pity that had begun to stir in him. No soldier, no officer, no hardened *Panzer* commander should look like this patchwork uniformed, hungry-faced man.

"Take one!"

"I may keep it for later?"

"If you wish."

The hand that stretched out shook. Two cigarettes were moved to his jacket breast pocket.

"How were you knocked out?"

"Typhoon rocket! I believe it was American, because we were against some of General Patton's divisions under United States number Five Corps. It does not matter. My driver was killed, the radio operator and gunner were wounded, and after I had helped them out, I was blown against the side

316

of the tank by a shell. There was a lot of confusion! The infantry were going down badly, my tanks were not all my own – perhaps you know what I mean, Lieutenant? They did not stay around – I think they thought I was dead. Those Typhoons are impossible! Unless we have flak divisions, we have no weapons to stop them! Where is the Luftwaffe?" The SS Major's face was twisting, he was coming across the table. To one side Max knew that Sergeant Sturman had moved in to stand beside his chair. The Major's hand suddenly struck the table in a pathetic gesture. "Nowhere to be seen! It was the same in Russia!" He fell back, spittle on his lips, his hand wiping his forehead.

"Why do you not all surrender now?" Max spoke quietly. "You have lost! You know that don't you?"

"There are still some reserves!" The Major whispered, as though there was some conspiracy between them. "We know there are two kinds of secret weapon nearly ready! They will drive your armies back into the sea. Then –" he paused, and looked round. The two guards were only just visible outside the entrance. "You will have to sue for peace! The Americans will go home, because the Japanese will be at their throats for a very long time. Perhaps we have even a weapon that will reach America. I do not know but I hear things! I am only a tank soldier, as I have told these idiots, when they ask always about our new weapons! You will have to join with us, to keep the Russians out of the West! You do not know them! We do!"

"They are giving you a bad time and you deserve it!" Max said. "What is your news from the Home front? How is morale there?"

"You have destroyed too much with your air forces! You are making it too easy for the Russians. Berlin is in ruins, I know it."

Max dug his fingernails into the palms of his hands, under the table. The pale-faced Major twisted his lips, showing a broken tooth, and both men stared at each other.

"You know Berlin perhaps?" It was hardly subtle.

"I was there as a child." Max knew that Sergeant Sturman did not understand a word, and the guards had spoken no German.

317

The SS Major was probably only a few years older than he was. It was his appearance and the circumstances that made more of the difference. But the reaction was unexpected, as the man rose, and stared at him with sudden, vivid contempt, and hissed one word.

"Traitor!" Then he stalked towards the tent opening as the two guards pushed in.

"You finished with this bastard, Mister?" One of them was pointing his carbine at the prisoner's stomach.

"Yes!" Max pressed his pencil too hard on the pad and broke the point. "You can bring the next!"

The military police guard who stayed inside the tent was watchful. Max spoke to him.

"Who is picking these fellows for us?"

"One of the dooty officers in the compound – they've got their numbers, regiments! We've had Canadians here wanting staff officers. Your infantry wanting certain regiments. The way we get it, Mister," the guard now seemed more communicative, "there's nearly quarter of a million Jerry prisoners couldn't cross the Seine river. They've lost two thousand tanks alone since the landings, one of their officers said!"

The prisoner that came in with the other guard wore the uniform of an ordinary soldier. He was stocky, with red hair, a bruised, bulbous nose, and had a green field dressing with a criss-cross plaster strip over one ear and part of his jaw. He had kept his cap, albeit devoid of badges, and with some show of presence had taken it off, tucked it under one arm and made a quick bow with his head in Max's direction. He recited his name, rank of lieutenant and number in a tired voice, then sat down willingly and took the proferred cigarette which he put in his mouth, patting pockets to show he had no matches. Reluctantly Sergeant Sturman put an old lighter on the table, and after it had been used, took it back.

"I'd like to say this, sir," Sergeant Sturman spoke from where he stood behind Max. "If any of these buggers need dusting-up, you just give the sign! I didn't like the Major, and I can't understand a word you're saying to them – bloody marvelous you are with the bloody language, sir! Just tell me if there's trouble!"

"I was with a unit of self-propelled guns," the German told Max. "That is four! But then three and one! We have no petrol, so we put hand grenades down the barrel yes? Then we try and get away. It is the General – not Model, he is a tough one, but the High Command, maybe even the Führer! Sepp Dietrich made the withdrawal. What a mess! He used to be a pork butcher they say!" The man seemed to want to babble on but Max stopped him. He asked quick questions about fuel supplies, food rations, mechanical maintenance routines, what he thought of American and or British tanks and their fighting capacity. He knew time was limited. These were the things that made up a picture, and he jotted quick notes.

The lieutenant, when he got up, holding onto the trousers of his borrowed uniform, said he was glad to be out of it all, and hoped he might be home by Christmas. He clicked his heels.

The next customer was SS again. Still in his close-fitting black uniform, but also with a black eye. The other eye glared at Max with thinly veiled hostility. He was a Captain he said, from the Second SS Panzer Corps. He had already been rapped on the shoulder by one of the guard's carbines to indicate he should sit down. Now speaking rapidly he flared.

"The Geneva Convention means nothing to these Americans! I have seen many of our SS lorried infantry shot with their hands up! I fought your eleventh division also! Yes? Near Caen! And Guards division in the area Chambois! We were units of several divisions under General Hausser. The Canadians fight like madmen, they take no prisoners!" He looked at Max's uniform with his one good eye. "You are British?"

"I'm doing the questioning, not you!" Max said. "Did you command Panzers? Tigers?" This one might be offered a cigarette, but only if he obliged.

"I do not have to answer that question!"

"That is stupid – we can always find out. The war is over for you now, Captain!" The man looked at him, and seemed to sag a little. He licked his thin lips. "Panther! I have had one Tiger in Russia. It is unbeatable. But the

319

Panther is my tank! You have nothing like it! Nor have the shit Ivans!"

Max asked questions. About the Panther's effective gun range, the mix of HE and AP ammo carried, the average length of service of tank crews now, and how confident the Captain was of victory, East or West.

He got most of the answers. But the Captain grew sullen. He leaned across the table.

"How come you speak such fine German eh? You talk like some damned flashy Berliner! When did you go over? You're Jewish aren't you? Filthy Jews, all of you! You have brought the world on our necks, with your money and your influence. We will get you though! Have no fear of that!" He rose, reaching across the table with both hands.

It was the nearest guard who yanked him backwards off the falling chair, just as the American Captain returned. Sergeant Sturman had pulled his revolver out of its holster, but put it behind his back.

"Trouble in here?" The Captain stood to one side, watching as the two guards worked swiftly to slip handcuffs on the prisoner, kicking him on the shins, pushing him out through the exit.

"Swine Jews!" He screamed at the American. Then at Max, as he turned his head, he tried to spit towards him, the spittle running down his chin.

Max felt a reaction of such cold anger seize him, that as he rose he knocked over his own chair. Two spots of high colour showed on his face.

"Easy lootenant!" The Captain held his arm. "We all get that from this lot! It's a pity they take them, I'm coming to believe! It would be better to blow their brains out! If it's any consolation, that bastard will be put on cool-down rations for two days when I report, and that's quite a gut ache – believe me!"

Max suddenly felt enormously weary. Moving slowly, with fingers he tried hard to steady, he collected the sheaf of cyclostyled papers on the way out. They were efficiently presented in a folder, made up of unwanted field maps. He thanked the US I Corps Captain, and returned silently with Sergeant Sturman to the scoutcar.

They stood and watched, as out of the main camp entrance came a convoy of big, sheeted US Army trucks, each one jammed full of grey uniformed prisoners, some still with field hats, some bareheaded. Their faces filled the open space of the truck tail-end, and some of them were singing. Armoured cars, with small calibre guns mounted, drove between the trucks, the helmeted figures at the guns turning them, watchfully. But as truck after truck lumbered and rolled along the track, out towards the main road the singing continued. It was a haunting tune, a marching song, with it's own weary, but still swaggering lilt. Max was trying to listen to the words.

"They used to sing that one in the desert!" Sergeant Sturman said, and licked his lips. Now he started to whistle quietly, the same tune. "Know it, sir? Most of us picked it up. I dunno why! *Lili Marlene* it's called!"

It was always little things that restored sanity. When they climbed back into the scoutcar, the familiar smells of steel-plate and petrol, the British instrument dials and the black deck of the radio 19 set were reassuring, but Max still felt a reaction of chill and his legs were shaking. He could not share with his sergeant the anti-semitic vituperation and hate. He had been stupid not to have expected that, as obviously the American Captain did. Now he was sorting maps, to keep his fingers busy, turning them over, while Sergeant Sturman waited. Max realised that this was still the old British regimental discipline. In the Royal Richmonds, drivers waited for orders to start up and move off. Even with his own troop sergeant, and poor Corporal Harris, or the new corporal, he could not be personally close. If at all, he was nearer to his own tank crew. With them he shared nights under a tarpaulin. But he did pass round his officer's monthly issue of whisky, with all of his Troop, splash by splash into all the mess tins. You knew most of the first names, but you did not use them. Perhaps this trip with Sturman would bring a useful dimension of something extra. God knows they depended on each other. The man was still whistling bits of that tune, adjusting his dusty black beret, wetting a finger and polishing the metal

321

stag badge. He too could have been thinking on the same lines.

"Didn't like you, them bastards didn't! I'd say it was partly on account of you sprekking the dootch! They didn't like that I could tell!" Sergeant Sturman was looking at him shrewdly. "Don't let it get at you! Next time you see any of that lot, you don't have to talk to them! Just leave 'em to the gunner! We done the job! Is it Gay Paree now?"

Max was grateful. But he noticed the absence of the punctuating, Sir.

"It's forty miles, but I don't know what sort of miles. If the Yanks have got the road sorted out, we could do it. You realise we're playing hookey on this bit, which I think it's only fair to say, in case anything goes wrong, but as I'm giving the orders you would be in the clear!"

"That's all right! Got to have something to tell the wife, other than looking forward to her cooking when I write home. Tell I saw Paris! How about that?"

"Start up! Get back on the road, turn right, put your foot down as much as you can, but for Christ's sake don't hit anything!"

Why did he want to make this dash for Paris? Max was unsure why he had such an obsession with the idea. The British had not liberated the city, and back in the mess, the talk was that they would move north at any moment in support of Guards Armoured, making for Brussels. Maybe he would never see Paris. That "never" bit was occurring now. There were a lot of soldiers who were never going to do anything again. Even that brief, direct contact with the German army had made him grimly aware that there was little chance of an easy end in sight. The fighting he had already seen had changed him, perhaps in some deep way, and he knew that nothing would ever be the same again.

The Daimler scoutcar was noisy. The studded sheet metal drumming and the heavy, wide tyres droning at speed, and Max fell into introverted reflection. Sometimes he felt elated, mentally strong, alert and unassailable in a new way, even when he was dead tired. But always there was the sickness of fear. You could not look at it, push it off, like the tiredness. You survived, with the impersonal risk calculation that demanded complete subservience of everything else. But there had to be courage in every decision, and often recklessness too. It was the waiting times, in the tank turret, when you could smell the fear, as a tangible thing. Sweat and pee and a taste in your mouth. Then when it was go, and everyone in the crew felt the surge of the engines, heard the blast of sound, the tracks churned round and the rocking movement of the heavy hull, purposeful with it's weapons and striking power, they had a closeness together, reassurance. When the tank spun round easily, like a heavy-weight boxer, you were on your toes, even tired and exhausted. You had nothing to beat, the feeling near to infallibility, helped by the benzadrine tablets the M.D. sometimes dished out to help keep you awake.

Next to him Sergeant Sturman was driving, his face rigid. They might get into trouble on this trip, but a quick look round Paris, and they could be back with the regiment. Doing the last bit in the dark possibly.

On the road they passed heavy traffic. Twice they were diverted into fields to bypass damage, or obstruction where US Army clearing machines were working. They crossed bailey bridges, and overtook long convoys of heavy trucks. It was not all American army. Painted unit signs showed there were Polish regiments, Canadians, and more French now. There seemed to be one main American sign, coding a route like their own system, the marker showing Donald Duck stencilled white on black, with the arrow upwards.

"We should be on the Bois de Bologne about now!" There was intercom in the scoutcar, but it was not worth using, so Max shouted. "There are the woods! I want to find a less popular way in. I've only got small scale of the city on these maps, but I want to come in at some place where we hit the Seine river bank. And then, if we buzz along that, it's easy map reading, the river on our right. That way we see the Eiffel Tower, get onto the Champs Elysees and round the Arc de Triomphe, or through it, or whatever you do. Then straight on out again at the top end!"

"Get a ribbon for that sir, don't we? Paris campaign? Sounds as though you speak the Frog too and all!" Sergeant Sturman was twisting and turning the steering wheel as they went round bends on a quieter road, then suddenly he was braking.

Looking ahead, Max saw why. In the middle of the cobbled road was a wooden marker, a four-foot high bollard painted with the tricolour blue-white-and-red in stripes, and surmounting it a French flag with the same pattern of colours.

Max took in the scene quickly. There was a small bistro by the side of the road, and in a field on the other side of a hedge, an army truck, and a few soldiers, chatting with civilians to one side of the bistro. Soldiers who wore British battledress, but the fore-and-aft cap that had long gone out in the British army.

From the Bistro strolled, a French army officer, more impressively uniformed, his fore-and-aft in black, with badge and white piping. He also wore white gloves, and a white webbing belt, on which hung his pistol holster, also blancoed white. From his shoulder epaulette hung a festoon of white cord lanyard with gilt tips.

As the scoutcar stopped, Max moved to stand up in his seat which thrust the top part of his body through the open hatch. He saluted, and received in return a gesture from one of the white gloves. French rank badges were unfamiliar. Was this a Captain?

"You have papers? The permit entry to the Command area of the Free French Forces of General de Gaulle?" The officer spoke in French.

"We are the British Army, Captain!" Max thought he might as well give the rank by proxy. "We need no permit!"

"The French army has liberated Paris, and has control of the city!" The officer had a chinless, pale face and a small moustache, and his manner was grand rather than severe. "Only the authorised documentation permits entry!"

"We are your allies, Monsieur!" Max was finding his French was coming as easily as his mounting irritation. "We have liberated your country!"

Sergeant Sturman spoke from somewhere in the depths of the scoutcar. Sturman, hot and dusty had driven hard. He had emptied his water-bottle and was already looking forward to a liberator's top-up at some grateful bar. He did not really care if it was wine or beer he had said, if the Frogs had nothing stronger. He switched off the engine.

"What's the silly fucker want?"

The white gloves had now, as no papers were proffered, started to wave the scoutcar back with an imperious gesture. Two of the soldiers had strolled to the entrance in the hedge. They were unarmed, and looked on grinning.

Max slithered down into his seat and shut the hatch. "Driver start up!" Sergeant Sturman glanced only briefly at his face and looked away. He had already selected reverse.

"How far sir?"

"Fifty yards!"

The Daimler went fast backwards. On reconnaissance that was its life-saving contribution. It thumped into forward gear as easily. Then, with engine flat out, it roared back towards the French officer, who leapt for his life.

Max Beaumont said afterwards, that he was tempted for a moment to take-out the bollard and flag, but with sharpened calculation at work, he knew that insult and injury were too different things. There is enough noise and fury inside a Daimler scoutcar in a hurry, but not so much that the crack of two or three shots hitting the rear end escaped either of the occupants.

"What's the matter with 'em? I'll go down this next cross-road to the left sir! In case they can get up something behind us! Bloody 'ell when do I get that drink?"

"There are two bets," Max said shortly. "Either they're pushing that bullshit, and we won't hear any more. Or we'll get picked up in the city!"

Max often said his first sight of Paris was so pleasant, that early September, it was never the same again. He took over the driving, jacking up the seat so that his head was above the hatch, and making decisions by well-trained directional instinct. They moved along the Seine embankment with military and other traffic including many civilians on bicycles. There were French army vehicles and soldiers on the street, but no attempt was made to stop them.

In a small alley they presently parked, and went into a darkened bistro. Much was made of them. With happy cries and screams from Madame and two girls, and back slapping from the handful of men at the bar. While Max drank two cognacs, Sergeant Sturman drank two beers, as there was no Scotch or gin, and bought two more bottles for the road. He gave Max some French Francs.

"You pay, sir! I don't understand them. They could rob me blind."

"They say it's on the house," Max told him quietly. Madame behind the bar came round to the front, and gave them both resounding kisses as they left, Sturman returned his with enthusiasm.

"The old wagon needs a drink too, sir!" Sturman heaved jerry cans out of the Daimler. "We could fill up here quietly like, in case we don't want to stop!"

They worked together with funnel and jerry cans, stowed the empties, and got back inside. Before he switched on the engine, Max thought for a moment.

"There's no number on this thing! Only regimental and div. signs."

"I had a look at the shot marks just now!" Sergeant Sturman grinned. "I'll square the driver on those when we get back. How d'you think they are on signals?"

"Let's take a look at Paris!"

They saw the Eiffel Tower that day, at first sight like a thin charcoal pencil line against the pale sky, then the whole soaring reach of the metalwork. They stopped, almost beneath it, the tower seeming to move gently, fingering the clouds. Max was surprised to find they could buy two picture postcards of it.

"Didn't they have no war 'ere then, sir?" Sergeant Sturman asked. Max told him about Paris being declared an Open City.

"Didn't make London that way. Nor Coventry!"

"Nor Berlin!" Max reminded him, then fell silent. Surprising how often now, that was in his thoughts.

They moved across to the *Concorde*, and after a moment's dithering, went up the *Champs Elysees*, empty of cars, with shop-fronts boarded, and only the pavements crowded, and military vehicles parked under the trees and at the *Rond Point*. At the *Etoile* the arch was spiked with flags of all the allies, French sentries marched and counter-marched, and the little scoutcar sped round and past them and up the route of *des Grandes Armees*, heading north.

They picked up with relief the Donald Duck sign, return arrow down, and joined a US Army convoy with headlamps on, crossing with them where the French Divisional area combined with the US Fifth and so without trouble. As Max continued to drive on, Sergeant Sturman was in high spirits.

"We'll be in Thirty Corps area soon, sir! Mind if I turn on the radio? We get Duffle Bag about now sir, if you like to put the earphones on."

"I've got to be a bit careful!" Max said. The road surface was bad. "We don't want any accidents now!" But he clipped on the black rubber earphones.

So it was that he first heard the melifluous magic of Duffle Bag, the new programme for the United States Army in Europe, bringing perhaps the finest music, the best bands, the biggest single lift to morale that any army ever had, at the turn of a radio dial.

"AFN it was called!" Max Beaumont looked round because the red light over the library door had changed from red to green.

"American Forces Network! Duffle Bag! One of those canvas holdall things that soldiers use. I date a lot of things from the sounds of Duffle Bag. It made you realise that there was another world outside there somewhere. Of power, plenty, peace and pulchritude, waiting for us! Who did we hear on Duffle Bag that day? Why, Glen Miller of course! Well, maybe if you never heard Glen Miller's band coming into your head, while your courage was running out of your boots you wouldn't know? And we should have tuned into regimental signals anyway!"

Max Beaumont got up, as Liz Charlton came through the door, followed by the PR man, Al Chemmy, with Liz holding a sheaf of papers in her hand, and Chemmy looking as though he was about to announce a death in the family. But Max Beaumont looked at them cheerfully, his head, characteristically a little on one side. His blue eyes bright, as though he might still be hearing Glen Miller.

"Are we advancing or retreating?"

327

God help us, I thought, he is still in the war.

Max was reading telexes and sheets of paper, handing them back quickly, with only a word or two. When he had finished, and Liz had gone quietly through the door he said: "Do you remember first hearing Glen Miller, Al?"

If Al Chemmy was surprised he didn't show it. "I certainly do." Al looked out of the window. *"Pennsylvania 6–5000! Tuxedo Junction! Deep Purple! Juke Box Saturday Night!* That do you?" Delighted, Max patted him on the shoulder.

"I was just saying! I think the British and the Americans won the war on those and the rest! There was Bing Crosby of course, and that upstart Frankie just coming along!"

"Sir, will you see what it's like at Battersea?" Al's voice was urgent. "In about two minutes there will be news on the box there!" He pointed across the room. "There are twenty or so police in hospital. And the rest. And more to come without any doubt."

He had stepped across the library, knowing his way, and was now opening panelled doors that concealed an outsize TV receiver. It lit up, and the preliminaries to the ITV News came on.

"Always the competition!" said Owen unhappily.

"The Battle of Battersea!" Max Beaumont stared at the screen, articulating carefully, repeating the newscaster, his voice oddly high pitched, as always when not guarding his emotion.

"Who's commentating?" I asked.

"Georgina Ponting," Owen said. He knew them all, of course. "The girls get the weekend duty. Christ, look at that!"

A wall of uniformed police struggled to hold back seething ranks of angry protesters. The cameras panned the crowd which stretched far beyond the railings of the park, blocking the bridge, the two sides surging and pressing like troops in some film reconstruction of an ancient battle. It was of course current history, here, now, and it was television. The tense voice of the girl commentator worked in with the camera crews.

"I am told there are perhaps five thousand protesters here this evening! And how many police we are not told. The mounted police are moving in now, they are clearing a way for another of the special coaches bringing in the newspaper staff who are defying the ban, journalists and others. Bricks, stones and home-made missiles, including the police say, fire bombs, have been hurled at these coaches! Now, yes! Something has gone off by one of the police horses! The horse is down! The rider is there on the ground! And now the others are beating off this tremendously angry crowd of protesters, the print workers and allied unions, but also we are told, many flying pickets and supporters from far afield!" There was a fudge, as the camera moved, but the uproar remained on sound. The girl newscaster's voice was back, hurried and more breathless now.

"Inside there is the line of vehicles that have brought staff in earlier, but many of the people at work inside have stayed the night, and will again. From here we can see the security people with their dogs, and there is floodlighting too, up on the posts beyond reach of that hail of stones. The riot police are in trouble, going down! There are more coming to their rescue, dragging them back! And casualties on the other side too! Ambulances trying to get through, two of them, and ambulance stretcher men braving this angry mob, the police trying to escort them forward . . ."

"That'll do!" Max Beaumont snapped. "Take it out will you!" He turned.

Al Chemmy switched the screen to darkness, and slowly closed the doors over the front.

"Well, Tolly – I suppose Publish and Kill will be the next headline someone will think up! Poor old Hugh Cudlip would turn in his grave. If his Fleet Street had ever stuck together – the proprietors I mean, all this could have been avoided!"

"Are you planning to get down there?" Owen asked quietly.

"The answer is, yes! But it seems I have to go in wearing a boiler-suit and a false beard, driven by minders in an armoured delivery van!" Max said, bitterly.

"Perhaps you should have kept a spare Sherman around?" Owen said.

Max stared at him with his eyes narrow and hard, his lips drawn back in a half-snarl.

"Why don't *you* drive me through! In one of your BBC vans, Mr. Owen?"

Al Chemmy as a good PR man decided to break up this little dialogue. We had all been a bit shaken by what he had decided to show on the screen.

"Sir, do I bring in the executives? They've been waiting a while? Just that our friends from the BBC are outside the Group!"

"Supposing we get up to date, Max? On or off the record!" I suggested. "We can quit if you want us to, but perhaps we could be allowed to learn what the hell is going on in Battersea?"

"Couldn't we have an O group?" It was Owen again. And I wondered whether Max Beaumont would go on taking it.

To my surprise, he looked at Owen with something like approval. "OK Al!" he said "Bring them in!"

They were familiar faces. Clive Bell, editor of *The World*, Laycock, Ricksdorf, Liz back again with notebook.

"Off the record," Max said. "The oldest phrase in the business. But right off! No privileges, no friendships, no tape-machines!"

We all watched as Owen, poker-face, put the black plastic box on the carpet at his feet and dropped a cushion on top of it. He sat back silently and folded his arms.

"Information," Max Beaumont said, quietly, and his dominance of the small group was total. "The unions have taken it the wrong way! They have not responded to any last offers, compromises on money, working conditions or necessities. There are now pickets at the plant, and they have asked for TGWU support. TUC meeting tomorrow. Information our side? The whole of the Battersea operation has gone live. Clive here has key staff editorial already with us and ready to go. The computer room and special link has been set up by our people from Chicago and there is a nucleus of our own, plus them, to work it! We shall recruit more this week. Accounts are OK. Ad. sales are OK. Platemaking and the composing room are on – both worked for the *Sunday World* and *Flash* last night. Intention," Max waited, fractionally. "Media International will produce all its formerly Fleet Street based papers at

Battersea and will fight off all opposition to that from whatever quarter!"

"I think fight is the word, Max!" Laycock said quietly. "We've got five thousand out there, not just bawling and yelling, but pushing the police back against the wire, with flying pickets from every militant union in the country, plus all the lefty MPs who want their faces shown!"

"We've just seen it, Dennis!" Max Beaumont was quiet but instilling confidence. "Next is Method! Remember, Owen? We have the finest automated computerised production set-up anywhere in Europe – thanks largely to our US and German know-how! Distribution will be by our own transport and will be guarded, fuelled and operated right down to retailer level by our own people! The plant is protected by our own Security Consultants! The high steel fence includes razor wire from Germany. If they storm the wire this will give time for more police reinforcements." He paused, looking quizzically at Owen Owen and myself. Neither of us spoke.

"Administration then! I shall be there tonight, at Battersea. It will not particularly help if I am known to be there, but next – Communication! I want all ranks, all levels, to understand what we are doing and why! Disruptions in the past have led to the loss of millions of pounds, sometimes bringing down whole related lines of companies! We have spent over one hundred million on this new set-up! It is going to secure the jobs and the future of a free press! I want all A level executives on bleep to me personally, Denis. Al! Make our story understood! Any questions?" Max was sticking to his old formula to the end.

"Is the Beeb going to allow this programme on at all?" It was Owen Owen to me, and now there was a short, pregnant silence.

"I've heard about it, Max," Al said shortly. "And I don't like it. Items, as *Time* magazine says! I get a phone call from TUC press office asking whether you're cancelling your TV appearance in view of the worsening crisis in Fleet Street – their description! Then our own TV columnist says he picked up a buzz yesterday from Bush House, that the Governors

331

want to be very neutral because the unions could spread this one!"

"What I don't like," Owen Owen said, and he still spoke directly to me, "is that I had a call from Roger Bullen, who said he'd been told to contact me. And that he would drop in for a chat tomorrow. I asked him what the hell that meant, and he said that you might be pulled off the show and the thing turned round into a survey of the situation generally. A piece he would be presenting! I told him that as Producer, when I had instructions on those lines, I might get with him, but tomorrow looked busy."

"He's after Mr. Tolly's job!" Clive Bell, editor of *The World* said in his hard, Scottish tones. "I can get onto this as soon as I'm back in the office. I can put half a dozen people onto it if you want!"

"Why do they want to drop you, Felix?" Bob Ricksdorf asked.

"Oh come on, Bob – you can see that one!" Max Beaumont said coldly pleasant. "The BBC's star presenter has been my personal friend for forty years! They fear that he will show bias! So now that we have people who do not like us on several sides, the fighting may get confused!"

With that it was over. And we were all drifting towards the door, together.

"The other old song of course, was Felix keeps on walking! And talking! That's the one I like!" Max paused as Chemmy opened the door for him, and looked round at me. "I hope afterwards, you'll come and work for me, Tolly! Part time and for twice the money? Think about it!"

Outside on the drive, with people getting into cars, and the lights from the big windows illuminating the front steps, Owen held my arm. "You're the only person he'll do this with!" he said quietly. "I suppose we'll know tomorrow if the balloon's going up!" He put on a droll face. "Christ, all this war stuff is really getting me now!"

332

CHAPTER FIFTEEN

I was thinking what Owen had said when I got back to the Richmond house early on the Sunday morning. At that hour the place seemed deserted. But I had been seen, and Rinski, immaculate in white coat, and as insensitive as ever, let me in. Obviously none of the others had yet arrived.

I went into the cloakroom off the main hall before going to look for Max Beaumont. It seemed as though I had been living in that Richmond residence for almost ever, somehow much more so than other places where I had spent far longer time on similar assignments.

The cloakroom was all marble toiletry, dark mahogany pots and bottles and silver-backed brushes, arranged in parade order like those damn toy solders. I thought about Max, and looked in the big glass, and wished that I appeared less like a ham actor playing Beethoven. That I could also have been born with his looks, that could still bring something of the strange, secret look into women's eyes. It did, because I had seen them. Even that tough little bird from German TV.

As I came out into the big hall, Max was coming from the other end, in his riding gear. He was not walking like a man with cares, instead with a quick lithe step, slightly swaying shoulders, that almost feline movement, as though he was taking in anything that might move to left or right. But I could see now from his face that he was tired.

"Up all night?" I said.

He looked at me sharply, as though it was criticism. Then he stopped only a yard away and gave his twisted smile.

"How did you know?"

"I didn't! But I can't think you were riding all night."

"When I got out of that place, Tolly, I remembered an old saying. It applies if you feel like I did. That the best thing for the inside of a man is the outside of a horse!"

Rinski brought Owen Owen into the hall. I saw Max take in Owen's Sunday look. The producer had not tried very hard with the razor and was wearing a black leather jacket over jeans.

"No Joe?" I said, hurriedly. Perhaps Joe's mirror would make him a credit to the regiment.

"Maybe later. He was with the cameras at Battersea a lot of the night."

"Come on!" Max said abruptly. "I want to get on! Let's get going, Tolly!"

He was still the only person who used my surname like that, as he had in those early days and it still sometimes seemed brusque. Now he did it to Owen.

"Let's get this thing tied up Owen the Owen!" he said. "Or is it Owen of Owen? And as it's just you two, and it's a nice morning, why don't we step through those doors, and sit in the stable yard? It's more fresh air I need, and some more black coffee!"

At the top end of the stable yard, there was a wooden table with heavy chairs round. It was a peaceful, old-fashioned place. Cobblestones and a black- and gold-faced clock on the roof tower, and the clinking, muffled noises of horses in stables made a comforting sound. Max must have had an idea of where we were going to be already, because Boris, in his short white steward's coat arrived, and put a tray with coffee in a silver thermos jug on the table.

"OK? If we need anything else you keep an eye on us, Boris!"

"Keeping eye!" said Boris in his thick accent. He did not offer to serve and left Max to pour for all three of us.

"Your Military Cross!" Owen said crisply without finesse. "I think Felix has definitely got to ask you that one, and we can wrap up any other bits from there."

Max slurped heavily from the steaming coffee cup, and looked at us over the rim with feigned concern.

"I hope nothing I say will perturb you! For instance I haven't told you how I saw a woman copulating with a donkey, shortly after that trip to Paris! It was in a brothel in Amiens."

"I didn't know you could get an MC in a brothel!" Owen said flat-faced and unsmiling. "How do we cover that?"

"Why not?" Max Beaumont still unprovoked, poured a little from the whisky bottle, which Boris had also provided, into his cup. "Of course some did die 'in the saddle' as I believe they said, in Cairo. Later, in the same month, the war got, well, too serious, for such things. Remember it? Operation *Market Garden!*"

"A Bridge Too Far!" I said to help Owen. "Arnhem!"

If it had come off well, we might have been home for Christmas. As that German prisoner hoped. Unfortunately a lot of his mates in the ninth SS Panzer were around when the drop went in at Oosterbeek. Nobody really knew they were so near to Arnhem. There's intelligence work for you! "Max Beaumont was looking through the stable archway towards Richmond Park from where he sat. "The country you can see to left and right, that view through the arch, is how it was there! And the trees were sparse, and no other cover. We pushed up the one and only road to Nijmegen. Early on, a couple of three-ton trucks following the tanks ahead had been destroyed by mines the Germans had laid in the verges, and some sapper unit had put up a notice: DON'T LET THIS HAPPEN TO YOU! KEEP ON THE ROAD! VERGES NOT CLEARED OF MINES!" That was why Max's own troop of three flail tanks, plus the remaining two of another troop, were pressed into the column attached to the Irish Guards, trying to get up the road to Nijmegen. If there were any more mines in front, Max Beaumont said, a Guards Armoured staff officer had told him, then his Bloody Things could deal with them!

It was just south of Nijmegen, that Sergeant Sturman and two of his crew had been killed. Hit by the deadly 88's, firing from the other side of the river, black smoke enveloped the tank, that was only fifty yards from Max's own, and he had jinked desperately in reverse, trying to evade the next shot. It never came, as the Guards Armoured on

335

the road had unleashed instant salvos, crashing and flaming from guns already traversed. 88's were usually sited in threes. For the moment there was no more counter-fire.

Max was out of his turret, crossing the short intervening space, stumbling over the bog-like ground, panting for breath. He knew the risk as he clawed onto the stricken tank, coughing, his eyes smarting in the smoke.

The sickening carnage in the turret was what one should never see, after the armour piercing shell had penetrated, then fragmented inside, whipping flakes of sharp metal off the turret wall, killing the crew in a hail of shrapnel. Pieces had killed the driver in front, a slumped shape in his seat. Only the co-driver was suddenly up there beside Max on the tank top.

"Get off it, sir! The ammo could blow! Get off!" He turned and leapt, sprawling on the ground below.

Sergeant Sturman's face was against the radio set. Most of one shoulder was blood-red pulp. His eyes stared open, seeing nothing. Somewhere below him, the other two were dead, wedged down below the gun breach.

In those seconds it seemed to Max he took in only the small things. Sturman's face was dirty. It was wrong that he should be dead and so grimed, and that one dangling leg had a boot on with the laces untied. The other foot was missing. For a second Max wondered if he should try to reach pockets, salvage anything for that family in Durham. Then he leaned in and grabbed instead the first-aid tin next to the radio. It was too late for use now, but each one contained the precious morphia phials for use on the wounded, and they were hard to get. There was nothing he could do for the dead.

Half-blinded now by smoke and tears he flung himself off the Sherman's hull, and ran to his own tank knowing he might be under fire, and had only the strength to pull himself up, and lay, holding the black tin first-aid set, feeling the tank moving again, jerking, twisting slowly. Miserably he felt his trousers wet inside. The radio operator was out of the turret beside him.

"Come on, sir!" The man's voice was hoarse and pleading. "Get inside, sir! It's safer inside, sir!"

336

Back in the turret, perched on the little drop-flap seat, a sudden crackle from his earphones hooked on the turret lid reached Max's brain.

It was loud enough to be on the nearest Guards Armoured channel, and he peered down into the comparative gloom of the turret to see his operator fingering the volume switches on the 19 set.

"I can see ant moving to cover now by those trees! West of 3484!" It was the excited voice of a young guards tank officer. There was silence as the radio played for a moment with its own mush. Then the high-pitched voice again. "It's a Tiger! All stations, King Tiger!"

Max tried to smile at the upturned face of Nobby Clark his gunner, their dirt engrained countenances sharing the same thought. When a first-timer saw the enemy, it always looked like a Royal Tiger.

"We will engage! Out!" It was theirs, Guards Armoured, not to reason why. "All stations Baker two! Cover me and I will flank left!"

His squadron command broke in immediately, to stop this brashness that was in the best Guards tradition. The Command voice was cool and imperative.

"Stay where you are Baker two! Our aim is forward. Keep on the road!"

And then, even as Max looked to that deadly road, the sharp unmistakable air-stripping crack of another German eighty-eight passed ahead, and with a hideous blast of noise an ammunition truck on the road was obliterated in red flame. Pieces of metal, and burning, smoking remnants rained down, and immediately the chattering of the Guards infantry machine guns broke out, seeking along the dykes and across the path towards the far farm buildings.

Presently, a jeep left the road, almost tumbling downward across the verge, and a steel helmeted figure with the shoulder pips of a Lieutenant Colonel stood up beside the driver, gesturing up to Max, whose head was just visible in the Sherman's turret.

"Who is the officer there?" He shouted. "A name! What is it?"

"Beaumont, sir!"

337

"Are you in trouble, Mr. Beaumont? What are you stopped here for? The Guards orders are to press on to Nijmegen bridge. But you could look for that Jerry tank! Get to it!"

The point was made, even as the jeep swung round in reverse, turning back towards the road. Another screaming shell went straight in front of it, to bounce off the road where a moment before one of the Irish Guards tanks had moved forward.

Max Beaumont felt as though he had a metal band tightening round his forehead, as he moved quickly and precisely, sliding down into the turret, breathing in the mix of damp metal, fuel and human sweat. Now he had the earphones on intercom, and his driver was swinging the Sherman round in a cloud of its own engine smoke and dirt from the tracks.

"Able One all stations!" On this net, his call sign was no longer Charlie. Max could see the other three tanks under his command, wheeling out of the comparative shelter of the gulley they had been in. "He's somewhere in those farm buildings! Movement and fire to cover us!" The rubber handset mouthpiece squeezed, black and greasy round his mouth. He switched to intercom again. "Smudger! Chuck her about! Make for those trees by the brickwork! Stop when we have cover there!"

Glancing behind him he could see now the chaos on the jam-packed road. The autumn light was just beginning to fall across the Dutch landscape. But the German tank gunner was not firing again. Why? Half a mile ahead, some of the Irish Guards tanks were ranging onto another cluster of half-ruined sheds and a dyke water pump. Had the Tiger moved? And how? There was no hull-down position or dead ground unless behind the dyke embankment. And what could inflict damage if it was a Tiger?

Now the earphones tight against his head were busy again. Max felt the vibration in his eardrums. He was dizzily light-headed, and his stomach was empty, tight with hunger as much as nerves. He would have to urinate again the moment they stopped, which meant using one of the empty shell cases, kept for the purpose. There was no getting out.

338

With a lurch the tank had stopped. They had reached the farmyard wall. Ahead and to his left, the other three Shermans were still crawling forward, leapfrogging, stopping, covering each other, gun turrets teetering and swinging when they halted.

"Switch off!" His own engine went quiet. Only the hum of the turret electrics whined on, as Max snatched off his earphones, and with his head above the turret cupola, listened. That was the snag with armour. You could not run, crouching and silent, and flop down out of sight, like the infantry. But you could switch off, and listen. From no distance away at all, half hidden by the ruined wall there was suddenly a flash, blast and instant shockwave with white light, that made Max close his eyes, shouting to his driver to start up again.

"He's got Corporal Barton, sir!" It was the gunner on the intercom. "They're trying to get out in front!" Now there was the searing, ripping noise of the German tank's machine guns as it sought to kill the escaping crew.

Round the corner of the partially destroyed barn, Max eased very slowly, talking softly to Smudger Smith through the wet rubber mouthpiece, crouching, with his eyes at the level of the cupola ring, the engine barely throbbing, tracks all but silent, carrying wet field mud over the sprockets.

"Stop!"

A hundred yards ahead and no more, the German tank waited, its high rear end facing them. It was not playing the listening game. A trickle of smoke came from the engine louvres. The long barrelled gun was traversed to the front, sighted on the flaming shape of the Sherman that had been its last target.

This was no Tiger. A Panther, Max saw in half an eye. But more acutely, the muzzle-weighted, long barrelled seventy-five that was the Panther's equivalent to the Tiger's eighty-eight, had started it's silent movement. Borne on by the wedge-shaped turret, it was coming round, towards him.

"Gun control! Fire!" Max whispered.

Unbelievably, Nobby Clark's first shell went straight over the top of the Panther turret. Max heard the clang of the empty shell case flung to the turret floor and the heavier, purposeful crash of the breech closing on the next round. Still, that hypnotisingly long barrel came round. Jerkily, slowly, and only then did Max grasp with sudden certainty that the wounded Panther had lost its hydraulic turret traverse. Lost the spinning speed of electricity, and was dependant on hand traverse, cranked by a desperate German gunner.

Nobby Clark had steadied. His second armour piercing shell hit the Panther at the one point that mattered, the joint between turret and hull, and this time, at that range, there could be no mistake. A white, blinding flash, and with a hideous, metallic jolt, the Panther turret tilted and jammed. The movement stopped and the long gun barrel slowly sagged.

A plume of thick black smoke began to drift from the stricken metal hull. As though himself in artificial slow motion, Max noticed that his own driver and co-driver had already baled out, and were crouching down by the tracks. He got out, and crouched behind the turret, feeling a cramping stiffness. He was followed out onto the engine hatch by the operator and gunner. "Nobby that was good!" was all Max could croak. All of them were looking at the stricken Panther. No order was necessary as the driver and mate scrambled up and back into their seats, and quickly all of them got back inside, as the Sherman's engines roared and it worked back, jerking as one track locked, then the other. If the Panther was on the point of a brew up, fuel and ammunition would blast a wide area of devastation.

One of the other flail tanks had rolled up now, and halted, covering the Panther from a short distance.

But Max gave the order. "Nobby – give it to them again! And the *co-ax!*"

He held on under the cupola edge as the seventy-five fired again, and the Browning sprayed away.

He suddenly felt that he was going to retch, and leaning out did so. There was not much to come up, because his stomach had been so empty. He had seen others succumb to this, and even more unpleasant forms of reaction, but it was humiliating in front of the troops, and there was never anywhere you could move away to, or get any privacy in a tank. If that Panther's gun had been on power traverse, he would not have been moving anywhere. Now they had stopped behind the barn, and he got out and jumped down to the ground, and leaned against the tank side.

Which was how the Regimental Commander found him, which made a story of it afterwards. Because Max had not noticed the arrival of one of those big American Command half-tracks, and there was a British Guards Brigadier, and an American airborne Colonel with him, with the pale-blue uniform flashes, looking extraordinarily crisp as he too jumped down. Also his own C.O., and it was, he supposed just his good luck that they should all have been on the road at that time. But when he saluted, the stiffness was still there, and his intestines heaved inside, and he wiped his mouth.

"Sorry for that, sir!"

"That's all right!" It was the Guards' Colonel, brisk, his voice a short bark.

"What did you say the lieutenant's name was?" The Brigadier asked.

"He did tell me sir, but I've forgotten! He came up with the flails, in case we had more trouble up the road!"

"It's Lieutenant Beaumont sir!" his Colonel had reported. "We call him Beaubum! He specialises in shooting Jerries up the backside!"

As the Brigadier had laughed, everyone else laughed quickly too, and Max was glad. There was nothing like any sort of joke at those times, and it settled the stomach.

"This is Trooper Clarke, sir!" Max said. "He is my gunner."

"I did miss first time, sir!" Clarke said. Then remembered to salute, and he and the other tanks crews moved away, and the Brigadier pulled a field notebook out of his pocket.

"Just keep that name for me," said the American. "We don't read and write in the eighty-second you know!" There was more short laughter.

"Why did you go on putting shells into him after he was knocked out?" The C.O. asked, his voice flat now. "Do you know ammo and fuel are short?"

"They might have gone on fighting!" From somewhere in the past, Max heard his own voice. The reply sounded as though someone else had made it.

341

"Get back on the road!" The Colonel was getting into the half-track with the others. "There are mines to the side of a road block! I'll give you a map ref. on the air."

Of course it was only good luck that the American airborne were with Thirty Corps. And handing out Purple Hearts. And some of their people would later get British equivalents. But Max never knew until later that he would also get the Military Cross out of it. When the corporal from the other tank came over with a mess tin of scalding tea, it was the colour of rust-water, and that was real.

On the other hand he pointed out, there weren't any Allied brass or Brigadiers to see him when they arranged the elaborate set-piece attack on Venlo that autumn. When he was blown up and trapped. Or later in the snow and ice cold wind of the Ardennes, sent to help the Americans in the Bulge breakthrough. Then he got frostbite, and later pneumonia. He had seen others, officers and men, who had suffered and done more in those realms cited as "beyond the call of duty" but who never got those decorations. They were rationed out, and he was luckier than most. In reality, there were those who did a lot, and said least, and he hoped we would understand that what he had described was only to give us what we had asked for.

As for bravery or courage, everyone was different, and there were enough theories. And fear was something that changed, and grew or shrank according to constantly changing circumstances. Really, the willingness to face death, to know that it meant the end of living, was something you could, in his view, do when you were at the end of caring. Or to achieve something with men you were close with, and who depended on you, and it was pride and leadership again, and there were different kinds of pride, if that was the right word, being responsible, a kind of conviction and loyalty to yourself.

Max Beaumont stopped talking. In the stableyard it was very quiet, with the old clock on the roof, its hands seeming to stand still, like the sky beyond with small, seemingly painted clouds, and only the snuffling, clinking sound of the horses out of sight in their stalls.

342

I was wondering how to get the same feeling from what we had just heard, with a question that would get across to millions of people. I could tell Owen had the same thing on his mind, although he had a folded piece of paper and a plastic ballpoint, and the paper was marked with tiny words.

There was also a new feeling I had, and I had it quite strongly, that Max needed to talk about experiences that were deep in his recollection now, as an antidote to events that were shaping his life at present. It was typical of his sometimes uncanny intuition that he appeared to pick up this notion independently, and looked round at me, smiling the old lop-sided smile, and offering the last of the coffee from the Thermos jug.

"My dear old Tolly!" he said laconically. "I remember you asked me once about Monty. How confident people were when they knew he had command, because everything that should have been done was done, and he used to go to sleep in his caravan, even as the battle started, saying there was no more he could do for the time, so he might as well get his Ovaltine! You're both probably wondering what the hell I'm doing with you blokes when I should be in that mêlée at Battersea! Well, we'll see how the campaign goes shortly! At the moment it is all in the hands of the line commanders. I might as well be in New York or on a yacht. But I prefer it here!" Max Beaumont rose, looking at his watch, with the usual small flick of his shirt cuff, and I never knew really why but inevitably Owen Owen and I were on our feet quite quickly too.

"You know – I wish I had seen action in that war of yours!" Owen was suddenly dead serious. "Not the sort of junk wars my generation wax indignant about. Do you think I could have made it at Sandhurst?"

Max Beaumont looked at him now, with cool assessment. "I dare say you could have done." His voice was its most affected. "As long as you could avoid saying the wrong thing at the wrong time perhaps? Now Tolly here, I don't think would make it! And quite rightly preferred to have his head in the clouds, rather than feet on the ground!"

"Where will you be?" I asked, grimly.

"In the Fortress? Where I spent last night, and shall again tonight. That is the most difficult time. Getting staff in, seeing all the systems are working, getting the newspapers out. Past the barbarians at the gate, shall we say?"

He left Owen Owen and I, standing on the cobblestones each of us for a moment casting about in our minds for something that had point, or seemed a professional conclusion to what was our last joint session before the actual filming scheduled for Thursday.

"Why didn't Joe turn up?" Owen fretted. "I'd like to have that bit about his MC on and I didn't even bring tape! And why does he still speak that kind of language? Know what I mean? 'That's it you fellows!' and 'So long, cheerio!' He even says Old Boy! And a lot of etiquette stuff with the girls. Is he permanently in the forties and fifties? He has always called you Tolly, and of course with my name, for which thank my humorous father, I never know whether he means me to call him Max, or whether I ought to insist on being called Mr. Owen!"

"Well there are bloody few who call him Max, if you've noticed!" I pointed out. "Not even the senior men he's had working with him for years. Even those Statesiders we met have to drop the Call me Buddy bit! No, I think when you learn a whole new language at a formative age, adapt and mould yourself, fight a war and survive, returning in that way to what was once your own country, well you could be acting a charade a lot of the time afterwards!"

"I hadn't thought of that! You could be dead right. If your life is unreal, all acting, suppressing your real feelings early in life, nothing afterwards is real. All a charade!" Owen's flat, broad-featured, unshaven face lit up, and he struck a pose.

"If you can dream and not make dreams your master!"

I rather thought Max Beaumont would have liked to hear Owen Owen declaiming *If* like that.

I had gone once again into the martial cloakroom, after Owen left, and was standing in the big hall for a moment, collecting further thoughts. It was of a size that could have taken in almost all the ground floor area of the Tolly home. The ceiling was a large, framed glass dome, not uncommon in those larger early Victorian places, and this goldfish bowl effect had produced a pleasing salon. The wide staircase made the same circular effect, and had been scraped down to the original mahogany, not unlike the subtle colour of the carpet. There were expensive modern paintings of the post-Impressionist kind on the walls, and a heavy golden yew table under the dome shone with the overhead light which also fell on a vast Chinese vase that held a great many tall and elegant flowers.

"I'm going to admit I was watching you!" Deborah Beaumont appeared without my noticing, standing in one of the several panelled doors round the hall. "And if I may say so, I think you were approving. Am I right?"

"So many of these houses can be like hotels," I agreed. "This one feels lived in."

"It's difficult! The boys have left home, of course. Max isn't here for stretches at a time, and often I make a quick trip to the States or somewhere, but you know, he needs a real home! And if he gets the chance, he'll hang up a picture himself, or even clean riding boots out there, or make one the of the dogs jump the sofa! I will say he has surprisingly good taste when he does bring home antiques or smaller things for me. Well, that sounds dumb of course, when you think of his original background. You never saw the original house, the one in Berlin? It was bombed pretty well flat I know. I've only seen some black and white old photographs, I think they belonged to his aunt, the one who more or less brought him up."

"Sybilla," I said.

"She had pictures, and to see some of those rooms in that house with heavy, tall, carved German pieces, and carpets and dark old furnishings with lace on, and drapes like a theatre. They give me the spooks! I don't know what they did to Max – perhaps you're finding out?"

"Yes," I said, "I think bit by bit I am."

"In a way I feel almost sort of jealous! We did agree Felix, didn't we? Although Max calls you Tolly. Why is that?"

"It was the same with the flying types I had been with. They all liked it – Pollywolly Tolly! It was a famous name,

Tolly's Ales – I think they believed I had something to do with it."

"He won't let you be dropped, you know," she said suddenly. "He's told me about it! That's what you were thinking about, when you were looking at the flowers, wasn't it? Max wanted me to give you this!" She held out a sealed buff envelope. "He said, as he left just now, that they would save time. They're letters. I don't think he particularly wanted them to go round any of the others, but he said you were to have them. I found them years ago, and kept them."

"They're not love letters?" Reluctantly I took the envelope.

"They're stuff he wrote during the war mostly."

"To his fiancée? The Navy girl he was engaged to?"

Deborah Beaumont rested a beringed hand on the big table, and tweaked for a moment at some of the flowers. "I think I know the one you mean. He was engaged a few times, you know. No, that one sent *him* the letter soon after he was wounded. I don't know if she knew that. She found a dashing sailor in the hand was more interesting than a Red Indian in the bush. That was the way Max put it." Deborah Beaumont smiled, and patted her hair, looking at her brocaded silk blouse. "How do I look this evening? I'm going to have some real friends in for lunch."

"You look great," I told her, and meant it. "I'm going to have a quiet day in the bosom."

For a moment she looked startled.

"The bosom of the family," I said quickly. "Always an expression I've liked!"

"Max's bosoms haven't always been family" Debby Beaumont said. "But we talked about that, you and me, I remember. I've known some of them, but we never discuss them. Rational discussion is the enemy of sin. And I think Max, for some reason, has to be sinful – but only in that way, Felix! And I sometimes think he has more discretion and natural reticence about it than if he was born British! Now you must go, and I will see you out."

"Are these letters indiscreet?" I held up the envelope.

"They were all to his Aunt – the one you mentioned. So I would say no, although I think the relationship they had must have been an interesting one."

346

The smile she gave me was not sphinx-like. It was the rewarding, All-American kind.

That evening in the study, I took the envelope, and pulled out the half dozen or so letters it contained. And though in many ways I needed a rest from the whole thing, there were some interesting new items and in a definite way they did help to round out the Max Beaumont persona.

Dearest Syb,   *Somewhere in N.W. Europe*
Well I've been made up to captain as of today, so don't forget to put that on the envelopes! It means I'm acting squadron second-in-command, partly because of the MC (thanks for the *Richmond Times* cutting, but why did you give them that drunken looking photo of me!) And because poor old Denis Skinner caught it. There's a lot of skwits about as usual (I can't spell the proper word) and he *had* to go, just when we had moved into a small orchard, and he trod on one of those AP mines. Lucky to lose only a leg. We went in turns to see him in the field hospital, and he was white as the sheets and bloody brave. They've pretty well finished off the flying bomb launchers, but we've heard about this rocket, you don't even hear it coming. You said in your last letter you had not been at all well – so we must be equal. If you mean you've copped it in some way, you *must* write and say so in clear. I might even get compassionate leave!

That bit about promotion was the good news, and now the not so good, because we did come unstuck on a big set-piece thing, and this was the first chance I've had to tell you, and *I am all right* now. All of which is to explain that I went on the sick list with a couple of the chaps too, and we had sleepy-times injections and they sent us off, back to X which is a big place. It used to be called shell-shock, being concussed, and now it's battle fatigue, and without going into the symptoms it's pretty gut-rotting. I was OK after a week, and we were put onto a miserable night train from somewhere back in Belgium. It was all blacked out, and we crawled along with no lights, there were troops from reinforcement depots, and the officers were cramped up, about a dozen of us, all sorts too, in a separate compartment. We stopped for the umpteenth time in some blacked out Belg. railway station, and in the dark the platform loudspeaker announced that the NAAFI had a hot tea trolley! Joy unconfined! We were going to be halted for half an hour, and get your mess tins ready! Carriages would be called forward in turn, officers first!

So of course, we woke up, and got our pannikins, and spruced up a bit. We went along the dimly lit platform, watched by all the troops leaning out of their windows as we passed, and then slowly they started to chant. It caught on, and I must say I didn't like the sound of it at all, and I never met anything like it before, because what they were repeating in a low-key chorus was "Officers first! Officers first!"

I suppose in my outfit, we never had anything like it, but these men were all sorts, infantry mostly, and as they went on chanting we slunk along. But we bumped into each other pretty smartly, because in front someone had stopped suddenly so we all did too. He was a Scot, this officer. About three foot nothing high, with his kilt, boots and gaiters, and his tam o'shanter all jaunty, and he put his hands on his hips, and looked along those carriage windows. And then he spoke. And I wish I could do the dialect, because apart from parade ground loudness, it puts an edge to it!

"Officers Fust, Officers Fust!" He turned his craggy, white little jock face, looking at them, one way then the other. "Yes! And when else is it Officers Furrst? When ye're all lyin' in the mud, with the shit comin' over us! And there's not one of ye'll make a move! Aye, who's furrst then? You know who's fuckin' furrst then!" And he turned smartly, stamping his boots. "That'll do lads! You'll get your turn!" And with his wee shoulders back, and his arms going, he stepped out, the rest of us behind him. In dead silence now, the faces that had crowded the windows fell back, just watching.

The trouble is, this war is going on too long. Winter in Holland is bitterly, horribly cold, and wet and dark. They promise us some new kind of tank suit, but they haven't arrived yet. I saw some of the Guards tank officers in their turrets with *umbrellas*. Sent out by their association at home! What the British army calls jammy.

Must stop now. Write to me all you can, you are the only one I have now. Love always, and don't fret about me. Max.

Another letter was about the Ardennes and the winter conditions there came to life on paper. It was odd to realise that the young Max Beaumont had only been using English for just ten years of his life. I knew there was censorship of mail from the front, and officers were charged with reading and checking the letters home from the troops, other than those in their own immediate command. Their own letters were supposed to be checked by brother officers, but the etiquette was to seal them down without reading. Certainly it might have been risky or embarrassing for Max to express his feelings about the Germans or the conduct of the war. Which made one letter of special significance.

Dear Syb,   N.W.E.
The other day we crossed the Rhine, somehow more of an entry into the land of my forebears than the messy strip of wet, cold Emsland we have been in and out of for weeks. We left from a place given the appropriate name of Amen Corner. The Jocks got most of the fighting. There was a foxhole (slit trench) with a dead German in it, and all his bits and pieces, helmet, waterbottle, pack-already he'd looted a blanket. He had been a machine gunner. There were pieces of that about too. But the point of telling you this is that he had been writing a letter home in spare moments, and there were muddy bits of lined writing paper about. Always a strange smell where the German troops have been, whether it's a farmhouse or a dugout or a big fortification. A stale, sweaty smell, like dishwater, quite queer. I wonder if we have our smell for them that is different?

I am telling you this because on one of the pages of this dead Jerry's letter it was the PS which said: I enclose a blade of grass from my machine-gun pit which I shall defend to the death for the Fatherland! Can you believe that? Well, he had done just what he wrote. I took a look at him and I would guess he was seventeen, if that. But Sibby – can you imagine a British Tommy writing, Dear Mum, I enclose a blade of grass etc. What *is* the difference between them and us? Or can I, of all people, ask that?
Your loving Max.

Dear Sibby,   Deutschland

Now it is looking like the end, some of the worst things have happened. Dick Winters squadron leader of A was knocked out in a messy job crossing the Dortmund Ems canal. You will see at the end of this, if I can scribble on, what that has meant. A German officer cadet school fought to stop the canal crossing, none of them more than fifteen and sixteen, and fanatics, like we have heard about the Japanese suicide airmen. The trouble honestly, is nobody wants to get knocked out now at this stage, and Dick had to do it again – Officers Furrst!

We did guard duty for a night in a place called Celle. I don't mind mentioning names now. The commandos had taken it early that day, after a terrible daylight bombing raid by a thousand US Flying Fortr~ss bombers – only because the SS were defending, and would not quit. They must know what their fate is going to be. Nobody is taking them prisoner now. Tanks don't usually do guard at night in built-up areas, and we crowded everything, tanks and lorries, into and round a school playground. As luck would have it I was on duty first, posting guards in places the commandos had marked on a map for us. The town was pitch black but still burning here and there, and the streets just tracks through the rubble. I went in the Daimler scoutcar (ex-Paris model), followed by a truck, with tank crews none too happy at this job. We had to guard a post office, railway station, a sugar factory and a distillery, and I put down an armed guard of NCO and three men at each. Guard against who, you will ask? Well the whole countryside now is lousy with German deserters, escaped slave workers, and Russian prisoners, and God knows what else, all armed as a rule. I don't really want to tell you this next bit, but I think I must for both of us.

There was nothing left of the railway station. With our torches, the corporal and I picked our way about in the black of the remains, and I realised that out there, on the tracks, there was a terrible mess where a whole train had been bombed that day. When I stepped off the platform rubble, I found I was walking on what I thought was soft ground but I was literally walking on bodies. But that was not just a normal passenger train. In the light of my torch I could

350

see they were all dressed the same. Blue and white striped pyjama suits, hundreds of bodies, all very dead. But as I swung the light round, some of the eyes glittered, and I can tell you how I felt, after everything else, that this time I was really going to pass out. I want to tell you this, because when I reported it, nobody seemed very sure what it was all about. A prison train they said. We were all exhausted anyway, and had orders to move on at first light when infantry would take over. But within three days we knew.

Our advance was across flat, heath country, with little opposition, and all the villages had white surrender bedsheets hanging out of the house windows. Then the tank wireless started a whole lot of special signals, coming and going, between Div. and our Reg. net, and even down to our level, with every unit of medics being called forward, and I thought there had been some terrible sort of setback in front, except there had been no O Group since early dawn, and no big artillery stonk or anything. You will have read it by now I suppose. Belsen lay right in front of us, and the fact was, we were going to run into it on our main center line. All the orders coming over the air demanded that we stop when we were able to sight what they called a barbed wire, enemy position. And then with less and less security on the air the word Typhus was being used, and the CO came up with an all stations call, which is highly unusual, and told us that it was a concentration camp, and that special precautions had to be taken to prevent the inmates from *getting out!!* I could hardly believe what I was hearing. But of course, typhus. And what else?

We waited for a while, that early Spring day, in the tanks, out there on the heath, and there was an odd kind of smell on the breeze that I didn't like, and then Sergeant Dasher who took over from Sturman, came over to me and said he and some of the crews wanted to go over and see what it was all about. The nearest barbed wire and those awful sentry boxes on posts we could see without binocs. about five hundred yards away, and I said if they heard our engines rev up loud, which they could at that distance, they must return at once at the double. And to take risk – I was going first.

351

I went with my driver, leaving the op. on the wireless. It is difficult to describe what we saw next. I suppose you must and will see pictures and descriptions in the newspapers back at home, and I would be glad if you would keep them for me.

The wire perimeter fence was fifteen-feet tall, and I was told later that originally it was electrified. When we got to within a shorter distance, the stench on the air was really awful. If I've got to tell you I must, because it was the smell of death and burning and excrement and something more, because all the shelling and burn smells I know. As we tramped up, a long line of desperate looking characters began to gather behind the wire as they saw us, and they were nearly all in those same bloody broad-striped convict tops and trousers that had been in that nightmare train in the dark at Celle. They hung on the wire and called to us. Not like people, but like bats, or rats or dirty trapped things. Their faces were not like any others I've seen dead or alive. Scared and sick men I have seen so often now, but it was their skin colour, grey-white, and others the shade of wrapping paper, and unshaven and dirty in a way different from soldiers. They jabbered in several languages, some crying, and using odd words like "Gentlemen!" and "Please me not German!" and *Essen*! and I got some talk going with a tall, skeleton thin Frenchman. He said all the guards had been rounded up and that our men were already surrounding the camp and inside there were not nearly enough medics. The camp was very big, he said. The SS had been killing and burying corpses for days, and they had been told food would be given to them before the end of the day, which he hoped it would be, because there were hundreds lying in the black tar huts that we could see, who were dying. I saw the ground inside the compound was just flat mud, and bodies were lying there, and some figures that looked like women came out, and just crouched to pee in the open.

I moved along the wire towards a corner where one of the guard boxes stood out against the sky, and beyond it outside the wire, I could see some of our uniforms, two or three Bren gun carriers, and army ambulance trucks with the usual red cross, and if they were there, I reckoned I could be too. I started to push along, and presently the awful smell got

352

worse, and old Smudger who was crashing along with me was trying to whistle in some odd way, to keep his spirits up, like he did in the tank when things were a bit off. He said to me, Christ! Is this what they've been up to, them bastards! Which about summed it up, except that it didn't at all. Because now we saw what was in front of us, and it was horrendous, being a huge long pit like a whole line of bomb craters joined in one, and it was half filled with literally hundreds of jumbled, naked bodies, tossed in, human skeletons, with shaven heads and arms and legs sticking up. For a moment I thought I was going to really pack it in, or throw up, because I thought of you and me and us, and for God's sake, some nightmare thought that Mama and Papa were in there. Which of course would be impossible, but perhaps you will understand why I just couldn't look any longer. There was a German bulldozer thing at the far end, and as far as I could see, they were still pushing more naked jumble in, and I wanted to scream across at somebody to stop them or shoot them or do something. And then I heard Smudger say, here you are sir, that's it! And a jeep had come behind us that I had not noticed, and a Provost Marshall swung out – that's a military police officer with the rank of Major, he was so bloody smart with his white belt and brasswear, and he said You're out of bounds and the trooper too! All this is out of bounds! Return to your unit that is an order. So I told him what to do with himself, and he said he hoped he wouldn't have to put me under arrest.

We got back to the others, and I told Dasher to keep a look out for the MPs, and to scarper across bloody quickly, ten minutes each. There was nothing to tell us what to do on the radio, only masses of special stuff was being brought up to help, and I got back into my turret and sat there, and felt a million years old and thought about many things and watched the crews darting across and coming back. No one interfered with them. Two of my men who have after all, seen a few things, were very quiet, and then suddenly sick. They lay on the grass. We brewed up tea, and they had a cigarette and everyone said that nothing was too bad for the Germans. I realised what that hideous train had been heading for.

This is what they have done, especially to us Syb, and I will say now Our People, and perhaps it was a good thing to have seen it, because it made some sense of what Sturman and those I knew in my own regiment, died for. Or does it? I just don't know any more. What if the Nazis had come to England and made their hell there too?

It must be over soon. For the first time I have seen on the map, Bremen and Hamburg, because usually our maps are big scale, and we also use aerial photos which are better. They will surely pack it in now? I hope we get leave *soon* when it does all stop. We ought to surely. I am very tired now, although we have good billets in an empty Jerry farmhouse. The inhabitants were killed by Russian DPs and laid out in the front garden, so helpful.

I love you,
Max
Maj.

The last little bit at the bottom under his signature was the final promotion that he was being modest about, or because perhaps, after all that, it probably didn't mean so much.

By now, I was tired myself, sitting there in the big chair by the desk in the study, with the reading lamp on, and the curtains undrawn and a certain chill in the room. It was going to be time to think about central heating again soon. All things being relevant or irrelevant depending on whether you were at Barnes or Belsen.

Chloe came in and stood by the open door.

"Tea?" She looked at the letters still lying on the desk. "Or Scotch and soda?"

But my mind had jumped back to the past again. "It's a hell of a time to remember," I said slowly to Chloe. "But there was a time I tried to kill Max Beaumont! Then a lot of things might have been different!"

CHAPTER SIXTEEN

My two years at Broadcasting House after I left school were due to pure nepotism. My father worked there. I did post boy, continuity and elementary research. In my case, it all ended when, unable to decide between Navy and Air Force I had gone for the Fleet Air Arm.

The war in Europe was over before I saw any action, but there was still Japan. Then my father told me Hugh Greene was setting up radio in Germany. He needed urgently to get service types who had some German and also experience with the Corporation. I volunteered, and was accepted, all by signals.

I flew over to Germany in a Dakota, in that summer of forty-five. An army Signal Corps driver picked me up in a Bedford truck, and took me into Hamburg. I had not been prepared for Hamburg. It was something I shall never forget. I had seen the London Blitz, and Coventry. Later I was to see Nagasaki. Hamburg was more like the Japanese version. The odd buildings that were standing round the Alster lakes stood up like rotting stumps in a black swamp. The little studios and transmitting centre of the new Nordwestdeutscherrundfunk were in a small green-domed building by the shattered mess of the main railway station.

The Atlantic Hotel nearby was the officers' club, where I had my first meal with two RAF types already working for Hugh Greene. "A miracle this place is standing," I said.

"No miracle," I was told politely, "The airforce was requested to leave something standing that would serve as an officers' club. They did the same thing at Kiel, for the Navy. Nightly bombing of the submarine pens strangely missed the yacht club there!"

For the first few days, I was busy getting instruction and I was glad not to have to walk the streets in a uniform with wing badges. Then I was sent to Hanover to do the special Job in Berlin with Max Beaumont. Some time later I was posted there, and returned to the Unit at Stingerstrasse.

The idea was to set up reporting and service facilities further south in the zone. To work with Signal Corps people and permitted German technicians to get relay going. To recruit any staff – not bogus rocket scientists – who could pass the denazification probe.

Hanover, in fact, looked little better than Hamburg. The people, shabby, hungry and dirty, worked ceaselessly at moving rubble, pushing little handcarts with belongings through the streets. Standard rations were less than 1000 calories a day. I had not seen Belsen then, as Max Beaumont had. Nor heard of the people of Rotterdam, driven to eating tulip bulbs.

I had a driver and the ubiquitous all Services fifteen-hundred-weight Bedford truck, which transported gear and bedding for both of us. Like the driver, I had been provided with an issue Lee Enfield 303 rifle and ammunition. At that stage in the occupation, no service personnel were to be unarmed, but I thought a pistol would have seemed a lot more practical. The occupying Forces were also officially not allowed to speak to Germans. No fraternising was being sternly enforced.

But this was not so in the world I now moved in, and nowhere more than in the Information Control Unit office building in Georgstrasse, Hanover. Here there was electric light and glass in the windows or most of them. The Germans who worked there on the reviving of a new, democratic press, radio, theatre and cinema, after fifteen years of Goebbels, were enthusiastic, comparatively well dressed and had lost that pale, sheeny complexion that I had seen on so many. The secretaries and other women workers were doing best, as I had learned early in Hamburg, and there was almost a scale of favours in the new currencies of cigarettes, extra rations, chocolate, even housing. Of course, working on the Information Unit's projects there had to be conversation, and that meant fraternising.

This strange new twilight world into which I had been pitched was totally different from anything in the trim, taut, world of the senior service's flying arm. Almost embarrassingly, I was the only non-Army type in that small officers' mess in which I had first met Max.

Stingerstrasse was on the outskirts of Hanover, at the far end of the Podbielskistrasse, where there was an almost untouched area of suburban housing, some blocks of flats, two or three streets of modest, three-storey, terraced houses. A row of these had been requisitioned for the accommodation of the unit. Most of the army's occupation troops were in barracks or camps on the outskirts, but we were living among German civilians! Those who had been thrown out to make room for us had to shift as they could, after all was it not what they had done, from Stalingrad to Paris?

The accommodation was not luxurious as I knew, but now, I unpacked in a comfortable room that was my own. The windows opened onto a small balcony which overlooked a back garden, now choked with debris and weeds, and beyond a path wound along the back of the houses. On the other side were the open fields. My driver was accommodated round the corner in Stingerplatz, with the other ranks, and having checked that he and the vehicle were taken care of, I walked along from my billet residence to the house in which the officers' mess was quartered. It was, of course, very different from Fleet Air Arm, Lee-on-Solent. The drawing room was the ante-room and bar, which I had seen before, and beyond was the dining room, with one table long enough to seat the dozen or so officers, who included two ATS, both with the rank of captain. They and the rest, all had one thing in common, they spoke German much better than I did.

A florid-faced officer in Scottish regimental trews invited me to have a drink. His accent was guttural.

"It would be a penk-chin for the Navy yes! Hora can do zat I think! He is sober this evening!"

Hora was the acceptable Hungarian dispossessed person, who functioned as barman and chief steward over the kitchen staff whom I had seen briefly on my first visit. He had red hair, a blankly expressionless face and still wore the smartly cut suit made entirely from army-issue grey blanket. The staff in the

357

kitchen, under his supervision, converted standard service rations, by the addition of black market supplements, into gourmet menus. All washed down with limitless champagne, or French and German wines confiscated from the defeated German army.

My new friend in the tartan trews introduced me to some of the others now assembling for the pre-dinner drink. This crowd was like nothing I had met before. They were certainly nearly all former German refugees, some wore uniforms of outfits I never knew existed, and they were civilian in manner and uninhibited in speech. They in turn had never met the Fleet Air Arm it seemed. They asked what I did. I told them, and they told me.

There was the theatre officer, who had plans for the Opera House and already half a dozen small theatres in the zone, with plays that were always sold out. The Cinema Captain, small, dark, with an East End accent, had an easier job, showing films in cellars and barns, but so far only one new film, made in Berlin *In Jenen Tagen*. The man who screened the Germans who were coming forward for jobs, drank beer at the bar, and indeed looked like a comfortable publican, speaking with a Bavarian accent, overlaid by public school.

Then Max Beaumont arrived with one of the ATS captains. He had tossed his cavalry peaked hat at Hora, in a slightly showy way, and the man had fielded it, putting it under the bar, and pouring the two glasses of champagne that Max requested.

"Where's MacNamara?" Max enquired. He did not seem to have noticed me.

This was the Lieut. Colonel who was the C.O. His real name was different but, as I was told, because he was the leader of the band, his Irish name had been bowdlerised.

"Can't go in to dinner until the C.O. wants to! Marvellous isn't it? No wonder we're all bloody pissed!" said the ATS captain elegantly.

Not for the first time, I found the emigrés liked using Anglo Saxon attitudes as often as possible, and also that Mess etiquette prevailed in this motley crew. The conversation turned to a burglary, a break-in at one of the billets, where an officer was away travelling. Clothes, shoes, a camera, cigarettes had been taken. Worst of all, some pistol ammunition.

"That's a court martial charge if the adjutant gets onto it!"

"Got no option!"

"Where is Bill anyway?"

"Berlin."

"Would it be DPs or Jerries on the run who broke in?"

"They picked up an SS Colonel in civvies this morning! On the Celle road!"

"They're getting away!" It was the beer drinking Captain, elbow on the bar, and he was listened to respectfully. As a member of "I" Corps he knew more than most. "Our American friends are recruiting some of the bastards for what they know – and I don't mean scientists and rocket stuff. We're doing that too!" It was then that Max looked and winked at me.

"For what they know about the Russians?"

"Or the werewolves?"

"Surely that's dried up?" The ATS girl sounded only slightly nervous. She got a hand pat from the officer in trews. Silently presiding, was the all listening Hora.

"Don't be so sure!" said the theatre Major. "If they can't do it overground, they could still go underground! Every other occupied country did it!"

"Half the bastards are living in the cellars already!" It was the first drawled, accented cynicism from Beaumont that evening. He still looked so young, and chillingly handsome with those ice-blue eyes and the tumbled black hair. The ATS girl, who had a clean, hockey-captain face, looked at him carefully as he poured some of the champagne from his own glass into hers.

"I should go to sleep with that nice issue .38 under your pillow, darling! By the way, Sarah's code for official entry, through the door, is four knocks," Max told everyone.

The Commanding Officer came in as the laughter greeted that one, and was immediately given a large whisky by Hora. He had thinning, sandy hair, and a rake's handsome, intelligent face. There were no identity flashes on his shoulders, only a parachute symbol on one arm, and a DSO among the medal ribbons.

"Why does everybody laugh when I come in?"

"Because you'll hardly believe it," Max Beaumont said. "But the Russkis have sent us some caviar for kick-off for our dinner, Colonel!"

"Let's go!" said the Colonel simply. He drained his glass in one, but then turned suddenly to me. "You sit next to me, as our newest member! Tolly isn't it? And Sarah can sit next to you, and hold your hand, in case you're nervous with all us brown jobs!"

Maybe I was nervous. Maybe that was why, when I retired to my billet room as it was getting dark, I thought of the burglary story and locked the door. I also pushed the magazine into my issue rifle, and snicked the first round up with the bolt. I had had little enough practice with the things, they were not really a Navy weapon.

I opened the windows onto the balcony, to check the fastenings, and peered out into the dark of an early autumn evening. Faint moonshine was up there, somewhere above the misty cloud, and the wilderness of the garden was in half darkness. Suddenly I kept very still. A person, or some sizeable creature was moving down there.

You did not have to be trained in any particular one of the services, you did certain things automatically, and I turned out the light. Then I picked the rifle up off the floor, and returned to one side of the open balcony doors by the curtain.

Now I was quite certain. I could hear someone moving out there. I decided to try some of my own German.

"Stop!" I shouted. "Or I shall fire!"

Whoever or whatever was moving out there, at the far end of the garden, stopped immediately, and all was silence. Nobody else appeared to have heard either the noise, or my challenge. But now I could hear a more careful movement along the end path.

"Come out with your hands up, or I shoot!" I shouted, and, as nothing happened, I pulled the trigger, then staggered back against the window frame with the recoil. So far, I had not had the luck to fire a shot in anger, but I reckoned if the SS or any other thieving enemy were still going to be about, I would get one.

360

Lights went on in neighbouring windows. A remarkable, illuminated top half of a figure rose from the scrub below, having had the sense to turn the flashlamp on himself, rather than at me. It was a figure in khaki, with a swashbuckling cavalry hat, and an arm pointing in my direction, who now switched off his torch and stood in the darkness, telling me in cold, steely, level English what he would do when he got to me. It was of course, Major Beaumont.

Slowly the window lights went out. In the rest of the locality, nobody seemed in the least degree interested in a stray rifle shot. Which was also vaguely disturbing. Shakily, mystified, I went to bed, after locking and bolting the balcony windows and drawing the curtains.

It was really because of that Beaumont the Burglar item, as it eventually and inevitably became known about in the Mess, that Max in a curious perverse sort of way seemed to take to me. Our clandestine trip to Berlin had been too brief to establish any friendship. I use the word take, rather than that he liked me, because I really do not believe anybody could tell with certainty whether Max Beaumont really cared for them or not. This was always one of the things I thought later, that made women crave for his attention in a quite extraordinary way.

But back in Hanover at that time, as I remember it, Max was not on scene next morning for breakfast, in that Mess of strange officers, with their polyglot voices and strange backgrounds, I was still the new member, and perhaps for that reason, found myself alone after dinner the following night, nursing a large brandy and soda. I wondered why the Mess emptied so rapidly, and where everyone went. Even the grey-blanket figure of Hora, the Hungarian barman, had faded away.

When Max came in suddenly, he nodded curtly, helped himself to whisky and sat on a bar stool, looking down at me. He wore service dress uniform, with the army's beautifully burnished Sam Browne leather belt and I thought at that moment he looked like someone playing Rupert Brooke from the First World War.

Some conversations stay in the mind long after more important dialogues have gone from the human retrieval system. Of course recent days of renewed contact with him may have sharpened memory, and I am not going to pretend that I could recall what was said by the young Major Beaumont, as he swung a leg nonchalantly on the bar stool, that evening in the empty officers' Mess in Stingerstrasse, as though I had it verbatim. But somehow recollection of that moment was a clearly retained image.

"You know of course why I'm togged out like this I suppose?"

I said, cautiously, that I had not the slightest idea.

"Because I'm duty officer tonight! *You* can go out if you like! One of us has to be here the whole time. You'll see the duty roster in the adjutant's office at number fourteen. Most of our chums here don't bother to dress properly for it, but it's the way we did it in my outfit, so I do. And when I have to go and inspect the NCOs' Mess, and the mens quarters up in Stingerplatz, I can see they think I'm a stuck-up twerp, aiming to stay on in the army and become a Field Marshal. Whereas nothing could be further from the truth. In this Mess, and the NCOs', they're all a lot of intellectuals in uniform, you see. Except the Sergeant Major who has nothing to do, and is a fat stupid sod. Why did you try to kill me last night?"

It was a good technique, and I daresay in the Fleet Air Arm we were less formalised than in his world, because I can remember answering with some disrespect that creeping about in the dark was not my idea of a joke, and it was a good thing I wasn't a better shot. Also that I was sorry.

"I know you're working for the new radio set-up in Hamburg. They said that would give bonafides to our Berlin trip. Also your German was not good enough for the dirty tricks game!"

"Not like yours and the others," I agreed. "But I've found a couple of people who will work in a small studio. I shall have to originate programmes and local news as soon as it's working. Do you still do the newspapers?"

"I start up newspapers!" Max said. "We've got to teach them press freedom! They haven't had any for twelve years or more under Goebbels. They gave me a packet of paperclips and a couple of good sergeants – one had been a teacher in Köln and the other a fashion designer – both Jewish of course. We went to Binneburg and started a newspaper. Not difficult there actually, because it hadn't been knocked about at all. The problem is finding German journalists who weren't Nazis."

"Like Berlin? Or like what you were doing last night?" I tried. It had occurred to me, in the intervening time since I had last seen him rising out of the garden in his own floodlight, that if I had shot him, I would certainly have been on a very nasty court martial.

The idea seemed to appeal to Max. He tilted his head back and laughed, the same illogical sense of humour that still stayed with him. The sound that came out was the high-pitched laugh, with no particular warmth.

"You must know what I was looking for! Or haven't you caught up with it yet? Why d'you think this place is totally empty every evening? Well, as you obviously know nothing about it, I'll tell you. Let me put a bit in your glass, as well as mine! You see, even Horrible Hora is away, doubtless on the same thing too!" He attended to the refilling of the glasses at the bar, and now he came and sat on the nearest chair before raising his drink briefly in my direction.

"Good luck!" he said. "It *was* good luck I think, don't you? I wouldn't want to be shot down by the Navy or whatever you are, at this stage!"

He toyed with his glass. "I was visiting a damsel in distress last night," he said shortly. "She lives in one of the houses along the street. They're packed out with people, all of them, and she's lucky to have a ground-floor room to herself, actually she's got two kids. It was fixed by one of the former press officers – older chap than you or me, and he's gone back home to change into a Control Commission type. You've seen some already I expect? Civil servants out here in a sort of fireman's uniform, keen to stay out too, for another century, if they can! Can't say I blame them. The trouble is," Max Beaumont paused, then looked at me suddenly with the twisted smile, and the bright gaze. "He's been crimed! They won't let him back! An official report went in to the adjutant, and he had to pass it on to the C.O. It was that bloody sergeant major, who had proof that Captain Jimmy Roots was supplying army food and liquor to the lady up the road, and had been doing so for months! Everybody's up to something, but they caught him. And that's it! Her name's Heidi by the way." For a moment he looked away for some reason. "She is the most beautiful thing you ever saw. Nearly red hair, grey eyes, moves like a panther. The real thing I mean, not the tank! Knows it all." Max Beaumont got up then, moving about in a restless way, then back onto the bar stool again. "Have you had any of the German women yet? I don't know why, but they're different. About sex, and men I mean. They seem to be cool and hot at the same time, they want it and they want you. And although they're all female, they seem to be making you too! As equals. Do you know what I mean?"

"This is my first time in any part of Europe," I said feeling as though I was out of nursery school. "We had flight training in Canada you know. That was my only overseas until this job. Some of the girls out there were pretty overboard about a uniform." I was not prepared to exchange any confidences with the cool young Major, for all his unexpected revelations.

"Two kids," I said. "When does husband come rolling in? And will he use the back garden entrance?"

This time Max was not amused. I saw the other side. His cheekbones appeared, his mouth tightened, his eyes went icy blue, calculating the degree of my impertinence.

"Listen!" he said. "I sometimes go that way from my billet, because I could still bump into any of the rest of the mess, or that sergeant major, going along the street outside! OK? And I don't care for everyone to know that I've taken up where the uncareful Captain Roots left off! Unfortunately, you have to know now. There are no husbands. At least there was one. He was killed in Russia. The second father was not married to her. He was in the SS, and she was madly in love with him, for which she has yet to apologise. But he was caught on the escape line to Spain, and shot by the French. At least that's the way it came through from another of them who did get away and told her."

I didn't know about Max's background, his war or his parents' end, when we shared the empty Mess that evening in Stingerstrasse, simply that I had, only the previous night, almost put a bullet in him. Later I realised that in a way that could have made him think, wrongly in fact, that I was a more hardened type, than when I had done the trip to Berlin with him.

Max explained then only that he had been picked for what he called a recruiting job because he had known Berlin before the war. I had since discovered that any probing with the strange and motley specialists in the Information Control Unit, was unwelcome. Max said he had to take one other member of the unit with him, as well as a driver. I wondered if perhaps he did not fancy the complex qualities of some of the others with whom he shared the Mess. I think I was not far wrong. Later, disarmingly, he told me.

"You had such a round, innocent baby face for that Berlin job. And that neat, dark-navy uniform was never meant for dirty work! Even the Russians wouldn't think we were up to anything that we shouldn't be with you along!" he smiled maliciously. "I know now of course, that if anything had popped up, you would have shot first and thought about it afterwards!"

In our house on a Monday morning, when the telephone rang before breakfast it was not usually good news. I was still upstairs in front of a mirror, trying to make a good knot in a bow tie. I heard it picked up downstairs. Then I heard Chloe come to the dressing room door.

"It's a Michael Lockley's P.A. I haven't said you're available. Do you want it?" Chloe held onto the door. "Somehow she sounds unfriendly. He's Portland Place isn't he?"

"The top," I said briefly. "But too early." I finished the tie fixing. "At that level they all sound like that. You're quite right, I don't want it, but I shall have to take it. He's Assistant Director General."

I sat on the bed and picked up the bedside phone. I knew Michael, although again he was new, and had moved up fast. When you have had my public recognition, there is nobody in any part of the hierarchy who is not prepared to be friendly, but like all power circuits there are switches and fuses, and since Girsten's little chat in the summer-house

I realised that I might not have the wiring diagram up to date.

I certainly did not know the secretary, but she was as I had said, the early shift. Some of the top brass had two or more of them.

"This is Felix Tolly speaking!"

She was of course sorry to trouble me, but the ADG wondered if I could find time to be with him at Portland Place, by say half past nine. He had a meeting at ten, and after that would be difficult. They would of course send a car. It was, she gathered, rather important, even urgent.

I said if the car was with me in half an hour I would do my best to be with Mr. Lockley on time, traffic permitting. And put the phone down. It rang again immediately.

This time I picked it up myself, and could tell who was asking for me, because this voice had become familiar. Obviously Liz Charlton was also on early shift.

"Or is it the late late shift?" I asked her.

"It's twenty-five hours at the minute." Liz sounded just a fraction tense. "I'm trying to fix his schedule, and that's day and night too. Could I just say he wants to see you here, at the new place, and what he calls wind up things. At the same time allowing you to see what the scene here has become."

"What has it become?"

"Pretty good hell for most of us! I think MB is the only one who is keeping cool and remembering what Shastakowitz would have done."

"Clausewitz!" I told her, and somehow I got the feeling, part of years of professional listening, that busy or not, Liz Charlton wanted to talk to me. "Outside – it looks more like Belfast than Battersea," she said. "It's great stuff if you like war!"

"Max was fighting for Press Freedom when I first met him forty years ago," I agreed easily enough, perhaps because of my recollections of the previous evening. I shifted the phone closer and waited. This was where Liz had wanted the conversation to go.

"Would that make him keen to show your German TV associate – things? To give her time right now? You haven't seen his office here. It has quite a lot of facilities."

"You can tell it all to me, Liz!" I said quietly. "There's been a big gap of years, but I think he hasn't changed. So Rita Henckman is still around?"

"We stayed with him," Liz Charlton said carefully. "We played it. The A Team here, who needed his say so, most of the night. She gave up and left, early this morning." Liz's voice was less tired than strained. "There are too many eyes watching, too many news grabbers and grubbers around, even our own people in this place. There's a lot in the balance, with all the journalists, and not everyone is on his side, you know?"

"I shall know more later," I said. "I cannot at this moment fix anything. I am summoned to Broadcasting House. When that's over I will get the car to take me to the Battle of Armageddon. Can we make a safe entrance?"

"I'll see Bob Dasher takes care of it. The police will know. They will stop you early where the bridge is closed, and you come in at speed. Sit in the back, and have something to cover your head, just in case they get the glass!

"I think I've got a suit of armour somewhere downstairs," I told her. "I must see if it still fits!"

"There's one more thing if you are seeing the Beeb! Mr Beaumont is working on what he calls your little problem too!" And Liz Charlton rang off.

In a way it was perhaps comforting to know that perhaps Clausewitz was safeguarding my line of retreat, when I entered in the Assistant Director General's large office. Michael Lockley was one of those people who shook hands, and then as we both sat down on the comfortable settee provided to set visitors at ease, he came briskly to the point.

"Graham Gitsen, I think must have given you the picture!"

"I didn't think much of what Gitsen had to say if that helps!" I waited for a moment. I should have known you cannot provoke at that level, although I have done it many times with bigger personalities, in front of cameras. But Lockley's smile was as smooth and empty as his desk-top.

"We get a lot slung at us these days, as you must know, Felix. I get very tired of it! The situation I'm putting to you is almost out of our hands now, because the Chairman and

367

the Board are into it. We – I'm sorry I can't mean you and me in this context – can after all only advise them. Bluntly, presenting Beaumont as some sort of hero this week, just won't do!"

I had thought he was going to say "at this point in time". Like people who use the "in this context" stuff so often do.

"That is not the programme, and not my style!" I told him. "Not what our producer has lined up either! This is a warts and all portrayal, the way it has gone into the printed outline and the two prelims we've run. I notice you've had plenty of news bulletins with T.U. and Opposition spokesmen shouting Foul! Plus analysis stuff on both our channels, of course so have ITV for that matter. Now let's see what sort of man Beaumont is! What made him, how it's worked out! I've known the man on and off for a long time. OK, the story intrigues me, but I can promise you there will be no slanted angles."

Lockley sighed. His gaze which had been unblinking, shifted, and he looked carefully at the backs of his hands. They appeared to give him no inspiration.

"I was hoping you would see it more broadly, more constructively, Felix. I know you've been told of rumblings in the Corporation. We don't want a sympathetic walk out, or any trouble, because we give prime-time to a one-sided programme."

"You won't get it!" I was suddenly weary of people like Lockley and whoever else was with him. "Check it out! You have staff working on this programme. Do you know Fleet Street? Do you know what it has really meant, to try and beat unions which have made British newspapers employ six times as many printing workers as are really needed? That have actually prevented news items being published that they didn't stand for? That the same dreary story has gone on for too long, with coal, steel production, manufacturing, railways! And you have had more than a whiff of it here in the Corporation! So Beaumont owns TV, here and in other countries, like most of the other media megalomaniacs. Except that I don't think he's like them. He had a different sort of schooling, but he could give jobs to quite a lot of people here."

368

"You aren't threatening me are you, Felix old boy?" Lockley's voice was like the hard-soft stuff they put on the walls of a sound-proof studio. I got up. This was not going to be the smooth exit that had faded me out on a thousand successful presentations.

"That's stupid! And if you are by chance taping, it will sound even more stupid to other people! I am going ahead with the programme unless and until I get a direct order not to. And don't put anyone else up as anchorman to my producer, or hold him up, or try to put on a substitute mish-mash! Or a so-called Balanced Look At The Dilemma for Britain's Newspapers! Or some sort of crap like that!"

Downstairs I walked through the swing doors and into the fresh air of Portland Place. I stood on the steps and took a few slow, deep breaths. It occurred to me suddenly that I had come in and out of those doors, and up and down those flat curved steps for a great many years. I looked up, to see the stone figures sculptured by Gill. There was the one that had caused such problems at the time, because of the size of his stone organs. Either you had balls or you didn't, I thought.

Somebody was hooting a car horn. A small black van, with no signwriting, came slowly along the kerb and stopped. I saw that it was being driven by a man in overalls. I also saw that it was Bob Dasher.

"Sorry about this get-up, Mr. Tolly!" Dasher said. He started to head down Regent Street. "You comfortable there in those seats in the back? You can see out through the screen, but nobody can see you.

He handed me over his shoulder, through an opening, a piece of plastic, like a credit card. But it also had my photo, in colour, about the size of a postage stamp. My miniature reflection winked and twinkled with some metallic, chemical quality.

"What's this?"

"Security pass. You can't get in without it, and you have to keep it on when you're inside the building. Once you're clear of the check-in, there's still places in there, stairs and corridors and elevators and the like, with lights and pick-up. They set off warnings on the security panels if someone is moving about without one. There's quite a few other gimmicks like that. Have you heard about the wire round the whole place? Razor wire it is, not ordinary barbed stuff. Cuts through clothes, cuts through anything, really nasty stuff."

"Who thought of all this?"

"It's American most of it. And German I'm told. They're the ones for that kind of thing! Mind you, if you could see the kind of crowd that's built up outside and the way they look, well I'm glad Mr. Beaumont told them to do the job properly. I reckon if they could get in, and get their hands on him and even the people working there, they'd string 'em up! And burn the place down, and smash all that new plant. I mean it!"

"I've seen it in other places," I told Bob Dasher. "Up North, and in the Midlands. Coal and steel. I saw Paris and the students, and then Frankfurt. India too, and trouble in Korea and Detroit.

"Did you ever see a book around over here called *Without a Trace?*" Bob Dasher talked, while manoeuvering the van out towards the Thames. "I was given a copy. It's the kind of thing that's going the rounds in some places. How to avoid detection, how to smash glass and break in without leaving a trace. How to use a camera flash to blind the cops' video cameras. They list the radio call signs of the Metropolitan Police and a lot of specialised units even I didn't know about."

"I get the feeling you know quite a lot about it, Bob!" I said. He was silent, as we waited for traffic lights to change, and moved on again, through the busy traffic around Victoria Station.

"The Hurricane Group," Dasher said. "That's one lot. Heard of them? There's some of their people outside the plant, along with the rest. They're not strikers. They just want to smash the whole country up, that lot and their kind!"

"And what about you, Bob? What are your politics?" I was on duty in my job, as much as Dasher was in his.

"I don't like Parties! At least, only the kind with dancing and a few drinks! Me? I like democracy – I've seen the other thing too, like you have, Mr. Tolly. I like England, I like English food, English girls –"

"And Mr Beaumont –?"

Again there was no immediate answer, and then Bob Dasher half turned, still keeping the traffic in view, but with his profile in shadow. "I've been with him more than forty years, I think I know how he is."

"Well – he's not English though is he, Bob?"

We were through the police barrier which had shut off the bridge, causing long delays on the embankment. Peering through the hole ahead, I could see that both sides of the road that led immediately to the riverside were really packed with heaving ranks of strikers struggling with police. The new building, squat and dark, was in the middle of remains of wharf-land, and the high wire defences loomed round it. Two ambulances were screaming away, and loudspeakers bawling, but it was impossible to hear what they were saying. They were being used by both police and demonstrators, and the background noise was the familiar, always ugly, continuous baying of crowd anger, with screams and sudden isolated cries breaking through. We jerked to a stop. In front a helmeted police face peered for a second and then as he waved us on, something that must have been a stone or brick struck the side of the van, and inside Dasher and I lurched instinctively the other way, so that I missed the raising of barriers, but saw guards, and some heavy gates on wheels pulled back to let us through.

Bob Dasher switched off the engine in an area shielded by a high brick wall. He helped me out, and for a moment we stood, both listening to the sounds behind us.

"Sods put one through the windscreen on Saturday!" Bob Dasher said. "Cut up one of the computer kids I went to bring in. American she was. Had to go straight to hospital. Anyway, now you're in, you can stay for as long as you like! There's enough food and drink in here for weeks they say. I'll take you straight up to Liz Charlton, because I'm ten minutes later than she said. OK?"

We passed a turnstile-type entrance inside the swing doors, where uniformed security guards, men and women stood armed with the usual squealer and quick frisking action. Obviously Bob Dasher's presence helped speed things along. I was asked to pin on my magnetic badge, and then we were

371

in a silent elevator, going up.

"Only four floors?"

"They're down too!" Bob Dasher grinned. "A lot's below ground, with the big machines, and enough electrics too. Here we are! All out for the Think Tank, Control Tower, Big Chief's Chambers, Liz's Lair and the rest! Everything in this set-up is kept in compartments, so that only a very few of the Major's top people have the whole picture."

We went through an office with wired glass windows and artificial lighting, where the effect was not unlike Newswatch's own staffroom, with half a dozen men and young women in front of processors, fax machines and transcribers, who scarcely bothered to look up as we headed for doors, at the end. A red light shone above the lintel. Bob Dasher unclipped his plastic passport and ran it through a slot box. The light changed to green. We went in.

Liz Charlton, looking unfamiliar with shaded spectacles, sat at a desk near to another door. One of the young men I thought I remembered from Park Lane, sat in a swivel chair nearby and regarded me thoughtfully. This was certainly not Park Lane. Very much otherwise, it was all functional, modern.

"OK, Liz? Cheerio, Mr Tolly!" Bob Dasher was clipping back his plastic onto his lapel.

Liz Charlton swung round her desk. "He's waiting for you! I've kept all at bay. But Al Chemmy may break in. Also you-know-who, the German Connection – he calls it that! D'you think she represents that to him?

"Let's go, Liz!" I said briefly. "This place is weird! The sooner I can get away and find the real world the better!"

At least Max Beaumont had continuity, when it came to his own habitat. The big room was not the Richmond library, and it was not Park Lane. But there was a conference table with Sheraton chairs, and two walls of the same real looking books. The curtains were heavy, honey-coloured velvet, and there was a pair of what had to be original Corot landscapes.

"Do you have books in New York too? And Paris, and Sydney and wherever?" On the other side of his outsize desk I sank into a modern but comfortable armchair without invitation. All this isolation from the horrendous stuff in the streets outside had me suddenly cynical.

"What's the point of it all, Max?" I said. "There must have been an easier way!"

Liz Charlton came in silently at that moment, bringing two flute glasses, and putting them on coasters, produced the half champagne bottle from a concealed fridge in the wall panelling.

"Give that to me, Liz my dear!" Max smiled. "You will tear your exquisitely painted fingertips."

"Already worked to the bone for you!" But she left us, and closed the door, and Max popped the cork and poured carefully. He raised the glass as fastidiously as he always did.

"Here's to substituting this stuff for tank shells!"

"Let them eat cake!" I said. Which did not stop me letting half the contents of the glass bubble down my throat.

"I wonder if you remember another thing?" Now Max Beaumont was being almost genially urbane, coming round the big rosewood desk to join me, standing looking at the top of the bridge just outside the windows. It was as though there was no drama, nothing to ruffle the unfolding of his recollections, no revolution in Fleet Street or casualties being taken away outside.

"This site," he said. "This piece of riverside, it's where those big old horses used to come, to bring the waste-paper to the Mills! The ones I was taken to see as a boy, when I lived on the other side of the river!"

"Great material, Max!" I said ungraciously. "The wheel makes a full turn. Is that the line? The grand old cart-horses brought in the waste-paper, and now you are churning it out again here, by the latest Luddite-smashing electronic magic! I must try and work it in!"

Max and I had, after all, been trained in the same sort of school, almost from that time. Basically we both spoke in the same trade language. He knew, that I was trying that morning to find some link between then and now, some turning point in his life, that when shown in the right way would be seen to formulate the character, make things comprehensible. But this was not it. Perhaps he felt my disapproval, perhaps by joint subconscious our minds were moving in a circuitous way on a similar track.

"I think you might be amused by this!" He stepped round behind me now, going over to one of the walls lined with books. He stopped there, and slowly I got up, half knowing what was coming. I saw him reach out, and move one of the books, but I did not see exactly how he did it.

The effect was what mattered, because with only a faint hum of motor, the whole bookcase section pivoted to make an opening like a door and Max watched with a happy smile. He could well have looked the same, as he enjoyed the detail of this construction, as when he was allowed to play with his father's electric train set.

"Come on in!"

It was a suite, artificially lit, because there were no windows. There was a large bed, beautifully covered in brocaded silk, antique furniture and pictures, soft carpeting, and a partly opened door to a bathroom. The circuitous psychology clicked.

"Does Rita like it?" I asked.

We stepped out into the main room again. The wall of books closed behind us, with a discreet thump. That Max Beaumont did not like what I had said I could tell. He stood, and it was the Medici look, untouchable, inscrutable. Like the first time he had measured my iconoclasm in Hanover.

"I could throw you out!" His face was turned my way, but he was not seeing me. "What do you know about me? Are you setting yourself up as a judge? Or jury?"

"Exactly!" I said, "you are like Ulysses! There are a hell of a lot of people in this building who are the crew. Or jury. And you want to stop up our ears so that you alone can hear the siren's song, and none of us are supposed to notice! I think it might be a good idea if you let German TV do just her job, and you do yours and I'll do mine!"

"Clever Tolly!" he said. "You were always clever!"

"I ask questions," I replied. "So what are you planning with Rita?"

"I tell you what! Let's see just how it works out! She was here last night, but so were a hell of a lot of other people.

374

Tonight could be the same. Or it could be different. Don't push me. What's that you've got there?"

"Letters," I said. I had remembered the fat envelope in my pocket and put it on the table. "I read them. And after that I started to remember our time in Hanover. Of course there was one name that came back from that time. It's the same story isn't it? See how it turns out?"

The silence that stretched between us was like brittle icing sugar.

"That was, of course, the Occupation time then, in Germany," he said at last, as though making up his own mind. "That was the end of the war – just as I think what is going on here, is the end of some sort of war perhaps. For me then, it was not just the starting up of papers, a new German press, but reviving a basic democratic freedom!"

"Combined very much at the same time, with another German girl with another name and a good deal of risk," I said. "Which as usual you didn't give a damn about!"

"Perhaps patterns of life will always repeat themselves?" Max said, softly.

CHAPTER SEVENTEEN

"I've never talked about it with anyone before," Max Beaumont was again not looking at me. "Do you know that strange thing? A sort of stabbing sense that comes up out of nowhere, unexpected, unannounced, and says: You have been here before! In this moment, exactly like this! You have been here before!"

"I know it – yes," I said. "It's a trick of the brain. A bit spooky. A chap called John Donne wrote a lot about it – the notion that you can, if you have the gift, see forward as well as backward in time. Aren't you really saying if you Had Your Time Again?"

"I got it again yesterday! When that girl was here. Rita. Do you remember by chance the other one? In Hanover? Sure, it's similar. A sort of film I've been through before!"

"I can see similarities," I said, but he was obviously fascinated by the comparison. I had never seen him so revealingly introverted about his own feelings.

"Get it back onto a reality plane Max!" I said harshly. "In Hanover you had a battle over the whole start up of that first magazine *Das Fenster*! Now you are brooding in here like Napoleon on St Helena, in the middle of another much bigger, vaster press freedom thing. You're uptight, tired, and a lot older! There was the one in Hanover, OK! The atoms in the brain get mixed up. When did you last see her anyway?"

"I was working that out, because as I began to look at that girl, Tolly, it first started that feeling going! Heidi and I had a totally unexpected meeting in New York, maybe twenty-five years ago. A weekend. She hadn't changed much either!"

"I remember her pretty well," I said. "This Hamburg girl – well," I paused. "I know what you mean, there are similarities. Do you know her background, have you asked her?"

"She evaded it, like shutting a door!"

"Max! I think this whole link-up in your mind, in present conditions is bound to be traumatic. You, in that Occupation time, must have been having mental back-flips that could trigger off again for the rest of your life. But I will ask another one. Did you come back as British? Or Jewish? Or as German in British uniform? What did you feel that time?" This was after all, important, and a lead question in any case.

"I don't think I ever got it right." Max had gone round the desk, and unusually for him, was slumped in his chair. "I walked along those battered streets, stepping round rubble and collapsed buildings, looped cables, burst mains, pipes and debris. You saw it all, Tolly! Uniform set you apart, the Germans avoided your eyes, or the few of them who did not, stared accusingly. All pale-faced, gnomes, trolls, witches, dressed in mixtures of clothing. They all carried something, little belongings or bags, or pushed prams or wooden wheeled carts loaded with sad jumble. It was like one of those Grimm's fairy stories the governess used to read me, come to life as some unreal vengenance!

When I first saw a street sign, the white lettering against a mauve-blue background in that gothic script again, I stopped and stared as though it had some message for me. Then there were the old mail boxes let into walls, the colour, suddenly, yellow, not red! Odd that such trifles were important! Tolly – I could hear what all those people in Hanover were talking about, what they were saying on the streets! It was the same in the offices of the Information Unit in Georgstrasse. They spoke *my* language! Can you understand? I had not been with my own people in that way since I was a child, and now I was different, so very changed! But I was one of them!" I had not heard Max Beaumont quite so emotional before. I watched as he poured the last of the little champagne bottle into his glass, and emptied it.

"Damn it, that's not true!" He almost banged down the empty glass. "I felt mixed up about it too! They were not my own people! They had killed most of them! I knew by then, what had happened to my parents. I had come back to

377

Berlin by then. It was so badly destroyed there was nothing left of the house or many of the streets by the Tiergarten. No answer there. I was alone! Until later, when there was Heidi in Stingerstrasse, and that at last made me belong! To myself!"

"What happened to Aunt Sybilla?" I remembered.

"Dead." Max Beaumont never stayed emotional for long. His voice went clipped, his eyes shuttered. I have never met anyone else who could blank off so instantly, a normally attentive, expressive face. "I got two days leave to go to London. She had cancer. She was shrunk, like a small, brown pigmy, and she couldn't smile. I knew she was all I had left at that time, and I held her hand as though that could keep her on this side. Don't go that way, Tolly my friend! Get out the whisky and the aspirin!"

"I've seen it," I said. "I know what you mean."

Max stared coldly for a moment. "I had forgotten we're on a job. Get on with it!"

"OK. What happened with *your* job in Hanover then? There was this transformation. Then and there, you stopped being a British tank officer."

"I was jumpy. Maybe it will never stop, once you have been in action. Other people who were, tell me that's not so. There were often times when I lived only with the binoculars in that bloody tank turret. Can you understand? When it was always like the I've Been Here Before bit! When you got to think you saw the enemy where there were none! Or was it yesterday you saw them? Or tomorrow? A hunch, a wrong guess, an instinct out of tune, and you and the rest were dead. They were ordering you on the earphones, ceaselessly telling you to push on! You were so tired you were near hallucinating. What *was* that in the binoculars?"

There was a longish silence, and I waited.

"I remember an officer older than me, at his demob send-off. He took me on one side and told me that as you got older it was much better and easier to do it in the morning, and it was important to know this! I thought he was talking about the war. Of course we were all as drunk as lords. I thought how perfectly revolting that anybody as old as forty should be even thinking about sex! Shall I tell you something, Tolly?

You can still do it, at different times for that matter, at my age! Does that encourage you?"

"I can't use that, Max!" I appealed to him now. "How about the paper you started in Binneburg? Anything there?"

"I had to revert to Captain you know, the army does that. I started up the newspaper there, yes! And there was enough newsprint for three times a week. Got some good staff too. It was there I learned not to screw your own secretary, an important lesson. I also saw the death of Himmler."

"Oh God, Max! Sex and death – keep in a straight line!" This whole session was getting unreal, but Max ploughed on.

"Himmler was picked up by the Intelligence Corps NCOs in Binneberg, really by accident, and they got him and one or two other suspects back to their place in a Jeep, and my own billet was two doors along the same street. I heard they had decided that it really was Himmler, in spite of disguise. By the time I got there he had bitten on the cyanide tooth filling, and they had him on the kitchen table, and for want of a stomach pump the three Intelligence Corps boys, German-Jewish of course, had an incendiary-bomb fire-pump shoved down his gullet and the place was swilling with blood and guts and water, and they were dragging him about and hitting him on the stomach. And then when they realised they had lost, and he lay there a mess on the floor, we were all quiet. How many of us did he kill? And only about four of us to see him go. Sometimes that one comes back and goes to and fro too, Tolly!"

Max looked at me, smiling ominously. "But you want a nice story? Ah yes! After that I went to Paderbrück to start the next paper! I liked Paderbrück. Not like Binneberg, because some of the problems of starting up a newspaper there were like they went on being for me ever after! In this country, the US, Commonwealth. Politics, religion, money, property, machines! They were all wrong, from the start. They had put off Paderbrück, because it was a city that had always been divided, Catholic and Protestant, with separate newspapers. We had hardly newsprint supplies for one, and the place was a ruin, no printing press really existed. I was sent up there with the usual packet of paperclips, and the team of staff sergeants. And when we got our requisitioned billets, there was supporting cast." Max smiled, and paused. And listening and jotting notes on my folded paper, I had the feeling that once again, he had gone off, moving away in his mind, this strangely divided man, looking into his own past, in that time of the Occupation.

The staff for the newspaper and the billet were recruited through the Military Labour Office. There were two sisters to do the cooking and housework. Arabella and Stephie.

In the ancient requisitioned house, next to the church, they had a room on the middle floor, by the kitchen. Max was on the top floor, the three NCOs had the ground floor front, and the two drivers were at the back. Military unit apartheid had to be kept up, even now the war was over. Tank-crews sleeping and feeding together was a thing of the past, and curiously, it sometimes seemed, not even the soldiers wanted it. He ate by himself, or at the officers' club, which as usual, had been established early in Paderbrück. It was in the ruins of a cloister.

Tacitly it was understood that as far as the two women were concerned, it was once again a case of officers first. Arabella was in any case it seemed, late officer's property. She had been the wife of a staff officer killed on the Russian front. She was tall and strongly built, upright, with a fine bosom, and as a widow she dressed in black from the small lace Käpchen on her dark hair, to buckled black shoes. Her sister who did the cooking was short and plump, with dimples in her cheeks which were a colour that suggested she had always come fresh from baking. Her hair was tousled, dark, a rich texture, and her eyes were small and brown like currants.

They told the Captain that together, and with their own servants and estate workers, they had left East Prussia in front of the advancing Red Army. With carts and a total of about three hundred horses. Sometimes Stephie said it was two hundred, and her older sister would say it was exactly three hundred and nine, including those that pulled carts. But by the time the German army in retreat had requisitioned, and others had pillaged, the sisters were lucky to cross the Elbe and reach distant relatives near Paderbrück, riding two horses and leading two more. These they had sold, and lived on the proceeds, until the job with the Herr Hauptmann was put to them as a command.

They were in every way all that was required, especially Arabella, who waited on him properly at a prepared table.

Of course she soon took turns with her sister to serve him in the bedroom too, with an air of polite inevitability. With her handsome, sweet face, strong but sad, wearing nothing but a grey-coloured overcoat with wooden buttons, she accepted the bedside glass of wine. Then the love-making, with a slow but rising ardour that embroiled them both. The strength of the woman, and the enfolding of her legs about him caused in Max a lustful, almost sadistic response. Thinking of the SS Colonel between those strong thighs, he thrust in her with an especial relish, but her strength could outlast his, and he was fascinated that she could orgasm at will, pulling him against her firm breasts, twisting and turning her head, with the tiny, bright teeth clenched as her lips drew apart.

At some point in the night, towards morning, she would go, and was next seen in the black dress and with expressionless, pale face to serve him coffee and breakfast in the little upstairs dining room.

The sergeants and other ranks collected their food from the kitchen. Each morning Max's driver, who was also his part-time batman, brought up his uniform jacket, polished brass and blancoed belt. Only later did Max learn that Arabella had done these too, in return for cigarettes.

There was otherwise, surprisingly little conversation between them. Max was out, busy with the newspaper problems often until late in the evening, and telephones were not yet working. Electricity was sporadic, heating depended on an army coal ration, food was army supplied too, but as usual, augmented by barter.

"You speak like a Prussian!" Arabella had said early on. "I can hear it clearly sometimes!"

"Berlin," Max told her shortly. She looked at him with her unusual black eyes, quizzically, her lips prim and straight.

"I think also you are Jewish! But then I am told Jewish men are cut. At the tip," she said, eyes downcast, "And you are not!"

Exceptionally, this conversation was one morning as he was getting ready to leave the bare little breakfast room and it was the only time the korrect *truce was breached, so Max did not trouble to enlighten her, finding her appearance and their relationship to his liking. The reality of droit de seigneur appealed to him as something very basic. He wondered. Could it be in both their Prussian genes, his and hers?*

"Before we came, if you had been found in bed with a Jew, was a crime! I am sure your husband told you that! Didn't he?" Max was saturnine.

Strong, upstanding creature though she was, for a moment she looked as though she feared he might strike her, then tossed her head in a curious, defiant way, seeking to outstare him.

"I never heard about such things!"

Her younger sister, the undeniably plump and roly-poly Stephie was altogether simpler. She had persuaded Max to give her one of his shirts for her nocturnal visiting. While her stout thighs and dimpled knees showed at the bottom, the generous breast spilled from the unbuttoned top like some cream confection prepared especially for him. Stephie wasted no time.

"Now! Quick! Quick!" was always her urging, as she lay back and laughed, her face like a china doll on the pillow. Max learned, and in turn was taught. To put on the army-issue French letter was the antithesis of now, and quick, in fact it was a passion killer. Only someone who could giggle and wriggle like Stephie could save the situation. He was told about withdrawal. Both sisters claimed Catholicism, and they knew about withdrawal. Max disliked its calculated retreat, a version that had nothing to do with Clausewitz. But apparently, there were days that were very much for now, and quick, or more, quickly or slowly, which had to do with the month, and was explained to him with Germanic simplicity by both sisters, who said that it was helpful for him to know why one or other of them might make a more acceptable substitute, depending how the Herr Hauptmann was inclined.

That they used his rank and title, in or out of bed was never questioned, nor found absurd, and only when he thought about it later, did it occur to him that his own German origin made it acceptable, indeed an essential part of the relationship. It restricted neither affection nor amour propre *on both sides. When he finally had to leave Paderbrück, to take up the job of Press Chief in Hanover, with the restoring of his rank of Major, Max knew he would miss them both.*

He bequeathed them to the local Military Government commanding Colonel, whose British wife, posted officially, as was now allowed the higher ranks, could hardly cook. She was grateful when Max sang praises of Stephie's dumplings. The sisters in turn regarded moving into service with a Colonel as promotion.

By the time he got to Hanover as Major and Press Chief, in that year of 1946, Max said, he had got not only a notion of how to start up newspapers from scratch because he had done it, but he also knew what the aim of the whole operation ought to be.

"If we were going to teach the Germans Press Freedom, then we had got to give them some!" Max Beaumont said. "It's the same thing right here and now! If that lot outside went on the way they've been doing Fleet Street for the last few decades there wouldn't be much press left at all! It's that old one about absolute Freedom and absolute Anarchy."

In his office in Georgstrasse Max told first only his two most trusted staff sergeants about his plans. The office was a small, cramped room. Paintwork peeling off the walls, army desks and chairs, metal filing cabinets, and naked light bulbs that hung from the ceiling, like onions.

"Information!" Max said. "We are going to start a new kind of newspaper! I shall be showing a dummy I made up in Paderbrück to the Colonel this afternoon. It will go for the usual Stage One approval to the Foreign Office. I don't know how much paper we can round up, but you can see what it's called. *Sieben Tage.* That is to give the idea to London that it is appearing as a newspaper, summarising the news, but not requiring as much newsprint as a daily. "Intention," he paused. "We're actually going to produce an illustrated magazine. The first! And fast!"

When he used the old style these days it was really just habit. The war was over. And these were not NCOs who had been at the sharp end, using the O Group language. But it was increasingly gratifying to him how it still got things done.

383

This job was going to call for different talent than the local newspapers. He had no junior officers on permanent staff at headquarters. They were a small handful, out doing what he had done, in Braunschweig, Oldenburg, Munster, Göttingen. The two staff sergeants who sat on the hard army chairs in front of him were Sergeant Brewer, originally Austrian and from the Pioneer Corps. His original name, Brauer, was not much more disguised than Max Beaumont's. The other staff sergeant, Caxton, formerly Krachstein, smaller, with the sad face of an intelligent monkey, had owned an antique business in Berlin. When he was told this and the address, Max could almost envision where the shop had been.

Between the three of them, the difference of rank meant little – these men, considerably older than Max, were very different, but shared one thing together. All three had returned to the land of their origin, and spoke German with total fluency. All three with no trace of self-consciousness, and equally fluently, but with varying degrees of accent, spoke on this occasion in English.

"The German language is a bore!" Max said lightly. He pushed a packet of issue cigarettes across the desk, moving some papers to one side, and all three lit up. "It is not really the language of journalists, I have come to think. You two blokes have done the job in one or two places. Have you tried to get them to write headlines, cross-heads, sub-edit stories like we do at home?"

Staff sergeant Brewer fingered the dummy that Max had created and printed in Paderbrück. Caxton peered round his shoulder, and cigarette smoke curled over the dummy as the three of them moved closer.

"Is it to be like the *Berliner Ilustrierte?*"

"Yes, and no! There will be more text. We must get pictures! The F.O. won't let us use the picture agencies, but I will get round that. We've only one news wire service as you know – Delmer's DND from Hamburg. I want to get a completely different style of writing into this thing. Crisp, colourful, factual. There will be no long-winded mixing of facts and opinions, or gothic typeface. We'll have to run domestic and foreign news stories by culling stuff out of the foreign press. You know the present line from

Control Commission in Berlin! I'm loaded with guidelines and instructions and censorship stuff. What I believe you two will agree, is that what the Germans now need is a dose of real Press Freedom! They've had none for twelve years under Hitler. If there had been a responsible, strong democratic press – the first victim of all dictators – the whole story could have been different!"

"Look at *Pravda!*" Little Sergeant Caxton waved his cigarette with his gentle elegance. "*Truth!* That for a joke!"

Max knew which of these two he had in mind for the jobs that would need to be done.

"Did you put this text together yourself?" Sergeant Brewer asked.

"Most of it, yes. Translated some. I got the Paderbrück secretaries to work on it, and of course I had the presses there and blockmakers for what pictures I used. Do you know the rules on the pix that we're getting?"

"No photos of Nazi leaders?" Brewer said.

"I heard that, but I was not involved with pictures at Munster. Is some red tape?" Caxton smiled his sad smile.

"The idea at the Foreign Offce, is that to show the Germans news photos of the former Nazi leaders might inflame the whole conquered populace into open rebellion!" Max said. "I have a good photo of Goering, in the dock at Nuremberg, for instance! Never mind, I'm working on that. I have contact with AP and Reuters through the American zone, and they might be able to supply pictures on a promise to pay later basis – I'll get photos somehow!"

"There's no more capacity for printing here in this building," Sergeant Brewer said. "The old rotaries are grinding away, and there's only two linotypes and three monos. You know they do the two local papers, and half-a-dozen specialist titles that have been licenced by London. Have you got powers to close down two or three of these? *New Thought, Re-education, Kunst und Kultur, New Medicine.* Jesus, what else!"

"Surely that's not one!" Max frowned. "I thought I knew them all!" The happy cackle from little Sergeant Caxton made him realise the joke was intended, and earned his own twisted smile.

385

"You two haven't seen the pile of licence applications for new titles! Quite a lot are inspired by London, and there's a whole Hampstead network putting on pressure for semi-religious, half political, Bloomsbury stuff which I'm fending off. Now listen, this is it! Intention! *Sieben Tage* will print in that odd-looking building behind the Opera."

"The Grünhaus," said Brewer. "I only know they're working on the machinery. I suppose you know more?"

Max let it go. These men were not tank sergeants.

"I've got a team I had in Paderbrück on the job, and sent signals through our zone and into the American and French zones for parts swapping. The office here is requisitioning paper, as well as the stuff we get from the only mill in Dusseldorf. That smart corporal Wottle, who used to be in scrap dealing, is making a central register of all printing parts everywhere. Those presses will be ready for us in three weeks!"

This impressed them. The non-combatants were sparse in their recognition of an operational approach, but he had not failed to notice the odd glance of respect the two older NCOs gave at the ribbons above his uniform pocket.

"We have only one floor that I can requisition. It will be ready tomorrow. But no heat. And light, only from an army generator from Signals. I got the favour of that in exchange for two crates of steinhager! OK?"

"Who is to staff the paper?" Brewer's face was deliberately blank. "Or is it just the three of us?"

"We shall recruit. You will do the initial screening. Of course we cannot do it ourselves! Any more really stupid questions can be asked standing to attention!" Max said easily. He knew men, damn it he should know them by now. There would be no trouble with Brewer and Caxton, they would help him get this show on the road, and would be proud, in their own right, to do so. And if there was any blame going round later, he would of course take it. It was still Officers First wasn't it?

If you worked hard, you played hard. From the beginning, Heidi and the start of the new magazine became a day and

*night affair, and it all moved together like a kaleidoscope in
its shapes and pieces and colours. Or was that because he was
now, at last, in his element? And conceivably, playing it out,
in his own country?*

*That first evening when he had the message at the Mess that
she needed urgently to see him, he had gone carefully along
Stingerstrasse stepping through the pitch darkness. There was
no street lighting. The message he had got, was that it was to
do with Captain Roots who had gone back to England and not
returned.*

*He went in uniform, loaded pistol in his holster. Number
seventeen was some distance along the terrace that was mainly
occupied by the Mess and the officers' quarters. He went
up the short flight of steps, pressed the doorbell and it
worked.*

*Although she had been expecting him, the door was not
opened immediately, but eventually just wide enough to allow
him to press through an unlit gap. Then the door was closed,
so that he stood in darkness that seemed only slightly less than
the street outside. He was instantly aware of two things. Scent,
the expensive kind that comes in bottles, and had never really
played a part in Max's wartime life, then a hand, with slim
fingers that he felt to be wearing rings and tipped with long
nails, slipped into his and took him through the darkness
towards an inner door, where a crack of light showed. As
she went ahead, guiding him, he saw that she was wearing a
fur coat, and in the dim light, that it was the heavy, ankle-length
kind. He supposed that without heating, a girl would feel the
cold.*

*In the room, the sparkle on the fur coat was provided by
candles, certainly a dozen or more, whose flames bent and
straightened as the door was shut, and the flames, provided
the only illumination, leaping, wavering, casting shadows.*

*Later, he would look back, and recognise the set-piece that
it was, but for now, this was the first time he had ever seen
a strikingly beautiful woman half naked, as the fur coat was
made to fall open. Max did hear his breath rasp, as his blood
surged, it was so deliberately erotic. The candlelight played on
the pale skin, contrasting shadow movements with the animal
ripple of the slowly moving fur.*

His hand was still held. He saw the made-up, actress face, the tumbling dark hair, that was the same colour as the fur, and that had the same quality of live sensuality.

"If you help me you can make love to me! But we must be quiet because of the children!" Her voice was a heavy, studied whisper. The fur coat was pulled silently together again, as she sat at a small table on an upright chair. Max sat opposite, looking round. In the candlelight he saw a settee, pictures on the dimly lit walls, and felt warmth, unknown in most German dwellings. A tall bottle and two glasses stood on the table, between them. Major Max Beaumont sat very still, and looked at the glasses and the bottle. In the war he had experienced what were called set-piece attacks. But not this kind.

Unless lighting was wholly conducive to illusion, this creature was the most disturbing, beautiful woman he had encountered up to now. No wonder old Roots had risked keeping this body and soul together, not only with a fur coat, but with stolen rations. And something had gone wrong, he now could not return, and she wanted Max's help. On terms so urgent they were being immediately offered. In silence he studied and recognised a shared blend of erotic frankness and the particular pride and pricing of the very beautiful. This one was no transacting whore in the normal sense.

"I came because I understood you wanted me to help you. About your friend – Captain Roots!" He spoke quietly and as she had, in English. And because that sounded like the remark of an unsophisticate pukka sahib, and suddenly aware of it, he struck out, staring openly now in the light from the candles, at her breasts, naked in the gaping front of the fur coat. "And you want us to cheat him, before we start?" Max was now growing angry with himself.

The little shrug she gave served to loosen the fur even lower, baring her shoulders, and he sensed disdain, and a secret humour at the knowledge of what she was doing to him.

"What is cheat?"

"Betrugen!" said Max.

Slowly she leant across the table, and slapped her hand mirthlessly across his face. It was calculated and effective, and Max's first experience of that form of arousal. Now they

388

*were staring silently at each other, the way that only two of a
kind do, before they start the love-hate.*

"Why do you sit there like a British?"

"If you must know, I am not one!"

*"Peter did not speak much German. He was kind and gentle
to me. Now they will not let him back here, and we shall not be
able to get married!"*

"Was that what you planned?"

*"What else is there for a future now in Germany?" Her lips
thinned, her voice bitter.*

"Where is your husband? You must have one I think?"

*"His son is asleep in the bedroom. He is four. His father was
killed on the Ostfront."*

"I'm sorry. For you and the boy."

*"He had no interest in his son! He was a sexual pervert." The
shrug again.*

*In silence, Max thought about this, but he was on unfamiliar
ground. He felt her knees touch his briefly, his khaki uniform
against the fur coat. Then it was gone.*

*"He was older than me. I did not love him!" The actress
face shaped savagely in the candlelight, the high cheekbones
stretched the pale skin, and her eyes moved away. Her mouth
moved at the same time, as though she was shaping words and
abandoning them.*

*"I was not married to the man who gave me my daughter!
She is only two, and he was a Colonel in the SS Ober-
kommand! He did not come back. Only a last visit, which
was here to get clothes and escape. I heard from his friends
that the Americans shot him. They took no SS prisoners."*

"Do you know for certain?"

*"I heard from Spain." Now she spoke listlessly. Max
watched and waited, seeing the face opposite him like a
mask, mobile, wax-like in the light of the candles. Her hand
came forward again and rested lightly on his knee.*

*"I think I have lost them all. But perhaps I have found you!
You are Jewish I think! Don't look like that! I can tell almost
anything about men! And your name is Max, and you have
blue eyes. And you will make love to me!"*

*And so it was, that first time. Heidi of the husky voice and an
arrogance he understood, the sensuality that flawed the poised*

389

*allure, and even the attempts at dignity, which collapsed swiftly
into adolescent giggles.*

*But it was the face slap that had triggered Max, as she knew
it would. And the near taunt that she knew he was Jewish. It
served to rouse in him a cold passion, controlled but lustful,
so that when his clothes were off, he pulled her roughly down
to the floor, rather than on the settee, neither of them speaking
a word, the fur coat held open only by her arms, as his hands
pinioned her wrists.*

*She brought to that encounter, experience and knowledge,
after the first, quick moments of passion, and provided for
Max a new unholy, pagan teaching. She strained her body
against his, holding him for moments, merging and parting in
rhythm and tensile strength, then soft surrender. Premeditated,
slowly, she initiated for him a knowledge of his whole being,
that was more than he had ever known of himself. The release
of her breath, warm and gentle in his ear, teeth that bit for a
second the lobe, long fingernails that mock-raked his shoulder
blades, and the soft fur of the coat sleeves that stroked passion,
through his skin, into his whole body.*

*Afterwards, when they were drinking the wine, sitting up
at the table, it was as though they were some naked Grecian
god and goddess, Max felt. This was the German of love
make-believe or real, and he knew with all his senses, that
he belonged to its special brand of romantic lust and studied
Sinnlichkeit.*

*Heidi putting on the fur coat again, moved barefoot and
silent into the next room, to check on the children. It was on
returning, they were back in reality.*

*"What can you do for Peter? Can you get him back? I need
food for myself and the children! Cigarettes! This is the last
bottle! A drink is always best afterwards not before! You have
a beautiful body, Max." She looked at him, lipstick gone, but
her eye make-up smudged like blue-black shadows on the high
cheeks.*

*He started slowly to get dressed. No other woman had ever
said that to him, as Heidi did, that first time.*

With a great deal more circumspection than her former
lover, Max obtained for Heidi the things she needed.

The necessities and luxuries that moved through the black markets of ruined Hanover, where the smell of war, and dirt and death still hung in the streets, and where gangs of thin, hungry, pale-faced men and women dealt in anything with anyone, who could pay in the right black market goods.

At the Information Control Unit there was a new Commanding Officer. He had arrived from India with his ADC, both men totally unfamiliar with any aspect of Europe, after years in the Far East as regular army. Their posting to Germany, to replace the increasingly rapid demobilisation of the senior ranks who had run the occupation administration was an absurd, but heaven-sent solution to the War Office. With an Indian continent now given its freedom, where else could these regulars be sent?

The new Colonel's face and general demeanour was absurdly like the horses that Max was still getting up most mornings to ride out. When the Colonel nodded, his ears seemed to move, and when he laughed, it was a whinnying sound. His ADC, a smaller figure, in his light colonial khaki, stood beside the new Commanding Officer's chair. With his curious pointed face, quick movements and stooping posture he seemed like a groom, ever ready to help the Colonel in and out of his stall.

Max pointed out that he needed to know the fate of Captain Roots, a useful officer who spoke fair German, and whether, on a point of military order, there was any charge against him.

"Isn't that the fella we've got on file, Nigel?"

The ADC said it was. He produced the usual buff-coloured file, and he and the Colonel read the contents.

Max watched the pair of them with growing impatience. He missed Colonel MacNamara who had been sent on to a new Berlin HQ. His knowledge of the unit, of Germany, its people and problems would have found some face-saving solution to this nonsense of Captain Roots, denied a Control Commission return.

"Recommended for demobilisation in the UK!" The CO closed the file. He looked at Max sideways. "We shan't see him back here! Bit of a black sheep wasn't he? Playing ducks and drakes with the natives? Flogging stores, the report says, or something like that! Used to get a lot of that out in India of course!"

Max got up, put on his regimental cap, saluted and departed. He had other, vital work. Most duty hours, Max was working tirelessly on the rapidly developing project of *Sieben Tage*. And most nights he spent with Heidi.

She took the news about Captain Roots philosophically. He had started to write letters to her in envelopes addressed via Max, by army post.

"He says that soon they will be allowing German girls to marry British," she told Max briefly. "Peter will tell me how to apply to join him, with the children in England. Then we shall go to Canada to start a new life. Unless," she pointedly paused. It was a moment when the small boy and girl were sitting like Hansel and Gretel, at the front room table, eating a supper of army cornflakes and black-market milk and apples. Heidi spoke in English. "You would like to marry me? Maxi?" She stood beside him, and unseen by the children gently massaged the back of his neck.

Max often told himself that he was in love with her. What did that mean in reality? Certainly he had never before known such a sense of bonding, the combination of lust, companionship and tenderness. Did it matter that she was eight years older than he was? And the children?

The candles were lit in the room, and the very polite, small children said their goodnights. As they must have done to Peter Roots. Even probably to their own real fathers. German children of all ages had been obliged to be polite. Memories stirred uneasily for Max as he drank a little whisky, and waited for Heidi to reappear. He could hear her singing some small song, a lullaby behind the dividing door, and suddenly he was no longer the philandering Major Max Beaumont MC, but back with Maria in Berlin, or Dairy Mary, another lifetime ago.

In the one other room, Heidi changed into a dated, sequinned three-quarter-length dress. They were going out, as they frequently did those evenings. To the 600 Club on the Hildesheimerstrasse. The elderly lady who lived in her one room, on the opposite side of the hall, sat, in exchange for items of food and a glass of schnapps, to take care of the children.

The 600 Club was the only, and totally unofficial, night club and meeting place for British officers and German girls. German men were there only as functionaries, dressed in tails and white ties. There was a small dance band, unlimited blackmarket drink, soft lights, small tables and sitting-out rooms. Such a place had become inevitable. Hidden away in the ruined city it was totally different in atmosphere and scope from the official Officers' Club, with its bright lighting, white-coated stewards, card-games, billiards, and essentially no women, except once a week, when a score of ATS and nursing sisters attended, and were overwhelmed by attention from those garrison officers who spoke no German, and had been rightly warned of the perils of VD that lurked on every street corner.

Heidi and Max drove to the 600 in his cabriolet Horch. It was one of the privileges of the quasi-military units like the I.C.U., to requisition these cars to supplement dwindling army transport, although they used army fuel. For Max there was his own private memory of the same make, older and even grander, that his father had owned.

But even this car was a black-market acquisition. The official requisition papers and windscreen label with its rubber stamp, Max had had manufactured by one of the older printers in Binneburg, who had found nothing unusual in the job, his ration coupon bribery, and being sworn to secrecy.

In the Club parking place a shabby ex-German army sergeant, the rank insignia now removed from the uniform jacket worn over civilian trousers, saluted, and, for ten cigarettes, promised to guard the car with his life.

Inside Max and Heidi sat at a small candle-lit table, drank Taintinger champagne, and danced among the other couples on the small, dimly lit floor. The music was a selection of old dance tunes known only to some of the German speaking officers, Die siebenten Himmel der Liebe, Ich bin die Fesche Lola, and other classics. Deep Purple, Buttons and Bows, La Vie en Rose, and always the haunting Lili Marlene, were contemporary.

393

A well-known black-market operator who had some con-
nection with the running of the club, came over to their table.
He had sleek dark hair, crooked teeth and a pock-marked
face, and proposed hand-made shoes that could be arranged
for Heidi, and somehow he knew too of Max's interests, and
offered him calf-leather riding boots.

"Made to measure! Five hundred cigarettes!"

They were politely declined. Max had already explained
to Heidi that black market could also mean blackmail.
As Captain Roots had discovered. But politeness was also
essential at the 600.

"Why do you not want to marry me, Max – du, liebling?"
Her voice was heavy, husky, deeply sad in her theatrical way.

"I have no job, no money, no home! After the army, when
I go back. Roots has private money, quite a lot I think from
what you told me!"

"Also a wife and two children to divorce! Then perhaps he
will have none!" Heidi pouted. "I think he loves me though!
More than you do!"

On such occasions a pang of real sadness hit Max. His ins-
tincts, combining premonition, self preservation, had become
fine-honed, and reluctantly he knew that he and Heidi were not
forever. Why could life not be just stopped sometimes, held like
a photograph, in the 600? Or the little warm room with the
candles at number 17 Stingerstrasse? It had earlier been, God
let me survive the War. Now it was, God let me understand the
Peace. He was getting too old, German or too Jewish, as he
looked at Heidi's candlelit profile and quoted her the Schiller
verse. "Ich sehe dein liebes Ansgesicht. Ich sehe die Schatten
der Zukunft nicht!" It was difficult, curiously how some things
did still go better in German. "I cannot see the shadows of the
future."

Impulsively he took her hand as the shabby quartet struck
up the music again with the low persistent throb of the tango.
Hör mein Lied! Violetta!

In the two rooms that were the crowded offices of *Sieben Tage*
the skills of little Staff Sergeant Caxton were clear. There
were desks, chairs, filing cabinets and the sound of type-
writers, German Adlers and old British army Imperials.

There were desk lights and the usual naked light-bulbs swinging from overhead, but only enough glass to put panes in some windows. The picked team of men and women journalists, a graphic designer, and the all important Picture Editor, two secretaries, an archive clerk, all smoked cigarettes provided by the sergeants, and to the smell of the smoke was added the mixed odour of unwashed clothes and garlic sausage. To Max the whole atmosphere was synonymous with his new endeavour, felt in the teamwork, tension, and excitement.

At one end of the room a partition made a small private office for the two staff sergeants. As requisitioning and scrounging was Caxton's job, he was out mostly. *"Er hat noch viel zu fixen!"* said the girl who was his secretary. The army Signals unit had promised field telephones, to wire into the civilian system that was slowly being restored. Then there was the whole question of distribution, because this was not just going to be a local paper.

"We have different points to reach, Herr Major!" the girl told him. Max reminded her coolly that she could speak her own language, and she blushed. They were on good terms with the two sergeants, all the staff, but they were still in awe, if not scared of him. "There will be some train possibilities, some British Army transport which you have arranged. Then also a little space on civilian food trucks and other road methods. We have bicycles, but at the moment no tyres, and in the *Land* also horse and cart they are using!"

"We are thinking of requisitioning two camels from the zoo," said Sergeant Brewer who came in at that moment. He smiled his little V-shaped smile. But the secretary looked sad.

"There are no camels!" She turned round to see she was not overheard. "There are no more animals! Mostly they were eaten!"

Staff Sergeant Brewer took Max out to a big trestle table set in the centre of the main room, and seeing it stand there on the bare boards of the floor, it reminded him of the long ago Bovington barracks. Round the table, working intensely, were the editorial and picture team. Piles of black and white photos, and cuttings, filled the space on the table. To one side, on makeshift desks of wooden crates there were photographs and paste pots and scissors, dummy make-up paper, the big white army mugs with remains of coffee.

"Begins to look a bit more like it!" Max said. He took a seat on an upturned tea-crate cushioned with an army blanket. Sergeant Brewer held up sheets of copy. In the other hand were long strips of galley proofs.

"See some of the try-outs first! Then the stuff that's gone for the final dummy. We have the block-makers going below. I think we will make the deadline."

"I want one more good dummy!" Max said, as he started reading the picture captions. But soon he was into the detail.

"This is hopeless! Listen! *It really will not do if the politicians are going to spend all day talking and scratching their backsides instead of getting results and solving problems. Take for example these Niedersachsen . . .* That is not good enough! It is not right! Just because there's a bit about scratching backsides! And this picture! *Hamburg: Never again a harbour?* And the caption with it. *It is said that it will take ten years to even clear the fairways of the Elbe as this picture shows.* Jesus, Sergeant Brewer! You won't meet any deadline with this sort of stuff! Deadbeat all of it!" His hard young face stared coldly round the group at the trestle table. They had stopped work, and one or two lit butt ends of cigarettes. They were a cool lot, but nervous of the young Major.

"How many of you can speak or read English?" Max asked. As though at school, half the hands went up. Carefully, upright. Avoiding any similarity to the old salute.

"Right! You've got English newspapers here! You bring them over from your Mess every day don't you?" He asked Sergeant Brewer. "Well those of you who can read them, forget about writing. Look at the construction, the headlines. Do you see how the intros go? The guts of the story. Well, we're not creating a newspaper but an illustrated magazine. Only the same principles apply. Colour! Interest! A compelling style, telling the truth, the facts, showing reality through the camera. I sometimes get the impression that as soon as anyone here is called an editor, or a writer, he lets his hair grow, puts on a bow tie, reads Goethe

396

and produces solemn rubbish!" He knew he was being deliberately provocative.

"My hair is long because I have no scissors to cut it!" A pale-faced young man with a fluent, weary English drawl, looked at him. Hunch-shouldered, his expression was blank. "There is only one pair of office scissors and they are blunt!"

"Who are you?" Max said tersely. Brewer had chosen this man and he did not know him.

"My name is Ludwig Wahrstimme. I am so far, the economics and business editor."

What is your lead feature for the second dummy?"

"How the British are stealing all the German patents! Dismantling whole factories."

"That's news!" Max agreed grimly. "I shall read it with interest! Perhaps when they dismantle, they will find a few dead slave-workers here and there!" There was an awkward silence and Max relented. "Any of you others more *Stimme* or *Wahr*? You know enough English! Teach the others who don't! Try and explain what we need, for the new style. Sergeant Brewer cannot do it alone, time is short!" He got up, and took the sheaf of proof pages. Whatever else were its failings, German was the language for giving orders.

"I'll look at these in your office!" he told Brewer

The copy, that had been set, was better. Max re-wrote some headlines, and put in cross-heads himself. He ringed some items for re-phrasing, and more for fact checking.

"It's the captions that are worst," he said finally. "I'll try and show that picture editor myself tomorrow. They've got to learn to look at pictures as experts, but to tell the simple reader what to look for!" He sat back, pushing original pictures across the desk.

"I should think you must be getting a bit shagged with this aren't you?" He relented, as Sergeant Brewer seemed to bow down, but was in fact reaching into the desk drawer. He came up again with a familiar brown stone bottle.

"Have a steinhager, sir! I am drinking it medicinally now! We only have a week to go!"

As he worked closely now with the project, Max became nervous. Central to success was the question of whether there was enough real talent to pull it off. The role of Editor in

Chief was the important one, because he would have to push and drive and swear at the others, tear up their work if need be, and go on doing this even after issue number one appeared.

In this own office, he interviewed one of the younger men, more or less his own age, called Wassermann. He had first met him working on the Paderbrück newspaper. There were things about him that might be what Max was looking for. In a few days he had to have a list of potential licensees for the final phase of London approval. Which was different again, because these were going to be the potential publishers. He had called the man over to his own office, for a final decision.

"I see your first name is Noah." Max had Wassermann's *fragebogen*, the questionnaire stamped by Intelligence security in front of him. "An odd name that, if you will allow me?"

The man standing in front of the desk, as Max had deliberately not yet invited him to sit, made an odd, but dignified figure. A tall, rakish scarecrow, the effect increased by his small, pale face shaped like a turnip, and wearing a pair of slightly twisted metal-rimmed glasses. They were German army issue, Max knew, as was Wassermann's greatcoat, which he kept on indoors, and wore over a British khaki shirt. There was no heating in the building and like most former German servicemen at the time, unless you had access to a lot of black market, there were no smart demob suits.

Wassermann was beginning to stare over the top of Max's head, an old military routine in all armies which Max disliked. He was told to sit. The man did so, taking off his battered spectacles and polishing them, gazing now with short-sighted, codfish eyes at Max's face.

"Jawohl, Herr Major! My name! My father, you see, was a *Pfarrer* – in the Lutheran church you know. I was born in nineteen twenty-five as you see on the paper there. He was a man of some humour, although I only knew him as a boy. But it was a time of disaster for Germany, the money had collapsed, people prophesied that we would go under." He put back his spectacles and gave Max a keen look. They were speaking in German, and the word he used was *untergehen*. "Perhaps you remember?"

398

This was subtly impertinent in the circumstances, implying as it did that Wassermann, on his side of the desk was not wholly without background information about Beaumont.

"Go on!" Max said coolly.

"My father thought that with such a name he could hope I would survive!"

"So you did, even the war!"

"The name was never helpful," said Wassermann sadly. "At school! In the army! I tried to use other names."

"You were in the Engineers, and on the Eastern front I see? Tough?"

"Cold!"

"But as you did survive, perhaps your father was right?"

"We could still go under now!" said Wassermann gloomily.

"I am looking for an optimist as acting Chief Editor for *Sieben Tage*! This paper's success means a lot to me! How do you get on with the others who work under you now?"

"Sometime they call me Ark. It is their joke! Also *Arsche* because I tear up their work!"

"You think you know what we are after? With this new style for *Sieben Tage*? Can you get the others to use these pictures I am getting by unofficial methods? Make something of them? Text that doesn't seem like a Goebbels' announcement or a military order?" Max was speaking with some intensity now. This man's own work was good, and the two staff sergeants had given him high marks. His English was almost non-existent, but that long, thin nose could, it seems, poke about, find stories and pull out interesting facts, and select the pictures for good make-up.

"Here you are!" Max said shortly. "I want you to do two stories! One is international – why are the British trying to stop Jews being shipping into Palestine? Stick to the known facts and what Bevin has said. Secondly a domestic piece. The Bishop of Paderbrück is supposed to have denounced people to the Gestapo. See if you can follow that up and get anything on it. I want to see the results by tomorrow with pictures! On this desk!"

"*Zum befehl!*" said Wasserman, standing up quickly. It was the stock German army reply. Tall and stiff in the blue-grey greatcoat, he lurched towards the door, but closed it behind him, with elaborate, pantomime quietness.

Max sat for a while, brooding. If he was to be editor, the man had to be allowed his individuality. It was what the new magazine was all about. Maybe it was thankless, even dangerous, giving this Wassermann and all the rest like him, any chance at all. He remembered again, as he had done every day since living in Occupied Germany, the sights, the smells and the heavy sense of evil of the Belsen camp. Perhaps it would be better to take all of the ones with any sign of leadership or independence into the Katyn Woods. Wasn't that what they said the Russians had done with all the Poles who might start something again?

Exactly a week later Max went to the Unit's Finance Officer. He needed completion of Phase Two forms for the final budget. A Major in the Ordnance Corps, who had been a partly qualified accountant, the Finance Officer had a reputation for being able to keep more sober after drinking more whisky than any other member of the Mess.

"Perhaps that's why they gave me the job, old boy!" He had once said to Max.

Now he looked at him with watery eyes, and took the forms. As always, he seemed to be faintly amazed to find himself responsible for financing all these strange plans for films, theatres, books.

"Is this enough?, he asked. "It's only *Reichmarks* you know? I suppose one day they'll change them for dollarmarks or some damn things! But they don't seem to be short of them, as far as London is concerned."

Two weeks after the forms had gone off, Max checked everything personally at the *Grünhaus*. Machinery, paper resources, the new and unofficial arrangements for photos from agencies who accepted that they might not be paid for some long time. He approved the final dummy. Then sent in for Phase Three approval, setting a date for the start of November. He also listed as potential licensees, Chief Editor Herr Noah Wassermann, the Production Manager, and the young Wahrstimme.

He had never told me much about his affair with Heidi,

during our time in Hanover, Max Beaumont said, because it all merged together in his recollection of that intense period of the Occupation. Of course there were a lot of things in everybody's life that were private, and I could not expect to be given every kind of detail, and he had forgotten some of his feelings at the time. He hoped I would not ask those sort of questions on the programme, either, but as it was just the two of us together at that moment – well he could give an idea of how it was then between him and Heidi, because he guessed we all knew – those of us who lived in Stingerstrasse at that time, that he and Heidi were pretty close. Max smiled at me.

The last weekend before Sieben Tage *was to start he took Heidi to the Hansel and Gretel wooden house in the woods. He had taken over this Tyrolean-style holiday hut from a Major in one of the Garrison infantry regiments, who was being demobilised, and who had accepted a camera that could have been surplus to press requirement, in exchange.*

"You'll like the little love nest old boy!" the other Major said. "I had to arrest some Polish DPs who were hanging out in it, playing at cops and robbers. And my bit of frat cleaned it up, and we had some happy times. I've left her to a chap in the Guards at Brunswick so you won't see her!"

Max and Heidi had happy times there too. She liked sleeping under the grey army blankets, naked, without covering or sheets, and bringing in wild flowers from the woods.

The children slept in another room with the old lady who had come with them from the flat in Stingerstrasse as Kindermädchen *and cook. Heidi did not like cooking.*

"I can get sheets and proper pillows." Max told her.

"I have often slept like this! It is right for this place. Besides, I can feel you better." That was typical for Heidi. "I feel myself better too! It is like having heavy, rough hands all over me, while I make love to you!" She twined her legs gently then tightly, pulling him slowly on top of her, so that he had to lift back to see the round perfection of her breasts, and could with one hand, fondle and shape them, tenderly, and take the nipples in his teeth.

"You have nice hands, Max! Because you are a sinliche Jude,

401

and you have never done any hard work with them!" She had learned that saying things like that could drive him on to the mildly sadistic, controlled thrusting that she loved, and holding her hips, he pressed her down, raping and conquering, so that her cries would have wakened the children if he had not smothered her mouth with his hand until she subsided under him.

"You must not do it again!" She was writhing and whispering. Which meant the opposite always, until her orgasm became almost continuous, and they were both spent and satiated and would lie side by side, and say nothing, until presently Max would fetch the champagne they both loved, and they would drink that, until the candles flickered, and burned low, when together they blew them out and slept.

On those autumn mornings the air was no longer warm, but Heidi seemed to love a pagan ritual of washing in cold water from a rain butt outside, splashing water from a bucket with the children, both of them, screaming with excitement and feigned fear, joined her naked in the game she made, and Max helped with rubbing down afterwards, with khaki army towels. Afterwards the old lady from Stingerstrasse, still silent, but oddly approving of such Kraft durch Freude goings on, would have lit the stove with paper and wood, and made coffee and eggs for breakfast.

It was in those days, Max Beaumont often thought, the time when he started his first really successful publishing, and his first love affair of timeless but futureless passion, that he would never be able to tell anyone how it had really been. Only that he knew himself it was a pattern he would always seek for the rest of his life.

CHAPTER EIGHTEEN

I remember realising that in unravelling the life of Max Beaumont I would know more about parts of it than others. And obviously the time in Germany after the war, the Occupation time, was one of them, because I had been there with him myself. But people would still be a long way from really knowing everything, and I became more certain as we went on, that there were large chunks that Max Beaumont was not telling.

For instance, nothing had been said by him in front of the others, about my attempt to shoot him down in the back gardens of Stingerstrasse. And when I thought about it, this made me more sure that there were other times, places and events along the years that he was editing out in the same way.

Professionally it irked me, because always, my whole reputation was based on getting the Kings and Commoners who sat with me in front of the cameras, to yield to careful prompting, to eventually be displayed, in the round, as it were, for what they were.

And this thought was followed again by the grim one, that this was the whole basis for some people's notion of why I should not do this programme anyway. The friend of Max Beaumont, who would conceal rather than reveal, and when I saw that Max was smiling I was tempted to challenge him. But it was not at me, but over my shoulder, at Liz Charlton who made one of her silent entrances, and was crossing the floor. Liz, who did not look in any way as though she too, must have missed sleep most of the previous night, and for whom tumult and the tension inside or outside this science-fiction fortress seemingly did not exist. As she passed the push-button bookcase bedroom, moving long-legged and silent across the carpet, I saw her untouchability and independence. Which was perhaps why Max employed her, so close to him, and why there would never be any hanky panky there.

"I'm afraid I've got to break it up!" Liz stood, poised by the edge of the desk. "Mr. Beaumont, the Chief of Police with a couple of aides is in number one conference now! He wants urgent talk with you!" She looked at him, the normally mobile face, expressionless. "They had about two dozen hospitalised yesterday, and last night!"

Max moved sharply towards the windows. "Send another fax into the bank – get Denis to sign it – for another quarter million!"

"Police Orphans' Fund?" I guessed aloud.

"Totally off the record damn you!" Max flared. "And what about the bloody horses wounded? What about them, Liz? Why the hell don't they use water-cannon in this country instead of playing out the battle of Agincourt? Can't you ask that, Tolly?"

"You ask the Police Chief as you're seeing him!" Liz said for me. She consulted her notebook.

"Mr. Tolly! There's an urgent signal for you from Mr. Owen. You can call him back from my office. And a Mr. Gitsen, also from the BBC."

"Surprise, surprise!" I said.

Max had walked round the desk and now was standing close by Liz, smiling, amiably.

"What do you think, Liz? Shall we let him go? Or lock him up in the bedroom there?" Then he went striding towards the door, buttoning his jacket, while Liz Charlton and I followed behind. It was as though all three of us were being pulled by some magnet, which is a way was true. Outside Liz put me in care of the young man with an open neck shirt and black leather jacket. His short cropped hair and pale face looked familiar.

"Where have I seen you before?"

"Park Lane office!" He was not, it seemed, one of my fan club. "In here!"

He showed me into a bare cubby-hole room, with a wired window, and a desk and two chairs, and pointed to the desk.

"Not quite the same as Mr. Beaumont's! But there's the phone. Dial nine for out!" He turned and left, closing the door.

It took some time for them to get Owen to come to the phone, and in the end it seemed he was not at the Nightwatch studio but at Shepherds Bush.

"I've had this call transferred," Owen said, speaking flatly. "Difficult to be alone in this place, but we're OK now. Listen, Felix! They must be in a twist over the Beaumont production. I was supposed to be hearing this afternoon about a whole new running order, with Roger Bullen doing the presentation. You heard that too, or something like it! Well, now I can't get anything definite! Graham Gitsen wants to talk to you, and if you can't be found the Assistant Director General wants to know why! From me, personally. After all I am billed as Producer, as his secretary said. Bloody uppity some of them!"

"Thanks, Owen!" I said, and meant it. "Be in touch!" I knew how Shepherds Bush and Portland Place worked. It was a pity. They had their chessboard and I was just one of the pieces. But I wanted to do Max Beaumont my way, not theirs.

I phoned out again and asked Gitsen's secretary where he would like to meet me. She had the grace to say that she was very glad I had called in. Because Mr. Gitsen was most anxious to get this programme problem settled. He would prefer lunch, and if it was convenient with me, how about Broadcasting House, executive dining suite, and would twelve forty-five be right? It sounded about as smoothly bad as it could be, but of course I said yes. I would have preferred the Garrick. But protocol held that even in the privacy of a London club, the sight of Felix Tolly with the ADG over a lunch table could reach a gossip columnist, and speculation, it was held, must be avoided. There was no need to send a cab, because where I was, people were throwing bricks at cars, and spitting on the windows, and the cabs were not keen.

It was of course Liz Charlton who provided me with the same incognito transport, where I sat concealed in the back,

405

unable to see, but hearing the sound effects of the large mob still in violent protest, close outside.

Even so, the driver was nervous until we crossed the river, the sound receded, and I also relaxed and even began to wonder what the Portland Place second floor might offer for lunch. It was never my own choice, for sluicing and browsing, but I realised that the public scene, even a club, where once again I would stand to attract more attention than others, might not be snoop-proof. One advantage of a private dining room on the Portland Place second floor is that all members and guests are treated at least as equal, and nobody stares.

There are four private dining rooms for top get-togethers at Broadcasting House. I found Graham had the Assistant Director General with him in the one that can seat up to eight, but was laid at one end for just the three of us. Which told me this had been fixed at short notice by the restaurant manageress who had the chore of arranging the executive bookings.

Graham Gitsen and Michael Lockley both got up when I was shown in, and I also saw that although they had obviously been talking together, the seat at the head of the table had been left for me. So I was to be pig in the middle. And of course Lockley shook my hand, and then, just as a tiny surprise I thought, thanked me for coming at short notice.

"We decided to skip drinks, Felix!" Graham said, waving a hand at the sideboard, with its collection of bottles, "But do help yourself if you feel like it."

"I notice you've got Sancerre on the table," I said, as the three of us sat down in a carefully synchronised way. They had, in fact, got the wine already in their glasses. The door opened, and one of the white-coated nanny figures who attends to the private rooms, moved purposefully forward.

"Good day, Mr. Tolly!" I took comfort. I did not know her, but she knew me, although I had not sluiced and browsed on the second floor for quite some time. "Will Mr. Tolly be drinking the wine?" It seemed to be like one of the quiz-show questions.

"Yes," I said. "He will." My glass was filled, and the small typewritten menu was put in front of me.

Without being disparaging about the Beeb's executive

406

catering, I had the private thought that this meeting could have been better in that, and several ways at the Garrick. All tables at the club would have been far apart enough for conversation not to be overheard, but this table and this room were indisputably best placed for privacy if I was to be quietly given the push, never mind the lunch.

Michael Lockley raised his glass in token salute but said nothing in a well-bred way. With his carefully brushed grey hair and neat face he could look important even when silent. Graham of course, said: "Cheers!"

I offered "Good Luck." It had been one of Max Beaumont's dictums, that it was the only worthwhile benediction, because it was the one element you could not plan for. And this whole thing was solely because of him.

The nanny of the table-waiting brigade was waiting patiently.

"We're eating fish!" Michael announced. "But have what you like, Felix"

We all ate fish, and drank a little more of the white wine, now accompanied by mineral water and more glasses in deference to our essential sobriety.

"I never have anything first, if I'm going to eat pudding, but perhaps you would have liked something, Felix?" Lockley said. I told him that I was quite happy, and might not even get as far as anything afterwards. It all depended.

There was nothing really depressing about the dining room we were in, which was plain and bright, with windows which looked out over elevations of the building. A pigeon landed on the windowsill outside and looked at us briefly, before sailing away to join others on a nearby ridge. The walls were bare of pictures and I felt faintly surprised that I had never noticed this.

"What happened to all the autographed close-ups of the famous?" I asked. "I seem to remember them being up on some wall, but perhaps it wasn't here?"

Both the men on either side of me were busy with their fish. Service up from the restaurant is quick, and perhaps because the waitress was now moving vegetable dishes onto the table nobody answered and the mystery of the pictures remained. I knew that the two of them were preserving silence, perhaps hoping that I might say something, ask something other than banalities, that would get us to the point of our meeting. But again, because the man had recently been so continuously on my mind the fact was that in Beaumont military terms, they were Staff, I was just Line, and Staff made the strategic moves. But Line could signal.

"Well how are things at Broadcasting House?" I said. "Or Bush come to that? Lot of interesting policy changes going on?"

"Felix, look!" Gitsen started. He then seemed to choke on the lemon sole that all three of us were eating, and gazed at me reproachfully, over his glass, as he took a quick swallow from his glass. "Can I ask you just one question?"

"Of course, yes," I said. "Go right ahead Graham!"

Gitsen looked at me sadly. He appeared not to have completed swallowing even now, and his eyes bulged slightly.

"The question really, can be put in a single word I suppose. I don't want to be reproachful or speak about double-dealing or anything that would seem to treat lightly of your integrity, Felix." He twisted a look at Michael Lockley who was gazing bleakly across my right shoulder. "Since our talk only this weekend, the question I want to ask you is just Why? Yes, why?"

"Why what Graham?" I asked.

Gitsen shook his head, poking at his plate, and a small sigh escaped him.

"Please Felix, don't prevaricate, don't push your terribly powerful position! You have been with the Corporation longer than either of us – you don't mind my saying that, Michael?" The neat grey head shook once, slightly impatiently I thought. "The thing is, we have responsibility! Policy responsibility, right across the board! Now that is not perhaps the right way to put it, because I don't mean the Board of Governors! And *you* know a number of them too. But the fact is, that as a result of some sort of misunderstanding – and it was only you and I together as I have told Michael – there has been a lot of follow up."

"Follow up?" I asked.

The comfortable middle-aged restaurant manageress had appeared through the door, smiling brightly, her head on one side. Almost like the pigeon I thought.

"Is everything all right, Mr. Lockley?"

As he nodded, I decided to give my nod to the winebottle. It was in a bucket on the sideboard, but I knew it was empty.

"How about a switch to Chablis?" I said. "Chablis still about?"

"For you, Mr. Tolly, I'm sure there is!" The manageress's tight little smile was at least recognition. She left, and we were undisturbed again.

"People!" Gitsen said. The rising impatience I had detected in Michael Lockley took over.

"The Corporation has to keep a lot of people satisfied, Felix! That we are not biased, not one-sided, not backing one party or one power centre at the expense of another! You understand that, Felix, I'm sure! I know Graham meant a number of people have talked with us, about this Beaumont programme. But what I have just said was the real need, we felt, for you to come and have a chat with us! You see a lot of people think Beaumont is the ugly face. Not just of capitalism, but our own world too – the media world. You can't just chuck thousands of people out of work because you don't like compromise or negotiating, or living with a balance of power."

The Chablis arrived, and there was fussing over new glasses.

"Don't bother!" Lockley almost became impatient with the manageress. He waved a hand at our existing glasses, and she looked slightly shocked and reproving. As though if somebody was going to behave badly, it might frighten the nannies, but not her.

"Let me be clear!" Lockley had started once again when she had departed, but I interrupted him.

"Do be clear!" I said. "I think that's important. Graham the other day was ominous, but not entirely clear. Do you mean the Trade Unions have been after you to say that a major life-story presentation of Beaumont would be unfair to them? Or has the Labour Party? Or the Governors collectively or individually?"

"I cannot see why you should be aggressive!" Michael Lockley said superciliously. "We are aware of all the people who could have interests in preserving a balance, and I'm not sure, Felix, whether you are one of them. With your trait – I think that's the right word – for sharpening up situations, getting your subject not just into focus, but reacting on a very personal basis to you – that you really understood either myself or Graham! The result has been some painful misunderstanding by other people!"

"Influential people?" I said. All three of us were still dissecting lemon sole, and as they had been rightly ordered on the bone, a certain messy informality was now developing on the plates.

"At one time I thought the next phone call would be from The Palace!" Graham said balefully.

"Policy!" I said hopefully. "That was the other word, wasn't it? After people, I mean. Which came first?"

"Felix you must accept that there are certain levels of BBC policy that you really haven't had to deal with! If there is any view taken – and really views are taken rather strongly these days, about broadcasting I mean, well, then the producer is involved first of all. But in this Beaumont programme, with you acting virtually as executive producer, and at short notice, the Corporation is really in a difficult position! With someone as eminent and well-connected as you are!"

"Well, that's a very nice and illuminating speech, Michael!" I said.

Lockley pulled his chin down onto his tie-knot and touched his spectacles so that he could half look over the top of them. "First of all there's Beaumont himself, who, as has been said, is *not* all things to all men. Jewish, an entrepreneur, rather mysterious in a lot of ways. Too much power for one man in media terms and had too much of it early in life. Warped by war would you say? A scent of scandals?"

"I wouldn't say anything – but it could be the reason I have done so much preparatory interviewing – more than I would ever normally do," I said. It was time to get to the point. "What's the score? Are we running?" Both men looked faintly pained.

410

"You may already know, that Beaumont got on to me directly, at home, yesterday, on a Sunday mark you. And said that if the programme was not going ahead as scheduled he was offering you a position with one of his TV companies in the USA at three times the money you made at peak earning. He would sue for the defamation implied in any change or postponement of the programme as advertised – his lawyers, he said, would take care of that. And he would take the programme with you and himself onto Independent Television here, within a few days!"

"Did he call it Seizing and Denying the High Ground?" I said, with genuine interest.

"What's that?" Lockley looked worried I thought, for the first time.

"A military expression."

"Talking of military, there were those curious calls from those Whitehall Press Officers the day before," Graham Gitsen said moodily. "Home Office and Number Ten. Expressing interest they said. I explained that our approach was as always neutral, while sounding the note of authority. Then I had the German Ambassador's Press Officer. The American Ambassador had apparently spoken to the Foreign Office already, and their Media man got onto me!"

"Look Felix, we just want to be friends about this!" Lockley said. "I think you've pulled too much to protect your position, which really was not threatened! We wanted you to exercise your talent across a wider spectrum of opinion and people on this issue, that's all."

I knew it was Max Beaumont I had to thank. I could at that moment have been at a loss. So I was especially grateful to him for my answer.

"Let's cut out the bullshit!" I said. "There's a saying by a man called Clausewitz, about first safeguarding your line of retreat! As you two went to University, which I missed because of the war, you probably know about him. He certainly has been useful for me, and now I come to think about it, I can well understand the United States Ambassador and the German too, returning a compliment would you say?"

"You have got so many connections, Felix! Enviably so!"

411

Lockley said. "I just wish you had expressed yourself to Graham and me, considered us your real friends, long before it started to escalate to high places, including the Board of Governors!"

"Well, I can only say I am encouraged that the highest levels are still concerned with high principles and not just levelling!" I told him. But it really was all over, and now it was time to go. I had no wish to delay over Michael's pudding or hear protestations of a new and better understanding.

"Thank you!" I said, standing up and laying down my napkin. "After Thursday, you can tell me what you think again. As it is, I must return to the Jewish entrepreneur!" I remembered that phrase. "Maybe I can use it? I must ask him whether he knew you were thinking of him that way!"

I left the executive dining room, with Gitsen and Lockley sitting much as they had been when we started. Somehow neither of their expressions had changed, and there seemed to be no sort of farewell that was useable.

Outside, along the passage where the waitresses were carrying things into the other private dining rooms, from which, as a door was opened, emerged happy sounds and even laughter, I met the Manageress who had come from the main restaurant once again, to see that all was well.

"Not leaving us so soon, Mr. Tolly?" If she meant anything more by that word the smile was genuine. "Was the Chablis not to your liking?"

"The best!" I told her. She looked round, like people do when there are others close at hand, and we might be standing in the way. "Well, I'll tell you what I would like then! Although I suppose you get asked often enough. I do have my own private collection you see! And if you do have a portrait picture you could sign for me –!"

"It won't look like me," I said. "But for that lunch you certainly shall have it!"

I decided to take a taxi from Portland Place straight to Battersea. Although what I really wanted to do was go home, to tell Chloe for instance, that it was going to be all right. Or even to Lime Grove, where Owen Owen and

412

the others ought to hear it from the horse's mouth, rather than the grapevine.

But Battersea, the place that one of the competing tabloids had headlined as Beaumont's Beleaguered Bunker, was pulling me. I had mixed, but strong motives, for returning there.

The taxi driver was less enthusiastic.

"You see what it's like down there?"

I said that I had. He relented.

"Felix Tolly, aint'cha?" His head half turned to nod at me.

"I had you in the back of the cab once before! Easy for me, but you wouldn't remember!"

"Glad to meet you again!" I said, and as we got underway I heard once again my voice, the one I was first hired for, steady, sincere, truthful, carrying conviction. "You can drop me over the bridge, you'll be out of harm's way there," I said kindly.

"They turned over a cab last night! Tried to set it on fire! Passenger was one of the reporters off the paper. Thinks he's still in Fleet Street! They got him! Stitches in his head too – cabby's all right, they left him alone."

"You'll be all right," I told him.

In the event the police cordon allowed us no further than the bridge, when they saw my security tag and photograph they became helpful. I paid off the cabby and thanked him.

"There's some of your people filming there now," a junior inspector said. "But they have to keep back with the cameras. There's a lot of that crowd don't want their faces on film, so you can't just walk in there, not with your face either sir, if you know what I mean!"

He talked into a two-way radio set, and presently the standard white car with blue light bar slid alongside. I climbed into the back, and as the car fairly surged away, I saw that the driver was hatless, and had as his companion in front, a WPC, who turned, all ready for talent spotting, with a swirl of short blonde hair, and a big smile.

"Just fold down onto the rear seat, Mr. Tolly! You might get your Equity pass torn up!"

413

But I wanted to watch the fast approaching sea of figures with banners pushing against the uniformed police cordon. They were angry faces, chanting. A roar of sound. Then so quickly, we were inside the tall, wired gates and down the ramp into the underground reception garage. It had taken all of three minutes.

"Thanks!" I said. I hadn't got time to get names, which was the usual form when the police helped TV. "Thanks both of you!" I got out, shut the door and watched the car swirl backward up the slope.

I showed my clip-on pass, was solemnly patted and security checked, and took the elevator to the third floor, walking the corridor with a uniformed security man, who deposited me inside Liz Charlton's office.

Liz and her two assistants were as always busy, and telephones, word processors and fax were noisy with it. But she swung round in her chair and got up.

"Fancy you here again!" Liz's smile could also be private humour. "I thought they were dropping you off the programme?"

"You thought nothing of the sort!" I said.

"You may have to wait a bit!" she said, jerking a thumb. There were lights on over the door to the inner Beaumont bunker. "There's a meeting on in there, with just about everybody who counts! I suppose you could go in – he's always said you, and only you, can see and hear anything you want. But honestly, all you'll see is a lot of jumpy executives round that desk and enough cigarette smoke to jam the air-conditioning! If you want my health and safety advice, keep out!"

In fact the meeting broke up a few minutes later. The lights over the door changed colours, and Liz moved forward swiftly.

"Come on!" she said. "Now's the moment! If you follow me in, that will be better than standing here when they'll all want to shake your hand and get your autograph!" After the catering manageress, even this seemed possible.

As Dennis Laycock, Rickdorf and Alistair whom I recognised, and some other faces that had seen at Park Lane, came out in the opposite direction, I saw Max Beaumont beyond them, still sitting. It seemed odd to see him in shirtsleeves, but I was beginning to know how he worked, and that he had taken off his jacket because the majority of the other men had too.

The air in the room was warm, and certainly there was the acrid trace of cigarette smoke, but also the undefinable lingering tension of collective action, a tangible thing that attends the end of difficult meetings. Perhaps Max Beaumont had see the expression on my face, because he got up, slipping his jacket on over the cream-coloured shirt.

"Liz, can you open one of these God-forsaken windows those security boys have fitted? There's a trick to it! Nobody seems to have told me what it is, but I've had enough of that recycled stuff! OK, put that paper on here, and I'll sign! Felix, I had an uneasy feeling we might not have you with us again!"

"OK! OK!" I said, watching Liz wrestle with the window on the far side of the room. "I'm not so sure I want to go on with you! Suppose I'm fed to the back teeth with TV? The power game? Every cab driver and kid police girl knowing my name! I can get off, if I want to!"

"It would be selfish though, Mr. Tolly!" Liz Charlton had come back from opening the window six inches or so, and stood by the desk. "Mr. Beaumont wants you to do the job! It's easier to let him have his way!"

I sat down in one of the leather chairs that surrounded the big desk, and noticed it was still warm from a vacated backside. Max finished his quick signing, and pushed some away for later.

"I might have decided I wanted to do it badly enough for myself!" I said, but the two of them were not listening.

"How much time have we got, Liz?"

"You and Mr. Tolly can have an hour. He's had lunch, you haven't."

"The small tin! And a half of the Widow. But Tolly needs a drop of the old eye-brightener, so bring two glasses!"

"A tin sandwich?" I asked, as Liz went out.

"Caviar doesn't keep, unless you finish the tin! The widow, of course is *Veuve Cliquot*." Max always seemed pleased to impart bits of arcane knowledge.

"You seem to forget that I have also been around!" I told him. "And drinking BBC Chablis! I read about caviar, but you read the consolidated balance sheets, and eat it!" But Max was looking at me kindly. Clearly in his mind now, he could afford to regard me, along with some thousands of others, as one of his creatures.

Mildly irritated, I got up, walked over to the opened window, and breathed in some fresh air, being also opposed to the conditioned and washed kind. Down below the Thames twinkled in the sunlight, rather like a moat at the castle walls.

One of the assistant secretaries appeared with a plain wooden tray and a white cloth, but on it were the luxury items, the small blue tin, the thin brown bread, the green bottle, and glasses.

"Max, I've got just a couple of questions!" I said. He had begun winding the top off the bottle, as the girl departed. I came and sat down again, moving away one of the other chairs, so that the sense of being part of a left-over meeting was in a way dispersed. "One is, that I think any time we could be interrupted by that German girl! You've been thinking about her?"

"Perhaps I have." Max poured champagne into the glasses, and pushed one across the desk in my direction. His eyelids drooped fractionally, his mouth twisted on the glass rim. No man at his age had the right to look even that pleased with himself.

"So think some more!" I said. "We'll be wasting a lot of time by presenting your life, if all we prove is that there is no fool like an old fool! If you have that girl in the hide-away bedroom, either she or one of the loyal crew will spill it within days!"

The seconds after that were the uncountable kind. Neither of us touched the champagne.

"I suppose, because I let you, you see a lot more than you should do my old friend!"

"You're not the Machiavellian character you sometimes think you are! It's a charade!" I told him.

Max Beaumont crashed a flat hand onto the desk.

"God almighty!" he said. "I really ought to chunk you out myself! There's only one thing I want understood from now

416

on! I don't need advice, Tolly, of any kind. Especially that kind, from you!"

"You won't get any!" I said. We went on facing each other for a short while, in silence. "Nothing much changes does it, Max? How did it go in Stingerstrasse in those days?"

"Everyone has to run it for himself! Haven't you learned that? A lot of the time I'm misunderstood! Maybe you're right. Last night she wanted that bit about being alone, in here, with me. OK! I said she could have the bed in the security room if it got late! All the time there were too many people about! I could have almost sworn they were bent on stopping it! In the end she went off in a huff, and I slept alone. If you can call it sleep!" Max grinned again.

"So to get your perspective on yourself, how did it go finally – in Hanover? With *Sieben Tage*, Heidi, anything else you like? Come on Max, let's get back to the job – not risk spoiling it!"

For a moment, Max Beaumont spooned caviar from the little tin onto toast, and into his mouth.

"Well that damn illustrated newspaper was my first. And last for a while! It cost me the job. I came into my little office rather different from this one if you may remember it, and that was on the morning we were due to run the first proper issue.

There was a telex from London on the desk, and it said that Phase Three approval, usually a rubber stamp by that time, was being delayed. More time was required – I can still remember the words – to consider some aspects of what was implied by the editorial policy! I ignored it. I went over to that battered little print shop in the Grünhaus, where the two staff sergeants and the German team had got a couple of bottles of champagne, and I pressed the button and we ran about twenty thousand copies!"

"You seem to have had the bubbly stuff with you whenever and whatever!" I said.

"When I got *Sieben Tage* out, all hell broke loose! I told London we could not recall the copies without losing face. The stuff bureaucrats dread! I was suspended from duty. Eventually after a few weeks, London decided the only thing

417

to do was to licence the publication quickly to the Germans, so that it was no longer strictly a British responsibility. All those stories about Gestapo Bishops, and how badly the French were treating German prisoners! When a publication which was started by the Occupation Powers finally became German, it had to change its name, so that everyone would know it was independent! It was Noah Wassermann who chose the title *Das Fenster*, instead of *Sieben Tage*."

"The window," I said, thoughtfully. "And the magazine has been seeing through things ever since. Did you ever get a slice of the action, Max?"

Max Beaumont looked at me almost coldly. "Did you get a slice of German radio? It was a job. I did my duty as I saw it. The Germans did get a taste of real press freedom. Today *Das Fenster* has a circulation of more than a million. And I have the satisfaction of knowing I was right!"

"What happened when you were fired for starting *Das Fenster*?"

"I was returned to my regiment! Remember the dreaded R.T.U.? It happened in the end! The bureaucrats had a heyday with the bit between their teeth. They decided for safety, that each and every German newspaper we had started in those days must belong to a political party. A real, tidy Foreign Office idea! They couldn't stop the magazine, but they could push me out, and they did."

"Second question, Max," I said, "Do you mind if I tell that bit about how the jumpy young Flight Lieutenant tried to shoot you in the garden?"

"You'd have to tell about Heidi, and about Peter Roots." Which was true.

"What happened to Heidi then?"

She married him in the end. "They went out to America. Remember, I told you in New York I saw her years later. We had one week-end. If we go in, it's off the record."

"If that's the way you want it," I said.

Max had not told me any of his life with Heidi. Now he seemed to feel he could, as there were just the two of us, perhaps. I had never before heard him talk so intimately.

In his own words, he said that in Stingerstrasse, when they got ready to go out in the evening, it was often dark, because electric light was still unreliable and candles were hard to get. She stood naked in front of the wardrobe cupboard in that little front room, and would rattle her few clothes along the rail, and ask Max what she might wear to please him.

And because more often than not, she meant it to happen, he would get up and come and stand beside her, and slide an arm round her waist, and there was a pleasing eroticism in feeling his uniformed body against her nakedness, and she told him that the German word for what he was doing was Frotten. More than once it led to a quick and premeditated love-making, if Heidi felt like it. Up against the wall by the cupboard, or on the table in the centre of the room, or if it was the floor with its rough, worn carpet, then she as the naked one, would ride him.

On one of the last evenings before he left to rejoin the regiment – although even afterwards Max had still managed to get away to see Heidi a few times – he had peered into the wardrobe, to help with the dress selection. Generally she chose anyway. There might be some dress in which she had not yet appeared.

"What is that black outfit? The one under the long dress?"

Heidi in underwear and the new nylon stockings Max had given her, looked indifferently at the long red dress which he lifted out from the rail. There was a much heavier outfit underneath it, and by the light of the candles, as Max pulled the sloped shoulders of the dress apart, it was easy for him to see what was underneath.

"That is Dieter's uniform," Heidi said indifferently. "I do not like the dress!".

"The uniform!" Max said.

"He wanted me to burn it, but I thought maybe I could sell it. For a souvenir! They sell badges and such things on the black market. I think I shall wear the dark-blue velvet!" She held up a shorter dress still on its hanger, against her nakedness, and looked at him, unsmilingly. But Max was rivetted by the black uniform, with the silver insignia of an SS staff colonel. The matching trousers, folded on the rail underneath, slid slowly off and fell to the carpet.

419

"Dieter was your husband?" He picked up the trousers from the floor.

"No!" Heidi sighed. She began to pull the velvet dress over her head. From beneath it she spoke in a muffled voice. "He was my lover. I have told you! And Sigi's father!"

"Why did he leave this here?"

"He had to get away didn't he?" She was doing up small buttons at the back of her neck, her two pale arms like an inverted triangle. "So he changed into civilian clothes, like many others. Here in this room! He had a friend with him, and Dieter lent him his only other things, a pullover and trousers. They had no shoes, but they pulled their trousers over their boots."

Heidi was pushing the low neckline of the dress into shape, wriggling her feet into high-heeled shoes at the same time. "Of course it was no good!" She sat down, suddenly, on one of the hard chairs and stared at the candle flames. "I told you, Max, the Americans shot him. They came to Hanover first you know, before you did."

"How do you know that? That they shot him, I mean? What about his friend?"

"They went different ways I suppose. Dieter was a fool! He was always sure he knew about everything. He took other things as well. His stupid iron cross with the oak leaves! You imagine! If the Americans caught him he wouldn't keep that for long I can tell you! Also his Mauser automatic."

"That was probably why he was shot," Max said briefly. "Perhaps he had a go at them, if they started to rough him up. But how do you even know that? Or do you just guess? He might turn up! A lot of people are saying hundreds of the SS have got abroad."

Heidi shook her head. "Let's have some whisky, Max! The bottle is there, in the bottom of the cupboard. The glasses are on the shelf. Only a little for me, it is so strong." When he had unscrewed the whisky and poured a little for each of them, she lifted hers a short way, and said jerkily, "Here's to Dieter!"

Max stopped short with his own glass, and tried to perceive the expression on her face. The candlelight did not help. But her eyes were perhaps extra bright.

420

"To hell with that! Just take care the boy never gets the same way!" He downed his Scotch in one. "How do you know he was shot Heidi? For sure?" Max said.

"Another friend came, once a few days after they had gone. At least, he said he was a friend of Dieter's, and I think he was. He came at night, and I would not let him in at first, I did not like his manner or his looks. He said he was a Colonel with Dieter, but he looked more like a rat! I do not think Colonels look like that."

"They come in all shapes," Max said.

"He wanted something. He said it was important and Dieter would have told me. He was unpleasant about it, because he did not know exactly what it was, and of course neither did I. I said Dieter had left nothing – I did not tell him about that uniform – because I did not want to get into any more SS trouble. And then I told him to go, because I said I had an American officer coming, who was sleeping with me, and I could see he believed that, and was scared. But he said if he thought I was lying, he would come back and kill me. That was when he told me Dieter had been shot, and somehow I could see it was the truth, because I think he wanted to hurt me. He went away then. I hope they shot him too. He made me cry."

"You haven't seen him since?"

"It is over a year ago, and he has never been back. Max, can we go to the 600 now? I want to laugh! I want only to see happy people, and dance with you! And old Frau Schrubber will not stay up with the children past midnight she said."

"Just let me have a look at that uniform again!" Max picked up the jacket from the chair back where he had draped it.

He could feel how the man had looked, his size and the slim shape off his shoulders. The SS officers always had tunic uniforms, tailored to perfect fit. He began to search through the flat pockets. There was a small car key, a single round of 1.5 mm for a pistol, a short piece of cord and an unused sticking plaster. He put them back. He found the inside breast pocket, with a small button, which he undid. His fingers felt inside and touched a piece of paper. All the other pockets were empty, he checked again, and the slip of

421

paper, when he took it under the candlelight, he could see, was a half-page torn from a German army field notebook. He recognised the lines, different from the arithmetic squares of the British field pads, and he studied the sets of figures written in the indelible purple pencil that was also German army standard, the sharp precise lines and strokes.

"Do you know what this is?" He held it up to her.

Heidi, impatient to get away now, had hooked the long red dress back over the discarded uniform, and put it back inside the wardrobe. She looked over her shoulder.

"I thought it was a telephone number. That is what it looks like! When Peter tried on his telephone it didn't work. I tried different ways. I think perhaps it was a military number of the German army once, but of course that would be finished." She came close and pressed herself slowly against him, holding his head up between her hands, then kissing his mouth quickly, twice. "Maxi! *Komm, lass uns tanzen gehen, liebling!*"

"What was the piece of paper? Did you ever find out?" I looked beyond Max Beaumont, who was facing away from me, towards the window Liz had opened, where shredded cloud moved against the sky and wind from the river brought a small stream of air into the room. Stingerstrasse and all its world, seemed a long time ago.

From somewhere nearer, came suddenly a whole series of small explosions, sounds that could be heard now that we were no longer in a state of sealed air-conditioning.

"Thunder flashes," Max Beaumont said briefly. He rotated in his chair, facing me again. "They chuck them under the police horses to make them rear up!" I did not like the look on his face.

"I studied that number for quite a time, maybe two days," Max said. "It had a sort of familiarity about it. There was an extra number underneath, just the figure thirty, then the letter m and a big E. I was slow, when you think I'd been using map references in a tank rather recently. The only thing was, of course, what map? And did it matter?"

"It would have to be a German map," I said. "An army one?"

"You're as smart as I was at that age!" Max rocked back gently, in his all-purpose chair. "To get such a map, or maps, in the end my friends in the I Corps obliged. They had collected quite a lot, with all sorts of markings and operations on them for future historians to delight in, and as I had begun to suspect, the one I wanted was not far north of Hanover. The reference number was a wooded area, just off the Uelzen road."

"Did you tell Heidi? Or the I Corps?"

"No, I kept an open mind. Scruff of paper in a uniform? It could have been a lost unit location, a hoped for rendezvous. But there had been the shifty Colonel who visited, wanting something. It could be weapons. Get away stuff. Incriminating stuff. We weren't into all they were up to then, and I was curious. But also careful." Max raised a tactful hand in case I was about to interrupt again. "You remember our Berlin trip? I thought a few things through on that occasion. Clausewitz you remember?"

"Don't tell me it again!" I begged.

"I had been ordered back to the regiment, and I had only a few days left. But the regiment – well it reminded me of mines again," said Max. "After all, that was not so odd was it? If I hadn't thought about mines I wouldn't be here now. And, if you care to get my meaning, dear Tolly, of course you wouldn't be sitting over there either!"

"I went to some other friends in the Engineers, and for a requisitioned German Press Leica they gave me, no questions asked, the loan of a simple mine detector. The poke and listen kind, which I had used in training too. I put it in a fifteen-hundredweight truck, which we often used to bring back bits of printing machinery, and told the transport sergeant I didn't need a driver. I found the map ref. easily."

"After dark I suppose?"

"No. Not really. You see after dark would have meant using a flashlight. And if by chance anyone saw that from a way off, they might be curious. I parked well off a track under the trees, and did the thirty metre bit which was that other figure. Taking it East from the track, as the letter E. There was no code involved. I guessed I might be looking for what the police nowadays call disturbed ground, don't they?"

"Your papers run those sort of stories," I said.

"The piece I found, wasn't so much disturbed as covered over. There were boot marks and some broken fir tree branches, probably some leaves had blown away. I went back to the truck and got the sweeper going. And although it could be just picking up escape gear, it clicked for me, bless it. The light was falling now, but I marked, lay down, and probed, the way we had been taught, and I pulled out three anti-personnel, the fat little bastards with the three-prong spike on them, that can blow a leg off or worse. You remember them probably? Just under the surface."

"Never saw them," I said. "What was underneath?"

"I defused the mines by hand, then I went back for the issue spade, strapped in the truck." Max was not to be hurried. "I got to the first crate underneath, and it wasn't even nailed down. In that one, when I got loose wood off, were only papers. I know now what they were but I didn't then. What in German are called *wertpapier*. Shares, stocks, bonds! Piles of them. It was the third crate that had the gold bars, wrapped in thin brown paper, like presents! Ten kilos each they weighed. I took one out and put it down beside me. There were more crates. I was on my knees, and thought a bit. If anyone had come along they might have imagined I was praying! Perhaps I was in a way. I used the spade to dig around a bit over a wider area, to get an idea of how much more there might be, and I wished I hadn't. I hit the bodies, you see. There were six of them, with not much shovelled on top, and far gone, and the stench was nasty. They had their heads blown in. Wearing German army greatcoats, but I think they must have been prisoners or slave-workers, poor bastards."

"What did you do about your little find, Max?" I kept my pen well away from the paper. He would see I was not taking notes.

"I chucked the mines in a lake on the way back." Max almost naturally returned to military report style. "I gave back the sweeper, and the fifteen-hundredweight." Max went quiet for a moment. "I know what you want to know! Yes, I took just one Midas bar. Up in my bedroom, I rubbed it down a bit, and studied it. Ever handled bullion?"

424

"I've seen it," I said.

"Of course it was stamped with the usual stuff you get on the bars, only more than usual. It had changed hands a few times. There were Nazi marks, and state numbers. And a few chips, where perhaps some lesser orders had taken the chance to scrape off a week's wage! Who knows? But Tolly! What I did see was a mark that was something different! And it hit me in a way I can't describe. Can you understand if I tell you that it was as though old Uncle Paul had suddenly crept into that little bedroom, and touched the back of my neck. There was a star stamped on that bar on one end, a five-pointed crude star. You know the one I think! With a letter S in the middle of it! I didn't need to think twice. I knew. One piece of Klieschen inheritance was back in fairly rightful hands! I didn't feel so bad then."

"Don't tell me you managed to get your hands on the whole lot of those poker chips?" It went through my mind in the same instant, that he might not tell me that. But it would explain a lot about Max Beaumont.

"Not a hope!" I saw the Beaumont blue eyes bright, as he swivelled round his chair to face the window again. "Work it out! The options I mean! If I had declared, and claimed, it would have gone on for years!" I think he did not want me to see his expression at that moment.

"I knew a bit about what had happened, after the bank was confiscated by the State. And from Aunt Sybilla that there was a remnant of family connection with banking, in New York. The more I thought about it, the less I liked the idea of just walking into Mil. Government House, in Hanover and telling all. I phoned – you could, in that press job, from the office, with a bit of difficulty. At first I didn't know if I had taken the right number from Aunt Sybilla's book. And I talked carefully at first, and then a second and a third time, when they called me. Again from my office, at night, when I had worked out the time difference. What I like about Americans," Max Beaumont said, "is that when it comes to practical action on practical problems, where money is concerned, they move faster and more effectively than even the Germans!"

"They seem to have lost the art a bit recently," I said.

"They hadn't then!" Max said tersely. "The Hanover area had been occupied by them in the first place, and by the next night, mark you, some very high connections had gone through the Pentagon, and that stuff was lifted and away to Frankfurt on two trucks. I kept out of the way. If it had failed, it would have been nothing to do with me. But it didn't."

"So you did get it damn you!"

"The shares and certificates were eventually part of restitution claims which took years, but in the end some original owners or descendants got them. Some were worthless of course. The gold – apart from one bar – went into Fort Knox I think. After some delay it did end up with original Jewish bank interests, in Israel, and the American end of such banks that could make claims too, I was told. I understand it put a lot of money into the lawyers' accounts on the way."

I put down the scratch pad and pen on his desk, because he had got up suddenly, and was going to the windows, looking out, then pacing round the desk, as though he was finished. He stopped and looked at me, his hands in his pocket.

"That lump of bullion you took! Was that what started you off? Literally that lump of capital?"

"That would make a nice story for you wouldn't it old Tolly! Wouldn't it? Funny you should ask what happened to that gold bar! No!" He sat down again, choosing his words, not trusting me, perhaps. Frowning at the desktop.

"The New York banks were helpful. I shan't tell you which ones. Although I suppose if you thought it was worth it you could check the Jewish connections of that time, or earlier. They were grateful! Grateful banks are better than talking ones, or listening ones or whatever they're all up to these days!"

"What did you do with the bloody bar?" I persisted. "Ten kilos did you say?"

"That German magazine, *Das Fenster*," Max spoke quietly, quickly. "It was licensed at about that time. Remember? I was in disgrace, for creating such a frightening example of the Fourth Estate in Occupied Germany, against the wishes of the Foreign Office! They wanted to disassociate from it, as quickly as possible, after they had fired me, and it was licensed to Noah Wassermann. It was to be a German

426

owned publication, and the name changed, as I told you, to signify this."

"You certainly floated Noah for life! Circulation over a million now you said?"

"It wasn't so easy then! The Foreign Office moves in devious ways. You remember how I got the start-up budget through the Finance Officer? Well he couldn't do any more when it became German. And surprisingly would you say, Noah and his mates found it curiously difficult to raise any money. They were all penniless of course. The licensing deal was always that they had to buy the publications we had started as a going concern, and probably go on pumping in cash until it did indeed float. But even with a licence, Noah couldn't get the banks of those days to play. They weren't remotely doing business. Mysteriously nobody was going to help this monster of Press Freedom! Perhaps the banks were genuinely hostile. Or it could be they had to listen, at that time, not to customers with gilt-edged propositions, but to other voices. Noah Wassermann came to me with defeat on his face. It's hard to remember," Max said with an expression of mock sadness, "but there was a lot of defeat syndrome about them all then! You were there. Perhaps you remember?"

"You gave him the gold bar!" I shouted. "You actually gave it to him?"

"Yes! I plonked it on his packing case desk."

"No strings, no hints, no nothing?"

"I told him that might help a bit. And not to ask any questions! And not to take it to any of the bloody bankers, but to shift it in what bankers so nicely call *tranches*, on the black market. I was after all still in uniform and still on duty," Max Beaumont said. "It was not for me to get involved in deals with any kind of Germans then! People change," Max said. He knew that he had changed. But that was the way he felt then.

At that moment I wished I could change established rules. I felt intensely irritated that I had given the off the record undertaking. People have told me that I have moments, interviewing on TV, when I assume what has been described as a pitiless or even merciless look, and spectacles that

427

are supposed to focus like laser beams. I adjusted them now.

"And you really expect me not to air this as part of the programme! The real Max Beaumont, the officer and gentleman in his Majesty's uniform, giving away stolen bullion?"

"It was not stolen," Max said quietly. "It was family wealth back in rightful hands! It made possible the start of a powerful voice of independence in those Occupation days, a voice that could right a lot of wrongs and prevent Hitlers from ever rising again! We who have enjoyed such privileges tend to forget in time that men have died to win them."

I watched him lean back gracefully into his tilting chair on the other side of the desk, and he put his fingertips together in the old way, and smiled the old twisted smile. "A free press, and radio and of course television, are among the best safeguards against tyranny in any country! That's why I'm still at it old, Tolly!"

"Bullshit!" I said.

"You gave your word!" Max leaned, crouching now in his chair, curled like a cobra.

"Did Wassermann keep quiet about it too?"

"Totally!" Max gestured angrily. "He sent me a telegram, after the official licensing, to say that my name would be for ever in golden letters over their door! I thought that was quite neat!"

"And you were demobbed and came back to London and went back to your old west London newspaper?"

"The owner was ailing, he'd been wounded in the blitz. I bought it from him."

"Being luckier than Noah, you did get some help from the bank?"

"There were the grateful ones!" Max agreed. "I bought a paper on the east side of the city, then started one in Hampstead and fairly soon in the south. I merged them. Then I moved into the provinces, then Canada. After that, I married Deborah, and she inherited the Chicago and West Coast stuff I rearranged. You know all that."

"And that led to TV, through radio stations – well that part of it is pretty well-known," I agreed.

428

But I was feeling suddenly, strangely tired, and perhaps I really was getting much too old for this stuff. Of what made sense of people's lives, and what could be spoken about and things that could not, and whether it mattered if the viewing public considered Max Beaumont a champion of basic freedoms, or saw him as an ageing mogul, charming, but basically a figure from the past, a product of out-of-date glories and values. It was my job to get it right, and now I must go away and get it all together for the programme.

Liz Charlton had returned, coming silently through the room and was now standing close beside me, so that without turning I knew, because she was close enough for me to pick up the expensive scent. Al Chemmy was more noisy. He plodded quickly round her, smiling his way bravely through his heavy responsibilities as Max's PR Officer at such a time.

"We gave you another fifteen minutes after you said, Max!" He hove to like a ship's figurehead at the desk, his face composed for any sort of reaction, one way or the other. "If you and Felix need more time, well you must have it of course! But the fact is we need to get another release out, and I'd like to sketch in the general lines!"

"I think we're through really," I said. "I'm still on Nightwatch for odd nights, and this is one of them, which means I ought to start finding out about the running order for that."

Which was when the door opened once more, and to nobody's very great surprise there was Rita Henckman. It was she who seemed rather more perturbed to find other people present. For a moment, as she closed the door by leaning back against it, while still looking at us, I almost thought she showed her resentment at not finding Max alone too plainly. She stood, her tanned face devoid of make-up, the wide-lipped mouth now almost pouting. Then it was to me that she spoke.

"I thought it was fixed that I would have the chance of a private interview for the ARD with Mr. Beaumont?"

She still wore the short black leather skirt and heavy, unzipped jacket of the same material, and carried a black sling handbag and the TV reporter's black cassette recorder. As though it too, was all part of the matching outfit.

As she came slowly across the floor, she shrugged perfunctorily at me, as I had not replied. She ignored the other two, and spoke only directly to Max. She spoke quickly in her usual husky voice, but there was no suggestion of the transatlantic note this time, because it was in German, and roughly speaking she asked him when there was going to be enough privacy in the office to continue her exclusive interview. The word she used was *gemeinsam*, which could mean like the more we are together, the better it would be.

"You know my dear, that Mr. Tolly speaks more than passable German, so we must stick to English for everyone!"

"Please forgive me! I have not got much time!" Now it was English.

I looked at Rita closely. I had guessed the exclusive interview bit some long time. I thought of Heidi, partly from the recent retelling, and I could see the attraction now. Little things, the small nervous hand with dark-red fingernails, that lifted her dark hair, always drifting over one side of her face.

"I will stay until you have finished then! Is it all right if I smoke?" As nobody seemed to care, she crossed her legs neatly, with a flash of black patent leather shoes. "Thanks, I'll use that!" Al Chemmy had moved the big desktop lighter towards her. Dear Al, who appointed himself guardian angel to all. Which I suppose in a way, was his job. But he spoke out otherwise.

"I have to say any exclusive was not cleared at all through my office, and Mr. Beaumont knows how I feel about that! There have been a hell of a lot of media requests! And I mean other than even our own people of course! All asking for that same thing. It would go down very badly if German TV were given facilities, Max! That is to say, it would make my life damn difficult!"

"Well now!" For once Max Beaumont had the grace to look forgiving, in a general sort of way. He put his hands clasped behind his head, and leaned back in the big chair. "We'll let Rita stay, and finish our little chat! After all she has been in on the interviewing before, and Tolly and I have closed down really. Am I right?" he asked me.

I saw Liz give me a look that was not seen by her boss, and decided to play along. I said that I would certainly like

430

to sit on for any further interviewing, because the whole connection had been arranged with that sort of thing in mind. I might skip Nightwatch. Liz Charlton murmured that she had a dozen quite confidential items that were demanding of Mr. Beaumont's immediate attention.

I could see a distinct air of tension in the face, and unusually expressive figure, of the German girl. It would be difficult for anyone not to get the message.

"Perhaps it is you all who need to have a cosy time, together then!" If my professional ear was any judge, her voice was struggling to remain even-tempered. Certainly you could hear the curious accent now. "I go then! But only the ladies washroom! Thanks, don't bother, I know the way!" She rose, stalking back towards the door, in a manner that could make impact on any male, Max being the main beneficiary facing that way. Then she was gone.

"Have you offered her a definite job, Max! Because if that's the way it is, I feel she has it over me!" I had not heard Al Chemmy openly aggrieved before.

"What bothers me, is that Security is getting a bit slack if she can come in just like that!" Liz Charlton frowned. "I don't think you should have got her issued with the gold label pass, Max, I must be honest!"

A small light went on with the low buzzer on the communication consul to one side of the desk, and Max Beaumont seemed glad of the interruption. He touched one of the row of small levers, and we could hear the operator's voice.

"Can Mr. Felix Tolly take a personal call in your office, sir?"

Max gave a quick look in my direction.

"It doesn't have to be here, Tolly! You can use outside?"

"Who is it?" I said cautiously. If Lockley or Gitsen had cooked up some afterthoughts, then they were not for here and now. The operator could obviously hear me from where I sat.

"It's a Mr. Owen, sir! Or maybe Owen and Owen if I got the company right! He says it's urgent he speak with you."

Some damn thing coming up on Nightwatch perhaps. I looked round. There was a flat curved thing on the desk, like a slimmed down tortoise, with buttons on its back.

"He'll take it on number two here!" Max nodded at the one-piece instrument, and flicked his switch.

"Is that you, Felix?" Owen sounded more troubled than just routine I thought. I could hear him breathing through his nose. "Listen – are you alone?"

"Obviously no," I told him.

"I don't like the sound of something!" He was talking with an unusually fast lilt now. "I called London office of German TV just now. They've promised clips of one or two background bits I wanted for the Beaumont production, but, that's not it. They said Hamburg had been worried at not hearing from that Rita Henckman, who was supposed to be over here, checking out interest in the programme for scheduling over there. Felix, listen. The reason they said they hadn't heard, was because she's been found in Munich. Dead!"

"Run that through again!" I said to Owen sharply. "They've got it wrong! They must have. She's here!"

"Felix listen, don't speak!" Owen's urgent voice in my ear was like a sharp probe. "They found her body in a car boot! Do you hear me, Felix? –"

I had put the phone down. Very slowly. I saw the other three round the desk were looking at me, curiously and in silence.

"Are you all right, Mr. Tolly?" It was an unsmiling but solicitous Liz Charlton. I had put a hand over my mouth in a stupid way, and I realised that it was shaking. And now Liz got up quite quickly and came over and touched my arm, and Al Chemmy was looking hard at me, while tapping the desktop with his fingertips. "Was that bad news, Felix? Anything we can do to help?"

It was not either of them I needed. I wanted Max Beaumont.

"Max!" I heard my own voice crack, "That girl!"

"That's enough!" His face had taken on a sudden harsh anger that I had not seen before. "I think you got what I said on that earlier! You can all of you get out!"

My glance went to the door at the far end of the room, then back to the three faces, all staring back at me, faces that showed anger, pity, caution. And as my own thoughts were

432

beginning to spin round I told them, although I hardly heard the jumble of my words, just what Owen Owen had told me.

For a moment there was silence, and nobody moved.

Then, perhaps because she was already on her feet beside me, Liz Charlton did. She walked away from where she stood with a slow, silent precision. To the empty chair, on which the black leather shoulder-strap handbag was where its owner had left it. Liz pulled open the catches that held the flap buttoned closed, and dipped her hand inside. Then she dropped the black bag on the chair, straightening up fast.

It must be my professional bit again, that will always make me hold action in frames, close in on details. The pale hand and dark nail-varnish of Liz Charlton, the fingers that wore no rings coming out of the handbag. And how her head turned on her elegant neck, with slow, careful grace as though she sought for something else. I saw what it was, at the same moment as the other two men. We followed Liz's movement as she reached out for the portable tape-recorder, half hidden on the floor beside the chair.

For a second she seemed to hesitate, her face turning even as her hand reached out, looking at Max Beaumont, and in that moment it was a look that totally changed her face, wiped out expression, her whole personality withdrawn somewhere inside.

Max Beaumont was on his feet as Liz's hand closed.

"Leave it!" His voice was like a whip crack. "Leave it, Liz! That's an order! Get out of here all of you!"

But Liz Charlton moved in one continuous motion, lifting the black box with both hands, the strap trailing, and she was upright now on those long legs which took her with swift grace the short distance to the one open window where she hurled the recorder through the narrow space, and then took two steps back into the room, standing, waiting.

In a curious way, the anticlimax when nothing happened seemed to stretch on. For a moment I experienced an unwelcome, but not unfamiliar, belt of pain across my midriff, and as though it was no part of my life, I watched Max Beaumont slam the window shut and pull Liz back, so that she seemed to lean on his arm. Gently Max kissed her on the cheek, squeezing her hand, saying nothing.

"It's gone in the water," she said dully. "It was best! I thought about it!" Her voice was trying to sound normal. "It had to be an electric fuse, you see, not mercury! Semtex of course as always, but there had to be time! If we left it here, some poor bastards would have to tackle it, and maybe the people below, if it went off before that. Not a bad throw would you say?" Then she sat down quickly.

"You mean that thing wasn't –?" Al Chemmy's florid face could never go pale, but now he seemed to have an unhappy outbreak of coughing. When it happened outside, there was the heavy thump of the explosion which ripped the air, and suddenly the double windows shook, and it was like when a gale slams rain on the glass, as they were heavily splashed with dripping water.

Abruptly Max moved to the communication box, pressing levers, even as alarm bells began to ring in the building, and a moment later police-car sirens could be heard joining in from out on the road.

"Get me front-gate security!" Max said harshly.

"She's been gone over ten minutes now!" I looked at Liz. "Where did you learn to pitch like that, Sunshine? And, by the way, thanks for saving me as well! Can I give you the kiss of life too?" Liz laughed, and when I bent to her, kissed me instead.

"It was throwing hand grenades I suppose!" I think it was then, she realised she might have said too much, and she turned and said something to Max Beaumont in a quick rattle of foreign language that was vaguely familiar, but which I could not place, although in my mind it was associated with tension and peril. And then, swiftly, now very much in control, she was up and making quickly away through the door.

Max on the phone was giving instructions to security people. He told Al Chemmy to get round the building and report back to him, on morale and damage. "I want you back in ten minutes, Al!"

"Where has Liz gone?" I wanted to ask more but it would do for starters. There was a short pause.

"The Israeli embassy!" Max said.

Somehow I was not surprised. "Mossad?"

434

"Liz is Mossad, yes!"

"*And* your PA Secretary?"

Max smiled. What was unspoken was that he knew we both, now, shared why Liz had been out of reach.

"Jack Dasher?" I said.

"He had a year's training out there."

"That young chap outside, of course!" I was thinking aloud. "The one I've seen at Park Lane too! Who are those two you have at Richmond? The Inside and Outside?"

"Boris and Rinsky." You could almost see Max making himself relax. "Mossad are, after all, simply the best! It's not a regular service you understand, but all countries have people who are doing double jobs."

"You must be worth a lot to them." I looked across the desk at him.

"Over the years, I have contributed several million pounds to Israel. Yes, some of that is known, so what the hell?"

"I don't see how that can be off the record after this latest – and what is it? Second failed attempt? A Shot in the Park as one of your competing tabloids called it so wittily! You can't keep this out of the programme! What was in that handbag, by the way? I see Liz Charlton took it with her."

"A rather practical line in sheath knives, and a tea-towel for cleaning up!"

"And you had in mind to get in that hide-and-seek bedroom with her!" I said slowly, unable to stop myself. "It's you that would have been screwed! With a butchers knife! Do you think we were right to try and cool your ardour, Max?"

God knows, he always had the last word.

"I don't see how you can tell me anything, my dear trigger-happy Tolly." The blue eyes were hard. "Don't forget, you tried to assassinate me once too!"

I told the driver to take me to Lime Grove and then as we moved through Fulham I changed my mind. There was time enough to look in at Barnes, and I wanted to see Chloe and tell her myself, instead of her hearing through all of the half dozen other ways she might. The script for Nightwatch would be done, this latest item would not be cleared for quite a while, in whatever form, and the running order only took ten minutes, when you had reached my stage in the game.

I went up the front steps two at a time. There were lights on upstairs, early for the evening and the wind seemed to rustle around the house, making moving shadows on the door. Chloe had always said she liked the sound of it in the Wistoria, and I was glad now that I had diverted, because the familiarity of the whole place seemed reassuring, a refuge of sanity. Leone, the older of the two au-pairs opened the door, as I had rung the bell rather than fumble for a key.

"Where is Mrs. Tolly?" I asked, taking off my coat, and giving it to her. I felt suddenly neglected that Chloe had not come into the hall, as she usually did. Although, of course she was not expecting me.

"She's in the drawing room," Leone said. "Is everything all right?"

By the time I walked into the big room off the inner hall, I was already planning just how I would tell her that I might not have walked in ever again. And then maybe I would find a suitable stiff drink for both of us.

Debby Beaumont was once more sitting on the settee, like a permanent still-life, and as usual working on some piece of tapestry. She seemed in no hurry with the needle, pushing it in.

"Felix! I didn't expect you!" Chloe said. "Here's Debby Beaumont!" Chloe's manner was rather as though I was part of an idiot TV audience, being prepared for a panel show.

"Don't get up!" I said. "Can I fetch us all an early-side drink?" It seemed a moment for the American expression. "I'm rather in need of one myself. Has Debby spoken with Max. Like very recently?"

"You must have one!" Chloe said, and there was a special, steady grace, about the way she looked at me.

"I just decided to call round, instead of telephoning, and Chloe was making a cup of tea, which we have had!" Debby Beaumont gave up stitching, and I looked at my wife who was standing up, and looking curiously posy by the mantlepiece, as the fireplace was empty. The heavy glass fireguard reflected the back of her legs, and I wished she would sit down, but I found the right glass, added Scotch and decided not to worry about water.

"Tea is best for shock, you know!" Deborah Beaumont said. I took a big slug at the heavy glass in my hand, and looked at both of them.

"You remember," I said. "That German TV girl, the one who was called Rita Henckman?"

"Yes indeed," Chloe was nodding, and looking at Mrs. Beaumont, rather than at me. "We've been talking about her just here and now!" Mrs. Beaumont was looking down now at her tapestry piece, turning it round.

"I know you have been a loyal friend of Max's over this whole thing!" she spoke suddenly. "After all, you knew him, before I did, even if only briefly that time you were together after the war! But don't be like everybody else, and tell me I don't know what's going on, because I haven't lived all my life arranging flowers! Like when you saw me the other day you know! In case you hadn't noticed, there's quite a lot of two-way sex in the higher echelons, Felix! There are divorced and unattached executives, right here in London, as well as New York or Sydney. There are the ones who are feeling lonely when they're on duty, and Max had to commute to the East Coast, there was somebody who wanted me to even leave Max! The times he had to go to Germany – and he's had to recently, about this new equipment, but now I needn't go on. This one has turned out well – differently!"

"We know about it, Felix dear!" Chloe said quickly. "Deborah knew what might have happened. And now what did happen. Because Al Chemmy phoned right away to tell her, and then Max told her more. And when she heard you had been with him, she came on over to tell me!" And now Chloe had come quickly across and was holding onto me, and some drink was spilled on the carpet. "Darling! Because just think! And Debby so calm I was ashamed! But you're all right! And I'm glad you're here! And Max Beaumont is too – all right I mean!"

"And Liz Charlton!" I said, as Chloe detached herself. "Whom I'm drinking to right now! As is Sefton I see." The dog had come to investigate the splash on the carpet, and was licking it in a tentative way.

"I still can't understand why Liz did it?" Chloe said. "To take that risk! You could have all been killed, the moment she moved it!"

"Max told me on the phone," Deborah Beaumont said. "He talked with Liz after she came back from seeing her people at the Embassy." Mrs. Beaumont was now patting Sefton's head, as though we were all engaged in tea-party small talk. "I suppose she was trained to know more about these things than other people."

"She said at once it could not be a mercury fuse, and must be electric with a time fuse, and probably set for the girl to get away." I told them. "But it was a gamble! I remember her once telling Max and me that it was one of her principles – don't do nothing, do something! Probably Clausewitz."

I saw the two women looking at me, uncertain, not amused, almost watchfully.

In the Lime Grove anchorman's room with its surrounding glass-paned windows, I glanced up at the clock with the sweep second hand, and saw there was plenty of time. Owen Owen had joined me, and Jane Milward had brought in the pink-coloured paper of the running order, which she put on the desk.

"We've got to go easy with the bomb attempt!" Owen said. He sat on the desk corner as there was only one spare chair, and swung one leg in the crumpled striped suit trousers. "You were lucky, boyo! That little cow might have had a hat trick! You and Max together would have finished this programme, wouldn't it? I'll tell you Jane here had a little cry when she heard, so you see how we all love you!"

"Owen don't!" It was only the second time I had seen Jane Milward blush, although I knew it might not be for me.

"Come here!" I said. And I gave the pink cheek a kiss.

"Trouble is, the story's pretty well blacked out," Owen gloomed. "Although it can't be for long, because the Germans have got the Munich end of it. What you've got there, is not even the Al Chemmy story, which has been stopped. Because the anti-terrorist people have not caught up with Black Rita, and the friends who got her away! All we've got is a piece about a mystery explosion at the Battersea

438

plant which is being investigated. But as there was also a big arson-type fire at one of the Beaumont paper warehouses earlier this evening, even the Unions have stopped shouting about explosions."

"Did Chemmy have anything else to say? Is all the personal stuff banned?" I fretted. "As I was there, I would have thought I was not bound by the same rules! No scoop?"

Owen Owen looked round the glass panels which surrounded us, and at the busy team outside, bent over processors, keyboards, tape-winders. Always so silent beyond our sound-proofed glass box. "Sure, Chemmy had plenty to say! All Top Secret. That girl, the one we all sat with so cosily, was checked out by Mossad computer files in Tel Aviv as soon as Liz reached them from the Embassy. It seems she even faxed them a picture from the security badge print out. Anyway, it didn't take them long. She was the sister of the girl Max Beaumont was so final to with the Bentley!"

I sat back in silence and stared. Not so much at the other two, but at my own realisation that nothing was ever going to change. "Fear, death, hatred, revenge! An eye for an eye! The son of man shall have no place to rest his head!" I moaned. I put my own head between my hands, resting my elbows on the desk, and Owen, like my earlier generation in our war, being as we had been, comforting, flippant, pretending. "And we can't even use that as a summary!" he lamented. He looked up at the wall clock. "Press on I think! There's fourteen minutes exactly before Felix keeps on talking!"

Somehow, the old studio gag *was* comforting.

For the next two days I had a feeling that Max Beaumont would phone. It seemed altogether odd, after being so close to him, he was suddenly not there in any real sense.

I still had to go over the scripted questions with the team's help, Joe Bailey on the early stuff, plus Jane and Owen. Because there was a deputy producer for Nightwatch, and Owen and I had to check out all the production – people who had pulled in background footage to the early Berlin times, London in the thirties, the war and during the occupation time afterwards, and then the steady build up of the

Beaumont empire at home and abroad. I wondered if they would find the bogus Rita Henckman in time to give the programme an extra shot of news. The murder in Munich by the Arabs and Red Army faction had already blown security on the main story via German Press and TV.

About half an hour before the scheduled time, I waited for Max in the reception room set up for VIPs, and wondered why it had to look even more plain than the same facility at Heathrow. Unlike most of them, Max Beaumont was punctual, to the point of being five minutes early.

"Keeping cavalry time, Tolly!" He looked unscathed, handsome, debonair, relaxed. He might have stepped in from some earlier success point in his life, the still slightly tumbled greying hair, the high cheekboned, tanned face, with the bright-blue eyes and the crinkles round them that went with the easy smile, and the strong cleft jaw. Because nothing he wore I now knew, was without recalling that Sandhurst mirror, I saw he had chosen a casual grey cashmere jacket, the mandatory blue shirt for the cameras, and an elegantly striped Hermes silk tie. No tycoon suit for Max Beaumont.

I had a copy of *Radio Times* on the table which I imagined he must already have seen – Al Chemmy would surely have taken care of that. Our picture on the cover was if anything, slightly less flattering, by the time the graphics boys had finished with it. I looked at the cover, and felt I looked, beside him, a hundred years old.

Max smiled at the young canteen waitress who had appeared with champagne, which I had ordered specially. She appeared flustered by the foil and wire.

"Here give that to me!" He took the bottle, and she looked relieved and disappeared, and he nodded over to where the crew-cut young man, whom I now knew was part of the security team, hovered by the door. "You can push on, and keep a look-out there thanks! I want Mr. Tolly to myself, before we go on his show!" He poured the two glasses.

"That's all you're allowed," I said. "Beeb rules! Good luck! You were right! Actually we are in luck with camera men tonight, because Owen has seen to that. It can always be tricky."

"I thought of calling you on it." Max looked round seriously. "I'm told by my people that an enemy behind the camera can kill you with two close-ups and a missed moment!"

"That's about it. But we'll be all right. One of these chaps has your kind of star sewn on his back, and the other one reckons if he does you well, you could be his fall-back position if the Beeb doesn't honour the next pay rise!"

"He's got the right idea," Max drained the last of the champagne glass. I had noticed that he too had a folded magazine that he had brought with him, but it was not another *Radio Times*.

"*Das Fenster*," Max said shortly. "This week's issue." It was folded open at a double-page spread with the Beaumont face large on one side. There were other, smaller photographs, but it was the headline that ran full across the two pages. *Feind, Freundin oder Familie?*

"Good stuff!" I said. "How would you translate that?"

"Enemy, Girlfriend –" Max paused only for a moment "– or Relation! German journalism to-day!"

"What the hell is that?"

"Press Freedom!" It was the way that Max said it. "They seem to have had their research dig that date I last met Heidi in New York. Work it out! Father unknown, mother German. Age about right! Red Army faction, and anti-Israel! Makes for circulation! They've even got me down as Schönberg here and there!"

Jane Milward put her head round the VIP room door. "Make-up!" She looked at Max Beaumont, and he rose, gallantly, to see the third blush, by my count.

"Surely not my dear Jane Milward with us! Would you say I need improving?" But he let her take his hand along the dim corridor, leading to the make-up room.

"Even the beautiful, and different and very truly sought after have to be just checked over," I said, following up behind them.

"That's *Just So Stories*! I didn't know you read Kipling!" Max Beaumont sounded genuinely surprised, as we moved down the darkened corridor towards the bright lights at the end. "Could you prompt me into quoting Kipling's *If*?"

Then Owen appeared, and the organisation moved into top gear.

We took up our places as was always the way, on the series that had made my name, as much as anybody elses. Sitting in the no-nonsense chairs on either side of the small table that kept us close together, as the lights were brightened to the point of nuclear explosion, then faded.

Production ran a test scan to Max Beaumont's face and then mine, the audio mike was clipped to the Hermes tie, and I could see the mobile cameras moving and tilting, the snaking cables on the floor, the faces in the shadows beyond. This was my world, where I was king.

"Good evening!" Now I heard my voice, the one that had earned the balanced, warm authority, firm-but-fair accolade, and it still sounded well, without my really understanding where the enthusiasm exactly came from, but it was there. If I hesitated or dried up, the BBC ground to a halt too. But I would not. At these times I had an extra existence that never seemed to be so sure in ordinary life, and now just Max Beaumont and myself were in that pool of bright light, surrounded by darkness. The monitor was just there, out of camera view, and I knew from the running order that we were starting with a close-up of Max and myself, followed by a quick black and white of his Berlin long ago. With streets, people, the Tiergarten, and then close-up of a big, horned gramophone playing its scratchy snatch of period music.

Owen Owen's music man had chosen a bit from *Cabaret*, the jaunty, sad, evocative, haunted tune from the Liza Minnelli film of Christopher Isherwood's Berlin of the twenties. Max could hear it, and I saw him smile, almost as though he could see it all again. Which was the idea.

But it was, I suppose, clever of Owen. Perhaps Max Beaumont's life really had been a charade. Had he been really sure, himself, who or what he really was, right from the beginning?

442